"Do you wish to stay with me for a time?"

If she heard that one more time, she would scream the house down, Morgana promised silently. What good would his gratitude do her? She didn't want his gratitude, she wanted his love, his confidence, his...

Morgana struggled against her rash tongue, against the sudden urge to fall into Brander's arms and confess everything.

It was no use trying, she reflected with a sigh. Then Brander stepped closer, so close her breasts almost brushed his broad chest, and she could feel his breath on her cheek.

His hands moved to her shoulders, pulling her slowly toward him...

Legacy of S

of S

D1115926

Legacy of Shadows

Virginia Brown

WARNER BOOKS

A Warner Communications Company

WARNER BOOKS EDITION

Cover illustration by Sharon Spiak

Warner Books, Inc.
666 Fifth Avenue
New York, N.Y. 10103

 A Warner Communications Company

Printed in the United States of America

First Printing: August, 1987

10 9 8 7 6 5 4 3 2 1

Dedicated to Bud McKinney,
who has never failed to encourage me,
and to my Aunt Virginia.
I love you both.

The
BEGINNING

Chapter
1

Tiny chips of sunlight danced erratically across the forest floor, evading the thick oak and beech limbs that formed a leafy canopy high overhead. Dead leaves and velvety moss cushioned the step of the girl who was slipping like a wraith through the silent wood. No twigs snapped beneath her bare feet to betray her presence, yet the animals knew she was there. Accustomed to her gentle hand and loving heart, they accepted her. Even the skittish doe would take food from the girl's outstretched hand. Fat swallows often fluttered to perch upon her shoulder, warbling happy tunes, and plump rabbits hopped near to sniff at her feet, cocking their furry heads to peer up at her with brightly alert eyes.

Tall and slender as a willow limb, the girl seemed more a woodland spirit than mortal flesh and bone. Indeed, old Kyna, her foster mother, had often called her Flidais, the spirit who commanded animals.

Deep purple flowers thrust fragile heads up from the leaf-strewn earth, seeking shafts of sunlight filtering through lacy branches. Kneeling, the girl opened her leather pouch and began to collect carefully selected plants, tugging gently until the leggy stems were uprooted.

"This will be enough," she told an interested rabbit. "My pouch is almost full." The rabbit's nose twitched in agreement, and she laughed softly as she pulled tight the thin leather strings binding the pouch's top. It was already full with foxglove, deadly nightshade, and henbane, and this monkshood would be the last addition. A whisper of wind sifted through the trees in a soft sigh, lifting a strand of dark hair from her brow as she sat back on her heels.

Smiling at the caress, she closed her eyes. It was a gentle touch like that of a lover stroking her cheek, she imagined, and her smile widened. A lover . . . He would be tall and strong, and as honorable a man as he was handsome, of course. The girl's mouth drooped suddenly, and long dark lashes lifted to reveal eyes as green as new spring leaves. She shouldn't even imagine such things. Old Kyna would scold her loudly, and perhaps even tell Conn that Morgana was daydreaming about mortal events again instead of concentrating upon her birth-gifts.

Silently regarding the quivering nose of a curious squirrel perched upon a knobby tree root, Morgana sighed. She felt much like a wild songbird who had been captured and put into a wicker cage, to sing only wistful melodies.

Rising, Morgana brushed clinging dirt and leaves from her woolen gown and tied the pouch at her waist. She'd best return quickly or Kyna would worry. The old woman feared the little people in the forest at night, the elves and fairies who could play mischievous tricks on unwary victims, and also the darker, more evil spirits who delighted in tormenting the unsuspecting.

Morgana's steps quickened on the faint path winding through tangles of bushes heavily laden with new berries. The muted calls of birds roosting for the night drifted to her ears through yew, oak, and beech leaves, mingling with the soft settling of the earth. In the shadows of trees older than time, it was not day, but not yet night. The light was diffused and soft, a shadowy green haze one could almost feel like a warm cloak pulled close.

In spite of the deep shadows, Morgana was not afraid. The forest held no fears for her, whether sunlit or shrouded with night. There was nothing lurking there to harm her, for the woodland creatures were her friends, and the villagers were too awed to approach one protected by Conn.

A faint smile curved the soft, full lines of her mouth as Morgana reflected on the advantages of being under Conn's protection. As chief priest in an order of the ancient druids, Conn held a strong power over his people. The tree religion was practiced in secret now, for most of the druids had been stamped out many years before. While Celtic customs had absorbed druid religion into their rites, and even the new Christian religion used some of the pagan rituals as theirs, the need for secrecy was great. Conn hoped that one day the religion of the sacred trees would return in full force as it had once been.

It took many years to become a druid, and few were chosen. Druids, Conn asserted, were born, not molded from unlikely individuals. They must be born with the veil over them to be a druid.

It was said that Morgana's mother, Eibhlin, had been a very powerful seer. She had studied since girlhood to be a priestess, and had been given the gift of prophecy as well as mystic powers by the gods. Eibhlin had proudly worn the outward signs of her calling, the intricate blue tattooing that covered her entire body, Morgana had been told. Mystical powers had shadowed Eibhlin's days and had been the sole legacy to her only child.

Of her father, Morgana knew nothing. He had been

chosen by fate, Conn had informed Morgana, and had been
a Celtic king. His identity was not necessary to her future.
Yet there were times when she wondered, and thought of the
parents she'd never known. Eibhlin had died in childbirth,
and Conn had taken her infant to the cottage of Kyna, in a
distant wood from her native clan. There Morgana had lived
in seclusion, with only Kyna and woodland creatures as
companions.

When Morgana had shown fulfillment of the promise
Conn had seen in her at birth, he had begun her training,
keeping her away from the disturbing influences of other
Celts. At first young Morgana had accepted Conn's verdict
and obeyed unquestioningly. Now she found a strange
restlessness in her soul, an unfulfilled yearning that Conn
was wont to dismiss as too earthly.

There were times when Morgana stood in the deep, still
wood beneath the sacred oaks and felt their power, felt the
visions that were gifts from the gods. These visions could
not be neither denied nor summoned, for they were not
under mortal man's control. Morgana understood and accepted this, even while she struggled against the invisible
chains of her gifts.

There were other times when she spied on the carefree
girls from the clan as they gathered at the well, laughing
and discussing well-favored young men who had caught their
eyes. Strong and sturdy, fair where she was dark, Morgana
envied them. They were so full of life, so caught up in the
daily routine of living, that they had no time for wondering
about the spirits that shaped their lives. Morgana found
herself torn between her destiny and her desire for
conventionality.

The passing years had frequently seen Morgana wandering in field and wood, befriending woodland creatures and
listening to voices in the wind and sea. Images danced in

the bright flames of a fire at times, and at other times she could see vague shapes of future events in her dreams. It was more a heightened sensitivity than a true prophecy, but Conn came daily to the tiny cottage to hear of any visions she might have seen.

He would be there now, at the cottage with Kyna, and she must hurry or he would draw himself up stiffly and look at her with those terrible eyes.

Long shadows had deepened to a purple twilight as Morgana reached the end of the path through the dark wood. She paused on a low rise overlooking the cottage where she'd spent the past eighteen years. Smoke curled in drifting wisps from the stone chimney jutting above the straw-thatched roof, and Morgana recognized the delicious scent of barley bread and stewed vegetables. Her stomach rumbled hungrily, reminding her that she hadn't eaten since early morn.

About to start down the gentle slope, Morgana heard a faint sound behind her, like the rustle of leaves stirred by an intruder. She half-turned to peer at the line of shadowed trees. Only thick silence and a filmy mist like morning fog greeted her. It must be the stealthy steps of a hunting animal, she decided, yet a vague disquiet settled around her in the mist. She was not alone. Her eyes narrowed as she detected a slight movement in a thick tangle of briars.

"Who is it?" she called softly, but there was no answer. Still she was not afraid. No one would harm one favored by the gods. She waited a few moments longer, and the mist slowly faded away, leaving her standing alone once more. Perplexed, Morgana shrugged and began walking through tall, dew-damp grasses toward the cottage.

The leather hinges of the wooden door creaked noisily as she pushed it open, and the sound drew the attention of two

figures seated at the table. Morgana stepped inside as Conn
and Kyna turned to greet her.

Touching the curve of gold necklace circling her slender
neck for reassurance, Morgana's mouth curved in a slight
smile as she moved forward.

"Greetings Conn, Kyna," she said softly. "Have you
waited long?"

"You know we have!" Conn snapped icily. The tiny
cottage seemed even smaller when he filled it with his
presence. Bony fingers drew back the cowl of his cloak as
Conn faced Morgana, and she was struck—as she always
was—by his appearance. The stark lines of his face were
almost cadaverous, the prominent bones of his cheeks standing out like the sun-bleached skulls of enemies left hanging
upon a Celtic house. Deep-set eyes were sunk far into their
sockets, burning with such intensity that they commanded
her gaze to meet his. "Well?" he demanded.

Knowing full well what he wanted, Morgana still hesitated. The irritation she felt was tempered with caution. It
would not do to provoke Conn into anger

"I have had no dreams today," she said quietly.

"Nothing?"

Again that vague disquiet that had disturbed her earlier,
but it was so tiny a prick that Morgana chose to ignore it.

"No. Nothing." Dragging her eyes from Conn's hypnotic
gaze, Morgana moved across the hard-packed dirt floor to
the crackling fire Kyna had burning on the hearth. It smelled
strongly of unseasoned wood, the thick smoke made by
still-green logs boiling up the stone chimney. The fire
always burned this way after Imbolc, which was the spring
lambing season, coming before the Beltane night on the first
of May signaled the summer season. Soon would be the
great celebration of fertility for cattle and crops, a high point
of the Celtic year.

"Morgana," Conn was saying gravely, and she turned in his direction. "You are drifting away from your teachings. Did you concentrate? Your mind must be open so that spirits can find a willing home in which to rest their secrets. . . ."

"I remember." Her forehead knit into a frown as she reluctantly faced Conn. For an instant Morgana perceived a difference about him; a bluish haze like that of the sea mists seemed to envelop him in a cloud, hiding him from her view. A chill wind blew sharply, taking away her breath as the mist disappeared.

"Morgana?" Conn reached out to grasp her by one arm, and his thin hard fingers gripped like the sharp talons of a hawk, making her wince with pain. "What did you see? I saw spirit-shadows in your eyes. . . ."

For some reason she didn't want to tell him, but the intensity of Conn's dark gaze forced her to speak.

"A blue cloud was around you, like distant sea mists or a storm over the water. That is all." Morgana pulled away from his grasp. "That is all," she repeated.

"Blue?" Conn echoed. He shifted uneasily and began to pace the cottage floor with measured, deliberate steps, as he always did when disturbed. He whirled back to demand, "Is it still there?"

"No. It is gone. . . . What was it?" she asked after a moment of smothering silence.

Instead of answering, Conn drew up the hood to his cloak. Sometimes he would make himself disappear or become invisible to the villagers, leaving them in awe. Only the priests and Morgana knew how the trick was done. Drawing together the edges of his heavy cloak, Conn quietly left the cottage without another word.

Kyna spoke for the first time, her thin, old-woman's voice querulous and strained.

"What was it, Morgana? What did you see to upset Conn so?"

Shrugging, Morgana shook her head. "I don't know. He will tell us when it is time, Kyna. Are there any more honeycakes? I'm starved, and I have not eaten since breaking fast early this morn."

"You're changing the subject again," Kyna grumbled, slowly lifting her brittle-boned body up from the wooden stool. "It's my lot, I suppose, always being left in the dark and never allowed into the light, but you'd think that since I brought you up from an infant—suckled you at my breast! —you'd have some sort of loyalty." A wooden spoon banged against an iron pot hanging from a hook over the fire as Kyna warmed to her argument. "But no! I am too old and ignorant to be told anything!" Hot stew was ladled into a rough wooden bowl and slammed to the surface of the table.

"Shall I get the bread?" Morgana offered in an attempt to stem Kyna's rebuke, but the old woman would not be distracted.

"I know there are some things I cannot hear, but your mother told me things." The spoon was jabbed in Morgana's direction. "She told me of the voices, and she told me of you before you were even planted in her womb. . . ." Kyna stumbled to a halt, realizing she'd said more than she'd intended.

"What did she tell you?" Morgana asked. Always eager to hear of her mother, she leaned close, but Kyna's thin mouth snapped tightly shut. It was closed so firmly that lines puckered at the corners. "You wretched old hag," Morgana sighed in resignation, "you do this on purpose, don't you!"

The wooden stool scraped across the floor as Morgana drew it back to sit at the planked table. Dipping her deer-bone spoon into the bowl, Morgana gingerly took a bite of the hot stew. Steam vapors rose in curling wisps above the bowl, wreathing the air in delicious clouds.

Kyna silently placed a platter of bread and a knife on the table, pushing it close to a round of goat cheese.

"You're like your mother, you know," she said after a few moments. "But where Eibhlin was hard, you are soft. And your dreams are not as hers were. She had the vision, a true gift from the gods, but it cost her dearly. Your dreams are too vague, but Conn hopes for more." Kyna looked at Morgana with sharply piercing eyes. "They are vague because you do not want the gift, Morgana. You reject what you have been given."

"And if I have?" Morgana said defensively. "Did anyone think to consult me before they decided that I was to spend my days in solitude and study?" The bone spoon paused halfway between mouth and bowl. Words spilled from her like water over a high ledge, tumbling over one another as she tried to make Kyna understand what she barely understood herself.

"I don't want this gift, Kyna! I want to be as the others are, drawing water from the well and baking bread, caring for a man and babies, and . . . and loving and being loved." Sudden tears sprang into her eyes, making them glow like green stones.

"But you are different, Morgana," Kyna pointed out. "You cannot be other than what you are, what the gods have made you. . . ."

"Yes, I can!" Morgana's fingers whitened as she gripped her spoon tightly, and she was surprised to hear the carved handle crack under the strain. "I can," she repeated, laying down the pieces of spoon.

Sympathy gleamed in Kyna's watery blue eyes as she slowly shook her head in denial.

"No, my child. There are none in this land who do not know of your gifts. You are respected, but none dare to come too near."

Morgana's throat ached. Kyna was right. Perhaps her destiny was that she would always feel hollow and empty and never be fulfilled. Conn told her over and over again that she must not question her precious gift, that dire consequences would occur should she deny what she had been given, and her immortal spirit might wander lost forever.

Turning her head to stare into the brightly leaping flames of the fire, Morgana wished bitterly for a chance to experience what others took for granted. One should be given a choice. . . .

A shrieking wind tore through the door left half-open by Conn, slamming it back on its hinges with a bang and startling Kyna and Morgana. Scurrying to close it, Kyna muttered under her breath that evil spirits seemed to lurk too close to the home of one protected by the gods.

" 'Tis a late wind that smells of winter," Kyna remarked as she leaned against the closed door. "And Beltane only a night away!"

Morgana did not hear Kyna's observation. She was staring into the flames of the fire with the inner vision Conn tried to encourage. Unbidden, the figures formed by flame and smoke writhed in front of her eyes.

A serpent skimming across the Irish Sea from lands of snow and ice . . . men, tall men, with hair of sunlight, horned helmets, and shoulders broad as oxen . . . flashing swords and howls of battle . . . dead Celts lying on the ground beneath stone crosses on a shore not far away . . . one man taller than the rest, with an aura of light surrounding and protecting him—the leader, an unknown enemy of the Celts, yet somehow familiar as he stood outside a Celtic monastery, his handsome face tilted upward and silvered by moonlight, his eyes troubled and watching . . . waching Conn, the blue fog swallowing up the druid like death . . .

Morgana blinked as the smoke stung her eyes, and the vision disappeared. She knew, as if the prophecy had been carved into a piece of hard wood, that the blue mist spelled death for Conn. Vivid impressions lingered in her mind as Morgana realized that she would meet the helmeted enemy leader who dealt death and destruction to Celts, and that somehow his destiny was entwined with hers. And most disconcerting of all—she had felt a strong sense of love emanating from the golden warrior. . . .

Her small hands clenched into fists as Morgana fought a wave of frustrating anger against the gods. If she must be burdened with the riddles, why not be given the answers? Now she would have to wait—and wonder.

Fear for the future rushed over Morgana like a tidal wave.

Chapter 2

Towers of wood were stacked on a hill overlooking the wild waves of the sea, waiting for the torch that would set them ablaze. Spectators gathered at the lip of the rocky ledge, waiting in hushed reverence for a member of the druids to light the fires that would usher in the Beltane.

Finally, when the sun slid into the cradle of the sea and the sky was the soft color of saffron, the Grand Bard stepped forward and lifted his hands skyward. A sea wind ruffled the flowing sleeves of his green robe and lifted the hem of the garment as he stood with outstretched arms. Long golden hair moved with the wind, and even his chest-long beard stirred with each gust. The bard's voice was deep and rich, as if springing from the very earth itself.

"Tan y'n cunys lemmyn gor uskys," came the command to set the pyres on fire. Crimson and orange flames leaped to consume the darkening shadows.

Morgana edged forward to toss a sacrifice of herbs and dried sheaves of grain into the flames, symbolizing their hopes for good crops. The acrid smoke stung her eyes, making them water, but she dared not flinch. To do so might be taken as an ill omen by those gathered to observe. Her arm arced outward and the offerings were accepted by the fires as she chanted, "Thousandfold let good seed spring. Wicked weeds, fast withering, let this fire kill."

Stepping back, Morgana caught Conn's faint glance of approval as she returned to Kyna's side. He had not spoken to her since the night before, when she had seen the blue mist, but his deep, dark eyes said what his lips did not. She was reluctant to tell him about her last vision.

Something was in the air this night that Morgana could not see—a difference, as if a storm were about to break over their heads. Even the air was heavy with it, though the darkening amethyst sky was unusually clear of clouds.

Children linked hands and circled to the right, in the direction of the sun's path across the Earth Mother, and their shadows danced against walls of flame. Across Erin similar beacons of yellow light burned from green hilltop to green hilltop, casting a glow over stone circles and fields of gorse.

Two fires of furze had been lit, and Morgana could hear the bawling of cattle as the country folk drove them through the purifying smoke with sticks before taking them out to wild pasture. It was a custom begun with the ancient ones, those druids so long before who had left their wisdom to be remembered.

It was reassuring to see the familiar rituals that had been one of her earliest memories, but Morgana was still unnerved by her recent visions. The blue mist around Conn was disturbing enough, but he was old and it was inevitable that he would one day join those who had gone before. It was the other vision that disturbed her most, the vision of the comely intruder who wielded savage weapons. Soon he would come to her village near Newgrange; she could feel the certainty like a soft cloak upon her shoulders. Somehow,

he had not seemed an enemy, but someone she should know
well.

A faint breeze smelling of sea and shadows skimmed like
a fat summer butterfly across her face, and Morgana's chin
lifted slightly as she turned to face the water. The wind
pressed her soft white gown to her curves, outlining long
slim legs and the proud thrust of her breasts. Late sun rays
glinted from the bracelets jangling around her slender wrists
and upper arms, and the heavy gold torque that she wore
around her neck glowed as if imbued with a fire of its own.
A matching girdle of thinly beaten gold circled her tiny
waist, tied with delicate chains that swayed gently with each
graceful step.

Watching, Kyna thought that Morgana was the most
beautiful woman in their tribe. Where most of the Celtic
women had fair hair, Morgana had hair as dark and soft as
night shadows. Her skin was darker too, a warm, golden
shade like late afternoon sunlight that warmed the earth
gently instead of harshly. Morgana was as luscious and ripe
as a summer apple, Kyna reflected. Sometimes . . . sometimes,
Conn was too harsh with her, expecting more than Morgana
could give, but who was she to argue? The mysteries of life
had never been revealed to such a simple old woman, and
so Kyna just watched and listened. 'Twas Morgana who
bore the burden of her mother's legacy. 'Twas Morgana who
saw dreams others could not. . . .

Chapter 3

Swirling gray mists came on silent cat paws, curling around the brooding rock faces of cliffs jutting into the sea. White-crested waves crashed against the night-dark stone, spraying spumes high into the air. The sea pulsed with mighty force, endlessly, relentlessly.

Sliding noiselessly through gossamer wisps of fog, a sleekly trim ship nosed past the steep edges of the bluffs as it sought lower land. The great serpent's head that formed the prow needed no guidance to these shrouded shores, though this was the first voyage past the cold reaches of the North Sea for the ship. The young leader had never before visited this land some called Hibernia, but was lured by fantastic tales about this strange land few Norsemen had seen. Celtic monasteries on this Gaelic stronghold were rumored to yield a wealth of plunder to any Vikings fierce enough to take it. The lure of rich prizes had been too great to resist.

Near the prow stood the Viking leader, a young man tall and strong, with eyes blazing the blue of the noonday sky and hair the color of light. He flexed his muscles beneath the rough, dun-colored tunic he wore and slid his sword from its scabbard. The whisking sound was echoed by the actions of his warriors.

"By Odin, we shall see our ends well met tonight." A man behind him laughed quietly, brandishing his drawn sword in a menacing gesture. "The foolish Celts sleep!"

A hard smile tugged at the mouth of the Viking leader, and his eyes narrowed as he swept the rugged shoreline with a piercing gaze.

"We chose the time well, Gunther. Tonight they honor Belenos, one of their old gods. 'Tis the eve of May Day, and they will have feasted, drinking mead and eating until they will be too slow to fight." His smile grew mocking as he sneered, "Even the Christian priests in the monastery will be among them in spite of their holy admonitions against the evils of drink and pagan rites!"

Brander tightened his fist around the ornately carved hilt of his sword and hefted a battle-ax. It had been many years since his father had witnessed a Celtic festival, but he had retold the same tale many times. Now Harald was old, and chief of his clan. Years ago, when he had been young, Harald had sought fame and fortune with fellow Norsemen interested in exploring the fabled coasts where gold and silver filled rough stone churches, and precious stones of amber dripped like rain from the branches of trees.

Brander had been but a small lad when Harald had stumbled across this green land of shrouded shores, yet his father's tales were still told over drinking horns during the long winter nights in Jutland. In spite of the dangers, he had been filled with a desire to match or even to better his father's exploits. Only recently had he been able to gather enough men to search for this land again. Brander had dreams of returning home in a blaze of glory to surpass Harald's.

The Celts were rumored to be quick-tempered and mighty warriors formidable in battle, but possessed of a weakness for intoxicating wine, beer, and mead. Shrugging, Brander reflected that 'twas a common weakness, and not one peculiar only to Celts. Tonight it would work in their favor.

A shadow darker than the rest rose abruptly before the serpent-prow, snaring Brander's wandering thoughts. They glided close to the shoreline now, and he squinted at the land shrouded with eerie shadows twisted into strange shapes. The Viking ship slipped into the shallows, scrunching against the sandy bottom as dark water lapped greedily at the sides. There was the muted clamber of feet against wood, and an occasional metallic clink as the warriors prepared to disembark.

Motioning, Brander silently urged his warriors from the longboat. There must be no sound to betray their presence to the Celts, no careless word nor rattle of sword to rouse them until it was too late.

The longboat rocked gently as the men went over the sides and dropped with hollow plops into the icy waters. At last the Vikings stood on the rock-strewn shores of Hibernia. Scudding clouds hid the moon's face, surely a favorable sign from Odin as they slipped unnoticed across grassy moors studded with wild flowers and briars.

Pausing, the men breathed quietly as Brander signaled them to a halt. Just ahead rose the steeply forbidding walls of the monastery which hid the sleeping Celts with their golden chalices and delicately carved statues embedded with precious stones. A drowsy, half-drunken guard met a silent death with the quick slice of a dagger, and heavily armored Vikings slipped quietly through massive wooden gates. No footsteps echoed in the stone-flagged corridors.

Silence lurked inside the monastery, leaving the Vikings uneasy. Where was their quarry—the fat priests and wine-sodden warriors? No one came to meet them. They stood, bewildered and with the juices of war still raging, staring at silent stone walls.

" 'Tis undefended," Gunther remarked at last, his tone as gloomy as the long, echoing corridors. His sword point flicked out to lop off the tip of a thick tallow candle spluttering in a golden holder upon the altar. "There's no sport in simple robbery, Brander. Where's the valor in theft?"

A frown creased the leader's brow. "I can't understand it. I was told that 'twas here, at the monastery of Monasterboice, that all came to sleep safely after a festival. . . ." His voice trailed off.

"They must have been warned," one warrior suggested at last. "Otherwise, they would have been here as fodder for our blades. . . ." He gave a vicious slice of his sword at an imaginary Celt.

"Perhaps," Brander agreed, "but all that really matters is that we pile our longboat high with gold, silver, carved chalices—seize whatever you can carry, warriors of Odin! We will go home much richer than when we came. . . ."

A sudden chill breeze came from nowhere, sweeping across Brander and causing him to shiver. A high moan like the keening of the winter wind jerked his head around to find the source.

"What was that?" he demanded sharply, but Gunther was concentrating on the Celtic treasures lying at hand.

"I did not hear anything, Brander." Gunther rocked back on his heels from where he squatted beside a knee-high statue embedded with precious stones. He shot his leader a quizzical glance. "What did it sound like?"

Shaking his head, and feeling a little foolish, Brander muttered, "The wind. That was all. It was the wind. . . ."

Uneasy now, Brander was in a hurry to leave this accursed place where the evil spirit of Loki seemed to dwell behind every gnarled tree and twisted bush. When the sun rose high in the morrow's sky, the Vikings would be gone, their proud ship gliding down the swiftly flowing river to the Irish Sea. If he never again saw this ancient monastery with its high stone crosses, he would be well pleased, Brander reflected. There was another place Harald had mentioned, farther south, where a band of druids were said to hold sway over the people.

"I thought the Romans wiped out all the druids several centuries ago," Brander had argued with his father, but Harald had been adamant.

"No, I met some when I was there. Believe me, they still exist, and they wear fantastic necklaces of gold and silver, with brooches bearing many valuable stones."

"Droichead Atha," Brander murmured aloud now, recalling the name his father had told him, "close to Newgrange. I will look there for more riches. . . ."

Again the wind shrilled through the halls, almost screaming down the stone corridors to chill Brander to the bone. The hair on the back of his neck stiffened, and he gripped his broadax more tightly.

"Did you hear it that time?" he asked Gunther hoarsely, but knew the answer when his companion turned a bewildered face up to him.

"Nay," Gunther finally laughed. "I think 'tis the lack of a woman that has finally softened your brain, Brander! Never fear—we will find many a Celtic woman before we leave this land!"

Oddly, Brander had no desire to bed a Celtic woman. Perhaps 'twas because his own mother had been a Celt from Gaul. But Bevin had not been as barbaric as these Celts seemed to be, with their strange rituals that only contradicted one another. Because of his mother, Brander was familiar with a few of the Celts' peculiar customs. Primitive rituals

honoring one of their ancient, discarded gods were conducted
in wild abandon, then the results of the pagan celebrations
were slept away in a Christian monastery. His mother had
been Christian, and Brander was familiar with the rival god
who claimed to be omnipotent.

But if a Norse god were to be insulted by being usurped
by a Christian deity, there would be swift and vengeful
action, Brander thought with grim amusement. The beginnings of a smile faded. Vengeance by any god made him
uneasy. Gripping his battle-ax, he shifted his glance back to
the dark hall where his men were enjoying their abundance
of wine and fruits of victory.

Suddenly Brander Eriksson could not stay a moment
longer in this dark and dank hall where mystery lurked in
silent echoes. He had to have air, fresh air that would clear
his brain and fill his lungs.

Pivoting, Brander walked away. He did not attempt to call
his warriors with him. To deny his men their sport would
bring protests from warriors accustomed to reward for their
efforts. Norsemen who went a-viking deserved proper
recompense.

His footsteps echoed hollowly down stone-flagged halls as
Brander found his way alone to the high stone arch leading
from the monastery. He would return to the longboat, and
his men could find him there on the morrow.

Once more standing outside, Brander took a deep breath
of sweet, gorse-scented air and turned his face upward. A
shimmering moon shone brightly down on him, with no
clouds to mask its silver face. Long shadows were thrown
across the small courtyard by high, carved crosses, stretching
almost to his booted feet as he stood in the portal of the
monastery.

For several long moments Brander stared at the brilliant
disc of the moon, his thoughts wandering. Clear, shimmering

light flooded over him, and he pondered the moon's cool beauty resembling a remote goddess. There were times when she wore the silver face of an enchantress, or perhaps the pristine features of the Valkyries, Odin's fair daughters. Should he ask for her continued good will?

The voyage had been surprisingly successful thus far. An omen, perhaps, pushing him toward even greater prizes, but at what price. . . . his ship . . . his men? No, 'twas bad luck even to think such thoughts . . . he would return to Jutland with a heavily laden longboat. The gods were on his side. So why did he have this foreboding?

Shifting from one foot to the other, Brander slid his glance to the murky gloom beyond the monastery walls. The shadows wheeled in a hazy pattern of trees and thick, ropy vines looping from towering branches. There was a muffled sound and he stiffened warily, waiting. A pale, brisk breeze once more whispered in a low moan, curling around his ears in a sibilant hiss like a serpent. Brander could not still his involuntary shudder of apprehension.

Chapter 4

Morgana heard the same whispering wind. Even while the Viking was standing at the monastery, listening, she was listening, too. The others of her clan had returned to their homes near Newgrange, but she had stayed behind, restless and unwilling to leave. She stood alone on a high ledge overlooking the dark curls of sea that washed against sharp, jagged rocks far below. It was a wind that pushed curls of hair from her face, whispering promises in her ears as it skimmed past, a white wind of premonition. Tonight the white wind had set in motion events that would alter her future. Morgana knew it as surely as she knew that one season followed another.

She turned slightly, sensing a presence behind her. Even before she saw him, Morgana knew that it would be Conn.

"You have seen more visions, Morgana." It was a flat statement without question. Conn's brows rose the tiniest bit. "Why have you not told me?"

"Perhaps I was waiting for the right time." Morgana slid her hands into the loose cuffs of her flowing sleeves and met the priest's night-dark gaze. The moon was low in the sky now, yet it still lit his face with a pale glow. Conn's thin lips twitched slightly at her evasive reply.

"Perhaps," he said, "but I do not think so. You don't want to tell me what you've seen."

"No. I don't." What would Conn care of blue, blue eyes and a fair face? Morgana thought. Or especially that warm wash of love that had enveloped her? He would scold her and call her ridiculous even to dream of such things.

Conn's brows rose higher. He stepped to the very edge of the precipice and stood with his back to Morgana. For several moments he said nothing as he watched the sea and sky and let the wind ruffle his hair. It was worn long in the style of Celtic warriors, falling over his shoulders in wavy tangles. He half-turned and the wind lifted it away from his thin, pointed face so that he looked much like a weasel with its ears laid close to its head.

"You are antagonizing the gods with your refusal to properly use your gifts," he said harshly. "When one cannot be grateful for what is given, the gods may take back the precious gifts that are so rudely refused."

Morgana's rounded chin lifted as Conn turned to stare into her eyes. Usually just his cold, hypnotic stare was enough to turn her knees to water and cause her throat to tighten, but this time it did not. There had been times when his will had superseded hers, but the clarity and reality of her recent vision gave her strength.

"I don't care if the gods take them back," she cried defiantly. "Truly, I hope they do! I never asked to see the things I see, or know the things I know, and I can't see that it has helped anyone at all." She forestalled Conn's acid reply by adding, "Besides, the Law says that one should not question those with the gifts. It is a bad omen."

Conn bristled. "The Law meant only that their visions

should not be questioned. You yourself are questioning the very essence of your being, your reason for walking the Earth Mother. . . ."

"No," Morgana interrupted, "that is not true. I question men like you, Conn, who will allow me no peace with myself. The gifts were meant to be used, not exploited. . . ."

"Do I exploit you?" Conn stepped closer. His voice was silky and slippery, reminding Morgana of the shimmering bolts of material that Eastern traders brought to Erin on their big-bellied ships. She had longed for a gown made of the exquisite material, but Conn had scornfully denounced the coveting of such worldly luxuries. "Do I exploit you, Morgana?" he repeated. "I only offer you the opportunity to help those around you."

"You offer me the opportunity to help *you*," she retorted, and wondered where she had gotten the courage to defy the chief druid. Never before had she gone this far and said the things she had just said! It was as if she were a stranger listening to someone else's words.

Her head began to throb with a dull pain that quickly grew worse, and Morgana tried to wrench her gaze away from Conn. She knew not to look into his eyes, that he could command anything, and she would follow him without a will of her own. Conn's power was in his eyes, in the terrible gaze that could pierce body and soul and force her to obey. But Morgana could not look away. She had waited too long and Conn's will was stronger than hers.

His eyes were dark liquid pools of night and his voice droned softly on, silky and suggestive, as slippery as an eel.

"You will tell me, Morgana, of the visions you saw and felt," he purred. And even though her mind rebelled, Morgana heard herself helplessly repeating what she had seen in the flames.

Conn's expression was intent and thoughtful. The lines

bracketing his thin lips and carved between his eyes deepened when she'd finished.

"So the Vikings come," he said, and there was a strange excitement in his voice. "I feared as much. It had been written that one day those warriors from the north will plague Erin. Though it seems that the time is near at hand, we must put it off as long as we can! I will warn our warriors so that they will be ready for them! Tonight, tomorrow, next year—we will kill these mighty few who dare to storm our shores with their puny weapons! There will be many nights of sacrifices and offerings to our gods for the victory!"

No, the Vikings could not die. . . . Morgana was pricked with the disloyal desire to protect the unknown invaders, and she wondered why. Undoubtedly, they would kill her without a qualm, yet she was drawn to that magnetic Viking in her dreams, and his destiny was hers. Could she protect him at the cost of her own people, her own country?

Her temples throbbed with pain, and closing her eyes, she put her fingers to her head in an effort to rub the pain away.

"More visions?" Conn asked sharply.

"No, just a headache caused by your insensitivity!" Morgana snapped. "It has been a long day, and I am weary, Conn. I must rest. . . ."

"No. There is not time for rest. You must concentrate and tell me where the invaders will land. And when. The interpretation is clear enough, but I need more details, Morgana. Think . . ."

"You know I can't force the visions, Conn. They must come willingly." Morgana stepped away from the tall, gaunt figure, drawing up the hem of her gown so that it would not become even more damp from the dew-wet grasses lacing the rocky ledge. Already sea mist had dampened the gown so that it clung to her body like a second skin, and she shivered.

Conn's fingers curled around her wrist, gripping with the sharp tenacity of a hawk as he sneered, "You will do it to spare those dear to you, Morgana."

"What do you mean?"

His grip loosened and he stepped away, drawing his cloak of concealment around him as he often did when he didn't wish to be seen. His voice floated to her from the darker shadows of close-wedged rocks, disembodied and eerie in the night.

"You will summon the visions for me, Morgana. I will seek you out on the morrow. . . ."

Then he was gone and Morgana was alone on the windswept ledge once more, troubled and confused. Of late, these hated confrontations with Conn had grown more bitter and intense, and part of her rebelled against his autocratic authority even while she knew she couldn't just meld into the clan without notice. She was a soothsayer, a priestess with the golden gift of prophecy, and no one would treat her as just another member of the clan. Kyna was right. She should accept her fate and become comfortable with it instead of struggling.

Morgana's shoulders drooped in resignation as she walked down the rocky path toward flatter land. Why weren't the visions ever about her life, her future? Must she always see for others instead?

Nightbirds twittered softly in the trees as she turned from the path into the woods. Friendly branches patted her arms in light whisks as she passed beneath low-hanging trees, and slices of moonlight played tag with shadows. In just a few hours the life-giving sun would smile down on the Earth Mother, and there would begin another day of herb-gathering and healings. Not that Morgana minded the healings, for it made her feel useful and needed when she heard a sick child's cough fade away, or when she healed a painful rash with one of her salves. Those were worthwhile things that brightened her days.

Pausing on the rise overlooking her cottage, Morgana saw the soft glow of light through the opened windows and smiled. Kyna would not rest until she knew Morgana was safe. In spite of the weight of her years, the old woman always waited on her charge, usually greeting Morgana with caustic comments to mask her relief. Kyna's loving anxiety for Morgana was transparent, a fact which both women tactfully ignored.

True to form, Kyna greeted Morgana sharply.

"I thought maybe the dark ones had come for you! I should have known you'd be too moon-scattered for them!"

The old wooden stool creaked a protest as Kyna rose. Her rough woolen shift barely reached ankles swollen with age, and she had discarded the belt that usually circled her waist. Kyna's creased face still showed evidence of the beauty of her youth, and for a brief instant Morgana was able to see her as she had once been.

"Why did you never marry, Kyna?" she asked idly, seating herself at the table. A loaf of dark bread and half a round of goat cheese still sat upon the table, and Morgana munched on a hard crust as she stared curiously at her old nurse.

"Who told you I never had?" Kyna bent beside the hearth, banking the coals so that the fire would not die. Soot streaked her forehead as she wiped at her eyes and slid Morgana a questioning glance.

"No one. I just assumed..." Morgana paused, realizing she knew very little about the woman who had nurtured her from birth. How selfish she was... too concerned about her own life and desires to show interest in another's. "Were you married, Kyna?" she prompted.

A soft smile transformed Kyna's face, making it appear much younger.

"Yes, child. I was already past my prime when married but he was a fine man, strong and tall, loving and kind. We were very happy together."

"What happened to him?"

"He was killed in battle, and I lost our child when they brought him home on his shield."

Suddenly Morgana could see it all, the bloodied body of a fine Celtic warrior draped over his shield, his weeping wife swollen with child. The images flashed quickly past.

"Conn brought me to you soon after, didn't he?" she asked quietly.

"Yes. I was tight and full with milk, and he knew I needed you." Kyna's smile was tender. 'The gods took away, but they gave back, too."

"I don't believe I could have loved my own mother more than I do you, Kyna," Morgana said. The words lay softly between them, never before spoken but understood. For some reason it was important that Kyna know how she felt.

Shaking her head, Kyna said gruffly, "I'm certain you would be just as careless a daughter, running about the woods at night without letting me know where you are!" Kyna's bent fingers reached out to touch Morgana lightly on her cheek, and her eyes were suspiciously bright. "Now eat something before you waste away to nothing," she added. "You're getting entirely too thin and bony. You look like a winter-starved calf!"

"What difference would it make? No man will look upon me anyway," Morgana sighed, obediently stuffing a hunk of cheese in her mouth.

Kyna rolled her eyes and snorted with exasperation. "Are we back to that again? Can't you think of anything else, child?"

"Yes," Morgana mumbled through a mouthful of cheese, "sleep!"

"Your bed is made with fresh straw and new hides. Eat a honeycake."

Shaking her head, Morgana rose and stretched, realizing how tired she was. The bed smelled of sweet, fresh grasses and fragrant herbs, beckoning to her.

"You're too good to me, Kyna." Morgana sank gratefully onto the low shelf cradling her bed.

"I know. I'm better than you deserve. Now sleep so I can. . . ."

Kyna smiled. Morgana was already asleep, one hand tucked beneath her chin like a small child, and her dark hair spread out like silk on the mattress. Kyna pulled a light woolen coverlet over Morgana to keep off the early morning chill. The old woman felt the bite of cold more deeply now, and knew it wouldn't be long before her tired body failed her. There was so little time and so much to do. . . .

Chapter
5

It was bright daylight when the Vikings came, so bold as to attack when none expected it. Even Conn was astounded at their audacity, belatedly rallying the warriors to a fever pitch of battle lust. Not that Celtic warriors needed much encouragement to enter the fray. They were madly fond of war.

Most fought entirely naked except for golden torques, or sacred collars, circling their throats, and bracelets on their arms. Still others wore chain mail, but nearly all stiffened their bleached hair with lime so that it stood out like a horse's mane. Formidable mustaches sprouted above their lips, of which the warriors were inordinately proud as they strutted in front of their enemies, taunting and boasting of their prowess in battle.

Expecting to take them by surprise, the Vikings were stunned by the display of concerted war power that confronted them.

As powerful and fierce as the Vikings were, the Celtic assault curdled their blood. They stood fast with spears and swords and battle-axes as the Celts charged with deafening blares from giant boar-headed war trumpets. The air was filled with the clatter of chariots, the hammer of hooves and whir of sling stones, the thud of spears and shock of shields, clanging swords and neighing horses, and full-throated shouts and screams. This battle was completely different from any other battle.

There were only twoscore of Vikings, and it seemed as if the entire land of Hibernia had met them on the rocky shores of their coasts. Even Celtic women joined the battle, and somehow they seemed the most fearsome. Accustomed to tall, healthy Viking women, Brander was still nonplussed to see the Celtic women fighting beside their men. They were a good match for the wild-haired, wild-eyed Celtic men; steely-eyed, the women were swelling their necks and gnashing their teeth while they flexed huge, pale biceps and pummeled Viking warriors with blows and kicks as powerful as if from the twisted cords of a catapult.

Seeking a break in Celtic ranks, Brander gave swift orders, and for a short space of time it seemed as if the Vikings might yet win the day. They slashed about them like the famed Viking berserkers, maddened with killing fever so that some would even bite upon their iron shields. But the Celts fought ferociously in defense of their homes, pushing the Vikings back and back until Brander decided to give the signal for temporary retreat and a chance to regroup.

Sweat poured down his face, stinging the numerous cuts and scrapes he had received. He glanced around him for a familiar face to pass along the order for retreat. Gunther was not far, standing amidst a half-circle of warriors and still swinging his battle-ax with hard, savage strokes.

The flat, grassy meadow was littered with bodies and discarded, broken weapons. Two-wheeled chariots bounced over mounds and rocks as the Celts raced about madly. Just beyond the meadow was a line of trees that promised shelter and possible vantage points, and Brander took several steps toward Gunther.

A horse jostled him, and Brander heard the familiar whir of a swung weapon. He whirled, slashing his sword at the unseen enemy. Then Brander recognized the bloody, gape-mouthed head of one of his men attached to the bridle of the Celtic horse. Gilby! He had known him since childhood, and the sight of his severed head prompted Brander to a fury that clouded his judgment.

Bellowing a war cry, Brander slashed out again and again, his sword biting into the horse's thick neck and bringing it crashing to the blood-soaked ground with a shrill scream of pain and terror. The Celtic rider rolled clear, whirling to face Brander afoot. He was grinning, beckoning to Brander to attack.

"Come, mighty Viking warrior! Attack if you dare! You have the heart of a bird, not a hawk, as I do."

"You are mistaken," Brander shot back, surprising the Celt by speaking his language. "You have the heart of a goose, not a hawk!" Kissing the edge of his broad-bladed war ax, Brander taunted, "Come, Celtic goose! Meet the Widow-Maker!"

Forgetting the sweat in his eyes and the nicks and cuts dotting his arms and bare legs, Brander fought with savage fury. He drove the Celt—who was as tall as Brander's larger-than-average height—back until he was pressed against the rough bark of a tree trunk. The Celt's sword had snapped in two from the force of one of Brander's blows, yet he still held the useless hilt and ragged blade in both hands, defying the Viking invader.

In spite of himself, Brander felt a wave of admiration for the Celt, and briefly considered taking him prisoner instead of killing him outright. His hesitation cost him dearly. A blow from behind sent Brander staggering to his knees, and the sky and trees whirled past at a dizzying rate as he struggled to rise. Another blow, and he measured his length on the grass beneath the tree.

Something warm trickled into his eyes. Sweat? No, this was sticky and red. Valhalla would welcome another warrior this day, Brander thought dimly. He was certain to die a warrior's death. Barely conscious, Brander heard the buzz of Celtic voices swim around him, and realized he was behind enemy lines and surrounded.

"The Vikings ran as if scalded dogs!"

"Aye, did you see them run in all directions like frightened sheep!"

"And when they saw that we had cut off their leader . . ."

The voices faded as the buzzing in his head grew louder, and the last detail Brander recalled was that he was circled by dozens of Celts with hot, triumphant eyes.

When he woke, he thought for a moment that he had descended into the lower world of Hel's regions, where the daughter of Loki reigned. There reposed the souls of all who had died of disease or old age, and at this moment, he felt afflicted with both those calamities. His head ached horribly, and his tongue was swollen with thirst. Lifting one hand, he gingerly touched a deep gash cut into his head by a war club. Brander winced, blinking his eyes to clear his vision. The din around him was enormous, like the bleating of a thousand deep-throated sheep. Where was he?

Firelight leaped erratically not far away, illuminating a circular area filled with big, brawny warriors. Brander realized with dismay that he was in the huge, thatch-roofed chieftain's hall where Celtic warriors had gathered for a victory banquet. A roast boar crackled on a spit over the fire, and gigantic bronze caldrons filled with foaming mead and wine squatted on each side of the hearth. Men sat cross-legged on piles of wolf skins, consuming vast amounts of wild boar and guzzling wine and mead. Some were already in a stupor, while others danced about drunkenly.

Jugglers and buffoons entertained in the crimson glow from the hearth, and in a distant corner opposite Brander a bard tentatively strummed his lyre. He was composing a recital enumerating the details of the day's battle, glorifying the Celtic victory over the Vikings.

Brander groaned softly. He had coveted glory, and now he was captured like a foolish puppy! He would be killed of course, instead of dying a hero's death, and now he would be denied a place in Valhalla. Only men who died a warrior's death earned the right to enter Odin's sacred palace.

No one had yet noticed that he was awake, but Brander knew escape was virtually impossible. The only entrance to the hall was across the open floor packed with Celtic warriors. Slightly turning his head, Brander saw his battle-ax propped against the wall near the door. Widow-Maker! —some Celt's battle trophy! If he could just inch his way close enough, he could yet die like a true Viking warrior. . . .

The incredible din inside the hall grew even louder as the chief stood up to present the hindquarters of the roasted boar. This was the traditional hero's portion; the thigh piece was given to the bravest hero of the day. Tempers flared and drawn swords glinted in the firelight as each man claimed the hero's portion and the chieftain bellowed for silence.

A horn sounded a long blast, and all grew silent for a moment. Eyes turned toward the man standing on a small, raised mound of hard-packed dirt.

The chieftain was tall, with the characteristic flowing mustache and hair. His short tunic was trimmed with rows of gold-embroidered designs, and his trousers were of the finest linen. A belt of huge gold links circled his lean waist, and even his soft, calfskin shoes were trimmed with beaten strips of gold. A wealthy man indeed, Brander observed with narrowed eyes. The gold torque around the chief's neck was the width of a man's hand, with heads of bulls carved on the ends. Jeweled eyes winked from the intricately carved heads.

Brander's attention was diverted from the chief's finery to what he was saying as an argument sprang up among several of the warriors. The chieftain held out his spread hands for silence, saying,

"I give the hero's portion to Caith. He fought the Viking leader and was responsible for his capture. . . ."

"But I was the one who struck him!" a man exclaimed, leaping to his feet in protest. "The hero's portion should go to me. . . ."

"It's easy enough to strike a man from behind, Garbhan," Caith said contemptuously. "*I* fought with a broken sword. . . ."

Pandemonium broke out as the man called Garbhan flashed a dagger, and Caith parried the lunge. It quickly erupted into a bloody brawl as Celt fought Celt.

No one had yet noticed that their prisoner was awake, and in the confusion, Brander inched his way along the walls toward the door. The hall was round in the shape of the sun, so that it was easy to escape notice behind the stacks of wolf pelts and straw-stuffed cushions.

Nearing the doorway propped opened to allow in gusts of

fresh air, Brander wrapped his fingers around the familiar contours of his battle-ax. Widow-Maker . . . how comforting she felt in his hands again.

Still on his knees with the ax in his fists, Brander's gaze raised to find a girl watching him intently. Dark jade eyes stared at him from a beautiful face, and he froze. She was just staring at him, and Brander's eyes narrowed, skimming over her. The girl was slight, tall but very slender, and she wore the Celtic dress that fit tightly to her breasts and hips, bound in place with a girdle of beaten gold. A wide necklace of gold circled her neck, and many bracelets jangled on her arms. Thrown back over one shoulder was a cape, fastened with an ornately carved brooch of gold and amber. The girl was obviously someone of consequence in this heathen Celtic land.

Tensing, Brander swiftly debated his next move. She would alert the others of his escape, of course, so he would have to fight after all. When he would have risen to his feet and prepared to defend himself, the girl shook her dark head slightly, and Brander could feel the intensity of her gaze resting upon him, as if she knew him and wanted to help. Bah, that could not be—but then she turned her face away and contemplated a far wall, ignoring him.

Puzzled, Brander dared not linger long enough to wonder about her motives. He took immediate advantage, and vaulted unnoticed out the door. Sucking in a deep breath to clear away the stale odors of sweat and smoke and burned meat from his lungs, Brander squinted into the darkness.

Not far from the hall was a line of trees with possible hiding places. He needed to get back to his longboat as quickly as he could, for the Celts would be in hot pursuit the moment they discovered his escape. Brander uttered a quick prayer to Odin that his men had not yet given up on him and still waited on the coast.

In spite of the throbbing in his head, Brander forced his unsteady legs into a jolting run toward the forest. Perhaps he would find safety there.

Not the trees . . .

Startled by the soft voice, Brander jerked to a halt. Who had spoken? He saw no one, and the jumbled noise in the chieftain's hall was a cacophony of sound. Uncertain, he took a few running steps toward the line of trees again.

Not the trees . . .

He decided it must be his own intuition that was warning him. The hair stood up on the back of his neck as Brander changed direction. He ran toward the open fields, blinding thrusts of pain jolting him with every step. His wounds must be more serious than he'd realized. Gasping for breath, Brander stumbled and fell, pushed himself to his feet and ran again. He must escape, must escape. . . .

At the far edge of the grassy field there was an outcropping of huge stones, flung as if from a giant's hand onto the ground. Staggering now, Brander sucked in ragged breaths of air to his tortured lungs, reaching out to lean on the still sun-warmed rocks with one hand. They felt so warm and comforting somehow, and he was tempted to lie down on the flat surface.

Feeling his way along in the dark, half-dragging Widow-Maker, Brander's hand suddenly encountered empty space between the smooth stones. Peering into the darkness, he could see a small cave formed by one rock leaning against two smaller ones, almost in the shape of a table. If he bent down and crawled in on his hands and knees, perhaps he could rest awhile, where none could see him.

Yielding to the demands of his injured flesh, Brander crept into the cave like a wounded animal. Clutching Widow-

Maker close, he curled up in the very back, where the granite roof sloped downward so that there was little room. Even if a Celt peered into the cave, it would be difficult to see him in the inverted V of the dark hole.

A shudder racked his body, and in spite of his intention to remain awake and alert, Brander drifted into a feverish sleep.

Chapter
6

That part of her that always knew, registered the fact that the Viking was hidden well, and a small, secret smile curved Morgana's lips. He was as brave, as handsome, and as daring as he'd been in her dream, and he did not deserve to die an ignominious death. She knew he wondered about her motives, but in truth, so did she. Instinct and that vague, voiceless whisper had prompted her actions, and Morgana had been trained to rely on her intuition. Would Conn condone what she'd done?

The answer was obvious. The chief druid would probably have a convulsion when he discovered that she'd aided an enemy.

Shrugging away her concern, Morgana slipped from the hall. She didn't wish to be present when those drunken Celts finally discovered their prisoner's escape. A hue and cry would be raised, and she would hear it soon enough. Now it was late, and she must return to her cottage.

Not bothering to lift her hem above the wet grasses of the meadow tickling her sandaled feet, Morgana strode swiftly toward her cottage. Blue, blue eyes and golden hair atop a sun-browned face kept appearing in her mind, and she thought of the wounded Viking. He was safe for a short time, but he was consumed with fever, and her teeth dug into her bottom lip as she racked her brain for a way to help him. Conn was too clever by far, and knew her moods and motives too well, so that she would be hindered in giving the man aid. Ah, but the Viking was so fair, so favored with comely looks, and his heart was good. This was not an evil man as were some of those who desired possessions that were not theirs.

And, Morgana recalled, this was the man she had seen in her vision two nights before. She'd known it the instant she'd seen him huddled against the far wall of the chieftain's hall. For a moment her heart had stopped beating, and every sense she possessed had sharpened. Perhaps this was the meaning of her vision, that she should help the Viking even though he was an enemy.

Shrugging, Morgana reflected that the Viking did no worse than other Celtic tribes had often done. Neighboring tribes were always warring on one another, planning cattle raids and sacking monasteries. Even monasteries warred against one another at times. The reason for this was simple: When a tribe attacked a monastery, they also attacked a king, whose brother was frequently the hereditary abbot, and thus appropriated the food supply stored there. There was nothing unusual about this method of warfare. But the threat of foreign invasion might bring together the warring Celtic tribes.

Conn hoped for unity among the Celts, unity and a return to the old ways, the religion of the trees. He hated the new Christian religion that had swept over his land, despised the monks and priests who propounded the theory of one God and the son who had given his life for all people on earth.

"Utterly ridiculous!" Conn would sneer. "One puny God, who can't even save his own son from being hung on a tree? I say that the sacred oaks are all-powerful, that one day we will rule not just Erin, but all the world!"

Morgana foresaw no hope for Conn's obsession. It was a smoke-dream, hazy and vague and just as insubstantial. The different tribes were satisfied as they were. Conn, of course, also saw himself in the role of chief druid reigning over all the tribes.

"You wander about at night like a cat," Kyna grumbled as Morgana pushed open the cottage door. "Do you search for mice in haystacks?"

A faint smile touched the corners of Morgana's mouth. "Don't fuss at me," she pleaded wearily. "I've had a tiring day, and the night has been as bad."

"Hmmph. You should stay closer to home then." Kyna slid Morgana an unsympathetic glance. "You are concerning yourself with matters you shouldn't, I'm afraid." She forestalled Morgana's surprised query with an upraised hand. "No. Don't bother explaining or denying. I don't know quite what it is that you're doing, Morgana, and I don't want to know, but you're endangering yourself. Please stop and think about what might happen."

"I don't really have a choice," Morgana said slowly. She pushed back a strand of dark hair from her eyes, lifting her face to Kyna. Strain was etched between her brows, and her soft mouth was tight with anxiety. "Forces war within me, Kyna, and I don't know how else to react. I can only do what I feel inside. . . ."

"Ah, you're so like your mother!" Kyna flapped her hands in resignation. Her woolen skirt bunched around knobby knees as Kyna sank to the stone hearth and clasped her hands in front of her, gazing at Morgana as if she was seeing her for the first time. "You're too much like her in some ways, and not enough in others. I would wish that you had Eibhlin's insight. . . ."

"Why won't you ever talk of my mother, Kyna?"

"It is not allowed."

"You mean Conn won't allow it."

"True," Kyna admitted, "but it is probably best that you not know too much. It might affect your future."

"Future?" Morgana's delicately arched brows rose so high that they disappeared beneath the wisps of dark hair on her forehead. "What kind of future do I have as Conn's minion? I will be exactly as he decrees I shall be, or suffer the consequences." Pacing the hard clay floor, Morgana's skirts swished about her trim ankles with each angry step.

"I will not be his . . . servant, Kyna! I will not! I mean nothing more to him than a vehicle of information!" Halting and swirling to face her nurse, Morgana stormed, "He uses me! I refuse to cooperate any longer."

"Really?"

The dark, dangerous voice was soft, so soft his observation might not have been spoken aloud. But Morgana heard him as clearly as she often heard the tower bells in the Christian monastery on their holy days. She stiffened, keeping her back to him, knowing better than to look the chief druid in his deep-set eyes. He had the power to drain her will with his gaze if she was foolish enough to turn her head in his direction.

"What do you want, Conn?" Morgana asked the far wall. It felt as if a hot iron was being pressed between her shoulder blades, and she knew his eyes bored into her like fire.

"It's not what I want, Morgana. It's what the gods want that should concern you."

"Are you the only mortal the gods will confer with? Perhaps they've spoken to me, too. After all, isn't that why you've trained me all these years—why I was never allowed to play childhood games nor romp and tumble in meadows and woods?"

"Ah, Morgana." Conn's voice was still soft and silky, slipping through the still cottage air as if on wings of light. "You blame me for your fate, when 'tis the gods who gave you the gift. . . ."

"You keep speaking of this gift, Conn, as if I were the only one in the world to have it! I'm not! Others can see beyond the veil into the future, just as I can. . . ."

"Yes, but not as well. And others haven't had your years of training in the arts. Don't deny what some would trade all that they possess to have."

"Like you?" Morgana asked sharply, and suddenly knew she had seized upon Conn's ultimate weakness. He masked his inability to foresee what would happen. That was why he relied upon Morgana—no, he *demanded* prophecies from her!

Conn's angry hiss told her she was right. Morgana's wry laughter rippled through the tiny cottage like the ringing of belled sheep.

"I've been so blind when all along, the answer was right before my nose! Oh, Conn, why didn't you just ask for my help instead of forcing me into an unhappy life of servitude? I'm certain I would have seen much more if my spirit had been willing. . . ."

"Enough! You are dreaming again, Morgana, for that is not the case!" Conn had drawn himself up into a stiff knot of fury, throwing one edge of his long, dark cape over his shoulder. He stalked toward Morgana, and she deftly managed to avoid his grasp while Kyna trembled in a corner, watching with eyes wide and fearful.

"Conn," Morgana warned, "do not be foolish. I am one of you, remember." She backed away from the druid, keeping her eyes trained on his hands instead of his face.

"Foolish? It would be foolish to listen to your childish prattle," Conn returned smoothly, seeming to catch himself. He halted in the middle of the cottage floor. "I intend you no harm, Morgana. Don't fear me. I was only angry because of the Viking's escape." His voice purred craftily, "Did you know that he had escaped?"

"Yes."

"Ah, but some say you left before his escape was discovered." Conn's hands meshed together, his forefingers pointing upward as he added thoughtfully, "I told them they must be mistaken when they suggested you had known of the Viking's plans. Some were angry that you had not warned them."

"Am I the shepherd of unruly sheep? Should I be responsible for all their mistakes? I think not, Conn," Morgana retorted. "Full-grown men should know better than to drink and quarrel. They can only blame themselves for the Viking's escape. I had nothing to do with it."

"Perhaps not, but you do know where he is."

Morgana still would not face the druid. In spite of her firm resolve, she wasn't certain how strong his powers would be, and she didn't want the Viking harmed.

"I saw him run toward the woods, and that is all I will tell you, Conn. Now go."

There was a moment of hesitation while Conn tried to perceive the truth; then, obviously satisfied that Morgana had spoken honestly, he nodded his head and left.

For several moments after the door slammed shut on its

leather hinges, the cottage was quiet. Neither Morgana nor Kyna moved or spoke as the fire crackled and popped on the stone hearth.

"You're making a powerful enemy, Morgana," Kyna said at last. "I beg of you, be careful! Did you really see the Viking run toward the woods?"

Nodding silently, Morgana stared into the familiar flames of the fire. The Viking *had* run toward the woods at first, until she had sent him a message to change his course. She had not dared to lie to the too perceptive Conn, but merely failed to tell the entire truth.

The fire popped loudly, spitting a spark onto the stone hearth where it quickly faded into ash. Conn reminded her of fire, Morgana mused, pragmatic until provoked, then deadly.

Unfastening the brooch that pinned together the edges of her cloak, Morgana swept it from her shoulder and to the back of a wooden chair. She had dressed in her best finery to go to the chieftain's hall, somehow knowing she would see the Viking. This fact had not escaped Kyna's notice.

" 'Tis your best cloak and gown, Morgana, that you wore to the victory banquet," the old woman commented slyly. "I wonder why that is?"

Gathering up her pouch of forgotten herbs from a dusty corner, Morgana chose to ignore Kyna. She tossed the pouch on her sleeping shelf and began shrugging out of her soft linen gown. The short, outgrown undertunic she wore beneath reached only halfway down her thighs, and she gave a brief sigh.

"At least I looked presentable on the outside," she murmured to no one in particular, but Kyna's sharp ears heard.

"Ah, and who would you be trying to impress, Morgana?"

"No one. I just wished to look my best for once."
Morgana's mouth tilted in a half-smile. She hadn't fooled
Kyna for one moment, and they both knew it.

" 'Tis the Viking!" Kyna cried, throwing her arms in the
air. "And us living on the edge of being wiped out by the
invaders!"

"It certainly didn't look that way at the battlefield today," Morgana observed dryly.

"You . . . you were there?" Kyna's eyes bulged as she
stared at Morgana.

"Of course. I wanted to see what happened, didn't I?
And why not? Some women fight beside their men."

"But you've no man to fight beside," Kyna pointed
out, "and I'm thinking you'd choose the Viking if you
did."

Morgana pulled a gown of rough, undyed wool over her
head and belted it with a thin strip of braided leather.

"No, Kyna, I wouldn't do that." She bent and tugged on
a pair of soft, kidskin boots that just covered her ankles.
"But I'll admit to you that I am extraordinarily attracted to
him, and I don't even know why." Pushing back a loose
strand of hip-length hair that had fallen over her shoulder,
Morgana's head lifted slightly. The small cleft in her chin
deepened as her mouth tightened. Her voice lowered to a
husky whisper that Kyna had to strain to hear.

"He is the man in my vision, Kyna, the one I saw coming
with weapons of death and a ship like a serpent. Our destiny
is somehow entwined, and I must know how and why. I will
go to him. . . ."

"No! Morgana, you can't! If Conn discovers it, both of
you will die. . . ." Kyna's voice rose to a shrill shriek as
Morgana took her warm cloak from its peg and drew it over
her head and shoulders.

"Death is just transition into another life, Kyna. Conn

taught me that,'' Morgana said with a brittle laugh. She hugged the old woman fiercely and told her not to worry, that she would return soon.

After the door had shut behind Morgana, Kyna discovered that the pouch of healing herbs had gone with her.

''Foolish girl! She has gone to heal a man who is just as likely to kill her as not!'' the old woman muttered, and tears of fear and frustration stung her tired old eyes.

Chapter 7

There was no moon. Rolling dark clouds hid its face from view, and a sharp wind tore through trees and bushes. Were the gods angry with her? Morgana wondered uneasily. No, they couldn't be, or they wouldn't have sent her the vision. She had listened to Conn and Kyna too much, and was beginning to doubt her own abilities.

Pointed briars tore her rough woolen gown as Morgana pushed through a patch of still-green berries. She should have thought to bring the Viking some food. He would be starving after the long day, and thirsty. She paused for a moment, then decided it was too late to go back, that Kyna would be asleep and she couldn't risk waking her.

The small rock crevice was pitch-black, and for a moment Morgana wondered if she had somehow been wrong in her intuition, and the Viking was not there. Then her sharp eyes caught the faint glimmer of metal, and she heard a soft sound like the rustling of mice in the wood.

"Viking!" she said softly, crouching down to peer into the black void. "Viking, are you awake?"

There was no answer, only a faint moaning sound and harsh breathing. He was more injured than she'd thought, then.

Kneeling close to the unconscious Viking, Morgana stacked twigs and leaves for a small fire, then used her stone to strike a spark. When it caught, she inched forward on hands and knees. The full pouch of healing plants belted at her waist dragged along the hard rock floor of the cave. Reaching out, Morgana touched the Viking with a tentative hand, letting the pads of her fingers skim lightly over his injured flesh.

Morgana stroked him as impersonally as she would touch a harp or flute, letting her wise fingers seek out his wounds and speak to her of their gravity. One cut in particular was bad, a nasty gash on his arm that went almost bone-deep. Anger scored Morgana's face with lines as she thought of the disregard with which the prisoner had been treated. Even one who was to be slain should have their wounds tended! It was the Law.

The gash still oozed hot and sticky, and had left the Viking feverish. The bleeding must be stopped and the fever cooled, before the Viking's spirit retreated from life. Quickly, she dug into her pouch, retrieving the monkshood that would reduce his fever and lessen the pain that was making him thrash about, reopening his wound.

It would take time to make another potion, using tannin derived from the bark of oak trees. The healing potion would retard the flow of blood oozing from the Viking's wounds. Morgana spared a brief hope that no Celtic warrior would see the smoke or light from the small fire she'd lit. She left the Viking briefly to search for the knobby galls which often decorated the bark of majestic, sacred oaks. This was done with careful ritual, explaining to the spirit of the trees what she needed as she removed the lumps with her dagger. Soon one boiled in a leather sling suspended over the small fire, while she tucked the others into her pouch for later use.

The Viking stirred in a restless sleep that drained instead of refreshed, and Morgana laid a cool hand upon his hot, perspiring brow.

"You are fairer than most, Viking," she murmured aloud, certain he could not hear. "But it is not just that which draws me to you." She wore a puzzled frown as she rocked back on her heels, staring at the man who had inhabited her dreams. His hair was as golden as light captured from the sun, falling in damp, heavy waves around his face; and he wore a mustache and beard as did most other Vikings, only closely trimmed and neat. Her fingers gently explored the rugged contours of his jaw and cheek, trailing lightly over the curve of bone and muscle.

When she encountered a wet, sticky patch, she turned his head slightly to examine another deep cut. Mingling with light golden sprouts in his beard were crimson smears of blood. . . . another wound . . . not serious, but needing her attention.

Morgana gently scraped away the hair from around the wound with the sharp edge of her dagger, taking care not to wake the Viking. He slept so soundly, with the sleep of the gravely wounded, that she fretted about his recovery. Surely he would not die! The gods would not have given her that vision if it was meant that he should die.

Deep emotion stirred within her breast, surprising Morgana. How could she feel so strongly about a man with whom she had not exchanged a single word? It seemed unlikely, yet it was true. She traced the arch of the Viking's brow with a tentative fingertip, admiring his facial structure. He was well-favored indeed, but beneath the outer shell of his pleasing form dwelled an honorable man. She sensed it, as she could ofttimes sense the silver dart of fish beneath murky waters of a stream.

Because of her highly refined sensitivity, Morgana was even more surprised when the Viking woke, fixing her with the gaze of an enemy instead of a friend. He should also sense that their destinies were entwined, but he did not.

Harsh, hurting fingers gripped her with surprising strength, threatening to crush the fragile bones in her wrist.

"Are you trying to poison me, wench?" the Viking demanded hoarsely. An expression of distrust marred his handsome face as he eyed the potion she was attempting to pour down his resisting throat. He gave her a rough shake. "Answer me!"

"And if I was, would I be foolish enough to confess to it?" Morgana countered coolly. "It should be obvious to even the most thick-skulled Viking that I am trying to help." She gestured to his bandaged wounds with her free hand.

Fever still burned bright in his eyes as the Viking turned his gaze to the aching wound on his forearm. It did feel better than it had done earlier, but Brander's sluggish brain resisted admitting that this girl might be a friend instead of his foe.

"And why would you help an invader in your land?" he sneered, his grip tightening.

Morgana winced at the pain, and managed to gasp, "I don't know! I only feel that I must . . ."

Derision curled the Viking's upper lip in disbelief. "I don't believe you. You must have another reason, wench. . . ." By all the gods, Thor's hammer was beating an incessant drumming within his skull, and he could hardly focus his eyes on the girl. From what he recalled, she was comely— aye, more than comely—beautiful. It had been a long time since he had been with a woman, and he could smell the fresh fragrance of her hair, the sweet scent of her wafting to his nose as if on a spring breeze. . . .

Brander's reaction startled both of them. He yanked Morgana close, so that she was pressed close to his chest, her breasts brushing against his rough tunic.

Morgana had never been held by a man, and the reality was much more breathtaking than the dreams had ever been. She had seen this man in her vision, had known she was destined to have her life intertwined with his, and now she yielded gladly. This was her destiny, her future, her very reason for existence. This man was the reason she had waited, had not taken another as did the other Celtic women. Celtic law provided that a woman could choose a man who pleased her, and now Morgana chose at last.

Somewhere in his brain Brander must have known her lack of resistance was not usual, but his pain-clouded mind only accepted Morgana's compliance as natural. The drugs and his injuries added to the confusion of the disordered day, so that he was aware of only the touch and taste of the woman in his arms.

His mouth was hot and searching, his hands tugging impatiently at Morgana's garments, tearing them in his haste. He wanted her, wanted to feel her soft skin and taste the sweetness of cherry-ripe lips. He needed to bury himself within her. . . .

Weak, but on fire with passion, Brander paid no heed to his injuries. He tore off his garments as well as hers, stripping them both so that they lay clothed only in the light from the fire. It was warm in the small cave, steamy with their desire, wrapping them close in hot, moist arms.

Though she had ofttimes witnessed the rutting of animals,

Morgana had never seen men and women couple. It was still a mystery to her, unexplained by Conn or Kyna. Why explain what they did not wish her to experience? Conn had once asked. She needed to concentrate on her gifts, not physical pleasure.

But now Morgana wished she had more knowledge than she possessed. She did not know what to expect, or how to react to the feverish caresses Brander was lavishing upon her willing body. And she didn't understand why her insides boiled like a hot, simmering stew, churning with an aching emptiness.

When Brander's mouth traced a warm, wet path from her lips to the hollow between her breasts, then moved to a pink crest, Morgana arched helplessly upward, craving something—anything to satisfy the confusing yearning she felt. She cried out softly, her voice a whisper against the heated angle of Brander's neck and shoulder.

Tender hands cut with the sureness of a scythe through her vague murmurs, rendering her powerless even to speak. What was he doing? Morgana wondered dimly, and why hadn't her powers ever prepared her for this—this sweet, hot magic that he was working with hands and mouth and hard male body?

She had never thought to solve the mystery of a man's body, even having witnessed the naked Celtic warriors as they fought with their manhoods jutting out with all the careless pride of a ram's horn. Now the mystery was prodding her insistently, demanding entrance into that secret place where no man had ever been before. Morgana turned into the Viking's body, straining against him, breasts pushing against his chest as he lay beside her, hip to groin, thigh to thigh, their mouths locked in a probing kiss.

Finding some untapped source of strength, Brander rolled

atop the girl, his long, lean body stretching over hers so closely that an oak leaf could not have been wedged between them.

"Ah, sweet," he muttered thickly, tangling his hands in the wealth of dark hair spread like a carpet of silk over the jumble of their clothes. Wide eyes the shimmering color of emeralds gazed up at him through sooty lashes, and her mouth was half-parted and smiling. Some sense jarred Brander, reminding him that he did not know this wench, but it quickly departed when the girl moved beneath him, wrapping satiny legs around his torso.

Nothing could have stopped him then. Passion surged through his veins in a thundering flood as he answered the appeal in those remarkable eyes, and Brander thrust forward. Dimly aware of the girl's sudden cry of pain and the tensing of her lithe body, he wondered at it, but could not stop. Again and again, moving with that age-old rhythm of man and woman, Brander rode to a crashing release.

Startled by that first hot stabbing of pain, Morgana had not been able to stifle her cry. Gradually, the pain subsided, but Brander did not. A strange feeling swept through her at his movements, leaving her yearning and unfulfilled when he finally shuddered and was still. He slumped against her, sweaty and warm, his harsh breath tickling her ear. Though she somehow knew there must be more, Morgana was content. The Viking had been sent by the gods for her, and she was now his in all ways. Her arms tightened tenderly, and wandering fingertips caressed and explored the smooth contours of his back.

When he wakened, still wrapped in Morgana's arms and atop her slender body, the Viking demanded harshly, as if just remembering their earlier conversation, "Why are you here, wench?"

"My name is Morgana," she answered, "not 'wench.'"

Pushing away, he tugged on his garments, keeping a wary eye on the still-nude girl watching him so calmly. "All right, Morgana. I would know your reasons," he said.

She recognized the weariness and confusion in his voice though his eyes were now much clearer. For some reason, he made her feel uneasy, discarded, and she drew up a torn length of her dress to cover her nudity, her chin lifting as she gazed back at him.

"And I would know your name, Viking. I can't continue to call you Viking, or invader, or lover. . . ."

"Brander Eriksson, from Jutland," was the quick, uneasy answer. A frown creased his forehead, peeping from beneath the bandage which Morgana had carefully wound around his head. In the cool light of sanity, the girl seemed young—too young. "What is your age, Morgana?"

Her mind moved quickly. Should she dare admit to eighteen winters? Most girls her age had been married for several years. The Viking would think her marred in some way, for no man to have spoken for her. He might not understand if she told him the truth. . . .

"I have seen fourteen winters," Morgana answered evasively, thinking guiltily that she *had* seen fourteen winters—plus four more.

Her answer stunned Brander. Fourteen? He had lain with a girl of only fourteen? By Odin, the gods would surely frown on him for this! It was not honorable for a man, a warrior, to take a child to his bed.

A faint groan escaped Brander, and Morgana stared at him in confusion. She knew that he was not pleased with her answer, and wondered if she should have claimed only twelve winters. But surely, the Vikings did not take girls that young to wife!

Seeing her confusion and hurt, Brander relented. He was

not a cruel man, nor did he like having violated a girl of
only fourteen. The proof of her virginity stained the white
kirtle she wore beneath her tunic, spread upon the rocks of
the cave for all to see.

"I have not thanked you for binding my wounds," he
said, awkward, unsure of how to speak to this girl who had
saved his life. "I tender my deep appreciation, and—" he
spoke through gritted teeth for he had never before apologized for anything—"I am sorry for . . . for . . . that." A
wave of his hand indicated the bloodstained garment at
Morgana's feet.

Morgana's gaze moved to her kirtle. "I'm not sorry," she
answered with mounting confusion. "Was . . . was it because I am inexperienced . . . ?"

Another deep groan. How could he make her understand
that it was only his natural urges which had made him take
her like an animal? She was so young, and so innocent.

"Please . . . I have to rest," he said. "We will talk of it
later, perhaps. I must leave quickly, before your warriors
find me."

"Nay! Stay here, or they will surely find you." Morgana
rose to her knees, forgetting the concealing gown she held,
facing Brander in the faint glow of the firelight. "If you
leave, Conn's men will find you, and you will be sacrificed
to our gods. . . . Stay, Brander, and I will bring you food
until the time is right for you to get away."

Staring at her, Brander found it difficult to believe that a
fourteen-year-old girl could possess such ripe curves and
lushness of body. Sweat popped out on his forehead in tiny
beads, and he swallowed hard. Irritable, he picked up her
discarded gown and tossed it back to her.

What choice did he have—when he did not know the
countryside and had only his battle-ax? Brander acquiesced,
accepting her help and hoping the girl's relatives would not

come after him with sword and spear for what he'd done. A wave of exhaustion left him weak, so that Brander only vaguely knew when Morgana dressed and left the small cave hidden beneath stone megaliths upon a rocky hill.

Chapter
8

The tiny cottage was quiet at last. Morgana waited until she was certain that Kyna was asleep, then slipped silently out the door. The old woman worried too much. She had seen Morgana's torn clothing, and the sudden anxiety in her eyes had pierced Morgana's conscience. But how could she explain how she felt when Kyna would only consider the fact that her lover was a Viking? And besides, it had only been once. Since that time, Brander had not touched her.

Scurrying through the darkened woods with food and wine for Brander, Morgana wondered why he had not shown her the same attentions he had the night of their meeting. She longed for him. Her pulse pounded with new blood when he accidentally touched her hand or brushed against her, yet he would jerk away as if burned. Perhaps it was because he was still weak, she reasoned. When he was stronger, he would respond to her. Wouldn't he?

But Brander showed no inclination in that direction. Sighing, Morgana watched with rapt attention as Brander devoured the venison and honeycakes she had managed to sneak from her cottage pantry.

"Do you know where my men wait? Or if they do?" he asked around a mouthful of savory meat. He lifted the skin of wine to wash down the last bite of venison. When Brander shifted position, moving his injured leg, he had to stifle a groan of pain.

"Aye, but you are not ready to join them yet. Wait, and I will do what I can to heal you quickly. Your men will wait."

"How do you know that? They may think me dead already, and sail away. . . ."

"No. They wait and discuss what to do. They are reluctant to return without you or evidence of your death."

Brander's eyes narrowed at Morgana's positive tone. "How do you know all this? Have you spoken to them?"

"Nay, but their voices speak in the wind. They will not leave without you, Brander Eriksson. You are the leader."

"You seem to know a lot for a Celt," he commented with a grunt. "I think you concoct wild stories just to satisfy me."

"If I have, you will know it soon enough. Then you may take your revenge upon me."

"How do I know you won't betray me to your people? There is nothing to keep you from doing so."

Staring at her in the dim, rosy light, Brander wondered about the motives of this beautiful Celt. He had not thought such loveliness would be found in this heathen land where men worshipped trees instead of proper gods. The dark beauty of this woman eclipsed any Celt—yea, any Viking woman he had yet seen! Brander wondered about enchantment as he gazed at the girl who moved with the gentle, quiet grace of a deer. Her movements were fluid and effortless, as if she were composed of air and water instead of flesh and bone. And her eyes—a clear, luminous green like the deep sea, or the soft sheen of summer grass. He flushed to find himself gazing at the soft lushness of her mouth, and the tempting dimple gracing a small, rounded chin. Her face was a marvel of sculptured curves covered by a rich, golden tapestry of flesh, all woven into perfection.

Brander's eyes reluctantly strayed from her face to her body, and oddly, it was as if he observed with an impartial gaze. She appeared to be a full-grown woman instead of only a child, and he recalled too well the satisfying feel of her body next to his; yet his blood did not quicken in his veins at the sight of full, firm breasts pressing against the rough wool of her gown, nor did his pulse race at the glimpse of long, silken legs and trim ankles. By Odin, had his manhood been destroyed by his injuries? he wondered dimly, and was startled by Morgana's throaty chuckle of mirth.

"You are still possessed of all your manly faculties, Brander Eriksson," she assured the astounded Viking. "Do not waste energy worrying on that score. Concentrate all your energies on regaining strength."

"How did you know what I was thinking?" His brows furrowed into a frown.

"'Twas easy enough. Your eyes say much about you." Morgana did not say aloud that she had heard his thoughts as clearly as if they were her own, and knew his reaction to her appearance. He was reluctant now, because of who he was and who she was, but he wanted her. Brander only stifled his desire, and time would change that. She wanted to preen like a conceited bird of gay plumage, who thinks it is the most beautiful creature ever invented. The Viking made her feel beautiful, when she had never felt so before. And because he saw her as beautiful, she was.

Thick, dark lashes shadowed her flushed cheeks as Morgana gazed at Brander. The gods had certainly answered her pleas after all. . . .

The next few days blended into a cycle of secret visits mixed with sleepless nights. Morgana's usual routine was interrupted as surreptitiously as possible so as not to alert Conn to her duplicity. Something drew her to the Viking as unerringly as the tide rushes back out to sea. She could not escape the overpowering emotion that filled her whenever she thought of Brander. And those nights when she could sleep, she dreamed of him. She saw them together, walking in a strange land, holding hands and talking like lovers do. Brander was her destiny. Weren't dreams the extension of one's hopes? If so, she would fulfill her hopes with Brander,

More and more food began disappearing from Kyna's small pantry, and she complained loudly about the return of Morgana's appetite.

"Entire haunches of venison are missing, and I'd swear we had another cheese," Kyna muttered one night as Morgana pretended to sleep. The old woman eyed her suspiciously. "You're home of an evening lately, child, and to bed early. While I appreciate the respite, I'd like to know why."

"Why?" Morgana turned her head to gaze innocently at Kyna. "Isn't this what you've wanted, what you've asked me to do so many times that I've lost count?"

"Aye."

"Then don't complain." Morgana turned her face back to the wall and hoped Kyna would retire quickly, so that she could rush to Brander's small cave. The hours went by so slowly when she wasn't with him!

Kyna stood tapping her foot against the floor for several minutes, mulling over the change in her foster daughter.

Then, sighing loudly so that Morgana could hear, she went to bed.

Long minutes after the ropes of Kyna's bed squeaked a final protest, Morgana rose and fumbled about in the dark, taking from their hiding place the haunches of venison and boiled vegetables as well as her pouch of healing herbs.

Still and silent, Kyna reflected on Morgana's actions. She knew what was happening, had heard how a Viking prisoner had inexplicably escaped and could not be found. Morgana's vision . . . The vulnerable girl had likely imbued this barbaric Viking with all manner of wonderful qualities he didn't possess, and was giving him food and aid. The cottage door creaked softly and Kyna winced. Should she inform Conn? The chief druid would be harsh in his judgment, and Morgana might suffer. But wouldn't she suffer when the Viking hurt her? A lump formed in the old woman's throat as the door shut with a slight click. She would pray to all the gods that the Viking would return Morgana's innocent, untarnished love. . . .

Brander was waiting, fretful because she was late, and ravenous. It didn't take him long to devour almost an entire haunch of venison and most of the boiled vegetables, and there was no conversation while he ate.

At last, full and satisfied, Brander pushed away the remains of his food and slanted Morgana a lazy glance as she gathered up the scraps for the night creatures. It was a starlit night when the thrushes sang outside the cave in full-throated harmony, and Morgana found herself absently humming their night songs. Because of the night's beauty, Morgana insisted they move toward the larger front of the cave.

"You can breathe in fresh air instead of the stale, dark air in this cave," she argued when Brander registered a suspicious protest. "And you'll still be hidden from view."

Relenting, Brander moved to the front and sat with his back propped against a slanting rock. It was much more pleasant than the air he had been breathing, fresh, with the sweet, sharp smell of beech and oak, and layers of fallen leaves over the night-damp earth.

"Celts are not so very different from Vikings," Brander observed idly, gazing at the stars from beneath an overhang of rock.

"No?" she answered his idle comment. A smile flickered briefly on her lips as she bent to the task of changing his bandages. "I would say there are some important differences, but underneath different shells, all men want the same. Each possesses similar values: a love of life and home, a desire to better himself."

"And a desire for glory."

"Is that what you desire, Brander?" Morgana finished tying the clean strip of linen binding his arm and cut off the loose ends with her sharp-edged dagger.

"Glory? Of course. 'Tis what all Vikings desire. It is our life."

"What of love, and home, and family? Are those not the most important to you?"

Shrugging, Brander replied, "They are important, of course, but the most important thing a man can do is to die a warrior's death and be assured of a place in Valhalla. The Valkyries, Odin's nine daughters," he explained at her puzzled expression, "ride their winged horses down a rainbow bridge to carry heroes slain in battle to the hall of heroes, or Valhalla. 'Tis on a sunlit plain of Asgard, high above the clouds, and there men feast on ever-replenished game each night, and recover from wounds incurred during

the day's battle-sports. Odin is our chief god, and to join
him in Valhalla is a great honor."

"I see," Morgana murmured in a tone that indicated that
she did not see at all.

"You don't agree. Is that not what your Celtic warriors
desire most?"

"The family is all-important to us. Though there are a
few who desire glory over all else," she added, thinking of
Conn. For a moment Conn's visage flashed in front of her
eyes; his cheekbones standing out as on a bleached skull,
and his prominent features rigid with fury and blood-lust.
Morgana shuddered.

Dark brows rose as Brander stared at her questioningly.
"What is it, Morgana?"

It was odd that in such a short time he had grown
sensitive to her moods, but he had. Now he recognized that
she had once more retreated into herself, to some hinterland
where no one could follow. Morgana's ability to withdraw
completely into the shell of her body, projecting only a
blank face and implacable wall, sometimes irritated Brander
beyond measure. He did not understand that ability, yet at
times he envied it. And she was capable of uncanny excur-
sions into his mind, reading him too well. He had the
inescapable feeling that this woman could be more dangerous than any Celtic warrior if she desired. Brander shifted
uneasily at the disturbing thought that he was totally in her
care.

"Why were you frightened?" he asked abruptly. "Did
something startle you?" He had seen her quick jerk when
she'd thought of Conn, and noted the smoky dark fret in her
wide eyes. Brander repressed the impulse to reach out and
stroke her cheek or trace the tempting outline of her parted
lips.

"Frightened?" Morgana echoed, and managed a wide

smile. "I . . . I was thinking of . . . of something. That's why I shuddered . . . no, I was thinking of some*one*, not some-*thing*." She sat forward, her face serious as she confessed. "Conn. He's the chief druid among our people, and very powerful."

"He will try to slay me?" Brander's lips curled in an indulgent smile as if to point out that it might be difficult for even a chief druid to accomplish.

"He will no doubt try to slay us both if he discovers that I have been giving you aid and shelter."

"I don't understand why you do this when it risks your life, too," Brander commented. His eyes, those wonderful blue eyes that could be the color of a summer sky or the delightful shade of a robin's egg, stared at her doubt-fully.

Didn't he? Didn't he remember that special night only four days before, when he had lain with her on a bed of rocks and discarded clothing, and made her into a complete woman? She remembered and would never forget. . . .

"There are some things one should just accept on blind faith, Brander." Morgana unfolded her lithe body and stretched her cramped muscles. "I have to go. The night is no longer young, and even the thrush's song is tired and sleepy. The sun will smile over the sea cliffs before I am home if I don't hurry."

"Wait . . ." Brander's quick fingers closed around her wrist, not painfully like that first time, but softly firm. Morgana met his eyes with a luminous gaze that seemed to see clear through him.

"Yes?"

"I am pleased that you think enough of me to risk your own life, Morgana—though I don't understand why—but perhaps it is best if you don't come again. I am almost healed, and it is time to rejoin my men. . . ."

She gasped as if hit in the belly. An odd, breathless feeling left her as empty as the depleted wineskin at Brander's feet.

"No! You are not strong enough yet! And . . . and your wounds may reopen, and you would bleed to death before you went more than two leagues. . . . Oh, I pray of you, Brander Eriksson, don't leave yet!"

To Morgana's horror, the words tumbled unbidden from her mouth, like the rush of a spring flood from the higher hills to the green valleys, and she was embarrassed. Flushing, she fidgeted with the dagger she still held in one hand; then, with crystalline tears trembling on thick, spiky lashes, she looked away from Brander's startled eyes.

Though cold logic bid her let him go, she couldn't. That wild, wonderful night remained hot and searing in her memory, so that she couldn't release him yet. He was hers, the gods had given him to her, but . . . Morgana knew how close to danger she stepped, that Conn might find the Viking at any time, and then she would not be able to save him. A shiver ripped through her tensed muscles, and Morgana bowed her head so that Brander couldn't see her eyes. She had to let him go.

"I'm sorry," she whispered thickly when he remained silent and watching. "You're right. You must go. It's just that . . . that . . ."

"It's just that you've made a complete fool of yourself over the Viking," a cruelly familiar voice said behind her. A rasping sound of sword leaving scabbard warned Brander not to reach for his battle ax lest he endanger both Morgana and himself.

"You must be Conn," Brander said evenly as a tall, robed figure stepped from the shadows into the light. He wasn't surprised; he had been expecting Conn, even anticipating his arrival, but now that the moment was here he realized how weak he still was, and cursed the fact.

"Aye. I must be. Stand back from the Viking, Morgana," the chief druid said sharply.

Still kneeling, holding the dagger she had used to slice through the linen bandages, Morgana stiffened. She had little choice. If she refused, Conn would have no qualms about killing her, and that would be no help at all to Brander. If she acquiesced, perhaps there would be a chance for both of them.

"Aye." Her own voice sounded in her ears as if it came from a great distance. Rising in a fluid motion. Morgana turned while bringing up the sharp dagger she still held in her right hand. She moved with the grace of one of the dancers who performed the midsummer rituals. She turned, balancing herself on the balls of her feet . . . lighter than air, it seemed.

But if she was lighter than air, Conn was swifter than light. His broadsword flashed upward, knocking Morgana's dagger into the air, where it spiraled down onto the rocks with a clink.

"You would attack me, Morgana?" His tone was ominous.

"No, but I would defend myself and the Viking," she answered truthfully. Conn was always able to perceive the truth, since he himself had little use for it.

"I see. The Viking has wedged between you and your powers, Morgana. You are weakened now, and useless to me." His hypnotic voice droned softly, persuasively, beating at Morgana's resistance like the erosive seep of water upon stone.

"You are bound by Law always to keep the truth, Conn, yet you twist and use it, ignore it when you wish," Morgana said to the empty space beside the druid. "You have given up the right to any power you might have had. . . ."

"That is not so!" The sword point reached out to touch Morgana lightly on warm, bare skin just above the scooped neck of her gown. The metal was cold, yet felt heated to a white-hot glow. He pressed harder, and a tiny drop of blood welled beneath the blade.

Still Morgana stared at him without flinching, knowing that to react was to lose. She must keep her wits, must not look him full in the face, or she and Brander were doomed to whatever fate Conn decreed.

Brander's voice was the growl of a cornered wolf as he said to Conn, "Remove your sword point from the girl before I remove it for you!"

"Do you think you can, Viking? How quickly can you move? 'Tis more likely that my blade will pierce her as neatly as soft butter before you could even rise from your pallet," Conn mocked. "Don't force me to it, though she would be better dead than with a Viking. I think you will both make excellent sacrifices to the god Taranis by the next moon, and I prefer keeping you alive until then."

Morgana jerked slightly at his words, dragging Brander's attention to her.

"Who is Taranis?" the Viking asked tersely. "And why should he demand the blood of a Celtic priestess and a Viking?"

Conn answered him, his voice a purr of pleasure. "Taranis demands sacrifice by burning, Viking, and even now there are men building the wicker frames which will imprison both of you. Morgana has sealed her own fate by giving aid to an invader. She is no longer one of us, but one of the enemy. Tomorrow, when the sun begins to set behind the sea, you will be enclosed inside a wicker frame shaped like a man—a Viking! Faggots will be set ablaze, and you will be engulfed in a sea of flame—both of you"

Brander's palms itched to snatch up his ax, but the paleness of Morgana's face made him pause. If he failed, they would surely die, and she had risked much for him. He must wait, must be certain that his slow-healing body would not fail him. Narrowed blue eyes as icy as the great bergs of the North Sea pierced the robed druid with a baleful glare.

Conn smiled, enjoying the sight of Morgana's fear-rigid face. She should not have defied him. . . . His gaze transferred from Morgana to Brander, those dark, dark eyes staring at the Viking in concentration.

"Don't look at him!" Morgana warned Brander, taking advantage of Conn's diverted attention to throw herself backward on the rocks. Her action took both men by surprise, but it was the Viking's battle-honed reflexes which recovered first.

Widow-Maker lay just beneath his waiting fingertips, and in an instant the battle-ax flashed upward. Conn was not there. The broad-bladed ax struck granite where he had been instead, sparks flying with a ringing sound. On his knees now, Brander scowled at the robed druid standing several feet away, meeting his dark gaze.

"Come, taste death," Brander taunted, beckoning with the ax. "Widow-Maker is not prejudiced about the men she sends into the next life. . . ."

"Is not your arm too numb to lift that ax?" Conn murmured in dulcet tones. "She grows heavier by the moment, doesn't she, Viking? Let your arm rest. . . rest. . . you are growing too weak to hold your ax. . . ."

"Nay!" Morgana shrilled, hoping to break Conn's spell over Brander. She had to be stronger, had to keep Conn from working his magic on the Viking. "Brander, listen to me," she babbled, her voice growing louder and louder as she saw his bemused expression and heavy-lidded eyes. "You must listen to me! Your men—they wait even now on you. You must go to them. . . ."

"The ax cannot be held up any longer, Viking . . . let it drop . . . let it rest upon the floor for only a moment because you are so tired . . . rest . . . rest. . . ."

Desperate, and seeing only one chance, Morgana stooped slightly, letting her fingers close over a loosened rock larger than a man's fist. Without pausing to think, she flung it as hard as she could at the druid, who was gazing with dark, hypnotic eyes at Brander.

The rock struck Conn in the temple, a serious blow that felled him like a great oak struck by lightning. He staggered a step, then crashed to the rock floor of the cave.

Immediately, Morgana flew to Brander. She gave him a rough shake, recognizing from glazed eyes and slackened jaw that Brander had listened to Conn's spellbinding voice too well.

" 'Tis time!" she hissed through clenched teeth, "Now, you must flee, Brander Eriksson! Go to your ship while you still can, before our warriors come."

"Warriors?" Brander repeated. He gave his golden head a slight shake as if just waking, clearing away the cobwebs.

"Yea, even now they arm themselves, and they will fall upon you with swords if you are not gone from here!"

"But . . . but what about you? Conn will kill you for this!"

Morgana wanted to smile a denial, but shrugged instead. Her throat ached painfully and she was dangerously near tears. She, Morgana, who could not remember even childhood tears, crying over a Viking invader. . . .

"I will protect myself," she said after a moment, "as soon as you are safe." Her head pounded, and the heels of her hands and her elbows were scraped raw from the rocks where she had thrown herself to avoid Conn's sword. But the worst pain was the one inside, where it felt as if a giant hand was squeezing the very blood from her heart. She'd known from the beginning that her association with the Viking was madness, and that she risked much for it, but she'd been willing to take the risk. Was life without love really living? She'd tasted a tiny portion of what it could be like with a man, and she was not willing to do without it now. "Come, Viking, we must get you safely to . . ."

A slight sound gave her an instant's warning, and Morgana felt a shadow on her back as she crouched beside Brander. She half-turned. Conn had found her dagger, and was poised to throw it. He aimed, not at the Viking, but at Morgana, his greatest threat.

This time Brander's reflexes were the quicker, and it seemed the Widow-Maker suddenly sprouted from Conn's chest as if by magic. Morgana had not been aware of Brander moving, nor of the smooth wrist flick that had sent the ax spinning through the air to embed in the druid's chest. She watched in awe as Conn fell slowly, his face incredulous, his mouth gaping. The bright light in his eyes began to dim as the spirit left his body, and Morgana turned her head away.

"Don't look," she whispered to Brander, "lest his spirit become angry and take revenge upon you."

Obeying, Brander looked instead at the dark, bowed head of the girl beside him. An unwilling tenderness rose in him, tinged with faint regret. She had a stout heart and did not deserve an unkind fate. Why did he feel as if he had known her much longer than three days?

"Hurry," Morgana urged, tugging at his arm, "before the warriors find you! They come this way, I can hear them."

Brander had learned not to doubt the girl's uncanny

ability to know things, and he stepped forward to remove Widow-Maker from Conn's chest. Though life was gone, the angry expression on the druid's face remained. His eyes were sightless now, staring up at Brander as if to remember his face through all eternity, to carry it into the next world with him. A shudder rippled through the Viking's large frame.

"Fever," Brander said when Morgana glanced at him quizzically. He did not want to admit to apprehension.

The path to the coast was dark and smelled of salty sea winds. Faint light sprinkled the eastern sky with a pearly mist, yet it was as dark as a tomb in the thickly leaved forest.

"I can't see a thing," Brander muttered once, groping for Morgana in the dark.

"You don't have to," her voice floated back, "just hold on to me. I know this path well."

By the time they stepped from the forest into open spaces, pale light flooded the sky. It glowed over a silver sea and shrouded hills, lighting swaying stems of furze that appeared as tiny chips of gold among spiny green leaves.

"My men?" Brander asked, breathing deeply. "Where are they?" He couldn't resist a glance over his shoulder to look for Celtic warriors.

"Ahead, not behind. Hurry." Morgana seemed to skim over the ground without touching it, floating on the salty winds of the sea.

Breathing heavily in spite of his efforts not to, Brander followed at a slower pace. His wounds still pained him, and he was weary from lack of exercise during his long days and nights in the cave.

They rounded a curve in the path, scrunching over ground that had become sandy and rock-strewn. Just ahead bobbed the familiar, grinning head of the serpent on Brander's longboat. Several of his men grouped around the ship, about to push it back out to sea.

"Wait!" Brander called, and their heads jerked around to stare with disbelief. Grinning, Brander half-pulled a now reluctant Morgana along with him as he joined his men.

"You are not dead...."

"We had given up hope...."

"By Odin, you escaped!"

Voices crowded him as all tried to speak at once, and he caught only disjointed fragments of their comments.

"Later, later," he remonstrated, holding up a broad hand. "Right now, there are Celtic warriors behind me—many of them—and I prefer not to fight in my weakened condition. Come," he turned and said to Morgana. "We have to hurry."

All heads turned toward the dark-haired girl who hung back slightly.

"I cannot go with you," she said, though her heart and senses urged differently. "This is my home. I would be a foreigner in a strange land, and there are things about me that you do not know. Your people would not understand...."

Brander dismissed her words with an impatient shake of his golden head.

"We don't have time for argument, Morgana. Listen . . ."

Morgana had already heard the unmistakable sounds of approaching Celtic warriors, the full-throated battle cries and stomping of feet over the meadow. A sad smile curved her mouth.

"I cannot," she repeated.

"You will be killed!" he exploded in frustration. "I cannot have your death on my conscience!" *Not when I've already shed your blood once* . . . the thought startled him.

"I will find a way to hide. Go," she urged, pushing at

him with delicate hands that held the art of healing in their fingertips. "Go, before they attack!"

Frustrated, he grasped her hands. "I need you, Morgana. None here know the art of healing as you do, and already I am feeling weak and faint. . . ."

She saw the paleness of his face, and the pinched, white lines around his mouth, and knew he spoke the truth.

"Here, take these herbs with you." She fumbled with the leather pouch at her waist, trying to unfasten it from her belt. Haste made her clumsy, but finally she handed him the pouch filled with plants and poultices. "You can recall which ones to use. . . ."

She placed the pouch into his outstretched hands, letting her fingers slide slowly back, reluctant to release this man she had known such a short time. Her sad smile and misted eyes told more than she knew.

Brander's fingers curled around goatskin pouch and small hands, holding tightly. Strong hands pressed into her skin as he took not only the pouch but Morgana's arms. Lifting her, he ignored her futile, angry protests and swung her over a broad shoulder. Vikings watched in stunned surprise as their leader waded into the sea, the water lapping at his ankles, knees, and then his thighs.

Morgana beat at Brander's shoulders, mindful of his injuries, demanding that he set her free. Dark hair hung like a curtain, shading her eyes, and she whipped it back.

"I am a daughter of the Celts!" she cried, "and I would die in a land of snow and ice! Put me down, Viking, before I call down a curse upon the heads of you and all your men!"

Brander's men muttered uneasily, recalling all the tales they'd heard of Celtic witches and their powers.

"She's a healer, not a witch," he snapped at his men, ignoring their dark glances. "And she goes with us."

None dared argue the matter, and they parted to allow their leader access to the longboat. Morgana was handed up the steep sides, then released immediately as if her skin burned those who had touched her. A bitter smile curved her mouth.

"I don't have to stay," she said softly when Brander pulled himself over the side of the ship and stood beside her with dripping tunic and trousers. He knew she was right.

"If you stay here, you will die," he said simply. "Doesn't that matter to you? I cannot countenance your death because of me. You saved my life, and I have the responsibility of you for all your days."

Morgana listened gravely. She could still leap over the side. It would be easy enough. Hadn't she often swam in the happy streams that babbled through green, green valleys? But she stood still. The memory of a golden night spent in Brander's arms tempered her choice.

A clamor on shore drew her attention. Celtic warriors gathered at the spot where the longboat had been beached, raising clenched fists, and a few threw ineffectual spears toward the Vikings as if warning them not to return.

But it was only when Morgana saw the slight, bent figure of a woman stumble into the shallow waters, holding up her arms in a beseeching gesture, that she wavered. Kyna. Kyna was calling to her, begging her not to leave with the Viking, and Morgana was torn with agony. How could she leave the only mother she had ever known?

Seeing the tortured expression on Morgana's face, and realizing the probable cause, Brander took pity on her. He would make the decision for her, so that she would have no regrets.

Morgana's arms were snared as she put tentative hands upon the rail of the ship, intending to vault over the side.

"I do this for you." Brander said into her furious, pained

eyes, "so that you will not die." Harsh ropes of hemp were quickly wound around her wrists and ankles, binding her tightly so that she could not leap from the longship.

Morgana sat like a stone on the deck, motionless. The ship drew farther away from the shore and still she did not move, letting wind blow across her face and rake its fingers through her hair. She sat with arms bound across her chest and stared at the shoreline of Erin as it faded into the distance, wondering if she would ever see her homeland again. Morgana's destiny had been chosen. . . .

The JOURNEY

Chapter 9

The longship rolled up the side of a wave, then sliced down into a trough between them. Water sluiced over high wooden rails to wet the decks, then trickled through the scuppers back into the Irish Sea.

They were in the open sea now, with no sign of land to guide them. Brander didn't need to direct his men in steering the ship; they were all well acquainted with time-tested techniques for guidance. The Vikings' navigation depended upon the stars and the relative direction of prevailing winds; warm wet winds were from the southwest, and cold wet winds came from the northeast. Thus, the feel of the wind could be roughly equated with direction. Hugging her knees as she perched on a fat cushion by the rail, Morgana watched curiously as the Vikings checked their estimates against the noon sun.

Water surrounded the ship in a never-ending blur of gray-green waves flecked with foam. Gusts of salty wind noisily billowed the red-striped sail into a graceful curve over the decks, sending the ship skimming like a seabird over sun-chipped water. Such a fragile vessel, Morgana mused, to dare the open reaches of the cold and angry sea, and such daring, bold adventurers to attempt the sailing of it.

The long wooden ship was curved in the shape of a broad smile, with fiercely grinning dragon heads at one end. Rowing benches lined the oak-planked decks at the curved prow, with a single bench at the stern, and the sides were pocked with small, square oarports for the broad-bladed oars. Rising from the exact center of the ship was a sturdy, smooth mast that held the sail and cross-beam. There was no protection from the elements, Morgana realized with selfish interest. The decks were bare of shelter for even the precious stolen cargo.

Goods from their raids had been stacked in the center of the ship, clustered around the mast which had been erected in a small, open cargo hold. Live chickens in flimsy wooden crates squawked and cackled, geese and ducks jostled in flurries of feathers for the same crowded space, and small pigs had been wedged between round wooden barrels. There were animal pelts, casks of wine and salted fish, skins filled with water, and bolts of material piled next to leather-bound chests filled with jewelry, chalices, and utensils of gold and silver. Basic tools for building and iron-forging—stolen from monasteries and Celtic towns—were stacked neatly in a box. Obviously, the Vikings appreciated Celtic ingenuity.

Stirring restlessly, Morgana decided to investigate the area she would be occupying for the coming weeks. Brander had released her wrists and ankles from their bindings with a mumbled apology, but she felt no rancor. All she felt was a deep sorrow, especially when she thought of Kyna.

Morgana was vaguely surprised to discover that she wasn't the only Celt aboard the Viking longship—nor was she the only woman. There had been few captives taken in the sporadic raids on Erin's shores, but one of the few was a girl younger than Morgana. She sat huddled alone against the rail near the prow. Morgana's curious gaze rested upon a small, pointed face like a cat's, with slit eyes that were contemptuous of all about her. Would she be a possible companion to while away the inevitable hours of boredom? Turning away from her survey of the ship, Morgana moved to kneel beside the disheveled girl.

"What is your name?" Morgana asked softly, then drew back as the girl tossed her mane of fiery hair and spat over the rail. Rebellious dark eyes glared from beneath bright red curls, gazing at Morgana with loathing.

Surprised at the unexpected reaction, Morgana withdrew. Retreating a few steps away, she paused. It was obvious from the red scratches on her face and arms that the girl had been dealt with harshly by the Vikings, and that she was furious with the entire world. Narrowing her eyes in concentration, Morgana tried to think what she would feel in her place. Fright? Certainly. Anger? That, too, and maybe even hatred against a force stronger than her own. . . .

Anger only masked the girl's shivering fear, and now Morgana perceived faint, flickering shadows in the stormy dark eyes. Thin brown arms wrapped around her body for protection from the wind, and the girl huddled next to the rail as if trying to meld unnoticed into the smooth wood. Her garments hung in ragged tatters, mute testimony to the nature of the attack against her even if one couldn't read the disillusion and disgust in those wide, expressive eyes. Bold hips gave the lie to her age, promising more than her immature body could deliver, and childishly scratched legs and bare feet thrust from beneath the hem of her gown.

Animosity glittered like molten iron, red-hot and glowing, each time she glanced toward Morgana. Her thoughts were obvious: A fellow Celt, supposedly a captive, yet after her initial capture, Morgana had been treated with respect, even kindness by the Viking invaders.

Morgana sighed. There was no way to explain, not without appearing even more traitorous to her people. How could she expect anyone to understand why she had aided the Vikings when she didn't understand the reason herself?

And worse, Brander hadn't spoken to her since he had released her. Was he purposely being remote and unapproachable? Morgana watched from afar, concerned, wanting to speak to him but not wanting to distract him. Occasionally he would pause in some task to rub at his injured arm, or readjust the bandage she had so carefully wound around the slash.

He was busy with his men, investigating the cargo and any possible damage to the ship, Morgana chided herself when she grew too impatient. And when he paused to lean against the rail with several companions, she reasoned that he was probably regaling them with the details of his capture and escape. Morgana regretted that she did not understand their strange Viking language, for she would have been extremely interested in hearing Brander's version of his misadventures.

From time to time a bearded Viking glanced in Morgana's direction, then quickly jerked his gaze away. They were afraid of her. She could sense it, a tangible thing, like a thick, insidious fog that ofttimes rolled over the land and enveloped everything in its path. Morgana tensed, then forced herself to relax. It would take time for the Vikings to learn that she was not like Conn, who would have enjoyed their fear.

Dragging her attention from Brander, Morgana avoided the surreptitious and guarded glances of the men and the girl. In two steps she was at the prow of the longship, presenting them with her back. Morgana lifted her face to the smile of the sun and let the wind whisper warmly across her tawny skin, pushing back long tendrils of ebony hair so that it blew wildly with a life of its own.

"Snakes," an uneasy Viking muttered under his breath, referring to the slithers of Morgana's streaming hair. " 'Tis said 'twill turn a man to stone to look upon a . . ."

"Enough!"

At Brander's growl, the man was silenced for the moment, but he still cast Morgana a suspicious glance in spite of his leader's warning.

"Thorfinn," Brander said quietly, and there was an undisguised warning in his tone, "I know that you are a good warrior and that you joined my father's clan by choice. You have been with us for several years, but you are still filled with superstitions gleaned from your years with the Greeks and Romans.

"The Celtic maid is under my protection," Brander added loudly so that all could hear, "and I will consider it a personal insult if any man should harm or offend her. She saved my life and nursed me until my strength returned."

All were quiet, except for the irrepressible Gunther, who was Brander's closest friend as well as best warrior.

"Aye, Brander," Gunther said, his blue eyes sparkling with mirth, "and I wouldn't mind having such a beauty nurse me back to health! 'Tis a wonder," he said into the rumbling laughter that rolled across the deck, "that you ever decided to get well!"

"Don't cast your wandering eye in her direction, Gunther. You have a woman of your own." Brander's grin eased the tension, but he couldn't halt the unwilling memory of long, tawny legs wrapped around him, and the feel of satiny flesh beneath his searching hands. Irritated, he dragged his attention back to the present.

Shrugging, Gunther observed that the Celtic woman he had brought with him preferred fighting to loving.

"She leaves me with so many claw marks, that 'tis as if I have bedded a wild panther," he said gloomily.

"I thought you liked women with spirit," Thorfinn interjected with a sly smile. "Isn't that what you said, Gunther?"

"Aye," Gunther defended himself in an aggrieved tone, "but I never desired a woman who leaves me feeling as if I've fought twenty berserkers!"

"Maybe you need the practice," his cousin Delling suggested. The Vikings bellowed with loud laughter, thumping one another on broad backs as they traded sharp-edged quips at Gunther's expense.

Morgana heard them, of course, and somehow sensed that the heated words had been about her. She held out her hands, letting sun rays slide over her fingers, a faint frown knitting her brow. Had she caused Brander trouble by being aboard? Perhaps she should have evaded him and fled—as she so easily could have done. But fragile threads held her to the Viking, threads that could not be easily ignored, for they existed not only in her mind but also in her heart. She would have to think, to let her unseen voices guide her. . . .

A low hiss from the Celtic girl captured Morgana's attention, surprising her, and she turned. Wind whipped sable hair into her eyes, obscuring her vision, and Morgana clawed it away so that she could see the girl clearly.

The girl glowered like a malevolent lump of coal, staring at the laughing knot of Vikings with undisguised hatred and murder in her heart, and for a moment Morgana feared for them all. The girl's enmity could bring no good to the voyage, and might well invite dark forces to bring destruction upon them.

" 'Tis a wasted emotion, hate," Morgana remarked casually, leaning over the rail but standing close enough for the girl to easily hear. "The one who harbors hatred burns with it, while those hated are rarely disturbed."

" 'Tis easy enough for you to say!" the girl spat. She whirled at last to face Morgana, her eyes narrowed to slits again and dangerous, wild hair flying about her stiff shoulders. "You have been cosseted since boarding this cursed ship, while I...I..." Anger and tears choked her so that she could not speak, and small hands clenched into fists at her sides.

Morgana remained silent for a few moments, testing the ribbons of understanding between herself and the girl. It was so easy for some to understand, and so hard for others. This girl wasn't ready to release her anger and hatred in a harmless manner.

Morgana's advice was succinct. "If you anger them, they will likely kill you, or at the least, sell you as soon as possible to someone who might be even crueler." The girl's eyes burned into her with dark intensity as Morgana continued. "There is no place to escape on this ship, and death is not always the answer."

Neither expecting nor waiting for a reply, Morgana turned back to observe the lace-edged waves that rose around the ship. The decision to leave Erin had been inevitable, spurred by her attraction to the Viking, and Morgana reflected on her fate had she remained. Aware of the wrenching pain at leaving Kyna, she wondered if she had done her best.

Staring over the rail and resting her elbows on the smooth wood, Morgana watched as the distant haze of land that was Erin finally disappeared. A floating mass of sea kelp caught on the crest of a wave captured her attention, and Morgana imagined herself to be as helpless. She was being tossed from crest to crest, each new wave more terrifying than the last. Her presence aboard the longship was irrevocable, and she must look ahead now, not look back. Still, it was hard not to think of her home, and a hundred different worries churned in her mind.

What was Kyna thinking? Morgana's last glimpse of her

foster mother haunted her, and she closed her eyes against
the pain. Unexpected tears stung her closed lids, and Morgana
blinked them furiously away.

"Tears, little one?"

Brander appeared beside her without warning, reaching
out a tender, calloused hand to brush away the wet teardrop
clinging to Morgana's tawny cheek.

"For whom do you cry?" His heavily accented Celtic
forestalled a fresh burst of tears, and Morgana sniffed
loudly, smiling in spite of herself.

"My old nurse. I didn't have a chance to bid her
farewell, or let her know that I was unharmed. She will
worry."

A slight frown creased Brander's broad forehead, and the
lines at the corners of his eyes deepened. "Does she not
have the same powers of insight that you do? Will she not
know that you are alive and well?"

Sun-daggers caught and held in Brander's hair, glinting
brightly. He had changed from his stained, torn tunic into a
fresh sleeveless garment of pale blue. It stretched across the
broad band of his chest tautly, molding to the flowing line of
skin and muscle. Gunther's muscles bulged in huge knots
on arms and thighs, but Brander's flowed more easily,
undulating like the smooth waters of a lake. He was so
handsome, a fusion of beauty and savage grace, that for a
moment she completely lost the thread of their conversation.

Bemused, Morgana had to give herself a mental shake
and concentrate on remembering his question. Ebony curls
encased her heart-shaped face in a velvet setting that vibrated with vivid intensity as she shook her head. Brander
leaned close to hear, "No. Only a chosen few have that gift."

"And you are one of them? How did you become one of
the chosen?"

Sooty brows that were thick and unruly lifted slightly as

he leaned a muscular forearm on the top strake of the ship, gazing with interest into Morgana's uplifted eyes. They were so green, reminding him of spring leaves and clear, sparkling emeralds set into a necklace of molten gold. The dark, soft curls straying winsomely into her face were the perfect foil for such loveliness, and Brander ground his teeth against his sudden desire to kiss the Celtic maid on the tip of her charmingly tilted nose. Nay. She was too young, a stranger from a heathen land, and he had already done her enough harm.

"I was born to it," Morgana was saying, and Brander's attention transferred to her mouth. He watched intently as her lips formed words, thinking how mobile they were, and quick to stretch with laughter or a smile. Or at least they had been. Now her lips drooped downward, and he was surprised at his desire to see them curve enchantingly upward again. Desire . . . the word startled him. The emotion startled him. He had been long from home and had denied himself a woman when his men had eased their appetites, and now his body was once again ruling his brain. He must be confusing desire with compassion, Brander decided, for who would desire a fourteen-year-old child?

"Who decides the future role of a newborn infant, Morgana?" he asked, and wondered at his lack of interest in the subject. Did her dimple show only when she smiled? There was a trace of impatience in his voice as he forced another question. "Does the mother?"

Morgana was still finding it difficult to keep her attention on the conversation. Her gaze skimmed the tiny details about Brander that she had previously missed in the dim light of fires in the cave. By firelight, he was a most striking man; in the broad light of day, he was devastating and dangerous at the same time. She had sensed the strong force of his personality, but the reality of it was as hot and searing as wildfire.

Sunlight picked out the myriad differences in him; the broad shoulders were fluidly muscled and leaner; the suntanned flesh woven in a marvelous tapestry of perfection over his facial bones was more taut, and his eyes—eyes that held a thousand messages in them, the windows to his inner spirit—gazed at her as if it were he who could see inside a person's mind and guess her thoughts. Morgana dragged her gaze from those sky-blue orbs that held her suspended and fumbled back into their conversation, trying to forget that magical night when their bodies and spirits had joined together.

What had he asked? Oh yes, he was asking her if the mother decided upon a child's future role in life. . . .

"Nay, 'tis the druid who officiates at the birth, usually a bard. He plays an instrument so that the first sounds a newborn child hears will be pleasing. Infants should be brought into a world filled with laughter and music, so that their spirit can easily make the transition from one life to another," she explained. "And the bard doesn't *decide* the future role, he merely defines the aura surrounding the child so that it is not forced into a role for which it is unfit."

"And did a bard decide that you were to be a prophet?"

Morgana hesitated. Conn had been present at her birth, and he had claimed the privilege of bestowing her name and announcing her destiny. But Conn had seen the veil, or caul, over her, as had the midwife summoned to the birthing. No other judgment could have been given. Everyone knew that the caul indicated powers of prophecy.

Her hesitation showed in the slight widening of her eyes, the pupils absorbing light like a mirror, and Brander made some slight movement that prompted her to answer.

"No," she finally murmured, "Conn decided."

"Conn? The druid who tried to kill you?" Brander gave a half-snort of disdain. "I wouldn't trust a man like that. . . ."

"Do you think I have no powers of prophecy, Brander?" Morgana cut in, unable to bear the thought of his ridicule. "Or that I do not have the sensitivity that allows me to feel what another person feels, or hear what they think?"

The bright square sail overhead slapped noisily in the wind, and the ship hammered through tons of greenish water with a loud shudder of timbers and pegged joints. Squinting against the press of wind and sunlight, Brander shook his head. "I never meant that. I only meant that I would never have trusted Conn's motives. Didn't your parents sense his true nature?" The shifting angles of Morgana's face warned Brander that he had somehow trod upon forbidden territory. "Did I ask the wrong question?"

"No, 'tis a natural enough question. My mother died within hours of my birth, and my father . . . my father is a Celtic king."

"Then you are a princess?" Brander's brows rose high. "How would your father allow. . . .'"

"I never met my father, nor did I even know his identity, except for what Conn told me." Morgana's tight lips relaxed slightly at the stricken expression on Brander's face. "It does not pain me anymore, Brander. Do not fret about it."

Brander's arm was warm, comforting, and maddeningly impersonal around Morgana's shoulders as he gave her a sympathetic squeeze.

"I seem to stumble from one bad subject to another like a lame horse, Morgana. Forgive me." He paused, then said in the tone of a man who has not divulged the information before, "I remember how I felt when my mother died, and the pain still haunts me at times. 'Tis not a feeling easily borne by even the broadest of shoulders."

A leaden shriek was the only warning as a bundle of infuriated rags and thin brown arms flung herself at Brander. The girl captured by Gunther surged to her feet in a lithe cat-like motion. Clawing fingers curved into talons intended to rake at his eyes. But Brander's reactions were too swift.

"Hold!" he bellowed in astonishment, grabbing her by the wrists. "What is the meaning of this, wench?"

"You speak of death, Viking, when I saw both my parents die only a few days ago at your hands! I would that 'twas you who had died in their stead!" Fiery hair tumbled in a wild spill over her shoulders as she struggled, panting and half-snarling Celtic oaths. She was crying with fury and her efforts, wriggling in Brander's iron clasp as he held her away from him.

Gunther appeared like magic at Brander's side, his face creased with anger. The girl was his captive, and her actions reflected upon him. He was furious that she would attack his leader without apparent cause. Reaching out, Gunther seized her with both strong hands.

"Stop this madness, Gwyneth!" He gave her a rough shake and a ringing slap that snapped her head to one side. Red welts in the shape of a handprint formed on the girl's cheek, and Morgana stiffened in outraged horror.

Her instinctive movement to help was forestalled by Brander's quick hand curling around one wrist, and Morgana pried futilely at his fingers. "But he will hurt her!" she insisted, quite unaware of the sudden quiet on the ship.

Gunther's normally cheerful face took on a grim expression and he slanted Brander a meaningful glance. The girl was a struggling handful, spitting and snarling like a scalded cat, and he didn't need more trouble heaped upon his head.

"Morgana, the girl belongs to Gunther. You have no right to interfere," Brander said calmly, drawing her closer to him and away from Gunther and Gwyneth.

"Belongs?" Morgana echoed in disbelief. "Is she a horse or a cow, to be . . . be owned and mistreated?" Her indignation swelled as she tried to shake loose his hand.

"Nay, Morgana," Brander half-growled, angry that she would question him in front of his men. "But her fate does not rest with us. Gunther is her captor . . ."

"And you are his leader! Have you no word in this matter?"

"I am the leader, yes. But we are a free society, and on board this ship, all men are considered equal. I have no right to rule Gunther's life. I have only the right to *lead* him," Brander explained.

"Under Celtic law, no man can own another." Morgana caught and held Brander's narrowed gaze with hard, jeweled eyes.

"Have you no slaves?"

"Not as you do."

"No captives?" Brander countered. "What do you do with the men you take prisoner in battle, Morgana?"

The sharp question caught her off guard. "We sacrifice them," she answered at last, reluctantly, and knew her answer was not one that would further her argument. But it was the truth, and druids were bound by years of training to the truth, as all Celts were supposed to be.

Brander's voice was filled with grim humor as he chided, "And being sacrificed is better than living a life of honest toil in the service of a kind master?"

"I didn't say I agreed with it! Does our error make it right to strike a slave?'

Morgana's eyes met his squarely, demanding he yield the point.

"Nay, but it is even less kind to slay one."

"We don't slay all captives. Some are accepted into

various households and even treated as members of the family. . . ."

"Like a slave?" Brander suggested, then smiled. "Not all our slaves are dealt with harshly." He signaled to Gunther to remove Gwyneth from Morgana's view, and his warrior complied with a darkling glance in Morgana's direction.

" 'Twill do little good to take her from sight. I know she is here." Morgana's face tilted, and the tight set of her mouth deepened the cleft in her rounded chin. Dark-fringed eyes blazed at him with green fires of judgment.

"If you have inner vision, then you will understand that she is not being mistreated, and that she attacked first," Brander said evenly.

The heated confrontation, on top of everything else that had occurred during the past few days, drained Morgana to the point of exhaustion. She was weary; weary of strife and secrecy and hiding from enemies. Morgana's battered spirit craved rest that would free her from those dark-winged bats that flew at her from all directions. How could she think when all was a jumble of words and half-formed impressions? —when everything was beginning to sound like she had heard it too many times before?

Pressing fingers to her aching brow, Morgana simply nodded in agreement because it was expected of her. She had lost the thread of the conversation somehow, and heard only a loud buzzing. The ship seemed to dip sharply between waves, falling, then rising, so that she swayed with its movements. She was young, and her experiences had never prepared her for such an exhausting ordeal as the past few days. One hand reached out for the ship's rail to steady herself, fumbling for a hold.

"Aye," she managed to say, and her voice sounded

distant and vague in her ears, like the rumbling of faraway thunder. "I know that your reasons are sound. . . ."

Brander caught her before she pitched to the rising deck. His glance at the warriors clustered a few feet away was startled, and Delling, the kindest of the group, stepped forward.

"Do you need help with the lady, my lord?"

"Aye. Find her some shelter from the elements," Brander answered, grateful that someone had recognized his need. He was obviously not accustomed to fainting females.

Chapter 10

The sky was dark when Morgana woke. She was amazed to find that she had slept the afternoon through without once waking. She winced at a pounding behind her brows like victory drums, and one hand rose to investigate the source of her misery. Searching fingertips grazed against a pillow of tasseled silk stuffed with goose down. Who had been thoughtful enough to cushion her head with such luxury? And when she shifted her legs, she discovered a lightly woven blanket had been spread over her to keep off the chill of damp, night air.

Morgana lay still for a few moments, staring up at the dark night sky peppered with tiny stars. An oil lamp burned near the prow, and she could her the soft rumble of men's voices. Knuckling sleep from her eyes, she noted several shadowy figures curved into the postures of sleep gracing the decks. The ship's damp sails wafted scent into the night air, a distinct, sharp fragrance as pungent as pine needles. Soaked hemp stank with a peculiar odor of its own, mixing with the smells of salted cod and an opened barrel of sour wine.

The decks rose and fell as though they were part of a great wooden cradle, and the hiss of wind and slapping of waves against the hull was comforting. A burst of laughter from the prow caught her attention. Even though she couldn't understand their language, the cheerful murmur of the Vikings sounded as friendly and familiar as the warble of spring robins. A tiny smile curved her mouth at the thought. The past few days must have driven her over the brink of sanity into madness. She should fear what lay ahead in a foreign land peopled with possibly hostile strangers, but she did not.

Rising slightly, Morgana shifted to rest her weight upon one elbow. Dark hair spilled into her eyes as she stared out over the top strake on the opposite side of the ship. Shrugging away the annoying wisps, her drifting gaze encountered nothing but sea swells and reflected moonlight. Now there wasn't even a distant haze on the horizon to remind her of home, and her face was slightly crestfallen when Gunther's cousin noticed her and stopped to inquire kindly how she felt.

Morgana mustered a slight smile. "My body feels well, except for a slight aching in my head, but 'tis my heart which pains me most."

The delicate, heart-shaped face mirrored her feelings, and Delling's imagination was caught. Some muttered that she was a Celtic sorceress, but he saw only weariness and a touching childishness in her features. Impulsively, he knelt beside her with a sympathetic expression gracing his broad face.

" 'Tis how I felt when first I left Jutland," he said in halting Celtic. "Then the excitement grew in me at the thought of seeing new and strange lands. You may grow to feel the same.''

"But you had an advantage," Morgana pointed out. "You knew you were returning home eventually. I do not."

"True," Delling admitted, "but you are with us. You already have friends in Jutland, but I never knew who I might meet." His ruddy face beamed with friendliness.

Warmed by Delling's kindness and sincerity, Morgana couldn't help offering him a matching smile. Mischievous fingers of wind tousled wisps of hair on her brow, and a curling strand waved forward across her face, tickling the tip of her nose.

"See?" Delling said. "Even the wind wishes to make you a friend!"

Morgana laughed and realized that her headache had disappeared.

"Your friendship has banished the pounding in my head," she said, "and I am grateful." Her dimple flashed for a moment, fascinating Delling. "What is your name, so that I can call you something other than Viking?"

"Delling Haardraksson. I am cousin to Gunther, who is Brander's closest companion."

"Gunther? The man who . . ." She paused, and Delling was quick to finish her sentence.

"Who captured the Celtic girl. Aye. He is a good man, my lady Morgana. Do not judge him harshly."

"I do not. I perceive the goodness in him." Shifting slightly, Morgana couldn't help glancing about the deck for a familiar, broad-shouldered figure. Was Brander already asleep, or did he sit with his men?

Noting her glance, Delling offered, "Brander and Gunther play at *hnefatafl*. Do you care to watch?"

"Hnefatafl?" Morgana's tongue curled awkwardly around the unfamiliar word. "What is that?"

" 'Tis a game played with playing pieces on a board. Come, I will show you," Delling said, catching Morgana's hand.

She hesitated, suddenly aware of how rumpled and untidy she must look. Vanity? she mocked herself silently. Rarely before had she bothered to worry about her appearance. There had been no one who would notice. Now she longed for Brander to notice.

Passing a hand over her wind-tumbled hair, Morgana attempted to finger-comb it to some order. Smears of red burned her cheeks when Delling gazed at her thoughtfully, and she was compelled to think of an adequate reason for her primping. The Viking forestalled an alibi by promptly producing an ivory comb and a small square of polished bronze to use as a mirror.

"You carry this with you?" she asked in surprise. He did not appear to be a man addicted to such vanity.

"Nay. I have a woman at home. This is for her. Disa is a good woman, and will not mind your using it."

Smiling her appreciation, Morgana managed to subdue her wild, thick mane into a semblance of order, and rubbed at the dark circles beneath her eyes. She gazed critically at her blurred reflection in the bronze mirror. Her face was thinner than usual, the eyes larger, giving her the appearance of a starving kitten.

"Ready?" Delling prompted, and sighing, Morgana gave him back the mirror and ivory comb. It was a hopeless task for now.

Her fingers smoothed the wrinkles from her gown as she walked with Delling toward the cluster of men. It was easy enough to pick Brander from the rest; his head rose higher, and his thick, tawny mane glittered like a polished bronze shield in the subtle light from the oil lamp. He was laughing, his well-shaped head thrown back and eyes sparkling with mirth. Brander's expression altered subtly when he noticed Morgana standing beside Delling.

"Ho, Morgana!" he said in a friendly tone. "Sit, and have a bite of salted fish and a skin of wine. You are more rested now?"

Must he be so casual and indifferent when her heart pounded at just the thought of him? Morgana tried to mimic Brander's insouciant attitude.

"Aye, I feel much better. Have I you to thank for bringing me a pillow and covering me with a blanket?"

Brander's surprise was evident. "No. Perhaps 'twas Delling. . . ."

"Aye," Delling confirmed. "She looked uncomfortable." His blunt fingertips pushed gently at Morgana's back, propelling her slightly forward. "The maid wishes to watch the game, Brander. You explain it; I have no gift for the Celtic tongue as you do."

A ready smile curved the sensual line of Brander's lips as he welcomed Morgana to a place beside him, pulling forward a cushion for her. Slim legs jackknifed as she dropped to the feather pillow, scooting close enough to lay a hand upon Brander's arm. An almost imperceptible grimace flickered for a moment on his face, and she leaned forward to ask if his wounds pained him.

"Not much," he admitted.

Morgana quickly produced a potion from the leather herb bag at her waist.

"Take this," she began, and one of the Vikings at the far edge of the lamp light gave a derisive snort.

"Be careful the wench does not poison you," Thorfinn warned with a sharp laugh. "She might wish revenge. . . ."

Brander's sudden cold stare stilled the man's words, and

he retreated from the circle of light, sitting back from the others. Morgana could feel Thorfinn's icy glare, and almost shivered from the force of it.

"Give it to me, Morgana," Brander was saying, and she slowly held out the potion.

Holding her gaze with his own, Brander swallowed the potion without another word. No one spoke. The men watched silently, digesting their leader's trust in the Celtic girl. It would be a serious breach of etiquette for any of them to question her motives now.

Turning, Brander motioned for the game to continue, and leaned forward to play. The atmosphere slowly thawed as the contest between Gunther and Brander raged, each testing the other's skill. From time to time, Brander would give Morgana a conspiratorial wink and a quick grin, and her heart would somersault.

The pressure of his hard-muscled thigh innocently brushing against her leg made Morgana's breath still, and she was grateful for the low light that wouldn't reveal the crimson flush staining her cheeks. The same light played over the pure angles and planes of Brander's face, trickling warmly over the shades of pastel in his hair. Morgana noted with surprise that he had shaved the light beard from his jaw. The tiny patch she had cleared with her dagger to clean his wound was unnoticeable now, and she reflected that he was even more handsome without his beard. Brander's was a face of Nordic purity, clean of line, with finely chiseled features. It would have been a hard face, aloof and cold, if it were not for the warmth and brilliance of his eyes.

Those eyes rested on her now, filled with polite friendliness, and Morgana felt a burst of frustration skim from head to foot. Did he *have* to stare at her as impersonally as if she were one of the . . . the dragonheads on the prow?

Morgana would have felt much better if she'd been able to see past her own and into Brander's thoughts. He was very much aware of her physically; the supple length of her thighs outlined by the thin woolen gown, the trim ankles peeking from beneath the too short hem, the feel of her shoulders and back when he reached out to scoot her closer to the game board. And the cloud of dark hair as fragrant and fine as early morning mist teased his senses.

A sister, he sternly reminded himself, he would have to think of her as a sister. She was so young, too young. . . .

"Have you ever played this game before?" Brander asked Morgana, and she shook her head.

"No, but we do have a game board that is similar. Only ours," she reached out to touch the wooden board with diagonally punched holes, "has none of these. We mark on a piece of wood instead of punching all these holes."

Smiling, Brander moved one of the finely crafted playing pieces. Carved from bone, the cone-shaped piece had the chiseled features of a man.

" 'Tis a king," Brander explained, "and I must protect him from attack by opposing forces, in this case, Gunther."

"Hah!" Gunther interjected. "Your king is as good as captured, Brander Eriksson! See? I'm attacking your flank thusly." He shoved forward a similarly carved playing piece, positioning it over one of the holes, and glanced up at Brander in triumph.

With a throaty chuckle, Brander swiftly made his move, expertly retrieving his king from danger and capturing Gunther's playing piece.

"You were saying?" Brander teased.

Gunther stared at the board incredulously. Finally he

slapped his thickly muscled thighs and roared with good-natured laughter.

"Aye, you have bested me yet again! And I did not even see it coming, Brander!" He shook his massive head from side to side and stroked his luxuriant mustache with a calloused forefinger. "I will win one day, take my word on that," he assured Brander. Turning to Morgana, Gunther complained, "He has always won at *hnefatafl*. Since we were small lads playing with wooden swords, he has won!"

"Your turn will come," Morgana assured him. "And even if it does not, can you not best him in something else?"

Gunther brightened immediately. "Aye! I can outdrink him any day," he boasted.

That statement seemed to be the cue for refilling their drinking horns, and a skin of wine was immediately passed from man to man.

"Do you wish a drink?" Delling offered Morgana, but she politely declined. She had observed the Viking method of drinking from horns that could not be set down, so must be continuously held or emptied at the expense of sobriety.

Wine muddled the brain, and besides, the Vikings were drinking sour wine which often curdled in her stomach. She sat upon the stuffed cushion close to Brander, watching and listening. They reminded her of Celtic warriors, who ofttimes whiled away the evenings trading tales of valor and glory, or listening to a bard recite ancient poems of Celtic history.

"Our poems are related by a *skald*," Brander told her, "and are probably mostly history, like those your bards tell. Of course, we recite poems about our gods and kings, also."

"Are you a king in your land?" Morgana asked, and
Brander grinned. She sucked in a deep breath at the trans-
formation when he grinned. He appeared to be a beautiful
god made of blinding sunlight, bright against the velvet
backdrop of night.

"Nay. My father is chieftain, or jarl. I have my own
home, my own lands."

"Oh." It was all Morgana could think of in reply, and she
knew it sounded lame and dull. Where had her usual
common sense fled? Why did she sit like a stone, with
nothing clever to say, no deft words to amuse this vitally
attractive Viking pirate? Viking pirate—that was wrong.
Vikings *were* pirates. That's what the name Viking meant, a
pirate or raider. The correct usage would be *vikingr,* she
recalled Conn once telling her. All Scandinavians were
referred to as Vikings, though actually they were divided
into different nationalities such as Swedes, Norse (from
Norway), Icelanders, or Danes. Brander had said he was
from Jutland, in Denmark, so he was a Dane.

Listening idly to the conversation humming around her,
Morgana recalled once mentioning that Viking raids on Erin
would soon increase, bringing a great change to their land.
Conn had scoffed at her vision.

"You are misreading it, Morgana," he had told her. "We
will repel the invaders, and Erin will gather into itself,
return to the old ways. . . ."

He had been wrong. These Vikings were just the beginning of a new age. Morgana sensed it without relying on a
vision or voices in the wind. These men were powerful, full
of energy and hungry for new conquests. They would not
stop with a few paltry visits, and would fan out into many
countries. Perhaps they already had.

"What do you seek, Brander?" Morgana asked during a

lull in their conversation. She lay back on her arms, held up by her elbows digging into the cushion.

"Do you mean in the way of glory or fortune?" Shrugging, Brander answered, "Self-satisfaction. I wish to be remembered as a fair man who lived and fought well; a wise man who ruled justly."

"Then you will inherit your father's position one day?"

"Aye, unless the Thing does not accept me."

"The Thing?" Morgana echoed. She stared at him blankly until he laughed.

" 'Tis a public assembly of free men, who consult on matters of importance, and legislate and administer justice," he explained. "Each region has its own Thing, and from these are elected royal kings. Succession is not automatic, for any candidate for the throne must be acceptable to the free men of the country. Do you think I'd be accepted?"

"Then, you are royal?" A frown knit Morgana's brows as she puzzled over this.

"Nay," he answered at last, and she saw that he had been teasing her. "My father is only jarl of a small clan, not an entire country. But we follow the same rules."

"Do you elect your kings?" Gunther leaned forward to ask Morgana. "Do they rule for a lifetime?"

A childhood memory flashed through her mind, and she hesitated. What would these Vikings think if she told them how Celts sometimes rejected their kings? Morgana still recalled the time she had seen an aging king deposed. The tribes' fortunes were failing, and the king had sired no offspring, so he was ritually slain. Inside a ring of human skulls taken from enemies, the totally naked king had stood facing Conn, the chief druid. Elaborately tattooed druidesses presented offerings and sacrificial animals as the king regally awaited his fate. A hush had fallen as Conn stepped forward with his ceremonial dagger. Morgana could still see sunlight flashing from the gold, carved handle of the bronze dagger as it swung high in the air, then descended. When the dying king writhed on the ground, Conn had knelt beside him, predicting the future by studying the convulsions of his body and the squirting of royal blood. It had been impressive and terrifying, an ancient custom now practiced by just a few small bands of Celts.

"Many Celtic kings gain their position by victory in battle," Morgana answered truthfully and evasively. "Some are chosen by the people, and others inherit."

"But what if the king is unfit?" Gunther pressed, and Morgana bit her lip in agitation. "Do you . . ."

A loud splash and peculiar hum vibrated through the entire vessel, followed by a rolling wave that sent the longship plunging into a watery trough. Immediately the deck was abuzz with activity as men lunged to their feet, the game and conversation forgotten. Morgana floundered about the deck like a landed fish, trying to rise.

Her heart pounded and her throat was dry as she struggled for balance, wondering what had caused the sudden commotion. Her stuffed cushion slid across the deck and disappeared into the open cargo hold as the ship tilted, and Morgana finally stood on her feet. Clumsily, still unused to the bucking motion of the wooden planks, she fought her way to the rail to peer over the side.

Moonlight flooded the dark, rolling swells of the sea, and in the midst of the endless space reaching as far as her eye could see, Morgana saw a glistening lump rise from beneath the waves. It was huge. It seemed as if she was witnessing the birth of a mountain from the watery womb of the cold Irish Sea. Nothing she had ever seen before had prepared her for this sight, and she realized that it must be a whale.

Or a sea monster. One heard of them, of course, so perhaps they were real after all, and not just figments of someone's imaginative mind.

The monster whale rose in a graceful arc of gleaming hide, soundless and beautiful; a geyser of living flesh that dwarfed the longship, glistening with a strange light. Then, with a deft twist of its fluked tail, the whale was gone, sliding back into the dark reaches of the sea. Again, the peculiar hum sounded, like the music of a long horn, distant and melancholy, echoing across the water as it disappeared from sight.

"Did you see it?" Brander asked from behind her, startling Morgana. She had been lost in some far-off region of her mind, thinking of the whale.

"Aye. It was beautiful," she replied softly, and turned to face him. "Did you think so?"

"'Tis not the first I've seen. For such large creatures, they seem so graceful."

"It is because they are in their element," Morgana observed. "Such an animal would be awkward and useless if it lived on land." For a moment Morgana felt a brief kinship with the whale. She was out of her element with this Viking, as awkward and useless as a beached whale. Yet, she had felt out of place in Erin, lost and floundering among her own people, searching for a comfortable niche.

Brander was smiling at her with the potent smile that made her pulses race and her throat constrict, and Morgana forgot about the whale.

"Only you would make such an observation, Morgana," he said. "Do you see inside every living creature?"

"No. I cannot see inside at will, only when the spirits command." Anyone could have read the expression of relief that skimmed Brander's face, and Morgana couldn't help a smile. "Does that make you feel better, Brander?" she teased, though she fervently wished she could see into his thoughts and read what he felt for her.

"Much! I could not feel comfortable with someone who knew my every thought."

One brawny arm reached out to drape casually over her shoulders, pulling her close to his long, hard body, and he turned her toward the spot where her pallet had lain beside the rail.

"Rest now, Morgana," he said. "It has been a long day filled with changes for you. You are so small and delicate, and I would not wish for you to become ill because of me. You have already lost much, and I shall always be grateful for the help you gave me."

"I don't want your gratitude, Brander, " Morgana managed to say through suddenly stiff lips. Gratitude! Was that the emotion he felt for her? She bit her lip against the rush of words that threatened to spill from her mouth, knowing that he would not understand. Brander was deliberately keeping her at arms length from him. If she tried to summon emotions he did not feel, she would only push him farther away.

"Then what do you want from me, Morgana?" he surprised her by asking . "I sense that you are unhappy, and I do not know how to put you at ease."

Slipping from beneath the disturbing pressure of his arm across her shoulders, Morgana stepped to the rail of the longship and turned to lean back against it, staring at his handsome face in the silver light from the moon. The deck was as bright as if lit with a hundred oil lamps, and her gaze could roam at will over the contours of his face and form. He was far too attractive a man for her to be able to concentrate on anything else, and she gave a half-sigh of discouragement. Hadn't she asked the gods for a man . . . a lover? And was this their answer? Well, she'd always known nothing was freely given. The gods had provided him, but they obviously expected her to use her own ingenuity to keep him.

Brander edged closer, the curved line of his dark brows knitting into a puzzled frown. She stood so still and silent, staring at him as if she'd never seen him before, and he wondered if the day's ordeal had disordered her mind. Enough had happened to derange anyone, especially a rather sheltered young girl who had been kept away from even the members of her own clan. And this girl was more sensitive than most, her spirit finely attuned to all around her, so that she would not escape the nuances of others' emotions. It must be exhausting to her still young spirit.

"What do you wish from me, Morgana?" he repeated softly, gently, his voice a whisper of sound.

"Your friendship for now," she answered at last. "All that you can freely give."

"And you have it. Now let me fix your pallet for you so that you can rest." In just a few moments he had her blanket spread upon the planked deck and a pillow positioned invitingly against the ship's side. Still kneeling beside it, he patted the cushion, motioning for her to lie down, and Morgana's pulse leaped. Did he intend to lie with her?

Sinking gracefully to the pallet, she glanced up at Brander, holding her breath, wondering if he would kiss her, hold her as he had that night in the cave. There was little privacy, but that didn't seem to matter to some, like Gunther who was rutting with the slave girl Gwyneth at the front of the ship. The sounds of their pleasure-making drifted through the night air to everyone's ears, Gunther's heated words and

Gwyneth's sharp protests mingling with the slap of sail and water.

Leaning slightly, Brander touched his lips to her forehead and murmured a goodnight. But when Morgana reached out for him he was gone, his tall, straight body momentarily blocking the moonlight as he rose.

A scowl puckered her forehead into unsightly creases as Morgana stared after his retreating figure, and her kick of frustration disarranged the blankets. Small fingers curved into disheveled folds of the blanket, and she sighed. At least the kiss signaled affection.

Later, lying alone on her pallet and gazing up at the sky, Morgana sleepily reflected that she was grateful that Brander could not read her thoughts.

Chapter 11

Days stretched longer now. The dragon heads gracing the prow pointed north, skimming over waves as the longship pushed toward home. They had stopped briefly on land, replenishing their water supply and gathering food in the Hebrides Islands before setting back out to sea.

Morgana watched from the rail of the ship as they passed the Orkneys, distant green lumps of land. Men strained at the oars when the wind died, bare backs gleaming with sweat in the sunlight as they leaned forward and pulled back, striking a cadence that surged the ship through waters as smooth as polished glass.

The sun beat down, hot and molten, leaving the captives weak and listless. Gwyneth still refused to look or speak to Morgana, turning her head away whenever she approached. The glistening fiery mane was dull and matted now, and her eyes lifeless lumps of coal that seemed to see right through Morgana.

Morgana could sense the Celtic captive's failing spirit,

but was helpless to assist. Any attempt to mention the girl to Brander met with resistance.

"She is Gunther's slave," he would say in a tone that invited no argument, and Morgana would bite back a reply.

So the captives crowded at one end of the ship, huddled in anxious knots as far away from the Vikings as possible. To Morgana's sorrow, she found herself to be an outsider still. She was not a Viking, and she would not be accepted by her own people who considered her a traitor. Would she ever belong, ever be made to feel part of a family?

Long days were spent staring over the ship's rail, thinking of Brander and fretting over the surplus of idle time. She paced the deck restlessly, pleating folds of her gown between her fingers until it creased into permanent wrinkles as she prowled from prow to stern. Diversion finally came in the form of a baby goose.

Bored as usual, Morgana skirted the cargo hold on her way from stern to prow, turning her head away from the noxious odor of animal droppings. A thin, pitiful peep filtered through the squawks, clucks, squeals, and hisses to snare Morgana's attention, and she halted.

Heavier mature geese jammed into the open wooden crates had trampled the gosling mercilessly, pecking him to bloody bits of bone and feathers. Bending, Morgana gently lifted him from the litter of feathers and offal. The tiny creature didn't even offer a croak of protest when she cradled him in the crook of an arm and took him to her pallet.

"What are you going to do with it?" Brander asked in thinly veiled amusement when he discovered Morgana's new pet. "Fatten him for the cooking pot?"

Unperturbed, Morgana continued spooning thin barley broth into the pale amber beak. Tiny pink legs twitched briefly as the gosling swallowed.

"I shall call him Smoke," she said, answering Brander's question about her intentions, "because of his color and size. He's hardly bigger than a smoke ring, don't you think?"

For a moment Brander's hand rested upon Morgana's downturned head in an affectionate, indulgent gesture, and her spooning motions ceased. Just the touch of his hand sent her pulse racing as madly as sea terns skimming over land and water. Looking up, she found his eyes crinkling down at her.

Brander shook his golden head in wry amusement. He had shed his confining tunic and wore only tight trousers clinched at his trim waist with a wide leather belt. The decorated brass buckle flashed sunlight and caught her eye. Then, involuntarily, her gaze dropped to his long, hard legs, with their blending of smooth muscles that flowed rhythmically with each movement. Disconcerted, her eyes flew upward again, only to encounter a wide expanse of sunbrowned bare chest. It had been not so long ago that his chest had been pressed close, his mouth trailing hot kisses over her breasts. . . .

Recognizing the widening awareness in her eyes, Brander felt the beginnings of a response stir in his belly. The heat had drenched Morgana's gown, molding it to her curves like a second skin so that the round fullness of ripe young breasts pressed urgently against the thin woolen material. A moist sheen dotted her arms and neck and face, and thin streams trickled into the mysterious shadows between her breasts. Brander's memory readily supplied the details of her body, and it took a great effort to jerk his thoughts in another direction. He moved several steps away.

"Just keep your pet from underfoot," he said in an unnecessarily harsh voice, then pivoted and walked to the ship's stern.

Morgana stared after him. Was she only hoping, or had there been the faintest response to her as a woman? One hand idly stroked the gray gosling as her eyes narrowed in thought. Perhaps the situation wasn't as hopeless as she had feared. . . .

The Vikings stopped for two days in the Shetlands before undertaking the last leg of their journey, going ashore to seek out fresh water and hot, cooked meals. The steady diet of salted fish and cold, flat cakes had staled. and they were all in jovial humor as they dragged the longship into the shallows.

Morgana was allowed ashore, but it was Delling who kindly offered to lift her over the side of the ship to carry her through the icy waters lapping at their legs. The warm-hearted Viking had spent the past days at sea teaching Morgana the rudiments of his native tongue and telling her what she might expect upon reaching Jutland. She had found in the man an unexpected source of friendship.

"Thank you," Morgana said when the burly Viking carried her ashore and gently lowered her to dry land. She stood awkwardly for a moment, then stumbled forward with a soft cry of surprise.

Laughing, Delling advised, " 'Twill take a bit to get used to solid land beneath your feet again. Go slowly, my lady."

Sinking to the rough hardness of a humped rock, Morgana joined him in laughter.

"I suppose I was more accustomed to unsteady footing than I thought!"

"Aye, you're a better sailor than you knew." Delling gazed at her in friendly affection, a smile hovering beneath his golden mustache. His smile faded when Morgana's searching glance did not find Brander and she turned to ask Delling bluntly,

"Delling, why does Brander avoid me? Is it something I've done?"

"Done?" he echoed. "What could you have done?" He dodged her direct gaze, and mumbled an explanation about going back to the ship to help drive the stock ashore to feed.

Morgana stared after him. He knew. Her mouth set into a straight, determined line. Before the voyage was over, she would find out from Delling why Brander avoided her. It would just take time. . . .

A familiar cry distracted Morgana. Her gosling had been left aboard in the small crate Delling had built for him. In just a few days he had grown much stronger, and she could hear his steady, tinny cries as he was left behind. *Poor Smoke*, she thought, *I know how you must feel. We're both outcasts, unwanted by our own kind*.

Leaning back on her elbows, Morgana let the sun drift over her in heated waves, closing her eyes against the brightness. She could hear the scrunching of the boat's hull against sand as the men pulled it onto the beach, heard their muffled grunts and comments as they strained brawny muscles. Waves hissed and roared in somber rhythm, softly then louder, lulling Morgana into a peaceful nap.

She woke with a start when cold, wet drops splattered onto her face and chest, eyes snapping open to see Brander grinning down at her.

"Lazy wench," he chided playfully, "do you sleep while we work?" He shook loose the remaining drops of seawater from his fingers, then dried his hands on his tunic.

A faint smile tugged at the corners of her mouth, then grew larger. "Aye," she retorted, "and I was enjoying it until now!"

"Come with me. We have a fire and hot food that you might enjoy." He caught her willing hands in his, pulling her up before he released his grip.

Morgana's fingers tingled at the brief contact, and she wished she dared hook her arm through his. Instead she walked beside him, trying to match his long stride, concentrating on the intoxicating closeness. Brander smelled of sea and sun and sweat, a pleasant smell that penetrated her senses and left her almost giddy.

Her free hand accidentally brushed against Brander, and Morgana was startled at the feel of cold metal. His sword was buckled at his waist, and he carried Widow-Maker in one fist.

"Do you expect trouble?" she asked.

"Nay, but I'm ready if it expects us." He pointed with his battle-ax at the distant line of trees. The land was flat and green, with marshy stretches of ground leading inland. Tall trees fringed the edges of the marsh with deep green shadows. "See? Trouble but awaits the cover of darkness."

A fresh pale wind passed over Morgana, bringing the sweet, sharp smell of pine, whispering gently over the contours of her face, and she heard herself say, "No. There is no trouble beyond this line. We will leave unmolested."

Brander started in surprise at the calm assurance in her tone. There were times when the girl was a bit unnerving, he thought irritably, but time should prove her right or wrong.

In the two days spent there, they saw no living creature but the small, shaggy ponies that inhabited the islands. The worrisome beasts crowded around the Viking camp, curiously nosing sleeping warriors and startling them into thinking they had been attacked. Morgana laughed long and heartily at the sheepish expression on Gunther's face when he realized he had attempted a defense against an unarmed pony.

Only Gwyneth's sullen temper spoiled Morgana's newer, lighter mood. When Gunther brought the Celtic captive ashore for fresh water and hot food, she sulkily refused to eat in spite of coaxing. Angered, Gunther boxed her ears soundly. Gwyneth jerked away and spun around as if to flee, then discovered Morgana gazing at her with sympathy.

"At least I don't play the willing whore!" Gwyneth shrilled, fixing Morgana with a baleful glare. "Take this Celtic whore if you desire to bed a woman...." Her words stopped abruptly when Brander leaped to his feet, eyes filled with rage.

"Shut her up, Gunther, or by Thor's hammer, I shall do it for you!"

The sight of a wrathful Brander left Gwyneth quaking and frightened, so that she immediately quieted. She didn't make a sound when Gunther furiously pulled her from camp.

" 'Tis no matter," Morgana said when Brander held out a conciliatory hand. "I know well what she thinks."

"I don't care for women's bickering," Brander said after a moment, "but I won't have her putting ideas into the heads of anyone else. You are not here for sport, Morgana, and I don't intend for you to be treated thusly."

Bowing her head, Morgana only nodded. How could she defend herself against an accusation that might be justified? She longed for Brander's touch to be more than brotherly and affectionate, longed for him to look at her as she had seen Gunther look at Gwyneth. What had happened to the man who had taken her so passionately? Did he regret it now? Or did he regret bringing her with him?

She should go to him boldly, Morgana thought, and tell him of her desire. 'Twas common practice for a Celtic woman to indicate her preference when a well-favored man pleased her, and no one thought anything of it. Knowing that, why did she hesitate now?

But Brander was different. His customs were not the same and he might misunderstand. 'Twould be a disaster to try.

The thin wail of her gosling still aboard the longship gave Morgana the perfect reason she needed for excusing herself from Brander's company. She needed more time, time to think about the days ahead.

Chapter 12

The Shetlands were several days behind them when a storm struck. Cold frigid air from the north swept across the sea, whipping waves against the ship like battering rams. Gray-green seawater sloshed over the decks, soaking everything aboard and leaving cargo and passengers crusted with salt.

Swirling and capering as if a wind-tossed autumn leaf, the longship hurled itself against the force of wind and water with a giddy violence that threatened to tear nails from the shuddering timbers. All around the ship the water gleamed dully, splotched with dark rain blisters. Oars glinted in the gray light as the Vikings rowed against the wind, and the square sail flapped with noisy desperation.

Huddled against one side, sheltering her sodden gray goose with a drenched cloak and her body, Morgana wiped at the streamers of seawater which were spat into her face by the wind. She was soaked to the skin and miserable. It was impossible to suck in air that wasn't laden with heavy moisture and the icy steam of pelting rain.

The dragon-head prow dipped low in the water, grinning, with rain drooling from fangs and carved wooden lips, then bucked over a wave before plunging downward again. Seawater rushed over the sides in a torrent of frothing kelp. Raindrops stung like arrows against her unprotected skin, and Morgana shivered at the intensity of the storm.

Dimly, through the roar of wind and rain and pounding waves, she heard Brander's voice and lifted her head.

"Morgana! Morgana, get into the cargo hold," he was telling her with curt gestures. The wind whipped at Brander's tunic and hair, and water sluicing over the ship's sides boiled around his feet. Impatiently, he jerked a thumb in the direction of the cargo area again, and Morgana obeyed.

She crawled across the slippery deck on hands and knees, cradling the squawking, frightened goose beneath one arm, and finally slid into the cargo hold. It held a few inches of water, but surprisingly enough, it was warmer than the wind-whipped deck. Terrified livestock clucked, squealed and hissed around her as Morgana waited out the fury of the storm.

Had she come this far only to die in the cold clutches of the sea? A pounding to equal the rattling of thunder and seawater sounded in her skull, making her wince against the racking pain. Rain blurred everything, so that it seemed as if she was already beneath the cold gray waves. A pervading sense of doom seeped into her bones with the chill, and Morgana reflected on the emptiness of her life. She would die without knowing if Brander loved her.

There were no comforting visions to deny such a fate, no certain assurance from her gods to aid her, and Morgana squatted in shivering misery amidst the pungent odors of wet feathers and animal droppings.

The thin timber separating livestock from cargo provided Morgana with leverage to brace her feet and keep from rolling about the hold. Barrels and casks crowded her from all directions, pressing against the restraint of hemp ropes holding them in place. Smoke, the gosling, quivered in Morgana's lap, occasionally piping shrilly, but otherwise reasonably well behaved. Idly, hardly realizing what she was doing to comfort him, Morgana began to stroke his wet, salt-sticky feathers, crooning a soft tune recalled from her childhood.

She was on the fourteenth verse when the storm finally abated. The wind lessened and the longship rode the waves more easily instead of diving like a heron into inky water. Only brief showers of rain spattered on the decks now, and the Vikings began the wearisome task of cleaning up.

Greenish black squiggles of sea kelp jelled on wooden planks, and salt began to crystallize on the cargo, human as well as animal. Brander came to stand beside Morgana, bending to ask if she was unharmed.

"Aye," she managed to answer through chattering teeth, and he noted the pale ashen pallor of her skin. Her hair was sticky with salt and seaweed, and dripped water like a sponge against the pressure of his cradling palm as he bent her head to examine her face with a critical eye.

Great green pools stared back at him, bruised and distended, salty crystals clinging like chips of pearl to her thick, spiky lashes. Violet shadows curved under her eyes like Turkish scimitars, and her lips were pinched and blue.

"You're going to be ill if we don't get you dry and warm," Brander muttered. His arms scooped under Morgana's thighs to lift her, startling the gosling curled in her lap so that he hissed a warning at the intrusion. "Quiet your bird, or I'll toss him overboard," Brander threatened, and Morgana's fingers began a rhythmic stroking on the gosling's back.

Thorfinn slanted a smirk in Brander's direction when the

Viking leader strode across the deck carrying Morgana and her drenched goose.

"It seems as if our fearless leader is smitten," he observed to no one in particular. The Finn's eyes narrowed as Brander lay Morgana gently on the deck and ordered a brass brazier rekindled to warm her.

Delling, working on an oar splintered by a crashing wave, lifted his head to glare at Thorfinn.

"The Celtic girl saved his life," Delling said. "Do you expect him to let her die from exposure?"

Thorfinn shrugged. "What does it matter? She is only a Celt, after all. . . ."

"You disgust me!" Delling shot back angrily. "You have loyalty to none, Thorfinn, and I wonder why you are still in our clan. Has no one offered you more prizes to sail with them?"

"No, not yet, Delling the Moral," Thorfinn mocked. "Do not fret yourself about it. All will know when I decide to sail on richer seas."

"No doubt." Delling stood abruptly, glaring down at the smirking Finn, then wheeled and strode to the opposite side of the ship. He'd never trusted that Finnish snake, ever since the day he'd seen Thorfinn substitute bad wine for good in the home of his hosts. It had been an ill omen that Delling had chosen not to relate, and now he regretted it.

Brander didn't notice Delling's preoccupation. He was deeply concerned with Morgana. She was so frail, so delicate, that he feared the storm had weakened her health. She shivered beneath a pile of blankets, and the delicate tracery of blue-veined lids closed over her eyes as her muscles contracted again and again. Holding one of her hands, Brander rubbed impatiently at the chilled skin, trying to rub warmth and life back into her body.

"Don't," she said crankily, pushing at him, her hands limp-wristed and flopping.

"You've taken a chill," Brander explained, as if to a small child, "and I am trying to help you, Morgana."

"I'll be fine." A crease wrinkled her forehead, sliding from her finely arched brows to her nose, so that she looked like she smelled something rotten. "Where's Smoke?"

"Smoke?" Brander stared at Morgana blankly, and she opened her eyes and asked again, fretfully. This time he remembered the gosling, and assured her that he was fine and drying his feathers in the crate Delling had made.

"Now close your eyes and rest," he instructed, and she willingly obeyed. Long lashes closed over her fevered eyes, hiding from view the sight of Brander's anxiety. She would have been pleased to know that he was concerned and worried, but instead Morgana drifted in a pleasant haze between sleep and awareness.

The steady rolling dip of the vessel lulled her into a somnolent state. Part of her mind remained alert, hearing the footfalls of the Vikings and the scramblings they made while repairing the storm's damage; another part of her mind insisted on a peaceful drifting as if she were floating through fields of clouds.

Gradually the motion of the ship became agonizing. At first she wake-dreamed that it was a reaction to her earlier fear of the storm and drowning; then, as the pain in her skull grew worse, she began to realize that it was not. Everything beyond her closed lids grew bright, and the very air began to throb with steam as wood and sails and animal hides began to dry in the sun. Steam rose in shimmering waves that she could feel, as if water had poured over fire-heated stones, and Morgana started to sweat like an ox pulling a plow. Even the thin trickle of perspiration over her brow and cheeks hurt.

She imagined that she was in a furnace, where a blacksmith's bellows pumped hot air so that the fire grew hotter and hotter. Opening her eyes, Morgana tried to focus but could not.

Her surroundings were blurred, as they had been when the rain poured in torrents over the ship and sea, and she saw only vague images that danced eerily across her field of vision. Bright lights exploded like thousands of tiny suns inside her head, spinning in showers of sparks across a pinwheel sky.

A faintly familiar face swam into view, slowly coming into focus as she stared with a puzzled expression. It was someone she should know, but who? His identity skidded past, wheeled and paused, and she recognized Delling's kind face.

"My lady?"

Dazzling sunlight concentrated on his golden head as Delling knelt beside her, and Morgana reached out a tentative hand. Her confusion was evident, and Delling turned a helpless face toward Brander.

"She doesn't know me," he said plaintively, woefully.

"It's the fever," Brander responded. His tone was brusque and businesslike, masking his concern as his hands felt Morgana's rapid pulse. Her breath was shallow and fast, and her skin felt hot and dry to the touch.

"How can she sicken so quickly?" Delling made awkward abortive motions with his hands, not knowing how to help but wanting to. "She was well enough before the storm. . . ."

Shrugging, Brander added another blanket to the pile atop Morgana. "Her condition was weak when we left Hibernia, Delling. Being cold and wet hastened illness."

"My wife is not so frail," Delling muttered doubtfully.

"Nay, but she is large and healthy as an ox!" Brander

tucked in the blankets around Morgana, then rocked back on his heels. She was still pale in spite of the fever, and she began to thrash about in her sleep.

Morgana dreamed wild dreams that mingled past and present. They faded into one another in a vivid blur of color and light, going from crimson to jet in a blinding flash. The dreams stretched endlessly, drifting from childhood to young adulthood in a slow-wheeling pattern of time frames.

She woke once to find Brander kneeling beside her, bathing her face with a wet cloth. Morgana attempted a smile, but fell back asleep before her tired brain could complete the signal to her mouth. When she woke again it was dark, and she could see only the vague outline of a profile against the yellow glow of an oil lamp. She blinkéd, slowly and lethargically, and when her eyelids lifted again it was morning.

Gradually, Morgana began to have longer periods of wakefulness. Time had little meaning to her, so that she wasn't aware of the passing of days, only of the changing weather. The air grew cooler and thinner, the wind lighter and the sky bluer, until it seemed as if they had passed through some sort of time warp and into another world.

Brander and Delling propped her against a tumbled pile of cushions and tucked her gosling at her side. Smoke had fattened considerably thanks to Delling's meticulous care, and he nestled by Morgana with a beady eye trained on anyone who dared to come near.

"You'd think the damned goose would be more grateful," Delling was heard to grumble when he rarely escaped being pecked on the back of one hand. "After all, I shared my food with the blasted bird!"

"You should have given him the best portions," Gunther suggested with a grin, and the other men laughed.

They were all in fine moods, exuberant and jovial and

glad to be so near home. Morgana was on the road to recovery, they had made a fine haul in Hibernia, and had lost only a very few men in the process. Their ship had weathered a violent storm and two weak squalls, and land was in sight. Aye, it had been a very profitable journey.

The longship's first stop was Kaupang, in Norway. They had skirted the coastline of Norway before rounding the southeastern tip toward Kaupang. Snow-capped mountains, rising abruptly from the fjord-indented coastline, turned rocky faces to the sea. Farther up the *Vikin*, or Oslofjord, the settlement nestled on the west side. Kaupang meant "marketplace," an apt title. There was a complex of houses and workshops by the waterside, and stone jetties.

A smoky haze hung over the settlement from the metal-working shops of iron, silver and bronze. Soapstone vessels were one of the major exports to Jutland and Hedeby. Northern merchant skippers came with cargoes of furs, skins, down, walrus ivory, and much prized walrus-hide ropes. Here, most of the slaves captured in Hibernia were traded for silver. From the settlement, they would be transported overland to Arabic countries of constant sunshine, and exchanged for silk, fruit, spices, wine, jewelry, and silver.

Close to home, the Vikings did not linger long in Kaupang. They conducted their business as swiftly as possible and sailed south. The next stop was Hedeby.

Morgana had heard of the settlement, called Slesvig by the Saxons, and knew it was a large market town, manufacturing center, and seaport. Perched on the shoreline of the Haddeby Nor, the inlet provided both a sheltered harbor and access to the Schlei fjord and Baltic Sea. This position at the base of the Jutland peninsula gave Hedeby control over the most important trade routes from Western Europe to the Baltic. Trans-European land routes passed near Hedeby through the Danevirke, a great system of earthworks protecting the Danish border.

Even more important, Delling told Morgana, was the flow of traders from the North Sea to the Baltic.

"Your tribe is rich, then?" Morgana, still weak from her recent bout with illness, curled her hand across the light blanket over her knees. The long fingers of her other hand softly stroked the grey goose as he perched at her side, and he lifted his head from beneath one wing.

From the corner of her eye, Morgana surreptitiously searched for Brander. He was at the front of the ship, standing with legs apart for balance, watching as the green sickle of land drew nearer. The dragon-head prow dipped gracefully, almost as if bowing, and the steady wind pushed it forward.

"No, not rich," Delling was saying, drawing Morgana's attention back to him, "but we do well. Supplying the Arabs with slaves in exchange for silver is very profitable, and it aids in the acquisition of other luxuries. There are furs, honey, wax, silk, and weapons. We get cloth from Frisia, black basalt from the Eifel regions for querns, and the Rhineland—ah!" He touched the tips of his fingers to his mouth and Morgana laughed. "The sweetest wines come from the grapes in Rhineland, as well as pottery and glass to pour it in!"

"I look forward to tasting this wine," she said. "Are we close to your home?"

Delling nodded and rose from his cushion by Morgana's side. "Aye, and I'd best help, or Brander will claim that I did not do my share on this voyage. . . ."

"Delling, wait." Morgana's voice had a sharp edge, and he paused to look at her curiously. "I need to know before we arrive—why does Brander avoid me?"

"He does not avoid you," Delling protested weakly.

"Did he not stay by your side when you were ill? And it was Brander who . . ."

"You know what I mean." Morgana twisted her fingers together until they were red. "Does he have a woman?" There. The question was out, and she held her breath waiting for an answer.

"A woman?" Sunlight broke over Delling's face in the form of a broad smile. "Nay, Morgana. Brander is not married. But I am, and my wife will be a widow if I don't go to help. I will talk to you later, I promise. . . ."

"Nay," Morgana forestalled his rapid departure. "I would know now why he avoids me. Is there some reason I do not understand?"

"Well . . ." Delling scratched his head and glanced desperately around, searching for rescue from unknown sources. There was none. "Perhaps it is your youth," he finally answered, wishing Brander had not said and Morgana had not asked. "You are overyoung, though you appear much more mature," he hastened to add.

Morgana blinked. "Too young??" she echoed. How was that possible? She had seen eighteen winters, and soon another would be added to her age! "That cannot be it, Delling! Why, I have eighteen winters upon me. . . ."

"Eighteen?" Delling's face registered his confusion. "But . . . but Brander said you were but fourteen."

" 'Tis what I told him, in a roundabout way. I didn't want him to think I had gotten this old without being spoken for," Morgana explained, noticing the bewildered expression on Delling's face. "Is that . . . that why he won't . . ." She stumbled to a halt. A pestilence upon her quick tongue! She had unwittingly provided Brander with the very excuse he needed to avoid her. But if she confessed, he would know she'd lied. Morgana's eyes met Delling's.

"Do not tell him," she begged. "He will never trust me again, and 'twas not exactly a lie, the way I told it."

"I won't," Delling promised, but his words set ill upon his mind. Brander's temper would be greatly improved if he but knew the truth. "I must join the others now, Morgana."

His voice trailed behind him as Delling strode swiftly to the prow to take his turn at the long oars. Morgana seized the opportunity to study Brander at length, letting her gaze linger over his tall frame and the bright sheen of his hair.

She had seen a lion once, a tawny, fierce creature with smooth muscles rippling beneath golden skin, baring fangs and arrogance at the world. It had been confined in a wooden cage and carried on a cart, and she had crept up to the animal under cover of darkness. Curiosity and a strange affinity had drawn her, and she had stood gazing at the lion for some time. He had gazed back at her with fierce eyes, hating his prison and the men who displayed him as if he was tame. Morgana had recognized that same wild look in Brander's eyes when she'd seen him in the Celtic chieftain's hall. Here, aboard the longship, he was in his element, and in control.

Brander turned, catching her eye, and motioned for Morgana to join him. She almost wriggled with delight, but decided she must act older, must let Brander guess that she was not a child but mature. Demurely holding down her skirt against capricious gusts of wind with one hand, and cradling the goose in her other, she made her way across the tilting deck past the rowing benches. Gwyneth, who Gunther had decided at the last moment not to sell with the other slaves, gazed spitefully as Morgana stood beside Brander.

Freshening wind blew across Morgana's pale cheeks, bringing back color, and her eyes sparkled as she tilted her head to look at Brander. He wore his conical leather helmet and was dressed in richly embroidered tunic and *braccae,* or trousers, with a heavy gold belt circling his waist. Leggings were laced to his knees, and he wore boots of the finest leather on his feet. Brander appeared every inch the conquering hero returning home.

Surveying her own garb, Morgana experienced a twinge at her appearance. She felt like a plain sparrow next to Brander's finery. Her rough woolen gown was dirty and tattered, and her soft leather boots were salt-stained and worn. Even her cape was in a sad state, and somehow she had lost the brooch used to hold it at one shoulder. The only possessions she brought to this new land were her pouch filled with herbs and a stolen goose.

The keen pressure of a smile tugged at Morgana's lips, and Brander glanced down and wondered what was amusing.

"I was thinking of the stark contrast we make," Morgana answered when he asked. "You, the finely dressed leader, and myself, plain as dirt and belonging to no one."

"And that is amusing?"

"Is it not?" Morgana's brows arched. "Won't your family be surprised at the company you keep?"

A smile widened to a grin as Brander considered that, and his fingers hooked beneath Morgana's chin to tilt her face upward.

"They'll be surprised, yea, but not as you think." How could she possibly call herself plain, when those great eyes glowed like emeralds, and her hair was as rich as the finest sable, flowing over her shoulders down her back? Even in the dingy, ragged garments she wore, Morgana would put to shame some of the finest women he'd known. His thumb lightly caressed the silken texture of her cheek, sliding over to her mouth.

A loud pop of bone against bone sounded, startling Morgana and causing Brander to jerk away as if he'd touched a live coal. Jealous, the gosling had reached from beneath Morgana's arm and pecked sharply at Brander's hand, leaving an angry red welt. Brander stood glaring at the bird and cursing in his own language.

" 'Tis an ill-tempered beast, and best eaten soon," Brander muttered darkly, giving the creature a hard look.

"Nay," Morgana said in spite of her frustration at the interruption. "He belongs to me. You said so when I was ill."

"Aye, I recall it, but if the bird wishes to enjoy continued good health, 'twould be best if he didn't peck at me like a viper!"

"I will tell him," Morgana promised, leaving Brander to muse on exactly how she would convey the message to a goose.

The ship nudged close to shore, diverting Brander's attention from the goose and widening Morgana's eyes. Hedeby was much cruder than she'd imagined, being a mere settlement of wooden houses flanked by smaller buildings and livestock sheds. Green fields stretched behind the settlement, dotted with more wooden houses. The rutted roads ribboned between them, and some were covered with walkways of oak logs.

Women, children, and dogs made up the majority of the crowd greeting the returning longship, and as Morgana watched, more stragglers streamed from the fields and low hills behind Hedeby. A ship was exciting; a ship belonging to husbands, brothers, and lovers was exhilarating as well. Throngs clamored at the edge of the harbor. Behind the semicircle of wooden buildings rose a huge rampart, curving protectively around the town and jutting into the Haddeby Nor in the form of a palisade. This rampart, Brander explained to Morgana as they stood at the rail, was linked to the Danevirke protecting the Danish border.

He pointed. Situated behind the rampart, just out of sight of the thriving, teeming settlement, was his home.

"That . . . that is where I will stay?" Morgana held her breath. Brander had never said where she would live, had never hinted that she might stay with him.

He frowned, as if the idea had just occurred to him.

"Aye, I suppose that is best for now. We can find another place for you later."

Morgana could almost hear her hopes and dreams splintering into a thousand pieces, the sound as loud in her ears as the crashing of a lightning-struck oak. He had been so concerned, almost like a lover, and now . . . She would not let him see her disappointment at the hint that she might be only a temporary visitor in his home.

Nor would she let him see her chagrin when he seemed to forget her existence in the excitement of greeting his family. A fixed smile remained on Morgana's face as Brander leaped from the longship and into the water, heedless of icy waves lapping at his finery. He splashed through the shallows with his men, laughing and talking, pausing to shove roughly at an acquaintance in that way men sometimes have, then clasping him on the shoulder with a friendly hand.

Pushing his way through the cluster of people, Brander finally reached his objective, and warmly clasped a tall man in an expansive hug. It must be his father, the jarl, Morgana decided. She stood at the prow, waiting, hoping for a sign from Brander to join him. Long minutes passed, and he moved farther away, standing on a stone jetty now, deep in conversation with several men and his father.

"He's forgotten you already," a Celtic voice hissed in her ear, and Morgana turned to see Gwyneth gazing at her with a tight smile.

"No, he hasn't!" Morgana answered before thinking.

She should not get into a discussion of this nature with the girl. No good would come of being forced into defending Brander. "Are you pleased at being kept by Gunther and not traded away like the others?" she asked finally.

"Aye!" The word was spat as if distasteful. "At least he covets me, which is more than you can say for the man you desire. . . ."

Her feelings were so obvious that even an enemy could sense her longing for Brander! Morgana shrugged, and held her goose more tightly. Her chin lifted as she gazed into Gwyneth's eyes, and any animosity she felt evaporated as she recognized the pain and fright hiding behind a mask of bravado and hate.

"I am glad for you then," Morgana answered simply. "Perhaps all will be well with you soon."

Her sincerity caught Gwyneth off guard. She stared at Morgana as if she couldn't believe what she'd heard. A puzzled expression creased her face for a moment. It quickly altered to the familiar sneer, and with a toss of fiery hair, Gwyneth held out one arm to show Morgana the jangling glitter of bracelets.

"Silver and gold, to mark my worth to him, Gunther says. I will trade them for passage home one day, but you shall remain here forever, sorceress!"

Morgana just watched as Gwyneth pivoted and strode to the rail to meet Gunther. He was waiting impatiently, and when she neared, he reached out a brawny arm and swept her from her feet to carry her ashore. The Viking seemed to be smitten with his Celtic slave, and Morgana knew a brief twinge of jealousy at the expression on his face when he looked at Gwyneth.

Would it be better to be a slave and coveted, than a friend who was not? She shook her head, and wished desperately for an answer. Where was her usual perceptiveness, the intuition that always aided her? Why didn't it come to her rescue now? She was lost, floundering in a sea of new emotions with no sign of familiar ground on which to rest.

It was Delling who carried Morgana ashore, lifting her and the goose in his kind, strong arms and splashing through knee-high water with them.

"Where is Brander?" Morgana wanted to know.

Delling cleared his throat in embarrassment. It was obvious that Morgana loved his leader, and he didn't know how to deal with the situation.

He made lame excuses about cargo and the longship, dividing their plunder and dealing with the men, then ended with sighing, "I will take you to his house myself. He will expect you to be there when he returns from his father's house."

A dull weight sat in Morgana's chest like lead. "He went to his father's house? Will he be there long, Delling?"

"I don't know, Morgana. Brander's father is the jarl, so he must give him an accounting of the voyage. You understand . . ."

"Aye. I understand." Holding her head stiffly erect, Morgana stood beside Delling once he set her down. She smiled politely as he introduced her to his wife, Disa, a large, jovial woman who genuinely seemed to like Morgana and exclaimed with laughter over the pet goose.

Disa's warmth gradually began to seep into Morgana so that she felt more at ease, and her cheerful chatter and matter-of-fact questions diverted her attention from Brander's abandonment.

"You are Celtic?" Disa asked, surprising Morgana with her command of the language.

"Aye, from Erin. How is it that you speak my tongue so well?"

Flapping a large white hand, Disa chuckled. "I came

from Frisia, where there are many Celtic slaves. One had to speak their language to give them directions. 'Twas easier than teaching them mine." She gave Delling an affectionate glance. "I've been trying to teach this one, but he has a head as thick as an iron cooking pot!"

"Aye, but look at my teacher! 'Tis easy enough to see why I find it hard to learn," Delling retorted.

It was impossible for Morgana not to smile at their loving banter, and she was grateful for their company on the trip to Brander's home. The Central Settlement of Hedeby had been established beside Hedeby stream, and the area teemed with construction.

"We are diverting the course of the stream," Delling explained, "and planking the sides. Hedeby is growing so large that we must expand somewhere! All the streets are being laid out at right angles and parallel to the stream, and our building plots are regulated in size. We are building a new rampart for protection, inside the old one. It will be much larger and stronger."

Vikings weren't as barbaric as she'd once thought, Morgana decided. They showed ingenuity and enterprise for things other than sea piracy and raiding monasteries. Indeed, the population seemed to be largely comprised of farmers and merchants.

Where was the land of snow and ice she'd envisioned? Green fields stretched as far as she could see, heavily wooded with oak and beech. The land was not mountainous as she'd thought, but undulated gently in soft rises, sand dunes, and grassy heaths.

Brander's home was beyond the grassy rampart curving some distance from the inlet. A crude road stretched from the harbor and around the rampart, winding through fields and woods. Delling provided a cart for the short journey, which took longer because of the curving road. The sun beat down warmly though the air was cool, and Morgana tilted back her head to let the sun smile on her face.

Birds chattered from thick-leaved branches, and the wind smelled of rich earth and fragrant grasses. Insects chirruped throatily, filled with urgency to complete their short life span, and the air hummed with activity.

The cart lurched around a bend in the rutted road, and Delling pointed out Brander's house to Morgana. It was large, built with stout timbers, and rectangular in shape. Instead of the usual roof opening for smoke that Morgana had noticed was common for Viking homes, Brander had erected several stone chimneys. The main house was flanked by smaller buildings; stables, pens, and sheds for livestock sprawled in a semicircle behind his home.

"Here we are," Delling announced cheerfully. He and Disa exchanged glances when Morgana climbed slowly down from the cart. She looked like a lost child, alone and frightened, and Delling felt a spasm of anger toward Brander that he would forget her so easily. Did he not care what happened to the girl? Why had he abandoned her in the excitement of their arrival? Delling grimly determined to ask his leader those questions as soon as he settled Morgana into his house.

"Perhaps we should take her home with us," Disa whispered in her husband's ear. "Does Brander intend to keep her here?"

Delling nodded. "Aye. Or so he said to me several times. He feels gratitude for . . . ah, I already told you that. I dislike leaving her, Disa, but what can I do? Brander would consider it an insult if we took her with us, and I don't want that."

"Well, I don't want to abandon her like an unwanted kitten on his doorstep!" Disa retorted. She tossed her head indignantly, fat blond braids flying about her plump cheeks with a life of their own. The cart creaked a protest as Disa's ample frame shifted.

"No, no," Delling interjected, alarmed that his wife might instigate a quarrel between himself and Brander. "I will take her inside and leave her in the capable hands of the woman who watches over his house." Delling forced a bright smile as he stepped down from the cart and joined Morgana.

She stood in the shadows of the house, gazing at the thick walls with interest. This house had windows, where most Viking homes did not. Perhaps it would not be as cold and dark inside as she had feared. Morgana turned at the slight pressure on her arm.

"My lady," Delling addressed her formally, "I will see you inside." He jerked his fingers away from her elbow when the gosling's head swiveled in his direction.

A faint smile touched the corners of Morgana's mouth. "'Tis not quite as I had thought it would be," she murmured. Smoke squawked a protest when she clutched him too tightly, and glared at Delling with black, beady eyes.

"Brander will be home soon," Delling promised. "He but finishes up necessary business with the jarl, his father."

Taking a deep breath, Morgana followed Delling into the house, blinking away the dust motes in her eyes. Her new life would begin in this great, timbered house where no one came to greet her.

Brander, sitting in his father's hall drinking mead from a horn and listening to his companions' tall tales, could not keep his mind from straying to Morgana. He kept seeing her at the rail of his ship, watching him, the slight breeze across the water lifting strands of silky hair as if in a caress, her eyes soft with gentle reproach.

But yet, even when he wanted her, wanted to feel her

beneath his arm, her head barely grazing his shoulder like a small trusting kitten, he knew he could not. She was so young in years if not body, and he could not bring dishonor upon himself or his father's clan by taking her again. He had already done so once, and he dreaded retribution by the gods.

Brander was jerked from his wandering thoughts by Harald's booming voice from the opposite end of the long table set in the center of the hall.

"Ho, my son the wandering hero, what's this I hear about your capture and escape?"

Brander shifted uneasily. He could see Thorfinn's quickly hidden smile and made a mental note to watch him more carefully in the future. The Finn seemed to enjoy baiting him.

Shrugging, Brander answered, "I lost my temper and fought my way into a trap. When the Celts captured me, I was taken to their hall . . ."

"And freed by one of their women!" Harald cut in with a hearty laugh. "Ah, 'tis your fair face which won her over, no doubt!"

A flash of irritation made Brander hold his tongue for a moment. His father meant well, but Morgana was not to be the butt of any man's jibes. His forbidding expression caught Harald's attention.

"Ho, have I struck a nerve, Brander? You don't seem to enjoy this play."

"I didn't enjoy being captured by the Celts," came the sharp answer, "and I shall go back one day to teach them a lesson."

Harald's brows rose. He'd never heard his son quite so vehement, and wondered what had happened in Hibernia. A battle was a battle, told and retold over winter fires, not to be taken personally. But Brander seemed to take it as a personal failure.

"It's not just the battle," Brander said, correctly reading his father's thoughts. "I killed one of their priests."

The hall grew quiet. It was the first time that Brander's companions had heard of Conn's death, and they exchanged glances of apprehension. The dead druid was no cause for alarm, but what of his very much alive protégé? Would Morgana seek vengeance?

A tall blond woman sitting near Brander reached across him to pick up a flagon of mead, letting her arm brush across his.

"So?" she said, favoring Brander with a honeyed smile. "If the priest is dead, what harm can he be?" Her hand dropped to Brander's arm in a light clasp. "He was no match for you alive, and should be even less so now. . . ."

"You don't understand, Erika." Brander's voice was impatient as he shook loose her hand. "His favorite pupil returned with me."

Erika stared with wide blue eyes. "You brought back a Celtic prisoner of war? Where is he?"

" 'Tis a she," Thorfinn cut in, "and a most comely wench she is, too."

"A woman?" Erika snapped. "Brander, how dare . . ."

His frigid gaze stilled her protest immediately. "I dare what I please, Erika."

Gytha, Harald's wife, leaned forward to pour oil on the troubled conversational waters, seeing her daughter's temper rise and fearing the worst.

"Then you mean to keep the girl a slave, Brander? I see the wisdom in your decision. We all need extra hands in the months before the snows set in. If you like, we will be glad to train her in the proper ways to behave. . . ."

"She is no slave, Gytha, but I appreciate your offer.

Morgana is the girl who aided me in escape. She saved my life, and in so doing left herself homeless. I owe her a great debt.''

Erika's eyes narrowed. This was worse than she'd imagined. The girl was not just a casual tumble on the sleeping mats but an actual threat. Any time a man felt a debt to a woman, deeper feelings followed. Forcing a smile, Erika caught her mother's warning gaze as she leaned closer to Brander.

"Then of course we shall honor her," Erika managed to say calmly. "Is she here with you?"

"Nay. Delling took her to my house. She will wait there until my return."

Which will be as many days as I can manage, Erika told herself silently, feeling the smile freeze upon her lips. She felt like a wood carving, stiff and unyielding, hatred for the unknown Celtic girl burning inside her breast like a live ember. It would not take much to get rid of the girl, then Brander would be hers. . . .

The
INTERLUDE

Chapter 13

Rain beat softly against glass windows as Morgana stared out at the dismal terrain. The sunshine and fat, fluffy clouds had disappeared, leaving the weather as gloomy as her mood.

Brander had yet to return. Each day that passed brought no sign of him, no hint of when he might return to his house and the lonely girl waiting there. Delling had come to visit one day, bringing fat, jovial Disa, and for a time Morgana's mood had lightened. When they left, they took her lighter mood with them.

Morgana idly traced the path of a raindrop as it slid over the thick, leaded window glass. One had to be wealthy to afford glassed windows, especially in this cold clime. Of course, she had known upon stepping inside Brander's home that he did not lack for riches.

Cold wooden walls were covered with fine tapestries, woven in far-off lands that Morgana had thought only existed in men's minds, and expertly carved furniture graced the huge main hall with quiet elegance. The house smelled of beeswax, and sweetly spiced rushes on the floors rustled a welcome when one walked over them. A huge stone hearth was flanked by comfortable benches and chairs for companionable conversation before the fire of an evening, and small tables stood waiting for foaming horns of mead or ale. A cheery room, a comfortable room, but empty without its master.

Pressing her nose to the cold glass, Morgana stared past the fields and earthen mounds of the Danevirke toward the harbor. She couldn't see the town or harbor, but knowing that it was there somehow comforted her.

Impatient for company, and restless, she turned away from the window, crossing her arms over her chest as she paced the floors.

"My lady?" A soft voice interrupted her reverie, and Morgana turned gratefully.

"Aye, Hlynn, what is it?"

"There is a messenger from the jarl. Shall I show him to you?"

Morgana made an eager movement with her hands. "Of course, Hlynn, of course!"

The maid hesitated. "His boots are muddy . . . the rain and wet grass . . . and I thought . . ."

"No, no, no matter! We can clean it. Now bring him to me. . . ."

Twisting her fingers in the soft woolen folds of her gown, Morgana took a few steps forward then stopped. The message would be from Brander, of course, for he knew she waited in his home. Should she appear overeager? No, that would be too obvious, and the messenger was certain to repeat everything she said and did. . . . Perhaps if she stood close to the fire, or even pretended to sew . . . no. That wouldn't do either. Then it might be repeated that she showed little interest in a messenger from the jarl.

White teeth dug into her bottom lip as Morgana quickly considered, and when the muddy and rain-spattered messenger was shown into the main hall, she waited calmly before the fire.

"Hlynn will bring you refreshment," Morgana told the weary messenger, "and when you are warmed, I would hear the news you bear."

A leather cap swept from his head as the messenger stood dripping onto the rushes and staring at the slim figure before him. By Odin, this Celtic woman was more beautiful than the rumors had named her! No one had told him that she had hair like the shadows of night, long and soft and thickly curling past her waist, looking for all the world like rich silk a man could bury his face in and be comforted. Was Brander Eriksson mad, that he should linger so long with his father? Did he not realize that this girl with the beautiful face of the goddess Freyja waited in his house?

"Your pardon," the messenger finally stammered when he realized he still stood dripping into the rushes, "but I was not expecting . . ." Words failed him, and he stood dumbly.

Morgana, accustomed to the scorn of others, flushed at the messenger's words.

" 'Tis a common happening," she answered, and the sad tone of her voice snared the youth's attention.

"Oh, no, my lady! I only meant that . . . that you are so fair, so much more lovely than even Delling reported you, that I was surprised. That is all."

The cherry blush staining her cheeks was most becoming, and made her eyes appear larger and greener, so that when she smiled with delight at his explanation, the messenger was truly at a loss for words.

"Oh!" she said, "that is what you meant. Then I am even more willing to extend my pardon for the puddles you

are making. If you will just step this way and let Hlynn
bring you a mat . . ."

The mat and mead were brought, and the messenger,
whose name he told Morgana was Tyburn, was quickly
seated before the fire to dry his wet clothes and body.

"Brander," Morgana brought up finally, delicately. "He
is well, Tyburn?"

"Aye, well and hearty! And he sends you his regards and
regrets, my lady."

"Regrets?" Dismay colored her voice with shades of
gray, and some of the sparkle in her eyes began to dim. "He
is not returning, then?"

"Nay, that is not what I meant," Tyburn hastened to
explain. "I only meant that he will be a day longer than
planned, and wishes you to forgive his failure to return
quickly. There was a meeting of the council, you see, that
detained him unexpectedly."

Relief flooded Morgana, and she sat back in the high
carved chair with a satisfied expression riding her features.
Her mouth, which had become accustomed to drooping,
turned up at the corners, and the dimple on one side of her
face winked for the first time since she had arrived in
Jutland. Long fingers curled under her chin as Morgana
gazed at Tyburn with the expression usually reserved for a
long-lost acquaintance.

"You are very kind, Tyburn, to bring me these glad
tidings. I can expect Brander within the next few days?"

"Aye, and he is bringing some guests home with him, so
he asked if you would see to their comforts. He said Hlynn
would help you, and Bothi and Kelda."

"Of course. More mead, Tyburn, or perhaps some spiced
wine?" Morgana's mind was whirling with tasks to be done
before Brander's arrival, the last few rooms to be cleared of
spider webs and insects, dust to be swept from the floors

and corners, wall hangings to be taken out and beaten, and bed linens to be washed and replaced. There would be food to prepare, of course—boar, goose, duck, and deer—and the bins to be checked for vegetables to cook. Bread would have to be baked, and the wine casks readied . . . so much to do in such a little time!

"How many are coming?" she asked idly, ticking off the tasks in her mind, counting on mental fingers which ones should be done first. "How many men and women?"

"Umm, his stepmother and stepsister, Gunther, whom I think you know, and two other men from the jarl's house." Tyburn shrugged. "That is all I was told."

Morgana's smile lifted the youth's heart to exhilarating heights as she thanked him. He wasn't even aware that he had been politely dismissed until later, so kindly and sweetly did she guide him to the door with soft words. Bemused, Tyburn spent the rainy night in the stables before returning to the jarl's house, dreaming of a slim girl with clouds of black hair and great green eyes like precious jewels.

Chapter 14

Upon her arrival in Brander's home, Morgana had found herself the astonished and unwilling caretaker. Gerda, who had usually seen to the smooth, orderly running of the house, had died during Brander's absence, leaving it in chaos and turmoil. Delling had immediately taken it upon himself to appoint Morgana as her successor until Brander's return.

"But I know little of running a house," Morgana had protested uselessly. "What do I do?"

"Whatever needs to be done," Disa had said with practical finality. "You are a woman."

When Brander did not return, Morgana discovered that she was grateful for the days full of activity, organizing food supplies and vegetable bins, seeing to the storage of grains and wines, procuring clean rushes for the floor and polish for furniture—the tasks had seemed endless at first.

At last they were done, so now all that remained was periodic checks for the day's dust.

Smoothing nonexistent wrinkles from the woolen gown

and overtunic she had borrowed from Hlynn, Morgana paced the floor in front of the windows. From time to time she glanced outside, cursing the drizzling rain and glowering clouds that pressed so gloomily to earth. If it was clear, she could see a great distance over the fields and in the direction of the jarl's home. It had been two days since the messenger had come to warn her of Brander's return, yet there was still no sign of him. When, she asked herself for the hundredth time, would Brander arrive?

Idly, she polished a bronze drinking cup and set it back on the long wooden table at one end of the hall. Smoothly polished benches stretched along the walls, offering repose to any who passed, and freshly cleaned velvet tapestries hung from high ceilings almost to the floor.

The rich, yeasty smell of fresh-baked bread drifted through halls and chambers, mingling with the delicious crackle of roast boar turning on the spit in the huge kitchen fireplace. A familiar, insistent honking from behind her made Morgana smile.

Smoke, the gosling turned tyrant, demanded to be fed. The arrogant feathered creature terrified gentle Hlynn, who avoided him whenever possible. Perversely, the gosling attached himself to the maidservant with grim tenacity, following her every step.

"Oh please," Hlynn had begged Morgana, "put him in the pens—or the cooking pots!"

Now Hlynn appeared in the arched doorway leading from the kitchen hall. Soft brown hair fell in disarray around her elfin face as she stared at Morgana with large brown eyes full of dismay.

"This wretched goose is distressed, my lady, and won't stop his incessant bleating!"

"Have you fed him?"

"Hourly. He paces back and forth, wobbling from side to side like a drunken sailor. . . ."

Morgana followed Hlynn, to find Smoke squatting on the threshold of the open door leading outside.

"See?" Hlynn exclaimed. "He lurches about in crazy circles, then stops. Do you think he knows we're cooking one of his relatives?" She indicated with a jerk of her head the golden brown goose roasted in rich gravy and placed on a platter in the middle of the table. Rich, satisfying smells emanated from the table crowded with gravies, sauces, vegetables, and meats.

Kneeling, Morgana's deft fingers probed feathers and fluff as gently as possible. Smoke squawked plaintively.

"I think I found the problem," she said after a moment. "It feels like a splinter wedged under his wing." She concentrated fiercely, trying to hold the struggling goose with one hand and pull the splinter with the other. Finally, "It's no use, Hlynn. You shall have to help me."

"That goose will peck me to pieces," Hlynn objected firmly, "and I'll just be bits of bloody bone and skin!"

Minutes of coaxing and several different promises later, Hlynn squatted beside the goose and Morgana, grumbling that she would sooner kiss a pig than help, but as Morgana was such a nice lady and fond of the goose, she'd do her best.

"Thank you, Hlynn. Now you hold him firmly, thus . . . no, if you squeeze too tightly he's liable to bolt away . . . yes, that's right. Here, just behind his neck and . . . er . . . tail feathers."

Hlynn closed her eyes at the indignity, muttering dire imprecations about the goose's arse as she obeyed.

Morgana pulled loose the splinter at the same time as Brander and his guests arrived. The goose shrieked loudly, reminding her, she was to think later, of a banshee wailing over crag and lough in Erin, then beat his great wings and pecked viciously at Hlynn. The maid released him immediately, stumbling back on hands and heels to bump her head on the heavily laden table. Bowls of pudding quivered violently on the table's edge, then tipped ever so slowly over the side to land with an interesting squish upon the stone floor, hapless maid, and charging goose.

The gosling floundered loudly in a shower of feathers and pudding, whipping about the kitchen in a frenzy as Morgana stared in horror.

"I see our dinner objects to being cooked," a familiar voice observed from the doorway. Resplendent in a turquoise tunic trimmed in silver, with loose trousers of the same blue color blousing from knee-high leather boots, Brander leaned casually against the door frame, gazing with more than mild interest at the scene before him. One hand rested upon the ornately carved sword hilt hanging from a wide belt at his lean waist, and the other curled over his mouth to hide a smile.

Conflicting reactions shadowed Morgana's face like the flicker of moonlight over the heaths. Delight at seeing Brander mingled with chagrin. Ranging behind him were several people she didn't know, staring at her with a mixture of amusement and incredulity.

Vaguely realizing what a ridiculous sight she must appear, sprawled on the kitchen floor with a fistful of goose feathers, Morgana flushed. How would she be able to rise gracefully? And what was the possibility of escaping Jutland in a hide-covered boat to avoid the embarrassing confrontation that was certain to follow?

Brander stepped forward and held out a hand, his lips twitching with wry humor.

"Delling assured me you would have things well in hand, Morgana, and I see that he was right."

" 'Twas the goose . . . a splinter . . . Hlynn fell . . ." The disjointed phrases fell randomly, like fat raindrops onto a heated pan, quickly sizzling into silence.

"So this is your little rescuer, Brander?" a feminine voice asked. "She seems very efficient. However did she manage to hide you from all those screaming Celts?"

Morgana's glance lifted to the tall figure of a striking woman with ivory braids quilted across the top of her regal head. She stood close to Brander, one hand resting upon his broad shoulder, her clear gray eyes filled with disdain and mocking laughter.

" 'Twas easy enough, Erika," Morgana heard him answer in a soft murmur. "She's very brave." His smile was warm and gentle. Did he smile for her—or for tall Erika?

"Get up, child," Brander was saying then, holding out a helping hand so that Morgana could rise from her undignified posture upon the kitchen floor.

Morgana couldn't halt the rushing protest that welled like a fountain from her lips.

"I'm not a child," she said sharply, but it was Erika, not Brander who agreed.

"No, you're not," Erika observed through narrowed eyes as Morgana was pulled to her feet and stood smoothing her borrowed gown. "I was expecting someone much younger, from your description, Brander," she directed to him. She sliced a disapproving glance at the hand Brander had laid upon Morgana's shoulder. "But then, it's easy enough to see how you might have mistaken her for a child. She's skinny as a willow switch, and uncommonly dark, isn't she?"

Plying the rough wool of her gown between her fingers, Morgana *felt* skinny and dark and plain. How could she hope to compete with a tall, full-figured woman like Erika, who obviously had her attention upon Brander? It might be hopeless, but Morgana, who had frequently confronted stone walls in her lifetime, strengthened her resolve. She would not give up until forced to.

"Brander," an older woman closely resembling Erika said, "this entertainment is amusing, but I am weary. . . ."

"Your chambers are ready," Morgana said in as efficient a tone as she could manage, "and dinner will be served in the main hall shortly. Is there anything else you desire for the moment?" Her eyes met Brander's gaze steadily, hoping he would not treat her as a child, that he would forget she had claimed a scant number of years and look on her as she was, a woman in love with him.

"Nay, not for the moment," he answered, and to Morgana's relief, there was no condescension in his voice. "In spite of the . . . er . . . scuffle . . . all appears to be well in order. Gerda could not have done better."

It was a supreme compliment, and Morgana flushed with pleasure. Her rush of pleasure was slightly deflated, however, when the older woman murmured a disparaging comment about men not knowing a thing about the smooth running of a house. There was no opportunity to offer a defense, as the guests quickly dispersed to find their rooms.

Gloom descended in a heavy cloud when Erika clung possessively to Brander's arm as they left the kitchen, and Morgana couldn't help a sigh.

"'Tis a wolf-bitch wearing a honeyed smile," Hlynn grumbled when the kitchen was empty of visitors again. "And I think you'd best watch your back, my lady!"

Kneeling, Morgana palmed a fistful of pudding-crusted goose feathers and frowned. She breathed on them, a slanting current of air that created a whirlwind of feathery down spinning in mad circles. Tiny bits of fluff still swirled in the air, carried by the fresh, wet breeze from the opened door. A plump, satisfied shadow moved as Smoke preened himself on the threshold, as blithe as if he had not caused Morgana a great deal of embarrassment and humiliation. Morgana rose and walked to the door, gently nudging Smoke outside with her foot.

"Who is she, Hlynn?" The question hung in the air for a moment like thick black smoke, soft and biting.

Finally Hlynn cleared her throat and shrugged. Her clear brown eyes concentrated upon the shimmering globs of pudding she was cleaning up as she said,

"Rumors fly as thick as gnats, my lady, and 'tis hard to tell which is truth and which fable. . . ."

"Tell me of them. I should hear them all."

Hlynn's hands stilled and she sighed. It was evident that Morgana favored the Viking leader. Too many times she'd seen Morgana stroking the rich nap of a velvet tunic belonging to Brander, smiling in that deep, significant way a woman has when she's thinking of a man she loves, and Hlynn had noticed the soft, vibrant tremor in her voice when she talked about the man who'd brought her to Jutland. And if those clues hadn't been enough to convince even the dullest of intellects, Morgana's face had positively glowed with love when Brander had come strolling into the kitchen. Hlynn, a slave most of her young life, had never formed an attachment to anyone, but she found it impossible not to care for Morgana. Who wouldn't love someone who asked instead of commanded, looked at her as if she was a human being instead of one of the work animals? Not even Brander, a master much kinder than most, had considered her as someone with feelings.

Soft hazel eyes glistened as Hlynn said, " 'Tis said that Erika wishes to wed him, and that her mother, Brander's stepmother, promotes the match." Hlynn's face darkened. "If you ask me, Loki himself spawned the daughter, for she has done nothing but ill since arriving in Harald's stronghold!"

"That's a harsh judgment, Hlynn. Loki is said to be a powerful god of darkness and evil."

"Aye. Only he's not a god, but a giant. Loki promotes strife and mischief between men. 'Tis the same with Erika, to my way of thinking."

Morgana was silent for several moments. She'd been so engrossed in Brander, filling her eyes with her first sight of him in many days and reveling in the touch of his hand, that she hadn't even tried to focus upon Erika. A vague sense of animosity was the only impression that remained, hanging like a hazy grey cloud.

"What are the other rumors, Hlynn? Does Brander have a dozen dead wives behind him, all murdered and stuffed in a closet, perhaps?"

There was a brittle edge to her determinedly light tone that did not escape Hlynn's notice.

"Oh, 'tis said he delights many women in the villages, and dawdles with them on cold winter evenings, sometimes staying away from his house for weeks at a time. And that he is now wealthier than his father, the jarl, who should be the wealthiest man in the hold. And it is whispered behind hands that no free woman has ever stayed in Brander's house, and won't until he takes a bride. . . ."

"Well, now he has two under his roof," Morgana said when Hlynn stumbled to a halt, realizing the portent of her words. "Which of us, I wonder, is to be the bride?" She swirled to face Hlynn. "What do the rumors say of Brander's intent? Does he plan to marry Erika?"

Hlynn looked at the roast goose, the pudding still smeared on the floor and the feathers lying like spent arrows on the hearth; she looked at the row of cheeses and breads, the stewed and boiled vegetables, and the remaining puddings; she thoughtfully regarded the casks of wine and mead, the invitingly open kitchen door, and the puddles of rainwater

standing in grass-bare spots outside; Hlynn looked everywhere but at Morgana.

"Hlynn?"

Wretched, miserable, angry, Hlynn blurted, "Aye, my
lady! He does plan to wed her!"

Morgana felt her eyes and nose begin to fill with tears.
No, she couldn't give in to the weakness of tears, not now.
Brander would see her red eyes and know she'd been
weeping, and she had no desire to try her hand at a
convincing explanation.

She should have asked. She should have asked Brander if
he planned to wed, then perhaps she would have saved
herself this crushing disappointment. But she should have
known. She should have sensed it somehow, that his mind
was preoccupied with another, but she had not. There had
been no clues, no hints that he might love another woman,
and she had dared hope that he would love her.

"Summon the others, Hlynn," she said quietly, pushing
away all thoughts of Brander. "We must serve the food
while it is still hot."

Hlynn watched Morgana in growing dismay. She had not
wanted to tell her, but a denial would only have delayed the
discovery of truth. It was kinder to know. Wasn't it?

Chapter
15

Brander was at a loss to understand why Morgana began avoiding him. Several times the following morning he attempted to draw her into conversation, only to find her sidling away from him like a crab on a hot rock, and escaping at the first lull in a painfully one-sided discussion.

By afternoon, he was completely puzzled. Retreating to the comparative safety and security of the main hall where he found two companions and a comforting horn of ale, he sat before the fire to ponder the situation. Time passed. Gunther and Delling—after an abortive attempt or two, fell silent, lost in their own thoughts.

Frowning, Brander drummed his fingers against the arms of his chair. There had been only brief glimpses of her in the past few hours, fleeting movements of a slender body passing just beyond the range of his sight like a wisp. He had forgotten how lovely she was, how he enjoyed just the sight of her. It had all come back in a rush when he'd seen her sitting on his kitchen floor amidst a shower of goose feathers and pudding. Somehow, the sight had made her even more desirable to him. She was a sorceress. A Celtic witch, who had snared his attention with her magic. Fingers drummed faster against the curved oak. Why did he think of her incessantly? She was constantly in his mind, like an insidious mist, posing and posturing, seeping past firmly erected barriers to dwell in his thoughts. In spite of his best intentions, Brander recalled silken limbs twined around him, the supple, erotic motions of her body beneath him, and cursed that night in the Celtic cave.

His moods ranged between anger and despair, bouncing erratically as sunbeams in a wooded copse.

"Did I offend Morgana, do you suppose, by laughing at her in the kitchen?" he asked Delling, who had, unfortunately for him, arrived for a visit early that morning and already heard all the details of Brander's arrival. "She hardly speaks to me. . . ."

By now inured to Brander's rapid mood changes, Delling faced exasperation with fortitude.

"Well, what do you expect?" he snapped. "Every time she sees you, you're wearing Erika like a fur-lined cape draped over you! Has the woman no feet of her own to use, that she hangs upon you like a summer cold?"

Brander blinked. He rocked back in his chair before the fire and exchanged a glance of mild surprise with Gunther— who was so caught up in his own troubles that he hadn't noticed Brander's erratic behavior. Brander considered Delling's words briefly, his fingers forming a steeple under his chin. Had he just been attacked by Delling, who was known for his temperance in manner? Thor's hammer, he must have offended someone, for even Delling to attack him!

"You object to Erika's closeness?" he asked carefully, thinking that he had asked about Morgana, not Erika. "Does it distress you that she enjoys being with me?"

"Why should that matter to me? I wouldn't care if you

mated with a she-wolf, which shows a remarkable resemblance to Erika, I might add!''

"Ho, Delling, such animosity from you is unusual. What has she done to warrant it?" Brander stared in amazement at the plump-faced man who had been with him for years. Except for Gunther, he was closer to Delling than any man of his acquaintance.

"Erika? She's done nothing to me. It's you, Brander, who has irritated me beyond belief. I always thought you a reasonably intelligent man . . ." Delling rambled into several disjointed phrases, some highly unfavorable to Brander, spicing his comments with frequent references to Morgana.

"Halt, Delling and give me a moment to digest this." A finger curled under his chin as Brander leaned forward to regard Delling from beneath dark, sooty brows drawn into a scowl. Gunther, emerging from his self-imposed preoccupation, saw the inevitable direction of the conversation and excused himself from the hall. Neither man noticed his departure.

"As I understand it," Brander began, "you are angry with me for ignoring Morgana. Is that correct? Yet, you are also angry with me because I try to speak to her. No? Then why are you angry?"

"Because you can't see what's obvious to anyone else!" Delling glared at him for a moment, his face as red as the glowing coals in the fire. "How is it that everyone else can see how Morgana feels, yet you trot home trailing that . . . that viper-tongued female behind you like a prize? How would . . ."

Brander's swiftly upraised hand forestalled the next deluge of comments. A thunderous expression creased his face as he half-growled, "Morgana is still young, and does not know what she wants. . . ." He blithely ignored the fact that *he* was quite old enough and knew exactly what *he* wanted— two facts not in his favor at this moment.

"Not as young as you think," Delling retorted. "And since when did age make a great deal of difference?"

"What do you mean—not as young as I think?"

"Bah, do you really believe that she is fourteen, Brander? Look at her! I mean *really* look at her. . . ."

There was a moment of nonplussed silence while Brander slowly digested this information. Then, "Why did she tell me she was only fourteen? How old is she?"

"I'm not certain. Eighteen, I think. She has some idea that you will scorn her for not having wed by this time," Delling explained irritably, as if Brander should already know all this. "Celts must marry early."

Brander's hand curled into a tight fist, and his mouth thinned. She had tricked him somehow, bewitched him with secret arts—bah! It was much simpler than that.

"She lied to me? After stressing how truthful she is?"

"I would think," Delling said slowly, "that she merely evaded the truth instead. 'Twould be easy enough to do without actually telling a lie."

Anger faded, and an unwilling smile began to tug at Brander's mouth as he recalled Morgana's exact words. She *had* said she'd seen fourteen winters, and that she'd done—plus some. The devious little wretch, he ought to give her a good enough shaking to rattle every tooth in her pretty little head. No. A confrontation would not be the answer right now.

Brander's fingers laced tightly, brushing against his chin as his brow furrowed in a thoughtful frown that Delling didn't particularly care for.

"What are you planning?" Delling began suspiciously, but interrogation was forestalled by Erika's arrival. Thor's hammer, but it was as if the woman instinctively knew the worst possible moment to descend upon them. Like a corpse-fed raven, Delling thought, slicing her an irritated glance.

The subject was dropped as Erika perched upon a stool at Brander's feet, smiling up at him with a practiced smile that reminded Delling of a hungry feline.

"And how are you this morning?" she asked brightly. "Did you sleep well, my lord?"

"Reasonably well, yes. And 'tis not morning, but afternoon, Erika. You must have slept soundly."

Brander was enjoying Delling's discomfiture, noting cheerfully how he glared at Erika and obviously wished her at the bottom of the nearest fjord.

"No," Erika objected, "I didn't sleep well." She launched into a detailed recital of complaints: the bed was too hard and the blankets smelled musty, her room had cobwebs and was disgustingly dusty, and did Brander know that his wine had soured in his absence? "You'd think someone would have tested it before serving it to guests," she declared with a sniff. "I could have gotten ill from it."

"Too bad you didn't drink more," Delling muttered, then covered his breach of good manners by abruptly excusing himself from the hall.

"What did he say?" Erika stared after Delling with narrowed eyes.

"Delling is a great jester," Brander said with a trace of impatience. Must Erika always be so critical? She constantly complained, droning on and on until he wanted to gag her. His tone was bored and slightly brusque when he said, "I apologize for the inconveniences you have suffered in my house. Perhaps I should arrange for your return home?"

"Oh, no!" Erika gazed at him in alarm. "I never meant that, Brander. I was only trying to point out the inadequacies of your staff. Perhaps you should procure a woman who is more . . . ah . . . efficient. . . ."

Brander's brows rose. "As you are surely aware, my housekeeper died in my absence, Erika. I had no control over such a thing, and am doing my best to replace her with a capable woman. I don't allow just anyone in my home."

"I know, I know." Aye, she knew full well no woman went to his house uninvited. Hadn't she been trying for almost a year? Rumor had it that the woman who wrangled an invitation would become Brander's wife, an honor she intended to have. Even so, in spite of several careful schemes and plans, she had only been invited because of her mother, Gytha. Thank the gods that Brander's housekeeper had died and left him in the lurch, or she still might be waiting! Clever Gytha, to have offered their help . . .

Not that his home was worth waiting for, she sneered to herself, glancing around the huge hall. It was too stark, with little evidence of a feminine touch. But all that would change when she became his wife. Then she would order those exquisite silks and fine linens, the glassware and soapstone, bronze statues and thick furs—it would all be costly, of course, but Brander would be grateful to her for her wifely efforts.

Sitting up straight so that Brander would receive the full effect of the exquisitely embroidered silk tunic that clung to her ripe curves, Erika preened, smoothing the ivory fall of her hair where it lay over one shoulder. The shimmering curtain of hair had been tied at the back of her neck with a length of silk, then left to drape a full, rounded breast, reaching to her waist, contrasting perfectly with the bright blue of her tunic. She smiled as Brander's idle gaze transferred to her hands. One of her best features, she accented them with jewels; huge rings winked in shades of ruby and sapphire, circling long slim fingers that tapped sensually against the smooth silk of tunic and underskirt, stroking the supple expanse of her thighs to capture Brander's attention.

Jeweled brooches glittered from her shoulders where they fastened her tunic, and silver bracelets jangled on her arms each time she moved, sliding up and down the soft white skin of her well-rounded arms.

He would ask her to be his bride soon, she could feel it in his eyes, could sense that he was more interested than he pretended. Hadn't she seen that same expression in other men's eyes? If there was one thing Erika had learned, it was how to snare a man's attention.

Leaning forward so that her breast brushed temptingly against Brander's knee, Erika rested her arms on his chair. She wet her lips, letting her eyelids lower lazily so that she stared up at him through her long lashes. The mood was perfect, and they were alone in the hall. . . .

Brander's hand dropped to caress Erika's gleaming hair, his fingers trailing in soft, sensual patterns over her ivory cheek. He smiled, letting his gaze rest on Erika, but he was seeing a tawny face full of life, a mobile mouth and wild mane of ebony hair, not this pale creature.

A shadow moved at the doorway, and his smile widened. Brander was aware of Morgana before she spoke, sensed her presence before she crossed the hall to his chair.

A pleasant expression rode his Nordic features as his head turned in her direction, admiring the slim sway of her hips and the way she tried so hard to keep her eyes cool and reserved.

Erika, concentrating on Brander, wasn't aware of Morgana. She was still dreaming satisfying images of a wedding, with Brander a powerful chieftain and her as his more powerful bride. The disruption shattered the delicious images into pieces, and made her aware of a possible rival. One glance at Brander's face when he looked at Morgana was enough to enrage Erika.

"Excuse me, Lord Brander, but Hlynn insists that I need

to ask your permission . . ." Morgana began softly, but Erika
whirled angrily to shrill at her.

"Must you sneak about like a cat!" she stormed before
Brander could open his mouth to intervene. "I ought to box
your ears for trying to listen to a private conversation!"

Morgana took one step back, but her eyes never left
Erika's face. She wanted to lash out at her, yank thick
strands of blond hair from her head and scratch her face, but
she didn't. Instead she remained deliberately calm.

"I wasn't trying to listen to your conversation," she said
evenly. "If you'd been paying attention to your surroundings instead of masculine knees, you could have heard me
walk across the rushes."

"Why, you impudent little . . ."

"Ah, ah," Brander warned when Erika surged to her feet
with fingers curved into claws to rake at Morgana's face.
One hand caught Erika's wrist in a bone-crushing grip.
"Don't, Erika."

The blonde vibrated with fury, glaring at Morgana through
slitted eyes.

"Are you favoring this . . . this ragged little slave over me,
Brander? Have you forgotten who I am?"

"I'm favoring no one. I simply refuse to let you attack
Morgana. And I haven't forgotten for a moment who you
are, Erika. Have you forgotten it?"

His mild reminder brought the angry woman up short,
and she tensed. No, she hadn't forgotten, nor had she
forgotten her reasons for being here. She must be careful,
must marry Brander so that she would one day be ruler of
her own clan. Bitter memories swirled in her head as Erika
recalled how Harald had conquered their clan, taking Gytha
as his bride and killing the chief—her uncle—then carelessly
bestowing the clan upon his own son. Brander had little use

for the small revenues which the impoverished clan brought, and he regarded it with the same disdain as his father.

Erika forced a smile. "Forgive me. Perhaps I overreacted, but I'm not accustomed to impudence from slaves. . . ."

"Morgana is not a slave," Brander pointed out. "She is a free woman. I don't expect to have to explain that to you again."

Realizing that Brander was truly angry, and that any favor she had gained was in danger, Erika retreated with as much dignity as possible. Better to yield the point than to lose all.

"I see," she murmured, looking down at her hands to hide the murderous gleam in her eyes. She felt like a child whose hands had just been slapped, and clenched her teeth at the humiliation. "No one told me, Brander. Had I known, I would not have spoken thusly."

Brander relaxed, and some of his anger faded.

"'Tis a matter best forgotten. After I consult with Morgana, we'll go for a ride. I know how you love to ride. Have Bothi choose a fine mare for you, Erika."

It was a small triumph, but an eagerly accepted one. Erika leaned forward to place a kiss upon Brander's cheek— not daring more in his present mood—and swept from the hall without so much as a glance in Morgana's direction, obviously dismissing her as someone of little importance.

Morgana strained to keep her tongue and temper in check until Erika was gone. The arrogance and brashness of the Viking woman was almost more than she could bear. And she had not missed that malicious gleam in Erika's eyes as she'd leaned forward to kiss Brander's cheek, nor the lingering glance. How dare Erika insinuate that she, Morgana, a Celtic princess, was little more than a slave, a . . . a . . . She wheeled on him abruptly.

"Brander, what is my place here? Am I to be your housekeeper? A slave? Will you sell me if I do not please you?'' Her voice was tight with anger, and her fingers dug into the folds of her gown, clenching and unclenching. ''I do not understand what it is that you want with me. . . .''

''Morgana.'' Brander took both her hands between his, stilling the quick, agitated movements. ''You are a friend, my rescuer, not a slave, nor even my housekeeper. I only want your comfort and happiness. What do you prefer? Do you wish to stay with me for a time or perhaps live elsewhere? I owe you my life. . . .''

If she heard that one more time, she would scream the house down, Morgana promised silently. What good would his gratitude do her? She didn't want gratitude, she wanted his love, his confidence, his . . . She suddenly envied Gwyneth, who at least knew what to expect.

''Brander,'' she said with grim patience, ''I need to think about it for a time.'' Retrieving her hands from his grasp, Morgana tucked them behind her. She couldn't bear his touch a moment longer. ''I am well satisfied for the present, however.''

''Are you? I'm glad.'' Brander's eyes crinkled at the corners. She was furious; he could sense the bubbling anger simmering just beneath her calm surface, and knew Delling had spoken the truth. Jealousy ill became Morgana's too transparent face. Add one more sin to a fast-growing list; when would she admit her age, or the attraction she felt toward him?

The air shimmered with a palpable tension that seemed thick enough to cut and stack for a stone wall. Morgana struggled against her rash tongue, against the sudden urge to fall into Brander's arms and confess everything. Instead, she looked at the velvet hangings on the wall, stared at the crackling logs in the mammoth fireplace and watched a shower of sparks fly up the stone chimney; she breathed in the sweet scent of fresh rushes strewn over the floor and the polish used on the tables—anything to divert her attention from the tall, handsome man standing before her, brilliantly attired in a blue the same color as his eyes.

It was no use trying, she reflected with a sigh, when Brander did his best to be a distraction. He stepped closer, so close that her breasts almost brushed his broad chest, and she could feel his breath on her cheek. Mumbling something—anything—she stepped back, blindly seeking relief from tension and her great longing.

"Where are you going, Morgana?"

"I have work . . . meals . . . animals to feed . . . Hlynn might need me. . . ."

"But you sought me out. What did you wish to ask?" He reached out, his touch warm, lingering, gently grasping her arm, and she flinched. The barely perceptible tightening of her features gave Morgana away, and Brander took quick advantage. His hands moved to her shoulders, pulling her slowly toward him. So she desired him, did she? Well, he would see how long it would take her to tell him as she'd apparently told others. . . .

The small space between them shimmered with the heat of their bodies, and the air seemed to be charged with tension and sparks. It was as if they stood on a hill with lightning crackling around them in slashing bolts.

If she moved, Morgana thought breathlessly, the mood would be broken, so she stood still, gazing up into Brander's eyes. She wanted him, wanted him as a woman wants a man, and she didn't care if he knew it. 'Twas time the Viking realized that she was a woman instead of a child. . . .

Half-mocking and half-serious, Brander leaned forward to place a chaste kiss upon Morgana's cheek, feeling the slight trembling of her body next to him. How could he have thought her a child for so long? The ripeness of her slim curves should have proven that lie to him, but he had been too willing to believe her. The reasons for that escaped him at the moment, but he would examine them later. His mouth moved from her soft cheek to one corner of her mouth, lightly tasting those honeyed lips.

"Well! Isn't this a pretty picture!"

Brander and Morgana both started, turning in unison toward the voice, one face mildly surprised, the other guilty.

Mild surprise altered to an expression of casual curiosity. "Gytha," Brander greeted his stepmother, "how are you this morn?"

"Not as well as you seem to be doing," she returned tartly. "Is this your new housekeeper or your new whore?"

Although Morgana didn't understand the language, she did understand the insult, and she stiffened. It was an obviously rude question, falling into the sudden cold silence like a stone. Brander's face hardened, his eyes growing flinty as he gazed at Gytha with marked dislike. No one spoke for a moment, and the only sound was the popping of logs in the fire.

It was Morgana who broke the silence finally, pulling from beneath his hands and gazing with quiet dignity at Brander.

"I will be in my chambers," she began, but he cut her off sharply.

"No. You will stay. If anyone leaves, it will be Gytha."

"What?"

Gytha strode forward with the loose, easy stride of a man, halting at Brander's side.

"I understood what you said, and I most certainly will not leave," she stated loudly, and Morgana had the thought that even her voice was deep and masculine.

Tall and large-boned, Gytha was well fleshed but not fat. Sharp facial features were softened by a generous bounty of flesh that Erika did not share, but it was easy to recognize their kinship. Morgana was reminded of the suspicious gaze of a ferret as Gytha surveyed her through pale eyes darkened with kohl; and the vivid paint glowing on her cheeks was too bright, which made her look slightly ridiculous.

Staring back as boldly as Gytha, Morgana had the brief, sarcastic thought that Brander's entire family must have a penchant for wearing blue. Was it a family quirk? His stepmother wore a turquoise tunic belted with a silver girdle, and silver threads glittered in her longer undertunic, an obvious statement concerning her station in life. And as if that weren't enough, an abundance of jewelry glittered on every finger and covered her arms from elbows to wrists. Ornate brooches held loops of crystal and cornelian beads on each shoulder, and three silver necklaces curved around her neck. Impressive, if one liked extravagance, Morgana decided.

"Gytha," Brander was saying through tight lips, "as you are my father's wife, you command my respect. In my home, it would serve you well to earn it. I do not tolerate rudeness to any of my guests."

Gytha's penciled brows rose, and Morgana could see the fury quivering in her eyes.

"Guest? This unkempt baggage? Are you in the habit of fondling 'guests' in your main hall, Brander? I thought more of you than that. 'Tis plain to see that your manners need mending. . . ."

"*My* manners?" Brander laughed shortly and unpleasantly, and Morgana wished herself far away from what was fast becoming an uncomfortable scene. She took a backward step, but Brander's arm snaked out to hold her still.

"Stay," he commanded without looking at her, and Morgana's lacerated temper suffered another biting lash.

"Brander," she began.

"And be quiet," he added harshly, adding yet another

blow. His attention and anger were channeled toward Gytha, but he couldn't stop to explain that to Morgana.

Eyes as icy as the northern fjords bored into his stepmother, and his tone invited no rash replies as he said, "You owe the maid an apology, Gytha. I would hear it now."

"Apology? To a Celtic slave? You must be mad, Brander. I will do no such thing," Gytha replied heedlessly. Her sneering gaze dared him to object as she reminded him, "Your father holds no great love for Celts and would agree with me. . . ."

"But my father is not here, and this is my house. I command here, Gytha, and will not tolerate the abuse of anyone under my roof."

"So I see," Gytha commented with another sharp glance in Morgana's direction. "This is the captive you brought back from Hibernia?"

"This is the maid who saved my life," was the short response. "I expect you to display more respect."

"Respect?" Gytha shrugged carelessly and lifted a cup from the table near Brander's chair. White fingers coiled around it as she stared over the rim at Morgana. "I shall *ooze* with respect if it pleases you, Brander," she said. "You always were one for coming home with stray dogs. Tell me," she said, switching to the Celtic tongue and turning to Morgana, "is it true that you claim to be a Celtic princess? Your dress hardly indicates wealth."

Morgana's first flush faded to white anger as she glared at Gytha. It was humiliating to be reminded of her status, and even more humiliating to know that even if she had met Gytha wearing one of her own gowns, it still wouldn't have been as beautiful as hers or decorated with silver threads. . . .

"I don't *claim* to be anything," Morgana answered coldly. "I am what I am."

"Obviously . . ."

"But at least I'm not rude!" Glints of green sparked dark fire as she continued, "It seems to me that if you are intelligent enough to learn my language, you could have spent more time on your manners. Now, if you'll excuse me, I have work to do. . . ."

"Morgana . . ."

"Leave me alone!" she flashed at Brander when he put out a hand. She was in no mood for any more confrontations with his family, and in no mood for explanations. Enough was enough.

She was gone before Brander could speak, and the black look he turned on his stepmother would have frightened any other woman.

"Why have you made it a point to be rude?" he demanded. "I should escort you back to my father without delay."

"Really?" One brow rose, and she smiled. "Then why don't you? I'm certain he would be interested in knowing that a slave merits more courtesy than the jarl's wife. . . ."

Her barb found its mark, as she'd intended it to, and Gytha's smile broadened. Harald would hear a jaundiced version of course, if she reached him first, and the damage would be done. There would be a rift, even if Harald suspected that she lied. Father against son, or husband against wife. Either situation would be intolerable.

"I find," Brander said coldly to end the conversation, "that I do not need your help after all, Gytha. My household is being run quite well. Delling will escort you and your daughter home before night's fall."

Surprise was evident, but quickly hidden. Shrugging, Gytha gazed steadily at Brander. When Erika had first come running to her, babbling about the Celtic girl, she had been alarmed. The girl threatened to upset her careful plans. Matters had seemed to be under control when Brander casually mentioned that Gerda had died, leaving him without a housekeeper, and she'd swiftly seized the opportunity. How could he have refused a kind offer of help to organize his household? Of course, it was only reasonable that Erika should accompany her. . . . Now the situation was worse than she'd imagined. Her daughter should be wed to Brander without delay, before that dark Celtic witch managed to spirit him away.

Pale eyes narrowed as Gytha gazed at Brander's impatient face. He was strongly attracted to Morgana; she'd seen it in the way he looked at her, touched her, defended her. All her plans were in danger of falling apart.

Chapter 16

"Morgana?" No response. Then, "Morgana," again, softly. Door hinges creaked, then the soft thump of wood on wood. No rushes covered the cold floor to muffle the distinct sound of footsteps on stone.

Shoulders stiffened as Morgana stood at the window of her small chamber, staring at the darkening sky. Faint sounds filtered from the kitchen, the banging of pots and chatter of serving maids seeping through the thin walls to her room. Close to the kitchen, the room combined privacy with proximity, the reason she'd chosen it on the night of her arrival. It seemed that she had erred, Morgana reflected bitterly, and should have taken a pallet in the slave quarters.

Turning, Morgana looked at Brander, regarding him as if he was a leper, and he smiled faintly. She was obviously ready for battle against him. Anger bristled from her every pore like the quills of a hedgehog.

"I apologize for my stepmother," he said. "She has a sharp tongue."

"So I noticed." Morgana turned back to the window

again. It had grown dark, and in the fields behind the house she could see the tall grasses outlined against a bright, new moon. The insistent honking of her gosling harmonized with a variety of other sounds peculiar to a yard filled with fowl, swine, and livestock. Morgana concentrated fiercely on the sounds, the sky, the moon—anything but Brander.

Why should he know how badly Gytha and Erika had upset her? It was bad enough that she felt this way; worse to allow anyone else to witness her distress. Harald hated Celts also . . . would Brander's father be as rude?

Morgana's fingers dug into the soft flesh of her upper arms as she held them tightly. Nothing had gone right since she'd had the vision in Kyna's cottage. The Vikings had come, as the vision had promised, and she had met the tall, handsome man she'd seen in the smoke. But where was the feeling of love she'd sensed? Had that been only a dream?

Morgana closed her eyes. Brander was so near, yet so far away he might as well be in Erin.

The touch of his hands on her shoulders startled her, and Morgana's pulses leaped. He was pulling her into his arms, holding her against his broad chest and murmuring soft words into the fragrant cloud of her dark hair, and Morgana's hurt and anger yielded.

"Everything I touch seems to go wrong. I should have stayed behind. . . ."

Her words were muffled against the soft material of his tunic, and her fingers curled into the velvet with the tiny kneading motions of a nursing kitten. Morgana reminded him of a kitten, at times showing her claws and spitting fury, but still soft and vulnerable. Brander smiled into the silky caress of her hair and smoothed it back from her forehead. Then, gently, he pushed her to arm's length, forcing her chin up so that she had to meet his eyes.

"No, I wouldn't have left you behind. You saved my life, remember? I owe you. . . ."

Exasperated, Morgana suppressed the sudden desire to shout at him, to tell this unusually stubborn Viking to forget the past, that he didn't owe her anything, that all she wanted was for him to see her as a woman. Her mind churned with several methods of gaining his attention, none of which would work, and her mouth tightened with frustration. What did she have to do to get him to see her as a desirable woman—strip naked and dance on his bed?

Brander noticed the sudden widening of her eyes, the way her pupils expanded to swallow light from the small oil lamp on the table, and wondered what she was thinking.

Of course, Morgana thought with a delicious smile pressing against her lips, *that is the answer!* Brander would *have* to see her as a woman, and then she would know whether she could hope for his love. It was such a simple plan, she wondered why it had taken her so long to think of it.

Uncertain about what had made her smile, Brander nonetheless smiled in response. When Morgana smiled, her entire face lit up as if a thousand candles were in her eyes. And there was the most fascinating dimple in her cheek, peeking at him winsomely, enticingly. . . . Why hadn't he yielded before? Conflict raged inside. He wanted her, wanted to hold her as he had that night in the cave, but it wasn't the right time. Instinct warned him that Morgana was still feeling her way into womanhood, that he shouldn't let her rush either of them into a relationship. That first night had been unfortunate, but he could make amends. When he held her again like that, it would be at the right time and in the right place.

Releasing her arms, Brander's tone was casual. "Gytha and Erika are gone," he said. "Delling escorted them back to my father."

What did he expect her to say? That she was glad? She was, but Morgana was reluctant to admit her dislike of the two women so openly.

"Perhaps they'll be more comfortable at home," she said noncommittally.

"Perhaps." Brander's tone indicated that he wasn't particularly concerned over their comfort. His expression softened. "Morgana, I would like for you to stay here, but if you are unhappy . . ."

"If I'm unhappy—what? You'll send me home? Find me another house in which I can be shunned?" Angry, inexplicably hurt by his words, she resisted even the suggestion that he would send her away. "Do what you like, Viking!" Jerking away from his hands, she stalked to the table where the oil lamp burned brightly.

Brander followed and whirled her back around to face him, his face set and hard.

"Don't rail at me for your misery," he growled. "I have done the best I know for you."

"Have you? Forgive me. I'm unaccustomed to such generosity, such . . ."

"Stop it!" He gave Morgana a rough shake that sent dark hair spilling into her eyes, clouding her vision. "What do you expect from me, woman?"

"This!"

Morgana's reaction was unexpected and startling. Flinging her body into his arms with the swiftness of a hawk, she stood on tiptoe and wrapped her arms around his neck, pulling his head down. Brander wasn't prepared for the soft warmth of her young body curving into him, nor the sweet, hot passion of her lips as they seared against his mouth. He was half-ashamed of his swift response, but coherent thought retreated into some dim corner of his brain like a wounded animal, and he kissed her back.

Round, firm breasts pressed against his chest, and he could feel the jut of her slim hips digging into his groin. Morgana's tongue flicked lightly over his lips, teasing, tasting, tempting, and Brander summoned his last vestige of strength. Uncurling her arms from around his neck, he set her gently away from him.

Stricken, Morgana could only stand and stare. Brander looked away from the hot wash of unshed tears in her eyes and said, " 'Tis not the time for that, Morgana."

"But you kissed me back!" Her voice was thick and accusing, her mouth trembling, and she felt ashamed.

"Aye, and I enjoyed it. But you aren't ready . . ."

"You mean *you* aren't ready!"

Anger made his voice rough. "If that pleases you better then—*I'm* not ready. Ah, Morgana," he relented at the sight of her pain, "you're young and inexperienced, far from home and alone in the world. 'Tis only natural that you should look to me for comfort."

"Comfort! Is that what you think it is?" A brittle laugh pealed through the shimmering shadows. "You know very little, Viking, though you think you're so wise. I knew . . ." Her voice halted abruptly. It wasn't the right time to tell him of her vision.

"You knew what?"

"I knew you'd act so stubborn."

His lips twitched. Never before had he had a woman throw herself into his arms, then rail at him like a fishwife when he rejected her charms. And for a brief instant, Brander wondered if he was crazy. Had there ever been so lovely a wench in his arms? Morgana's fresh young beauty startled him each time he saw her, and her nature was sweet and loving, in spite of an occasional outburst.

Unfamiliar tenderness flooded him when she turned away again, presenting him with a view of her back. Raven hair

flowed down her back to tickle her tiny waist, and the
borrowed gown curved tautly over shapely hips and but-
tocks, clinging to slender thighs. How could he ever have
believed her to be a child? Brander marveled, watching as
she stepped to the small table near her bed.

She stood for a few moments, idly toying with a hair-
brush Hlynn had given her, light from the oil lamp flowing
over her in a bright flood. The tiny flame flickered briefly in
the breeze caused by her movements, then grew steady.
Morgana stared at it, her attention caught and held. Light
pushed shadows from a small circle in weaving patterns,
cavorting like children at play. Bright then dim, the circle of
lamplight beckoned to Morgana.

The brass bowl holding oil and wick began to glow
brighter and hotter, and the flame became white then blue. In
the heated sphere around the bowl, Morgana saw vague
shapes that quickly sharpened into focus, and she leaned
forward eagerly. A man . . . several women . . . then nothing.
They were gone before she could recognize them, and she
gave a soft cry of disappointment.

Slowly aware that Brander watched, Morgana realized
that the vision was gone and would not return. Her eyes
widened. Had her gift abandoned her? Where were the
visions, the prophecies she had always held in the palm of
her hand, so that the simple uncurling of her fingers would
release them?

Brander recognized the smoky dark fret in her eyes, the
set of her mouth and the simmering frustration. Morgana's
dark hair tumbled forward, hiding her face from him as her
fingers curled over her brow to cover her eyes.

"You were searching and could not see?"

Long fingers uncurled to expose eyes the color of sea
water, green and swirling with shadows. Morgana nodded.

Her shoulders hunched forward like an old woman's, and she was suddenly very tired.

"Please...I am weary and would be alone, Brander...will you...?"

"Aye. For now." A comforting hand touched her briefly with understanding, then dropped away.

Morgana heard the closing of the door a moment later. She was shaken by her experience, though she knew well enough that the sight did not always come when summoned. Perhaps her frustration with Brander had seeped into that private world of shadows where she sometimes wandered.

Whirling, Morgana stepped to the polished bronze mirror hanging on the wall. She stared into it, seeing a disheveled, wide-eyed girl who bore little resemblance to that person she had been only a few weeks before. She had changed a great deal; it showed in her face.

Chapter 17

"What is the matter with you lately?" Gunther asked in exasperation. His gaze narrowed at Brander, sitting back in his chair before the fire, fingers wrapped around a horn of ale. "You're as testy as a bee-stung hound."

Shrugging, Brander ignored Gunther. He lifted his half-empty horn of ale and drained it, then called for more. Hlynn hastened to refill it, then escaped to the kitchen as quickly as possible.

"It's the Celtic wench, isn't it?" Gunther's observation didn't demand an answer, and he received none. "At least you don't bear claw marks, nor do you have to listen to hours of gibberish that you can barely understand. Enjoy your good fortune . . ."

"Gunther, I would rather we did not speak of it." Brander's tone was flat and final, and his request was granted. Gunther sat staring morosely into space, watching a fly crawl up the wall. When his fingers began to drum a melody on the wooden arms of his chair, and he hummed an accompaniment, Brander's brows rose in irritation. Gunther paused. Time ticked slowly past. The fly on the opposite wall flew away, and Gunther's gaze wandered. Absently, he began to hum a tuneless melody. This time, Brander fixed him with a piercing glare.

"I think I'll search for Gwyneth," Gunther finally mumbled, pushing up from the chair.

"For someone who complains about her like you do, you certainly seem eager for her company," Brander commented sourly.

"Aye, well it's better than sitting here with a foul-tempered warthog!" Gunther glared at Brander, almost daring him to reply, hoping that anger would clear the air and release their frustrations. He was disappointed.

"Warthog?" Brander echoed in a thoughtful tone. "Yea, most certainly! Now leave . . ." He waved an irritated hand, and Gunther stomped impatiently from the hall.

Brander's fingers curled under his chin. He kept seeing green eyes flecked with gold, staring at him with a stricken expression in their depths. He'd half-expected Morgana to approach him, but instead she'd avoided him once more, fleeing as a hare before the hounds. Plague it! Did the wench think he was of no consequence—that he could be toyed with at her will? No. He was a man, a Viking, not some weak, puling creature to be taken lightly!

Chair legs scraped harshly across the floor as Brander rose in a fluid motion. The day's ale made him reel, and it blurred his vision so that he had to shake his head to clear it. That motion sent him stumbling backward, and he tripped on the hem of his long cape and had to catch himself against a chair. Swaying with drunken dignity, Brander squinted across the hall. He would find Morgana, and she *would* talk to him, whether she was in the mood to or not.

As luck would have it, Morgana was outside with her goose. She stood on an island of dirt amidst the muck and ooze of the stableyard, throwing Smoke handfuls of grain. She didn't see Brander coming, and only heard his arrival when he misstepped into a pile of odorous animal droppings. The attendant commotion caused her to gaze with rapt attention while the tall Viking hopped clumsily on one foot, arms flailing like a crippled windmill, swearing and narrowly avoiding imminent collision with two pigs and a goat.

Finally, breathing heavily and with fire in his eyes, Brander stood at Morgana's side. He reeked of ale, sweat, and manure, and had difficulty focusing his pupils in her direction. He flopped forward from the waist.

In Brander's mind, he had made a courtly bow worthy of any who had ever attended a king. In reality, Morgana held her breath as his feet shuffled in the mud, and he seemed in danger of tipping over. Brander straightened slowly to stare at Morgana, his eyes struggling to find her. Successful at last, he managed a lopsided smile.

Late sunlight glinted from the top of his head like old gold coins, muted and soft and shimmering with elusive light. His eyes, those bright blue eyes, shone like pieces of sky, and but for the singular glassy stare, would have appeared lively and intelligent.

One delicate brow rose as Morgana gazed at him. "Aye, my lord Viking? Did you wish to speak with me?" Her gaze dropped to his feet. Brander stood ankle-deep in a puddle of mire and muddy water, ruining his fine calfskin leather boots. Spatters of mud stained his trousers and long cape of fine wool. When her eyes returned to his face, the green orbs were awash with laughter.

"You laugh?" Brander's tone held the injured dignity of a petulant child. "Laugh, but at least you will listen now, and not avoid speaking."

"I have not avoided you."

"By Odin, don't lie!"

"I never lie. . . ."

"Hah!" He leaned close, and Morgana's nose wrinkled at the strong smell of ale. "You lied," he said, punching a finger at her with each word, "when you said you were fourteen!"

"No. I claimed fourteen winters, and I have seen fourteen winters. I just never said how many more I had seen. . . ."

"It's the same as a lie!" Brander's eyes were narrowed and his tone belligerent, and Morgana wisely decided not to argue. In this state, Brander was not likely to be objective.

"If you say so," she said calmly.

"I say so."

"Then, it is the same as a lie." Morgana tossed the last of her grain to Smoke, then wiped her hands on the skirt of her gown. An amused smile played at the corners of her mouth, threatening to break into a wide grin at any moment.

"I warn you," Brander muttered through clenched teeth, "not to laugh aloud. You will regret it if you do. . . ." He was uncomfortably aware that he stood in a puddle of rainwater, but his ale-sodden mind couldn't grasp the technicalities involved in extricating himself. It was late afternoon, and he had sat in his chair in the main hall drinking ale all day. Now he was reaping the results.

"I'm not laughing," Morgana lied blithely, ignoring the fact that she had just claimed not to be a liar. "But I must go in. Will you go with me?" It was probably the only way he would be able to navigate his way back to the house, and she marveled that he had found her in the first place.

"Aye, take me to my chambers." Brander lifted an arm to put it on her shoulder, and immediately became tangled in the folds of his cape. He struggled valiantly against the vicious beast for a moment before finally yielding to a stronger force than his, and slanted Morgana a mute appeal

for help. Gently, fighting laughter, she disentangled his arm
and moved to his right side where the cape hung open,
pinned with a brooch on his shoulder. A man's sword arm
was always left free. Morgana patiently put his hand on her
shoulder, indicating that he should lean on her, then took
several cautious steps through the mud. Brander squished
beside her.

It was a miracle, she was to reflect later, that they made it
across the stableyard without mishap. Brander was a big,
heavy man, and she had great difficulty keeping her balance
while guiding him.

Negotiating the long corridor leading to his room was
relatively simple after the stableyard, and Morgana wedged
Brander through the door and halfway across the floor
before he stumbled. Momentum carried him forward, and
she barely managed to lead him to the large bed piled high
with furs. He sprawled in a big X across the pillows and bed
coverings, head down, muffling an unintelligible comment
to a hundred thousand goose feathers.

"What did you say, Brander?" Morgana made no effort
to keep back the smile that threatened to become a huge
mirthful grin. There was no answer, and with a shake of her
head, she sat on the edge of his bed to disrobe him.

Immediately, he rolled toward her with clutching arms,
frowning as he found himself holding an armful of furs and
bed coverings instead of the elusive Morgana.

"Be still, Brander," she directed, and was relieved when
he obeyed. She pulled the furs and bed coverings from his
grasp, then squealed in surprise as she was engulfed by
brawny arms that almost knocked her to the floor. She
rapped him sharply on the head with her knuckles, exasperated, and this time he waited patiently while she tugged off
his filthy boots, then released the leather bindings to his
leggings. It took several minutes of labor to remove his

cape, belt, and tunic, and, puffing for breath, she decided he could sleep in his trousers. Nothing was worth the effort it would cost to remove them, and he wouldn't know if he was comfortable or uncomfortable anyway. Not until morning. Or maybe even the next afternoon . . .

"I said lie down with me," Brander said distinctly, his arms curling around Morgana's startled form with surprising strength. "I wanna feel you nex' t'me. . . ." His words slurred together as he patted clumsily in the direction of Morgana's head, missing by about a foot.

"Not tonight, Brander." She firmly removed his hand from her breast, where it lay like a piece of wood, leaden and inert. "Maybe another night . . ."

"Nay. Tonight!" His eyes narrowed, and he repeated stubbornly, "Tonight . . ."

"Fine. Just let me get comfortable, and I'll lie here with you." Her mind worked fast. If she could calm him, then she could lie with him until he went to sleep. He'd never know the difference until later, and in the cold light of day, he would think differently.

Morgana managed to arrange Brander in a more suitable posture upon the bed, then curled next to him. Her back pressed into his hard angles, curving to fit his chest and thighs. This was the most difficult thing she'd ever done; lying next to Brander, it took great effort not to reach out and caress him or smooth back the tumbled, damp curves of hair on his forehead.

If he woke, would he recall the last time she had lain with him—that night in the cave? She'd known then that he was her magic, that she would love him, but he still didn't realize it. Or did he? Did he know, somehow, that they were meant to be—that fate had decreed it?

Brander's breath began to come more regularly, the gentle

rise and fall of his chest indicating a deep sleep. Satisfied that he wouldn't wake, Morgana tried to ease from the bed.

Her feet were hanging over the side when Brander's heavy arm fell across her chest, crushing the breath from her lungs. Wriggling uncomfortably, she tried to move and couldn't. Puffs of breath left her like air from a blacksmith's bellows as she shoved at him until she was weary and gasping. Finally, Morgana managed to dislodge his arm.

"Where y'goin'?" a slurred voice demanded to know, and curved fingers tangled in her hair, holding her as she attempted to rise.

Yielding with a sigh, Morgana lay back upon the soft mattress and curled into Brander's side. He was warm and safe and familiar, and if the truth were to be known, she wanted nothing more than to lie with him. Of course, she had somehow thought it would be different, more like the last time perhaps, but this would have to do for now.

In the morning, bright rays of sunlight pricked Morgana's eyelids, waking her. For a moment she was confused, not remembering where she was, then memory came flooding back. She turned her head to Brander and found him regarding her with red, swollen eyes. A cheerful greeting died unspoken on her lips.

"Close the windows," Brander muttered. His voice was forced through clenched teeth. "The light is blinding."

Morgana slid from the bed and closed the shutters, darkening the room. The cold stone floors were chilly even with the thick carpets Brander had brought back from Eastern lands, and she scampered across the floor to leap back into the bed.

Brander fixed her with a baleful eye. "Must you jump about like a rabid hare? My head is swollen to the size of a war shield, and you prance about on the bed like a horse!"

"My apologies," Morgana said in a most unapologetic tone. "Are you ill?"

"Aye." This last was a half-groan, so that she really did feel a twinge of sympathy for him.

"I can ease your pain," Morgana offered, "though the cure is near as bad as the cause. Are you willing?"

Recalling her skill with healing medicines, Brander eagerly accepted.

"Anything, only ease this cursed pounding in my skull and scrape the burr from my tongue. . . ."

Once more Morgana rose from the bed, this time leaving Brander's chamber. He had almost decided that she would not return when the door opened and she entered with a tray. A thick cup stood in the middle, steam rising from it and dispelling an unsavory odor.

"What is it?" Brander's nose wrinkled with disgust as he stared doubtfully at the cup. Thin vapors writhed above the cup like snakes, winding and twisting, and he briefly closed his eyes.

"Drink it all at once, quickly, or you will not be able to finish it," Morgana instructed. She lifted the cup to his mouth, ignoring his pleading gaze and plaintive sigh. "All of it," she repeated, watching with narrowed eyes as he obeyed. The bottom tilted up as he drained it.

Brander lowered the cup and belched loudly, surprising himself. His startled expression quickly altered to alarm as the herbs seared into his belly. Morgana stepped aside as Brander tore from the bed and flew to the chamber pot in the corner. Discretion won out over curiosity, and she silently let herself out the door. He would let her know soon enough if the potion had worked adequately.

It was some time later when Brander found Morgana in the kitchen.

"You are," he said in a voice that held much more

energy than it had when he'd last spoken with her, "a heartless wretch. Why didn't you warn me of the effects of your potion?"

"Do you feel better?" Morgana countered, noting his healthy color and bright eyes.

"Aye, but I almost died from the cure."

"I did warn you, remember. Did I not say that the cure was almost as bad as the cause?"

" 'Tis a simple case of understatement," Brander grumbled. He reached out and tore off the end from a loaf of fresh-baked bread. "For a time, I preferred dying."

"The herbs cleanse your body, and leave you free of the poisons you so blithely imbibed." A faint smile curved her mouth at his grunt of acceptance, and Morgana continued stirring a savory stew.

Brander, gazing at her delicate profile, knew a moment of gratitude that she had been wiser than he. To have taken her in that drunken state would have been a cruel mockery of what he was beginning to feel—nay, what he already felt for her, and he thanked whatever gods were listening that spirit and flesh had failed him.

Hlynn, stuffing a cloth with pudding, slanted Brander a curious glance from her spot in the corner. He seemed much more amenable than usual, though he had never been actually surly to her. Morgana brought out the best and the worst in him, so that he was always on one end of the scale or the other. Was there no in-between that could make for a happy compromise?

Her brow furrowed as she contemplated a way for them to resolve their differences. Perhaps . . .

Chapter 18

Under the hazy sunlight of a cloudy sky, Morgana stood on the flagged stones of the path leading to the front door, watching as Brander examined a fine horse. The animal stepped nervously, snorting, nostrils like pink blossoms flaring in the soft light.

"High-strung," the seller observed unnecessarily, and Brander just grunted. The seller, Ben Abdu, was a short, swarthy man wrapped in stifling, dingy robes. He didn't appear to be entirely reputable, but his renown for selling excellent horses made him a good amount of silver.

And, Morgana thought, this horse was beautiful. He was solid white, with brown eyes like velvet, and a finely molded head. His neck arched when he pranced, and a long, flowing tail lifted proudly high. Brander's hands skimmed over the animal's legs, touching and testing for strength.

"He's strong enough," Ben Abdu said, hovering like a mother hen over its only chick. "Came from Holmgard, in the land of the Rus, but was sired in Arabia. See the chest? Wide, with greater lungs than ordinary, and..."

"But the legs are thinner," Brander pointed out.

"Aye, but stronger! It is true," Ben Abdu insisted, seeing a sale and silver slip away from him. "These horses have bones as strong as ivory!"

When Brander would have opened the animal's mouth to check its teeth for age, the horse shied away, screaming shrilly and rearing.

"Down with you!" Ben Abdu cried, jerking viciously on the leather reins. "You lop-eared son of a jackass! Get down I say!" He yanked again and blood spurted from where the metal bit cut into the horse's soft mouth.

"Stop it!" Morgana cried, unable to stand silently another moment. "Can't you see what you're doing to his mouth?"

She came to stand beside the horse, ignoring Brander's warning, and ran a soothing hand over the trembling legs. Whites of his eyes showed as the stallion quieted, sensing friendship, but when the swarthy Arab stepped near, ears were laid back and teeth bared.

Brander watched quietly as Morgana talked to the horse, blowing her breath in his flared nostrils, and scratching his jaw. A faint smile curved Brander's mouth. They made a good contrast: Morgana, so dark and slim and tawny, against the snowy white of the horse. An idea began to form in his mind, and his senses quickened.

Ben Abdu rubbed his hands together greedily. This horse had been nothing but trouble to him since he'd wrestled him onto the ship, and now he sensed a sale. He would raise his price to cover the cost of the boards broken by sharp, flashing hooves, and the leather straps that had been snapped in two. . . .

"Twenty pieces of silver," Ben Abdu said with a smile, "for this magnificent animal! This creature is faster than the wind, yet able to carry two men of your size, Brander

Eriksson! I will even"—he waved a hand to include the trappings of silk and leather on the stallion's back—"part with all of this for only a few pieces more. . . ."

"Fifteen," Brander countered, "plus the saddle and harness."

Ben Abdu was aghast. "Fifteen?" His voice croaked like a toad's, and he put the back of one hand to his forehead as if he was in extreme pain, which, in truth, he was. "Fifteen? You must be jesting!"

"Nay. The animal is too small for me. I would look ridiculous upon his back. Forget it." Brander pivoted, and began walking away.

Morgana patted the arched neck regretfully, letting her fingers tangle in the silken mane that fell over the stallion's high withers. She looked into the soft eyes and felt as if she was attuned with his spirit, and wanted to shout after Brander to come back. But she didn't dare. She had no money, and nothing of value, not even one gold bracelet. . . .

"Brander Eriksson," Ben Abdu called after him. "Your lady could ride the animal. See how docile he is with her? She has a way with him, and already she likes him. Is that not so?" he turned to ask Morgana.

But Morgana understood very little of his heavily accented Danish, and could only shake her head and shrug her shoulders. Ben Abdu's dark eyes narrowed even more.

"You are . . . a Pict?" he asked in a strange language, and she shook her head. Ben Abdu's brow furrowed as he tried to recall what she'd spoken earlier. "Celtic?" he tried again, and this time Morgana understood.

"Aye."

"Ah." Ben Abdu made a steeple of his fingers and smiled widely, baring broken, charred teeth. "You admire the horse, mistress?"

"Aye. I would be foolish not to admire a lovely animal

such as this. But 'tis not my money to spend. Make your bargains with Brander Eriksson.''

Morgana started as Brander's hand lay softly upon her shoulder, and his eyes crinkled at the corners when she turned to gaze up at him.

"Not one piece more than fifteen for horse and harness," he told Ben Abdu without taking his eyes from the slim girl at his side. "And 'tis a crime you are committing by even asking.''

"Aiii," Ben Abdu moaned. "May Allah forgive me for being such a fool, but I will sell him to you for that! He costs me too much to feed, and I set sail for home tomorrow. The silver, please?'' He held out a dark hand, palm up, waiting for his coins.

Brander hefted a purse from his belt, and counted out fifteen pieces of silver.

"Ah," Ben Abdu grunted with pleasure. "Kufic coins!" He palmed the coins, testing one between the stumps of his teeth, then dropped them in his purse. Gathering the folds of his many robes tighter in his twisted cloth belt, Ben Abdu waved a quick farewell and started back down the road to Hedeby as if he thought they might change their minds. "Kufic coins," he muttered again, pleased at this reminder of home.

Brander explained at Morgana's questioning glance, "Kufic simply means they bear script named after the city of Kufah in Mesopotamia. 'Tis good silver.''

"Oh." Morgana didn't care, at that moment, how good the silver was. She was delighted that Brander had bought this horse. "He has heart," she murmured softly, "and will serve you well, Brander.'' Her fingertips slid lightly over the horse's satiny hide, marveling at the sheen and luster.

Brander took the leather reins. "I bought him as a gift.'' He tilted his head to see her reaction, but Morgana's expression was carefully blank. "Do you think the lady will like him?"

Lady . . . Erika? Morgana's chin quivered with her effort to hold back a harsh retort. "If the lady likes horses at all, she'll like this one," she managed to answer calmly. "He's a fine animal."

"The lady obviously likes horses . . ."

Morgana recalled Brander's promise to Erika to take her riding. . . ."

"And also geese, especially fowl-tempered ones, excuse the bad joke," Brander continued.

Geese? Ah, he was talking about *her*!

"For me, Brander—this horse?" She smiled with delight and flung herself into his arms when he nodded. "I never thought . . . He's so beautiful . . . and you're so kind, Brander, to buy him for me. . . ."

Chuckling at her incoherent phrases, Brander halted and swung Morgana into his arms. She caught her breath, staring down at him in the hazy gray light of the day, wondering what he meant to do.

"Don't you want to ride him?" Brander didn't wait for an answer but swung Morgana onto the animal's back, letting her sit amidst bright silk trappings. He stepped back to admire her, his gaze drifting from Morgana's tumbled sable hair to her feet. A slight frown puckered his brow. Against the backdrop of silk, Morgana's gown of undyed wool seemed even more ragged than ever. Why hadn't he noticed how she was dressed before? He'd looked only at that small, beautiful face, not her garments.

Morgana, excited with her gift, didn't notice Brander's preoccupation. She nudged the stallion with her heels and he bounded forward, passing Ben Abdu a short way down the road.

"The horse!" the trader called after her, and Morgana

turned to hear, "He is called Trska. It means swift in my language." Satisfied that he had fulfilled all obligations toward horse, buyer, and deal, Ben Abdu returned to his ruminations about what he would buy to take home to his fat little wife and seven chubby children. *"Habaytik, wa na arifti . . ."* he sang off-key, singing of a love who didn't know how he felt.

Morgana let the stallion have his head, racing across grassy fields toward the Haddeby Nor. Hooves thundered and dirt clods flew in spiraling chunks behind horse and rider. Faster and faster she rode, free as the wind and birds and clouds skimming overhead, until at last Morgana pulled Trska to a halt. He stood with heaving chest, fine flecks of white foam lathering his satin sides and the silk trappings he wore.

Even with the clouds it was warm, a condition Hlynn claimed would not last long. Morgana tilted back her head to stare at the sky, then slowly surveyed her surroundings. Yea, she could feel it in the air, the crisp bite of the wind that presaged cold weather, and behind the dull gray clouds lurked more, bigger, and fat with rain or sleet. Winter came much quicker in Jutland than in Erin, it seemed.

Leaves fell from the trees, scudding on brisk breezes to whisk across golden fields, ending in rustling piles against the high, semicircular rampart guarding Hedeby. Reaching out to pat Trska on his wet neck, Morgana urged him forward with a mental command the animal responded to immediately. There was no need to use the reins or her heels, or even pressure from her knees. Trska answered to Morgana's unspoken directions.

The roads in Hedeby were paved with logs, and Trska's hooves clattered noisily across them. A few people paused to stare at Morgana curiously, but most scurried busily about their tasks. The settlement bustled with activity. The *Hærvej*, a long northern extension of an important trade route, passed through the Danevirke near Hedeby. This brought in travelers from the land routes. More important was the flow of traffic from the North Sea to the Baltic, which avoided the dangerous coastal journey round Jutland by traveling the short distance overland behind the protection of the Danevirke, and thus through Hedeby.

Should she ever decide to flee Jutland, Morgana reflected, 'twould be quite simple to do. Sea traffic abounded, and there would be no difficulty in securing passage somewhere, even if not to Erin. A small smile appeared at that thought. Where could she go that she would not be haunted by memories of Brander?

As if conjured by her thoughts, Brander magically appeared at her side. He was riding a large bay, and reined his animal beside Trska.

"Escaping me already?" he asked jokingly, startling Morgana. It was *she* who had the gift of insight, not Brander, wasn't it? "Ride with me," he said without giving her time to reply. "I have a spot I'd like to show you."

Hoofbeats hammered a solid rhythm against wood roads, then dirt as Brander veered from the main thoroughfare and over tree-lined slopes. Following, Morgana admired the way he sat his mount, straight and tall, riding as easily as if he was part of the horse.

When he halted, she gave a small cry of delight. For a moment she could have thought herself back in Erin. Tall oak trees formed a canopy that blotted out the gray sky, and a thick carpet of leaves lay on the ground.

Brander grinned. "I thought you might like this spot. Let's sit a while." The idea had come to him when he'd watched her ride off, hair flying on the breeze, one with the graceful animal she rode. A powerful surge of desire had prompted him to action, and he'd known it was the right time; now they were in the right place. . . .

Dismounting, they sat on a comfortable cushion of dead leaves, staring up at small patches of sky barely visible through thick branches.

"How did you know I missed my friends?" Morgana asked idly. "I grew up with the trees and feel a kinship with them." Lazily, she rolled to one side and propped her chin in the palm of a hand. A drift of hair spilled over her fingers in a graceful fall.

"I simply remembered how I felt, lying in that cold stone cave in Hibernia and thinking of Jutland. I longed for flat land free of so many stones, and open spaces where I could see almost from one side of the country to the other." He shrugged, half-embarrassed by his thoughtfulness. "I thought it might be the same with you."

"Did you?" Morgana was remembering that cold stone cave, too, and the first night she had gone to find Brander. Didn't he recall that at all? Was she just another woman to him, a conquest, perhaps, as some men considered the women they'd known?

Questions trembled on the tip of Morgana's tongue, and she was startled when Brander said softly, "The only good thing I think of when I recall that cave is you, Morgana. You made the time sweeter just by being with me. And . . ." He stopped, his mouth firming to a straight line.

"And what?" Surely he knew how she felt; after all, she hadn't tried to keep it a secret. Must she instigate every confrontation? Only when Brander was full of too much good ale did he come to her! Morgana's hand clenched into a small fist of frustration.

Noting her tensed posture, Brander reached out, gently uncurling her fingers. He touched his lips to her palm, hearing her quickly indrawn breath, and smiled against her hand. Blue eyes darkened when he looked up into her face.

"Open for me, love."

"Have I not already, Brander?" Aye, she had opened her hand, her body, her heart to him—could he not see it?

"Yea. That you have." White teeth nibbled on the soft underside of her arm in tiny bites up to her elbow. "And would you again?" he asked against her satin skin, lips tickling vulnerable flesh.

Morgana was hardly aware of their horses' soft nickers from where Brander had tethered them. Her heart was beating so fast that it seemed as if it would leap from her body, and the shallow pulse at the base of her throat fluttered wildly. Brander, lifting his head, saw that hollow of trembling flesh and smiled.

His hand shifted from her arm, his palm testing the sweet curve of her back, fingers riding the tiny ridge of her spine. Brander spread his fingers, reveling in the thought of the velvety soft skin that he knew lay beneath her rough woolen gown.

Morgana moaned softly when his palm slid to cup the firm ripeness of her breast. She remembered now, how odd and pleasurable it was to have him touch her, how her insides began to burn and grow tighter and tighter, forming a hard knot. And Brander knew by the staccato breaths she took when he found the right motions. Slowly, he lifted a hand to unfasten the straps of her gown and let the garment fall. A belt held the tunic at her waist, and he released it. Morgana's long undertunic was open at the neck, the longer sleeves covering her arms almost to the elbows. Brander drew it over her head, and proud breasts sprang free of confinement, gilded a soft peachy color by hazy light from the cloudy sky and lacy tree branches.

Morgana sat amidst a pile of garments, as bare as the day

she'd been born, gazing at Brander with her heart in her eyes.

"And now you," she said, reaching out with trembling fingers to undo his wide belt. He sat still, but was surprised how he shook inside like a lad with his first woman, letting Morgana's clumsy fingers tug at the leather.

"Here," he said finally, helping her with the belt, and before a minute or two had passed, he was pulling off his clothes with her. Cape, overtunic, short-sleeved undertunic, then boots, leggings, and trousers were added to the pile of clothing.

Brander spread his fine wool cape over a particularly thick mound of leaves and drew Morgana down with him to this bed of leaves. They lay for a moment in mutual admiration. She admired his long, lean body with its superb curvature of muscle and bone; he feasted his eyes on soft skin, slim legs, and full breasts like ripe apples.

This was the way it should be, Morgana just had time to think before Brander drew her close again, under life-giving trees and sky and clouds, with the wind as a sweet accompaniment to gentle sighs and loving whispers.

Then time and place receded as Brander coaxed a response from her with hands and mouth and body, caressing her skin with his fingers as a musician plays a harp. Intoxicating lips, honeyed with moisture from her kisses, strayed to the peak of a breast, pausing to tease the pink crest with his tongue. Morgana's sudden arching gasp for air fit her breast more tightly against his searching mouth, and her fingers dug into his shoulders.

Minutes passed while neither thought of anything but their need for each other. For Brander, desire had not been so sharp and sweet for many years; Morgana was realizing the consummation of a long-awaited moment.

Suddenly unable to wait, needing to feel him bury himself within her, Morgana surged upward, pressing her hips against his groin, feeling the heat of him against her belly.

"Brander..." she said against his lips, pleading.

Recognizing through the thick, heated mist that she was urging him, Brander responded. With his mouth still fastened on hers, he moved between her thighs. Morgana only dimly realized that there was a world beyond hot, damp ecstasy, vaguely knew that earth and sky and trees cartwheeled somewhere just past her field of vision; she could barely follow Brander's light explorations with mouth and clever tongue, or recognize that they lay upon a crackling mattress of pungently scented leaves.

Slim arms, honey-colored and soft, lifted to twine around his neck, holding him, and Brander could hold back no longer. Morgana saw him smile softly down at her as he entered, sending shivering currents radiating to the tips of her toes and fingers, cradling her hips with his hands and murmuring sweetly, "Now, love... now."

Answering his thrusts with quivering anticipation, Morgana matched his rhythm, her heels digging mounds into the soft material of his cape, bunching it into little humps of leaf and wool. Head, hips, heels, burned into the cape, surely leaving a charred imprint that would never be scrubbed away. Passion scorched them, scorched everything around them, burning brighter and hotter until the very air shimmered with the heat of it.

Distantly, as if once more in her dreams, Morgana heard and felt Brander's voice, thick and husky, shifting damp strands of errant hair straying over her neck and shoulders, mutter against her throat, "That's right, my love, my heart... just like that...."

This time Morgana experienced the same shattering release as Brander. When he soared to those heights she'd never seen, she soared with him; and when they were suspended for a heartbeat on that sweet, wild precipice, she knew what it meant to be loved. Together they floated back to reality, pearled with a mist of love and satiated, Brander relaxed and fulfilled, Morgana limp and wonderfully content.

As her heart slowed its rapid beat and her senses returned to normal, she curved her body to his in the way lovers do. Brander caught the edge of his cape and drew it over them, wrapping them in a soft cocoon of wool and repletion.

Love, Morgana reflected drowsily, was much more fitting under the roof of sky and leaves than it would have been beneath an uncaring ceiling of timber and mud. How had Brander known? She cuddled closer, feeling the regular thud of his heart and the strength of his arms around her. The gods could not have invented anything better than this.

Chapter
19

Dry brown leaves curled and fell, drifting into piles against gates and walls, riding brisk winds, and crackling sharply underfoot. The air was sharp and biting, sweeping in across the fjord with a salty tang, full of wide-winged gulls that drifted lazily on slanting currents. Fields that had swayed with rich green stems were now melded into a brittle gold hue that glittered beneath gloomy skies. Winter roared across Jutland with clouds of frost and towering cumulus.

It was already much colder than Erin had ever been, Morgana decided as she shivered beneath a loose fur cape. She held her hands to the fire, palms out, fingers spread. Light, in ever-changing patterns, capered on the hearth and walls of the main hall. It slanted across her hair, picking out the deep, rich highlights, reflecting them to any who looked as bluish glints peeping from thick waves.

"Still cold, my lady?"

Morgana half-turned, a smile on her mouth, and cheeks flushed from the fire's heat.

"Aye, Hlynn. It seems to seep into my bones."

"I felt the same way when I first came to Jutland," the little maid said cheerily. She lifted a metal poker and jabbed at the burning logs, sending a shower of sparks up the stone chimney.

Morgana propped her chin in the cradle of one palm, gazing at Hlynn curiously.

"Where did you come from, Hlynn?" Memories of home assailed her as she asked, fresh and bittersweet. Green copses shrouded with tree shadows, sacred groves of oak hung with mistletoe, high rocky crags and deep running streams, fields of gorse like yellow stars flung onto the ground—Morgana couldn't still the sudden soft sigh and Hlynn heard it.

"I don't miss Northumbria like you do Erin," she said into the crackling silence. "I was brought here as a very young girl, and my brother was with me, so it wasn't so bad." Hlynn pushed back a limp strand of soft brown hair and poked at a smoldering log with the fire tongs.

"Where is your brother now? Does he speak the Viking tongue as well as you?" Morgana thought of Kyna, the only person who had truly cared for her, and fought a hot wash of tears.

"We should both speak it well," Hlynn laughed, "as the Danes invaded Northumbria some years back. It was just another language by the time we were brought here. Rowan now lives with Brander's father, Harald. 'Tis not far, and sometimes, when Brander goes to his father's home, he takes me." She smiled at Morgana. "He would have taken me this time, except he knew how close we've become."

"Oh Hlynn, I'm sorry. If I'd known . . ."

"Oh no, he asked, my lady, but I wanted to stay with you," Hlynn assured her. "There are times my brother is a pain in the arse, believe me! I visit him because he's my only living kin."

The fire blazing properly again, Hlynn rocked back on her heels and wiped sooty hands on the rough wool of her gown. She tugged at the belt binding her shapeless gown at the waist, then readjusted the thongs which laced her leggings above cloth and leather boots. A cape of sheepskin hung over one shoulder, pinned with a bronze brooch, swinging with every movement.

"Perhaps the next time Brander visits his father you can go with him," Morgana offered.

Examining the carved brooch on her shoulder, Hlynn looked up and said with a sly grin, "Perhaps 'twill be you who goes."

"Me?" The thought startled Morgana. Would she want to go to Harald's home—knowing he disliked Celts? When Brander had received the message summoning him to his father, he had made the half-hearted suggestion that Morgana accompany him. It had, thankfully, been ignored and forgotten.

"Why would I wish to go hunting with the men?" she asked Hlynn now. "I have an affinity with the creatures, and cannot stand to see them suffer and die, even though I know they give themselves to us for sustenance."

" 'Tis not the hunting I was thinking of, but the fact that Brander wishes you by his side constantly now," Hlynn pointed out with a broad grin. "Ever since that day . . ."

"I know, I know!" Morgana's cheeks flamed. She and Brander had ridden back from their tryst in the woods with leaves clinging to their hair and a content expression in their eyes that no one could have misinterpreted. Everyone, including Smoke, had recognized the difference in them at once. And her feelings for Brander were so transparent that no one needed the inner sight that she possessed to see how she loved him.

She recalled how, when he'd left, he had held her to him so tightly that it felt as if her ribs would surely crack, and had whispered teasingly into her ear, "Try to miss me, little one!"

Oh, she did, and it had been only a fortnight since he'd ridden to Harald's to join the hunt. Even her dreams were more vivid with Brander not beside her at night now, curled into her with a fierce possessiveness that she missed sorely. These dreams were peopled with strange creatures and events, swirling in mysterious shadows at times or stepping into blinding light so that she couldn't discern features or identities. And there was a recurring dream on several nights, of a white horse—Trska?—and a dark one, chasing her until she pitched headlong over a cliff and into total oblivion, falling, falling, never reaching bottom—which was ridiculous, of course, because there were no cliffs in Jutland.

She would be glad, Morgana thought with a longing sigh, when Brander returned.

Since it was the warmest place in the house, Morgana was in the cooking area when Brander came back. She was watching Hlynn and Kelda cut up a rabbit for stew, and sneaking tidbits to Smoke at her feet, while idly scraping vegetables for the cooking pot. The gosling honked noisily for another bite, and Morgana fed him while she chattered of Erin and Kyna, and her beloved loughs and crags.

"Crags rise like jagged teeth from the sea," she was saying when she felt warm lips upon the back of her neck where sable hair pulled into a knot had left bare skin. Her quick, indrawn breath had barely filled her lungs before the lips were replaced by broad hands curving tenderly around her throat.

Breathlessly she cried, "I thought you were never coming back, Brander . . . !"

"How did you know it was me?" A smile crinkled

ice-blue eyes and stretched his mouth as he filled his sight and arms with Morgana. "I could have been anyone."

"But you aren't. You're back. And I'm glad to see you," she added unnecessarily.

Anyone would have noticed her joy at seeing Brander. Morgana was wrapped around him like a vine, clinging and kissing his eyes, lips, and chin—anything she could reach. She vibrated with pleasure, and wondered how she had survived the past days without him.

"Are you hungry? Thirsty? Or do you wish to retire . . . ?" She stopped short, blushing furiously at the thoughts which attended that suggestion.

Grinning, Brander caught and understood her abrupt sputter into silence. Aye, in the past weeks he had thought continuously of her slim body and vibrant face. Kitchen firelight graced her tawny cheeks with a rosy glow, refining and coloring the unblemished texture of her skin, soft and sweet as a baby's. Sometimes, as now, her eyes grew so wide and credulous, looking at him with the unblinking gaze of a newborn, that it was almost as if some piquant spirit had painted them overlarge in her face. Flecks of green and gold deepened, softened, swallowing firelight like a polished bronze mirror until she simply radiated. It still surprised Brander how she could turn his insides to a melting pot of mixed emotions when she smiled at him.

"I do find myself a bit weary," he murmured against the sweet curve of her ear, blowing aside the wisps of sable hair that tickled his nose and lips.

Stew and unscraped vegetables forgotten, Morgana slid her arm into Brander's and pulled him from the kitchen.

Kelda watched with wide eyes, clapping one hand over her mouth as she turned to Hlynn.

"Hmmph," Hlynn said to the disgruntled gosling at her

feet. " 'Tis a safe bet that Morgana will not see her crags and loughs again, nor will she want to!"

"Honk," Smoke said with beady eyes fastened on his mistress's back. "Honk..."

The
CONFRONTATION

Chapter 20

Brander and Morgana lay in a cocoon of soft heated breath and warm furs and blankets, wrapped up in each other like two tussling puppies. She squealed, laughing, when he tickled her bare rib cage, blunt fingers digging into her skin with quick jabs. The strange hump of blankets on the wide bed shifted, swayed, and lunged sideways as Morgana tried to escape, ending up on the cold stone floor with a thud. Two bodies tumbled from the covers, gasping for air, faces alight with laughter.

"'Tis not fair!" a breathless voice gasped. "You're bigger . . . and stronger!"

"But you wriggle like a greased eel," Brander objected, "so that I can hardly lay a hand on you. . . ."

The hump of blankets and furs lifted as he stood like an Arab, swathed in thick robes.

"You look," Morgana said between giggles, "like Ben Abdu!"

"Ah, for twenty pieces of silver . . ." Brander began when Morgana managed to hook her foot behind his ankle and tug. He fell, half across her squirming body and half across the bed. "Oof," he said.

But when he would have turned to exact revenge upon her by tickling her into submission, Morgana grabbed his face between her palms and kissed him, long and hard, pressing the tip of her tongue between his lips to tease and tantalize.

Relaxing, Brander responded. Softly, he palmed a full breast, kneading and caressing the mound that burned under his touch. Morgana moaned throatily, curling into him, luxuriating in the touch of his hands and mouth against her fevered skin.

She felt his hands spreading sable curls drifting over neck and shoulder, uncovering that tiny ridge at the high point of her spine. Brander's tongue was as rough as a kitten's, rasping over her flesh in small circles, hot and full of liquid fire that sent shivering tingles from spine to toes. Morgana moaned again, deeply and richly, and felt the shifting of his breath from her back to her ear when he heard it.

"I love the sounds you make," he murmured against her ear, "and I've missed hearing them. . . ."

Now his hands were cupping under her hips to lift her, laying her back on the bed, moving lightly and sending waterfalls of shivers through bone and muscle. One hand trailed down the bumps of her spine to caress the swell of her hip, while the other wooed a response from the sensitive flesh on her nape, tunneling under a wealth of hair to stroke her before moving lazily to her mouth with his fingers.

"Open for me, love," he coaxed. "Like this . . . yea, is that not better?" Brander's thumb dragged slowly over her bottom lip, sliding gently into the hot, moist interior, blunt fingers tilting back her chin. His hand tangled in her hair, slipping downward, back to the gentle rise of her breast, cupping and caressing, teasing until Morgana could not catch her breath.

"Brander . . ." The word was more a sigh than a spoken word, whispered against him, against tense-muscled flesh, spiced with the scent of tobacco, wine, and wind.

"Aye, love?" Brander's thumb moved agonizingly slow, circling the taut peak of her breast, dewing it with moisture, the dampness enhancing the whirling impact of his contact.

When she arched against his palm, rosebud hot against the curved flesh, he moved his other hand in a slow, teasing sweep down and over tawny skin, smoothing over the soft swell of her belly to massage the firm flesh. Morgana could feel his breath on her cheek, on the nape of her neck, and on the shadows between her breasts, until she was on fire with urgency.

Smiling at her in the dim light from fire and lamps, Brander pressed her backward into the tumbled nest of furs and blankets. She couldn't remember, later, how long he explored her contours with hands and mouth; all she could recall was the sweet ecstasy of her responses, the wild, hot sensation that welled until only Brander could satisfy it, and she was pulling him closer and closer, pleading with him to end the torment.

"Now . . . Brander . . . now . . ."

"Aye, love. Now," he promised, yielding to his raging desire, sliding his body over hers in a sensuous, tantalizing motion. Husky laughter whisked over a taut peak when Morgana whimpered, his two-day-old beard scratching erotically across the aroused point until she writhed helplessly. Wet kisses pranced over breasts and ribs, trailing down the curve of her belly and lower, ignoring Morgana's small, shocked cry of protest. Sensitive, searching fingers explored her, firmly kneading the shapely contours of thighs and hips, then shifting so that his cupped palm fit to the soft rise of inky curls, lingering, bringing Morgana to a shivering release with the firm, smooth motions of his hand.

When she clung to him, still trembling, he slid slowly across her body, touching every inch of her, forehead to forehead, mouth to mouth, then chests, bellies, and thighs. They fit together like pieces of an Oriental puzzle, tightly meshed, glued with a mist of hot, moist desire.

Seeking Brander's warmth, the comforting closeness of him that made her complete, Morgana arched upward, heels digging into the mattress like burrowing moles. Ready and yearning, she cried out with a mixture of relief and heady pleasure when he thrust forward, and passion soared to new heights.

Brander's voice was a hoarse murmur in her ear, cajoling and warm with desire, "Ah Morgana, you are sweet . . . so sweet . . . yes, do that . . . and that . . ." as he entered her fully, as deeply as he could. The rhythm of hearts and lungs altered rapidly, quickening to swift tempos like the cadence of drums.

Nuzzling her neck, that slim fragrant column supporting such a marvel of bone and skin and clouds of dark hair, Brander reveled in the feel of her beneath him and around him. He'd never experienced such a fusion of mind and body, and while it pleased him, it was confusing and unsettling. They were so attuned, so perfectly in rhythm, that it was as if they were one being, one creature intent only upon loving and being loved.

Jeweled eyes glittered in fragments of light and shadow, smiling up at him, mirroring his own face in their smoky depths, and Brander lost himself in Morgana. There were no more thoughts of anything but the sweet release that exploded into a thousand splinters of delight, racing through every part of their bodies to bathe them in golden mists of satisfaction.

New to the play, Morgana recovered first. She rubbed

against Brander like a kitten, almost purring with happiness and fulfillment, wanting to experience it again.

Brander opened one eye, slightly disgruntled and staring at her with the glassy gaze of a fish upon a platter.

"Greedy wench," he muttered, curling one arm around her to draw her closer to him. "I cannot again . . . so soon."

Her question was simple and direct. "Why not?"

A ragged breath preceded his answer. "Because a man . . . a man must take . . . take time, Morgana."

"Time for what?" Long fingers drifted through golden hairs on his chest, stirring her interest as she watched them twine around her fingertips. Her voice was drowsy, replete, the soft silken purr of a kitten. "How much time?"

"How much . . . ?" His groan mingled with laughter. It was crazy, but he could feel the return of desire, sparked by the lingering touch of her fingertips along the ridges of his ribs, and the soft trailings of sable hair across his belly. "Ah, Morgana." This last was thick, mixed with a sighing sound of pleasure when her fingers found and caressed him.

"See?" she said. "It wants to . . ."

"So it does," he agreed, rolling over to tuck her beneath him, "so it does. . . ."

The last dying rays of afternoon sunshine slanted through glass windows in a hundred tiny rainbows, transforming dull architecture of stone walls and floor to a wonderland of beauty. Mist, gathered in the light, hung shimmering in the air, bathing Morgana's face in a rosy glow as she slept.

Was there ever, Brander wondered with a faint smile, a more complex, fascinating creature than Morgana? Innocent, worldly, bold, shy—she was all those things enfolded into a bundle of curves and rich flesh. How could he resist her? Or why would he want to?

Leaning forward, he blew lightly on Morgana's upturned

face, disturbing a stray tendril of hair so that it tickled her nose. Still asleep, her brows puckered into a tiny frown and her nose wrinkled. He blew again, and this time long lashes fluttered and lifted to reveal eyes still hazy with sleep-shadows.

"Lazybones," he chided in a soft, indulgent tone, "it's time to rise for our supper. The next meal won't be until morn, and I find myself hungry."

Morgana's lips curved into a satisfied smile. She stretched, loosening muscles in her arms and legs, then curled her fingers under her chin while she gazed at him in loving regard.

" 'Tis night?" Her eyes flicked toward the window where purple shadows colored the glass.

"Almost. Aren't you hungry?"

"Umm, hmm. But not for food, Viking."

Brander laughed, his eyes crinkling at the corners in the way Morgana loved.

"You are greedy," he said in a much different tone than he had earlier.

"Aye," she readily agreed. " 'Tis hard not to be, with you as the banquet."

That comment conjured up tempting images, and for several moments they played upon it with a variety of ridiculous phrases that left them helpless with laughter at their cleverness. They might have toyed with words even longer if a knock on the chamber door hadn't halted their fun.

"Enter," Brander called out, tucking a thick blanket around Morgana and still chuckling at her latest quip. The bar lifted and the door opened to admit a wide-eyed Hlynn. In her hands was a tray heavily laden with steaming dishes.

"I've brought you enough food for a banquet," she said, then stared in confusion as the pair on the bed exploded into gusts of laughter.

"Thank you," Morgana finally managed to say between giggles. "We were just talking about supper. . . ." She lapsed into laughter again, and Hlynn couldn't help a wide grin at their merriment even though she didn't understand the cause.

" 'Tis enough to last 'til morning unless you're greedy," Hlynn said into a fresh burst of laughter, then set down the tray to back out of the room, still smiling. It was good to see them so happy, she reflected, shutting the door behind her. Brander had always seemed on the harsh side, with little laughter or joy in him. Morgana certainly brought out his best.

Muffled laughter followed her down the hall, reinforcing her pleasant thoughts, so that she never saw the shadowed shape waiting just ahead. A loud squawk made her gasp and grab her throat with one hand, and then scowl at the cause of her momentary fear.

"Hush," Hlynn rebuked Smoke. He waited at the turn in the dim corridor. She flapped her skirt at him as he tried to dodge past. The gosling was obviously searching for Morgana, and it took some doing to shoo him back to the kitchen.

Bothi, in from the stables for a hot meal, looked up from his bowl and slanted a narrow glance at the squawking goose and Hlynn as they entered the kitchen with a flurry of tail feathers and harsh words.

" 'Tis a wretched creature, and fit only for eating," he muttered to Hlynn. "The petted, pampered beast!"

Hlynn quickly wrested a hunk of bread from a flat loaf and threw it to Smoke.

"Aye," she agreed, "but Morgana finds him lovable. And to his credit, the stupid goose adores her."

"Hmmph. 'Tis of no use to anyone. What can a goose do? Nothing but eat and lose feathers, if you ask me, and good only for dining and stuffing pillows." Dark brows lowered as he slurped noisily at his stew. He finished, sat back in his chair and eyed Smoke. "Good for nothing," Bothi repeated firmly.

"But Morgana has an affinity for poor, dumb creatures. She claims they're far more intelligent than given credit for being, and that . . ."

"Hah! The lady may be pretty, and may have our lord tangled around her tiny little finger, but the truth is, she ain't no smarter than that goose." Bothi lit his pipe and blew out a large cloud of smoke, then glanced up to find Hlynn's face creased into a wrathful glare.

"You . . . !" Her finger pointed in quivering fury. "You have sheep dung for brains! Your head is filled with horse droppings! You . . ."

"Enough," Bothi said in amazement. "I understand. I only meant that if she longs for more than she has now, she won't get it. Brander intends to marry Erika, and that's that. The little Celt had best understand that he only plays a pleasant game for a while, and that he knows where profit lies."

"And what profit in wedding that overblown wench with the tongue of an adder?"

"Lands," was the prompt answer, "and taxes and men to fight—does Morgana have those?"

The answer was obvious. Morgana's treasure was in her eyes and hair, in the curve of face and form and sweet temperament, not in lands or silver. Hlynn shifted uneasily, hoping that Bothi was wrong.

Chapter
21

Warm green eyes slid to Brander's face, lingering, searching for hidden meaning behind his words. He had just asked, quite simply and straightforwardly, if Morgana would care to accompany him to his father's home for a celebration.

"What kind of celebration?"

"Winter solstice. We feast, play games, and talk, and if the weather holds, we sled to Hedeby." His palm covered one of her hands where her fingers curled into the edge of her bodice. "Have you ever skated on ice, Morgana?"

"No. It rarely snows in Erin." What about Erika? And Gytha? Would they be at Harald's also? She dreaded facing them again, especially in her old, worn gowns that shouted of her low status in Brander's household. Hlynn had urged her to ask for new gowns, or material to make them, but Morgana still hesitated. Her relationship with Brander was so new, so fragile, that she dared not test it for such a trivial matter. Besides, what did it matter what she wore in the privacy of his home? But now...

"You don't seem pleased by the idea, Morgana." Warm

breath, wine-spiced, whispered across her cheek as Brander leaned close. "Don't you want to go?"

" 'Tis not that. . . ." Oh, why were his hands so distracting, brushing at her hair, lingering on the sensitive nape of her neck?

"Then it's settled. We shall be there for a few weeks, so pack enough for both of us."

Morgana was appalled, and wondered how Brander, who was usually thoughtful and considerate, could be so obtuse as not to notice the state of her limited wardrobe. Besides the rough woolen gown borrowed from Hlynn, she had only her outgrown chemise and the gown and cape she'd been wearing when she left Erin. Bright color infused her cheeks when she envisioned the ridicule certain to be directed at her from Erika and Gytha.

But Fate took a kindly hand in the form of Hlynn, who informed Brander in no uncertain terms that to subject Morgana to the derision of others was the cruelest thing imaginable.

"What are you talking about?" He eyed the maidservant with a hard stare. "Who would dare?"

"Gytha and Erika," Hlynn answered promptly even though her insides were quaking with fear. "They would delight in making her appear ridiculous with her rough garments of undyed wool. You may not have noticed, but women put much stock in beautiful clothing."

"Ah," Brander said in the tone of one enlightened to the truth. "I see now why she hesitated." He frowned, then brightened. "Hlynn, in one of the storerooms, I believe you will find several bolts of material. . . ."

In only two days, Hlynn had managed to fashion three beautiful gowns, with the help of Kelda and another slave. Speechless and near tears, Morgana could only stare at the gowns draped over the bed. As if not quite believing they wouldn't disappear, she reached out tentatively, stroking the shimmering folds of a silk gown. Silk, that Byzantine gift of the gods, beautiful to behold and luxurious to wear, sensuous and divine.

"I've never had a new gown, especially one so beautiful," she murmured finally, and Hlynn was rewarded for all her patient hours of sewing in the fickle light of oil lamps.

"And that's not all," Hlynn said, bubbling with excitement as if the gifts were from her instead of Brander. "Look what I found in a trunk in the storeroom, my lady!" She lifted a long cape trimmed around the hood and edges with ermine.

"Oh, but that can't . . . I mean, surely Brander means that for someone else. . . ."

"Nay, my lady. He said 'twas to be yours. I asked." Hlynn wiggled it invitingly. "Come," she coaxed. "Try it on."

It fit perfectly. Morgana felt regal and beautiful, and asked so many times how she looked that Hlynn sent Kelda for an overlarge mirror of polished bronze.

"See for yourself," she said when the mirror was brought and propped against a wall.

Preening and turning, Morgana admitted that she looked entirely different.

"Who would have thought it?" she murmured, more to herself than anyone else. Ah, if only Kyna could see her now! Her old nurse would probably mutter a tart comment about the foolishness of admiring one's reflection, but she would still appreciate the beauty of the cape.

Brander, upon entering his bedchamber, was attacked by a whirlwind of white-caped beauty, kissing him and capering about like a puppy.

"Do you like it?" he asked dryly when she paused for a moment.

"Oh yes, Brander. It's . . . it's beautiful, and see? Hlynn fashioned these for me and they fit perfectly! I don't see how she did it without my knowing. . . ." Morgana's voice trailed away as she thought of long cold nights spent sewing by the feeble light of lamps, and the hundreds of tiny pricks from needles on Hlynn's thumbs and fingers. "I would like for Hlynn to go with us," she said into the soft silence, "to see her brother."

"I have no one else to take charge of the house while we're gone," Brander objected mildly. "Another time, perhaps."

Morgana shook her head, and when she looked into Brander's eyes he recognized obstinate lights.

"She has given much of herself, Brander, so that I would not be shamed. Don't you think I know who must have thought of my lack of garments? Ah, I don't mean to sound unappreciative, but 'tis Hlynn who went without sleep and pricked her fingers—please allow her to go with us!"

A smile crinkled his eyes and pressed his lips into a curve. "Aye, there will be people left to manage for a few weeks I suppose. And tell Hlynn to find herself some suitable garments also. . . ." He cleared his throat then, and pulled a velvet pouch from the folds of his cape. "These are for you."

Curious, and unaccountably shy, Morgana took the pouch he offered. She pulled it open with trembling fingers and gasped. A glittering jumble greeted her eyes; silver bracelets, rings, beads, and brooches sparkled within the depths. A small, bone-handled dagger lay among the gold and silver in the bag, meant for a lady's girdle, more of an eating utensil than a weapon. Morgana stared, remembering her dagger lost upon the floor of the small cave where Brander had hidden.

"For . . . me?"

"They're certainly not for Hlynn," was the gruff answer before the rest of his sentence was muffled by Morgana's mouth against his and was soon forgotten.

It was a strange caravan that set out for Harald's house. Bothi grumbled that they all looked like Arab traders as he loaded the last of the bundles into a cart and handed the reins to Hlynn.

"And there'll be snow afore you get there," he added ominously, tugging his cap more tightly over his head. His glance said that was what they deserved for appearing so ridiculous.

Snow clouds hung heavily in the sky, almost brushing the ground, it seemed to Morgana, and she pulled her cape more tightly against the press of wind and chill. Trska, frisky at the promised exercise, pranced prettily, and Brander's bay snorted his displeasure at being so close. Hlynn was wrapped in so many wolfskins that one could barely see her nose and eyes, and she resembled a round, furry barrel with arms and legs.

"Let's go," Brander said, ignoring Bothi. "We have eleven or twelve miles to travel before we arrive, and I don't want to battle snow."

Frosted ground crunched under horses' hooves and cart wheels, popping and crackling as they moved forward. In the back of the cart in a large wicker basket lined with fur reposed a noisy bundle. It honked, poking its head from under the lid to glare at Hlynn with black, beady eyes, obviously blaming her for its discomfort.

"Hush, you miserable wretch," Hlynn muttered to the goose, "at least you're out of the wind!" She sighed and reflected that if the goose hadn't made such a pest of himself in the barnyard, perhaps he could have been left behind. To have left Smoke behind with Bothi would have been certain disaster, and it had been Hlynn's decision to take him along.

"I don't want to feel responsible for your well-deserved murder, or Morgana's distress," she'd told the goose, and so he'd been tucked, protesting loudly, into the basket.

Gaily colored blankets topped the bundles stowed in the cart behind Hlynn, bright splotches of color against the dull browns and golds of fields and roads. The sturdy, large-boned animal pulling the cart was dun, blending in with its surroundings so well, it seemed to Morgana, that the cart almost rolled of its own accord.

The little caravan of Brander, Morgana and Hlynn wound along the hard, rutted road curving toward Hedeby. North, beyond the town and broad scythe of rampart, was another small settlement. This one was inhabited by Harald and his clan, in a fort upon a man-made hill overlooking harbor and fjord. Not far away a leg of land jutted out into the lip of the Haddeby Nor, separating it from the Schlei fjord, almost blending with gray sky and gray-green water.

It was late afternoon before they arrived at Harald's, having had problems with a wheel of the cart which had caused Brander no end of disgust and was only fixed with much swearing and at the cost of a bloody thumb.

"Bothi should have checked that axle," Hlynn said to no one in particular when she'd gotten back into the cart and it jolted forward again, "instead of making weather predictions about snow. . . ."

As if on cue, fat white flakes began to fall from the sky, thicker and faster until it looked as if a fleecy blanket of wool had been draped over the land. Morgana watched in fascination as trees, bushes, ditches, and roads were changed from ordinary colors to glistening hues of sharp crystal white. It looked, she thought, like a frosted honeycake.

Pinpoints of lamplight guided them the last mile to Harald's, shining from stout wooden walls, spearing gloom and opalescent dusk. Thick doors were thrown back and Brander dismounted, stepping forward to greet the cluster of men in the open doorway. Hearty Danish words filled the air, punctuated by friendly slaps on the back while Morgana and Hlynn waited patiently.

Finally, too cold to sit longer, and clapping mitten-clad hands together to knock away the snow, Morgana attempted to dismount on her own and almost fell from Trska's back. The silk draperies so generously included with the sale of the horse had been abandoned for practicality's sake, but a heavy robe of wool had been thrown over the saddle in their place. It now tangled in Morgana's legs and skirts so that she tumbled forward very ungracefully, sprawling facedown into the snow. Cold-numbed legs and brain were slow to respond to her mental commands, and she was both embarrassed and relieved when male hands hauled her upward, kindly knocking snow away from the hood of her cape so that she could see.

"Hallo, Brander, this must be the clumsy wench Gytha told me about," a voice boomed, and Morgana felt but didn't show a wince of despair. *Harald?*

It was. Her frost-rimmed eyes focused on a huge bear of a man who was—amazingly—wearing only a sleeveless tunic and loose trousers. The resemblance to Brander was undeniable. There were the same dark, straight brows like hawk wings, the same thinly molded nose and deep-set eyes. Harald's jaw was graced with a thick beard liberally sprinkled with gray, but long hair brushing his shoulders showed only a few strands of silver among the pale, shining length. He was grinning, and his eyes crinkled in almost the same way as Brander's did, sunbursts fanning from the corners.

All this was noticed in a fraction of time as she was hauled upward, brushed free of snow, and her rumpled cape straightened. It was probably the most embarrassing way she had ever met anyone in her entire eighteen years, Morgana decided with a shivering sigh. At least the incident in Brander's kitchen had been inspired by a goose and not her inherent clumsiness.

"Welcome," the friendly giant was booming, easing some of Morgana's tension, and she managed a smile through purple lips and chattering teeth. "Come inside before you freeze," he added in oddly accented Celtic. "My son can see to the rest."

Morgana found her left arm tucked firmly in his as Harald led her into the house, which, like most Viking homes, was windowless and built of wooden timbers. Brander's home was stone, but possessed of the added factor of inside insulation in the form of wooden walls built a foot inside the outer stone walls. His father's home was not as airtight, and cold drafts whistled into the main hall with howling frequency. It was also smoky, with only a small hole in the roof as a main outlet for smoke from the blazing fire. Snow and ice just as often filtered through the hole as not, or froze over it, so that the hall constantly remained in a haze of smoke.

Morgana stood in the middle of a room full of people and noise, staring about her. It reminded her of Celtic celebrations, with loud laughter, dripping bowls of mead and wine, and blazing fires. In the middle of the room stood a square fireplace, open so that all could crowd around it, smoke blackening the roof and walls, and sleeping benches lining four sides of the long chamber. How, she wondered, dripping melting snow onto the floor, could anyone possibly sleep in such chaos? It would be impossible.

Harald's heavy arm descended upon her shoulder as he turned her around, speaking in his tongue to his wife. Though Morgana could not understand his words, she definitely understood the haughty expression on Gytha's face, and stiffened. The chief felt the tensing of her slight body even through the thick cape trimmed in ermine, and grew angry.

"I demand that you show hospitality, Gytha! It does not matter how you feel—no one is turned away from my door cold and hungry, especially not a visitor my son has brought. . . ."

"Visitor?" Gytha's brows rose and her chin lifted as she stared down the length of her aquiline nose at Morgana. "This, my wise husband, is no visitor, but your son's convenient . . . ride-under. I am supposed to accept her?"

"Aye." Harald's mouth tightened. "And you will see that she has no cause for complaint. Brander asked my permission before he brought the wench, and it was given."

Some of the din and confusion in the room quieted as those nearest their leader witnessed the confrontation, and Morgana felt many eyes turn toward her. Her cheeks grew hot, and she began to wish she hadn't come, but she would allow no one to see her humiliation. Her small round chin with its tiny cleft lifted just as regally as Gytha's, and against the rosy glow of her wind-reddened face her eyes appeared even larger and greener, glittering like rare jewels.

She shifted slightly away from Harald, and the hood to her cape fell back, releasing a tumble of dark sable curls halfway down her back. Harald was to remember later that Morgana looked like a feral creature bristling with animosity, and primitively beautiful as she rounded on them with harsh Celtic words.

Angrily she declared, "I don't need forced hospitality. I am quite capable of returning . . ."

"Don't be silly, child," Gytha broke in. "I wasn't suggesting that you should return home." Penciled brows rose and her painted mouth curved in a caricature of an indulgent smile. Behind the pleasant façade, Gytha wondered if the chit understood more of their language than she pretended, or if she was—as claimed by that hot-tempered Celtic wench of Gunther's—a witch, a sorceress who could read thoughts.

Morgana's body drew into a tight knot as she gazed at Gytha, sensing the animosity and hatred and even the slightest trace of fear. What was behind Gytha's actions that made her fear Morgana's sight?

She concentrated fiercely, her emerald eyes narrowing on Gytha, trying to penetrate the inexplicable aura; but it was too noisy, too distracting in the room, with everyone watching and muttering, and dogs barking and snarling over scraps of food.

A hand lightly laid upon her arm snapped Morgana back to the present, and her field of vision slowly altered to focus upon Brander and snow-covered Hlynn. The maidservant hung back, still holding the large wicker basket in tiring arms, while Brander gazed searchingly at Morgana.

"Have you insulted her again, Gytha?" He was speaking to his stepmother but still looking at Morgana. "I would not take it well. . . ."

"Nay, Brander. She misunderstood, 'tis all," Gytha answered, and Harald agreed with a slight hesitation.

The tension might have stretched longer if it hadn't been for the goose. Weary of travel and cold and being knocked about in a confining basket, Smoke slithered his long neck from under the top and pecked sharply at the nearest object, which happened to be Harald's arm.

Startled by the vicious jab, and not at all sure where it

had originated, the Viking swung warily toward Hlynn, bristling with anger.

"'Twas not me, my lord," the poor girl half-gasped, slicing Morgana and Brander a pleading glance. "'Twas...the goose!"

"Goose?" the deep voice boomed incredulously, and titters rippled through the crowded hall. "What goose?"

"Morgana's goose," Brander answered, and his lips twitched with amusement. The amusement deepened to belly-rumbling laughter when a muffled *honk* erupted from the basket.

"It's a pet," Morgana offered with only the slightest trace of a smile hovering on her mouth, and Harald nodded, jovially accepting the explanation.

Gytha, standing with her mouth twisted, could say nothing as Brander took his leave and led Morgana and Hlynn from the hall. She stared after them, eyeing the rich ermine-trimmed cape Morgana wore and thinking furiously.

"No tricks," Harald growled softly, startling Gytha into staring at him with guilt in her eyes. He hovered over her. "I know your little games, and I won't have you playing them with my son. Do you understand?"

"Nay, lord, I don't. What do you mean—games?" Gytha's expression subtly altered to innocence and bewilderment.

"I feel no need to explain, wife. You know."

She did know; and her intentions were to continue just as she pleased with all her plans. That Celtic woman would not put a spoke into the smoothly oiled wheels of her scheme.

Someone else stared after Morgana; hidden in a dark corner, watching intently, the Celtic girl who had been captured at Monasterboice felt a wash of hatred. Why had Morgana, the enchantress, been favored over her? Aye, now she was garbed richly with her handsome Viking lover on her arm, while Gwyneth, who had never known aught but the love of her parents, was fondled by a man she didn't love and was a captive sneered at by others. The spark of hatred flared higher, threatening to consume her.

Morgana couldn't remember later just how she got to the small chamber she and Brander were to share; she had only a vague memory of long dark halls filled with intermittent light from oil lamps and smoke. Hlynn had gone to the slave quarters to seek out her brother, taking the bothersome goose with her, and promised to return at first light for Morgana.

"I would not throw you to those wolves alone, my lady," she murmured in Morgana's ear when she bid her good night. " 'Twould be too cruel. . . ."

"Does Hlynn think I would abandon you?" Brander asked when they were in their chamber. He leaned an arm against a tall carved bedpost, watching Morgana.

She fumbled with the carved brooch at the shoulder of her cape, finally releasing the clasp and sliding from under the weight of fur and cloth. It was draped carefully over the high back of a chair to dry, then she turned to Brander.

"Nay," she answered at last. "She only worries that I will feel uncomfortable among those who dislike me." Her slight shoulders lifted in a shrug.

"But you don't?"

Morgana smiled. "Why should I worry about what I cannot change? I shall only worry about what I can. . . ."

"And what can you change, little one? What miracles can you work?" Brander teased, his expression softening as he pushed away from the bedpost to cross to Morgana. Her answer was muffled against the rich velvet of his long tunic, her lips pressed against his chest as he held her close. Clouds of dark hair were still cool from the bite of wind and snow, slipping through his fingers with a silky tumble as he lifted the wisps from her neck, massaging her skin with a gentle, erotic motion.

Worries of time and place ceased to exist for either of them as they lost themselves in the sweet void of sensual exploration, a world of sight, taste, and tactile senses.

The problem was not, Morgana thought hazily, as she burrowed into the wide feather mattress with Brander, a matter of concern.

Chapter
22

Hlynn tapped early on the bedchamber door, rousing Morgana who slipped quietly from the bed without waking Brander.

"I thought you might wish to be up before the others," Hlynn whispered, and Morgana agreed.

"Give me a few moments to get dressed, and I'll meet you in the cooking area, Hlynn."

It took only a short space of time to don one of her new gowns and warm shoes, and she washed her face with a quick splash of water from the pewter bowl beside the huge iron brazier in one corner of the room. Checking her appearance in the small mirror on one wall, Morgana decided that she was presentable and let herself quietly out the door.

Even in daylight the halls were still dim and shadowy, necessitating light from oil lamps. A faint haze hung in the air, smelling of stale smoke, damp garments, and the memories of yesterday's food and wine. Did they ever air out the house? A brief vision of Kyna's small cottage with its door and windows and fresh, clean breezes made Morgana sigh.

She wandered as quietly as possible through the main hall where snoring men graced the long benches on each side of the hearth and sour wine soaked into the rushes. Dogs lapped at spilled food and an occasional face, or curled close to warm bodies and the smoldering fire. Several women lay among the men, faces sagging in sleep and exhaustion, and Morgana felt a pang of pity. It was not an easy life for some of the slaves.

The cooking area was separated from the main house by a small square corridor, and it emanated an entirely different atmosphere than the other. Here, there were fresh delicious smells of bread and vegetables, and the happy chatter of women. The buzz of conversation slowed when Morgana appeared in the doorway.

Hlynn's brown head, noticeable among the many fair ones, bobbed into view as she spied Morgana.

"Come and eat," she urged, tugging Morgana into the middle of the room. The others just stared. This girl was different from them; she was not a slave—that was evident from the gown of soft, dyed wool that clung to her slender frame—nor was she a lady, and they were uneasy.

"She is a free woman," Hlynn clarified for them when they remained silently staring, and some of the tension eased. The chatter resumed after a few desultory glances, and Morgana and Hlynn moved to a far table.

The kitchen area was a place of great interest to Morgana, for she had never seen its like. Even Brander's home did not possess a cooking area of this size, but then, he wasn't the chief and accustomed to housing and feeding great numbers of people.

Cauldrons of iron and soapstone were suspended over the fire from a tripod, and some hung on chains from a solid

roof beam. More clay pots and soapstone bowls were among
the hot embers of the stone-lined hearth, steaming with
substantial meat stews, broths, and porridges. Meat and fish
baked in ovens heated with warm stones; mutton, lamb,
beef, and veal, pigs, goats, and a wild boar roasted on
several spits turned with a long-handled fork.

Unleavened barley bread quickly became hard and inedi-
ble, so that baking bread was a daily chore. Several Viking
women were using the rotary hand querns for grinding the
coarse flour, while some kneaded dough in a wooden trough
and then slapped it onto a long-handled iron plate among the
embers of the open fire to bake.

Milk was set aside for drinking or made into butter and
cheese, with the separated whey being saved for pickling.
Great vats in a small room off the kitchen were used for
storage, and their contents ladled out into buckets for
serving. Since the winter solstice would bring many to
Harald's, beer had been brewed for the festivals and feasts.
Honey was used as the base for sweet, fermented mead;
beer was made from malted barley, and hops added for
flavor. There were also barrels of fruit wines stacked in the
storage area.

Wooden bins contained salted fish, wheat, oats, cress,
wild apples, and hazelnuts, and earthenware jars were filled
with herbs and spices such as cumin, mustard, and horse-
radish. Strings of onion and garlic hung from the beams;
cherries, plums, sloes, elderberries, blackberries, raspber-
ries, and strawberries were clustered in more jars. Few
would go hungry this winter, for it had been a good year for
crops and hunting and commerce.

Sitting on a high stool, Morgana watched as Hlynn deftly
prepared a wooden tray piled high with food "For you or
Brander," she said, laughing. Hot, flat loaves of barley
bread were added, and salted cod and smoked herring

nestled beside thick slabs of cheese and dried apples. Steaming wooden bowls of porridge completed the feast, and it was borne through the kitchen balanced on Hlynn's shoulder.

It would have been a delicious way to break their fast had the tray not been knocked from Hlynn's grasp to splatter upon the stone floor. A hand came from nowhere as she stepped into the hall, unbalancing the tray and Hlynn. She stood, gasping with shock and outrage, staring into the amused eyes of a wild-haired woman she had never seen before.

"Too bad your meal is ruined," a spiteful Celtic voice said into the suddenly still air, and Morgana looked into Gwyneth's narrowed dark eyes and sighed.

"We meet again, I see. Is Gunther still treating you well?"

"What do you care?" Fiery hair was tossed carelessly. "I see your lover is clothing you in fine garments, but it still doesn't hide your black spirit. . . ."

"Enough," Hlynn cut in, angered by Gwyneth's sharp words and spite. "You have the venomous tongue of an adder and would do well to curb it. Since you saw fit to knock the tray from my hands, you may see fit to clean it up. . . ."

"Oh? And who will make me? You?" This last was said with a laugh, a challenge issued in front of witnesses crowded in the doorway with bulging eyes and gaping mouths.

Tension vibrated in the air, thick and tangible, roiling like black smoke to shroud the hallway. It was not, Morgana decided, the sort of scene that was likely to make friends of strangers.

"I'll clean it up," she said into the hostile silence, and bent to do so. No one moved for a moment, then Hlynn bent to help her pick up shards of broken pottery and chipped wooden bowls sticky with porridge. Then another woman stepped forward to help, and another, and muttering a vicious Celtic oath, Gwyneth disappeared from the hall.

"Who was that?" Hlynn asked when they had cleaned up the mess, thanked their helpers, and left the kitchen. "And why does she dislike you?"

With a mystified shrug, Morgana replied, "She was captured from another clan in Erin, and brought on Brander's ship by Gunther. At first she was not treated well—and I thought that was why she disliked me. After all, I was not ill treated." She sighed and continued, "When I tried to talk to her, she rejected me, and her hatred has obviously not lessened at all."

"Could she be jealous, perhaps, because you have Brander?"

"Nay. Gunther treats her well, I believe. There must be another reason for her enmity, Hlynn."

The main hall was stirring with life when they passed through, men yawning and stretching, dogs with tails and tongues curling, and the fire feeding on new logs. It was going to be another long day of feasting and celebrating, Hlynn observed gloomily.

"Don't you like celebrations?"

"When I'm the one celebrating," she answered with a grin. " 'Twill be Vikings celebrating, and Celts and Gaels and Saxons cleaning up after them."

"What of your brother? Is he here?"

"Aye, he's watching after your goose. Rowan is a good-natured soul, but lazy. I promise you he will make such a project out of guarding your goose that none of us will see much of him at all."

"That will surely make Harald even happier with me and

my goose," Morgana murmured. "I feel I am straining the boundaries of his hospitality just by being with Brander."

"Don't believe that." Hlynn halted in the corridor outside Morgana's room. "He will deny his only son nothing, my lady. Oh, he may huff and bluster, but whatever Brander wishes for will be his." She bit her lip, grasping Morgana's hands between her own, and leaned forward. "My lady, I do hope . . ."

Whatever she wanted to say had to wait because the heavy wooden door swung open to frame Brander in the opening.

"Where have you been?" His face was dark with irritation, surprising Morgana and wiping away her smile as she turned to face him.

"Why, you were asleep, and I went to bring you some food. . . ."

He glanced at her empty hands, his mouth curling into a mocking smile.

"So I see."

"Nay," Morgana blurted, growing angry, "you don't see! There was an accident, and the food was spilled . . ."

"You don't appear to be soiled. . . ."

"All over Hlynn," Morgana finished tightly. This was a Brander she had never seen before, tight-lipped with anger that was directed toward her, and she could think of no cause for it. Some sixth sense in the back of her mind warned her that someone had deliberately caused mischief, but she couldn't think of who or how.

"We won't need you for a while," Brander was saying curtly to Hlynn, tugging Morgana inside and closing the door. They stood for a moment in tense silence, facing each other like weasels fighting over the same scrap, taut and angry. A coal hissed and sputtered in the huge brazier, and outside the house the wind blew in long, sighing shrills, curling through wood and chinking. Somewhere a shutter banged, vaguely surprising Morgana as she had supposed there were no windows at all in Harald's house. It registered dimly, for most of her attention was on the tall man standing with arms crossed over his chest, gazing at her as if she were a stranger.

"Someone has said something." It was a flat statement of the kind Morgana was known to make, and it lay in the silence like a hot stone.

"Aye," Brander admitted at last, still looking at her.

"What has been said? It doesn't matter who said it, but I would have the chance to admit or deny. . . ."

"Why did you steal from the room so quietly this morn without waking me? Did you go to meet someone?"

"Ahhh." The one word was rich with understanding. A wry smile tugged at her mouth, and Morgana's chin lifted a trifle higher. "You think I go to meet another man? Would that bother you?"

Harsh, hurting hands clasped around her wrists, reminding her of that first night when Brander had woken and found her bent over him with herbs. His fingers dug painfully into tender skin, bruising it, and she flinched. Immediately, he released her, then demanded, "Answer me!" even when he already knew the answer.

Thor's hammer, Brander swore silently, why did it flay him so badly to think she might be interested in another? When the woman had come to him with such a wild story he had laughed, then her facts had weighed with truth. How could he not believe?

"Nay." Morgana's chin jutted out proudly, and her eyes flashed fury and disbelief. "I refuse to answer such a ridiculous question, even to you, Brander. You dishonor me by asking."

"And you dishonor me by your actions!" He flung her

wrists from him and stalked away, moving to stand beside the coal brazier. It radiated heat he didn't feel, so flushed with anger as he was, and he whirled to face Morgana again.

"Don't say it," she forestalled him, sensing the harsh words on the tip of his tongue. "Wait until you are less angry so that there will be no regrets."

Something in her face made him hesitate. Even when defiant and furious she was vulnerable. There was an inner strength in this Celtic maid that had nothing to do with her powers of insight, and Brander often found himself admiring more than her face and form.

Schooling his unruly tongue, Brander pivoted on one foot and left the room without speaking, softly closing the door behind him. The tiny click of wood sounded as loud as a clap of thunder to Morgana, who watched wide-eyed with amazement.

She still wasn't quite sure what had happened. Their happy, comfortable relationship had shattered in a matter of minutes, and she didn't even know why. Somehow—she wasn't sure how—she was sitting on the edge of the still unmade bed where they had slept only a few hours before, and contemplating their first fight.

Chapter 23

The main hall was crowded with men, women, children, and dogs. A huge log burned merrily in the open hearth, and the sleeping benches lining the room were filled. Delling was there, and Gunther and Gwyneth sat close together at the middle of the long table that was overloaded with meats, peas, onions, cabbage, and breads. Morgana sat at one end of a long table beside Brander, toying idly with her food, looking at no one. Occasionally she would toss a piece of meat to a large black hound who sat on his haunches watching her intently. Animals were always drawn to Morgana.

"Don't you like the venison?" Brander asked after she gave the dog a particularly large chunk of meat. He eyed the dog and her half-empty plate. " 'Tis fresh."

Morgana slid her eyes to his, wondering how he could behave as if nothing had happened. In private, he had been cold and distant, but now, in front of his family and friends, he was being solicitous.

"Do you wear two faces, Brander, that one moment you can talk one way, and the next moment another way?"

Her unflinching gaze made him flush and grind his teeth, and a small muscle in his lean jaw twitched angrily.

"Don't, Morgana."

The two words were short and clipped, but managed to convey his fury quite effectively. Morgana, too hurt and angry to care, ignored the unspoken warning.

"Don't what?—ask the obvious?" She waved a hand at the crowded hall. "You had nothing nice to say to me just a few hours ago; now, in front of your friends, you kindly ask how I like my meal?"

Standing abruptly, Brander's hand curled around her arm and pulled her up with him. The movement, so quick and smacking of repressed violence, gained him the instant attention of his father.

"Are you ill?" the giant voice boomed down the length of the table. "Or do you drink too much wine?" Laughter rippled in the wake of Harald's words.

"Nay," came the answer, quick and hard, "I am not ill." Brander's eyes, icy as winter, fastened on Morgana, and his voice was almost a whisper. "Do you come quietly?"

A scene could only make matters worse and give Gytha and Erika—who smiled like a feline from the opposite end of the table—much satisfaction.

"Of course," Morgana answered, smiling through narrowed eyes, "was there any doubt?"

The long walk to their chamber was made in silence. It was only when the door closed behind them that the quiet was broken.

"Don't try to make a fool of me in front of my friends and family," Brander said. He leaned back against the wall and waited for her response, letting his gaze drift from her partially braided hair to her feet. She was, as always, beautiful. Even in ragged garments she was lovely; but clad in a soft clinging velvet gown that outlined and enhanced every curve, she was stunning. A wide belt of silver links circled her slim waist, and the matching brooches that had been a gift from Brander were pinned at her shoulders.

"A man cannot be made a fool of without his cooperation," Morgana said, dragging his attention from her appearance to the situation.

"No," Brander agreed, "he cannot. And you, my lovely Celt? Can you be made a fool of?" Blue eyes flared with smoky glints as he stepped nearer. Before long Morgana felt his hands curling on her shoulders, pulling her forward into his chest. The contact was light, neither forced nor suggestive, but casual, as if they had not just been fighting. Blunt fingers searched blindly in her hair, found and bared the tender nape of her neck and one ear, and she could feel his warm breath.

"Ah, Morgana," he said into the heavy silence, "I find I cannot remain angry with you though I know I should. Why is that, I wonder?"

This last more to himself than her, but Morgana took the liberty of answering.

"Because you know I haven't done anything," she said into his velvet tunic, feeling her trapped breath curl upward over her lips and nose.

With a wry chuckle, he said, "I don't possess your intuition and insight, child, so don't suppose I know anything."

Light-headed just from his proximity and the feel of his hands on her, Morgana nodded. A cupped palm lifted her chin so that she stared into his eyes, seeing the gentle humor there.

"I still don't know what the disagreement was about," she said, "and it was our first fight so I'd like to—so it won't happen again. . . ."

"Someone—I won't say who—told me that you were seen with a man this morning, cuddled in a very . . . loving . . . posture in a shadowed alcove. I am ashamed to say that I did not stop to ask many questions, but I believed the story."

"Without asking me?" Outrage colored her words with wrath. "How could you?"

"Morgana," he said as he took her hands between his, holding her still, "I have no excuse. It won't happen again."

"And if that person comes with other words to turn you away from me, what then?"

Brander caressed her hair away from her face, pushing the silky tendrils back and letting them slide through his fingers. Inky, even against his tanned skin, the curls tumbled carelessly into his cupped palm like a sable pool, and he lifted his hand to his mouth, tasting, breathing in the soft, sweet fragrance.

"I won't listen," he said into the swirl of dark hair, and then, " 'Twas only my jealousy that made me listen. Shall we flay the beast?"

"Aye," Morgana said, her voice thick with relief and laughter. "Jealousy is a beast, indeed."

She felt Brander's tense muscles ease as he held her close, but dark shadows swirled behind him, curling into even darker corners of the room and seeming to chase away the light. This was not the end of it.

Two nights passed before another incident occurred. During that time Morgana was able to brace herself for the worst. She still wasn't sure, still didn't know who had lied to Brander, and the shadows were so vague and unreadable.

Hlynn saw to it that Morgana was well occupied while the men went hunting to replenish fast-dwindling food supplies,

taking her one morning to the small room just off the
kitchen area where the weaving was done. In the cold days
of winter, the chamber was filled with women, free and
slave, who helped with the looms and carding. Spinning and
weaving were year-round tasks, both to clothe families and
to produce cloth for other essential purposes, such as sails
for the longships.

Morgana was fascinated. She'd never seen looms like
these, since most of the garments Kyna had fashioned were
hand-me-downs from other clan members. Hlynn explained
the various objects and their functions. There was a special
comb with long iron teeth that was used to card the roughly
cleaned wool, then attached to a distaff, a wooden stick held
in the left hand or the crook of the arm. Fibers teased from
it were fastened to a spindle, and weighted at the bottom
with a spindle-whorl of clay or stone. When the spindle was
set turning and dropped to the ground, it slowly drew out
the wool into a thread. This was wound into a ball or a
skein, if it was intended for dyeing. Skeins were made with
the aid of a reel—a handle with a curved bat at either
end—onto which the wool was wound crosswise from
corner to corner. The finished wool was woven on a warp-
weighted loom, which was an upright structure leaning
against one wall. There were other tools, such as a weaving
batten of whalebone, and small, pointed pin-beaters of
wood used to make detailed adjustments to the threads.

"Do you think I could learn?" Morgana asked Hlynn,
reaching out to stroke the smooth oak of the massive frame.
"Then I could fashion my own garments, perhaps."

"I could easily teach you. . . ." Hlynn began when another voice cut in.

"Ladies," the voice said, stressing the word, "only do
tablet-weaving of ornamental braid, or embroidery. Slaves
weave common cloth."

Morgana turned with a sigh to face Erika, the meeting inevitable.

"Good morn to you," she said, then waved a hand toward the loom. "I would like to learn all aspects, as I have never seen it done before."

"What did you wear in Hibernia—oak leaves?" Erika's haughty tone rasped in the air, catching the attention of all those near enough to hear. Heads turned and eyes grew large as the Viking woman stepped close to Morgana, hands on her hips and eyes flashing spitefully.

"Nay," Morgana managed to answer calmly enough, "we wear the same materials as you: woolens from our sheep, silks from Byzantium, linen from flax, and of course, velvet and furs."

"Ah yes, furs," Erika broke in. "Like the ermine cape you wear? 'Tis beautiful, obviously not fashioned in a barbaric country like Hibernia."

Fully aware of their rapt audience, Morgana spoke softly, "You are right. It was a gift."

"A gift?" Erika's shoulders stiffened, and her blue eyes sharpened on Morgana's small face. "From Brander?"

Morgana hesitated. She had no desire for a scene, and to answer honestly would certainly bring one about. As it happened, an answer from her was unnecessary.

"Aye," Hlynn blurted, "the cape was a gift from Brander, and the beautiful gowns she wears, and the jewelry also. . . . He likes to give her such things."

"Does he?" Erika's tone was venomous, her smile brittle. The sharpness of her Nordic features was accented by a frigid expression of hatred. Her entire body vibrated with hostility until it actually seemed to Morgana to quiver, finally erupting into action as Erika took a quick step forward, one hand lifted to strike Hlynn.

Watching and waiting, Morgana wedged herself between them so swiftly that Erika recoiled in surprise.

"Nay, you shall not harm Hlynn for speaking her mind," she said.

"She is a slave," Erika shot back, "and will do what she is told when she is told! *You* are in no position to dictate orders!"

"Neither are you—not to a slave who does not belong to you." Morgana stood her ground, gazing into Erika's angry blue eyes.

For a moment all watching held their breath, certain that Erika was about to strike the impudent Celt and start a furious row, but it seemed that Erika entertained second thoughts. A harsh curse hissed into the still air, then she pivoted on her heel and stalked regally from the room, ivory braids flapping against her back with each step.

"What does Brander see in that slut?" Erika raged, pacing her mother's bedchamber floor in quick, angry steps. Pausing, she flung herself onto a highbacked chair to pout like a petulant child.

"She's convenient," was the prompt answer. Gytha lifted a silver bowl filled with wine, narrowing her eyes and staring at a bronze brazier glowing with hot embers. "Perhaps we should arrange that she isn't quite so . . . convenient . . . after all."

Erika gazed at her mother hopefully. "I want him," she said, "and I don't care how I get him. But that ragged little Celt shall *not* have him!"

"She won't," Gytha soothed. "Now straighten your gown where it's wrinkled and comb your hair. You must look perfect, Erika. I wasn't expecting Brander to bring the little wretch with him to the celebrations, but since he has, maybe it's the best thing." She leaned forward to stare into her daughter's eyes. "There are . . . things . . . that can happen to discourage both of them. Do you understand what I mean?"

"Aye," Erika answered with a sly smile. "I *do* understand."

Fatigued from hours of hunting for fresh game in snow and ice and wind, Brander eased himself inside the door of his bedchamber. He leaned back against the solid wood for support, eyes widening as he noted a huge wooden tub standing in the middle of the room.

"A bath?" he murmured hopefully, searching for and finding Morgana waiting in the shadows against one wall.

"Aye, 'tis the best cure for cold and aches." She stepped into the light, smiling, dark hair tumbling forward over her shoulders and breasts like a silk mantle. Her skirts swished softly against the floor, rippling with every movement as she knelt in front of him and began untying his leather leggings.

Brander laid an affectionate hand upon her head, enjoying the soft feel of her hair beneath his fingers.

"You take good care of me," he said, eyeing the steaming bath and a well-laden tray of food with appreciation. He lifted his arms, allowing Morgana to unbuckle his heavy sword belt and remove it, then pull off his stained and dirty tunic. Leather boots and warm wool trousers were added to the growing pile of wet clothes, until Brander was stripped and stepping into the huge tub.

Lowering his lean body into the hot water, he lay back with a sigh, closing his eyes and resting his tawny head on the high side. Picking up his garments, Morgana smiled over one shoulder at him, her eyes alight with warmth and mischief.

"I've not had much experience with taking care of anyone but animals," she said, flinging his snow-stained cape over one arm, "and I find that I rather enjoy this."

"Do you?" One eye opened to gaze at her. "There *is* a lot of difference between a man and an animal."

"Not as much as you'd think. Both require food, drink, shelter, and . . . love." She smiled obliquely. "Do you see that hound in the corner?"

For the first time, Brander took note of the huge black dog sitting in a corner of the room. The light from oil lamps and coal brazier flickered over his ebony coat, highlighting the white fur on his chest and tipping his massive paws as the dog met Brander's surprised stare with a calm, regal gaze then stepped forward to sit at Morgana's feet.

"Aye," he answered at last, flicking Morgana a puzzled glance, "I see the dog. 'Tis the animal you were feeding at the table not long ago. What is he doing here?"

"He had food, water, and shelter, but he was still hungry for something else." She laid her hand upon the hound's head, and he opened his mouth, baring wicked fangs and a pink, drooling tongue.

Alarmed, Brander half-rose from the tub, dripping water in a shower as he stuck one leg over the side. The dog's head swung in his direction and the thick fur on the back of his neck bristled.

"Morgana . . . !"

"The dog will not harm me, Brander, but I can't speak for you. Please, be still while I talk to him. He isn't used to you. . . ."

"Isn't used to me! That dog was whelped by my favorite bitch two years ago. He's the barn dog. . . ."

"He doesn't know you, and he knows me." Morgana's calm, matter-of-fact tone finally penetrated Brander's objections, and he sank back into the tub, glowering at both of them.

"First, a demented goose, now a hound that threatens to savage me in my own bedchamber," he grumbled loudly, sloshing water over the sides of the tub. "Your strange affinity with animals is unnerving, Morgana."

"I apologize," she said most unapologetically, still stroking the hound's head. Burying her face in the thick fur around his neck, Morgana smiled. The dog had come back with her from the main hall, tail wagging and eyes pleading, and she sensed his loneliness. Hadn't she felt the same way many, many times before? Even amidst a hall crowded with people and dogs, amidst laughter, song, and dance, one could still be lonely for that special attention and affection. Perhaps Brander, who had grown up around dozens of family members and friends, couldn't understand that empty, bereft feeling.

Morgana gave the dog a final pat on his great head and rose to fetch Brander a towel. He was still watching her from the tub, eyes narrowed against the light of a lamp that glowed over his body with gold and crimson hues, when she brought him the towel.

"My thanks," he murmured, and reached for it. Brander's big hands grabbed not only a fistful of towel but Morgana's fine-boned wrist, yanking sharply so that she tumbled into the tub with a loud splash. A geyser of water spewed into the air then settled around them in a heavy mist. Bath water dripped from Morgana's hair and thick eyelashes, clinging like crystal drops from her nose and squared, angry chin. She glared at Brander.

"You have ruined my gown," she stated icily, "and 'tis not as if I have that many."

"I can buy you a dozen if you want." Brander's wet face pressed close to hers, brow to brow. "I was lonesome for you, and you were so far away. . . ."

His words, mirroring her own thoughts, startled Morgana so that she began to smile in spite of her irritation.

"You're impossible. . . ."

"Aye, and hungry. . . ." His mouth nibbled at her earlobe, cheek, and the velvet hollow at the base of her throat.

"Brander," Morgana said with a breathy little moan, "what are you about?"

He had pushed away the clinging, wet material of her gown, baring one shoulder, and was fumbling with her bronze brooch, unpinning it to let it fall into the water.

"This," he said against the ripe swell of her breast, moving lower, "and this. . . ."

Morgana arched closer, trembling as he teased her with lips and tongue, until nothing mattered but Brander. In spite of the rapidly cooling bath water, she was flaming hotter and hotter, until it seemed as if the water should steam and sizzle. Somehow wet garments were peeled away like the layers of an onion, joining puddles of water upon the stone floor.

In a far corner sat the barn dog, watching with cocked ears and tilted head at the two playing in the water like children. He didn't recall the man that well, but the woman had fed him and, more important, had talked kindly and affectionately. The dog's sense of loyalty was concentrated on Morgana, and he watched over her with anxious brown eyes, hackles rising when she squealed.

"Stop it, Brander!" Morgana splashed him with water, laughing at the face he made. "You almost got soap in . . ."

"Morgana—the dog." Brander's voice was tense, catching her attention. "Call him off." He sat rigid and still, not quite daring to move, staring past Morgana.

Turning, Morgana saw that the great dog had moved to the edge of the tub, his eyes fixed on Brander, hackles raised and teeth bared.

"It's all right, dog," she said softly, "go sit down. Sit, dog. . . ."

The dog sat, but his eyes were still fastened on the arm Brander had around Morgana.

"What is his name?" she asked.

Brander's shoulders lifted slightly in a shrug. "He's just always been called the barn dog."

"Barn Dog," Morgana said again, *"Go lie down!"*

The hound understood and trotted back to the corner near the brazier and curled up in a ball, the tip of his tail touching his black nose.

Brander breathed easier, relaxing and shaking his head. "I'm worried," he complained, "that when I touch you, I'll be attacked by an angry goose, a surly dog, or even a raging chicken. You've become a dangerous quest, Morgana."

"Dare you attempt it then?" she murmured against his ear, the tip of her tongue flicking in light movements. She wriggled upward, breasts rubbing against his chest, her hips in the angle of his thighs.

"Aye," he rasped, "just try and stop me!"

Chapter 24

Nights were long, and what daylight there was left to the land was gray-white with snow and clouds. Naked tree branches thrust their arms into the churning sky and moaned in wistful agony as a powerful north wind swept across Jutland. Paths from house to barn to byre were covered with a drifting sea of snow that was waist-high in places. Bear, wolf, fox, and other furs covered warm garments for further protection, and the main hall reeked of freshly killed game. Thick smoke choked corridors and chambers until Morgana longed for fresh, clean air.

"Please," she asked Brander again, "can't we go outside for a time?" They sat in chairs before the fire in the main hall, only half-listening to a saga related by Harald's favorite skald. Morgana's feet were propped on the same stool as Brander's, and the hound sat at her side, his tail occasionally wagging and brushing rushes strewn over the floor. "This hall is so smoky and stifling...."

"When it grows a bit warmer, I will take you riding," he relented. "Until then, just try to enjoy the festivities."

That was difficult to do, Morgana reflected silently, when Gytha or Erika did everything in their power to make them joyless for her. Barbed comments or sly innuendos followed her whenever Brander was not present, so that she felt ready to explode with suppressed anger and resentment.

Little things had been done to aggravate Morgana. She had found a hare's foot in the bottom of her wine cup, she had listened to the mistaken suggestion that the roast goose she was eating was the one she had brought with her, and—the worst so far—she had discovered that her ermine cape was missing.

"I'm certain I haven't seen it," Erika chimed in when Morgana once more searched the hall for the cape. The tone of her voice, spiteful and malignant, gloating, captured Morgana's attention immediately.

"Then perhaps you know someone who has, Erika." Morgana faced the blond Viking woman with raised brows.

"You probably sold it," Erika said rudely, "and want to place the blame elsewhere."

"And who would I have sold it to? Everyone here knows Brander and knows of me. Who would purchase such a well-known item?"

"Then perhaps you burned it. I don't know! It's your problem, little Celt, not mine."

For several moments Morgana stared at Erika. There were times when she was besieged with the weight of others' enmity; Gytha, Erika, and Gwyneth all seemed to hate her for no fault of her own, and she longed for peace.

"Nay," Morgana answered at last, " 'tis not just my problem, Erika. This house is large, but still not large enough to hold strife among its occupants. I would have peace. . . ."

"There will be peace," Erika cut in, "when you are gone! And not until then!" Whirling, she left the hall.

Morgana had not spoken to her since that time four days before, and did not look forward to their next conflict. She sighed, wishing Brander understood the urgency behind her request for fresh air. Accustomed to the freedom of wood and field and wild sea winds, the confines of the house were stifling. Dropping her hand, Morgana idly stroked the barn dog's head, toying with his drooping ears.

Seeing her dejection, Brander had a thought. He reached out to caress a silky curl where it lay upon her shoulder.

"Would you like to learn to skate, Morgana?"

"Skate?" She thought of those she had seen, skimming over ice on wings of leather and bone, and nodded. "Aye, it would be fun, I think."

Within a short length of time, she was wrapped in furs and accompanying Brander down the hill gently sloping away from the house. Not far away was a small pond for cattle and horses, and Brander stopped at its edge. They were knee-deep in snow, crusting in white lace edges over their feet and legs. Morgana's breath was frosty clouds in front of her face, and her nose was already pink from the bite of the wind and frigid air. Gray clouds hung low, speared on the tops of tall trees like banners.

"Cold?" Brander asked cheerfully, grinning at the sight of her eyes and nose peeping from generous swaths of wool.

The furry bundle that was Morgana nodded. "I'm not sure I can do this," came a muffled voice accompanied by frosty clouds. "I can barely move. . . ."

"Sure you can. It's like flying." Brander pushed her gently to a seat on a log and knelt to fasten on her feet the skates he held. A leather boot was attached to a long animal bone, and when Morgana tried to stand she found herself wobbling like an infant taking first steps. "Here," Brander said, thrusting long poles in her hands, "use these."

Finally, with the aid of the poles and Brander's arm,

Morgana was able to slide a few feet across the frozen pond. Elated, she turned to flash him a triumphant grin and slipped, arms flailing and poles tumbling several feet away as her feet flew from beneath her. She landed in a disgruntled heap of furs, wool, and flying snow.

"You could have caught me," she accused hotly, eyeing Brander's mirth with narrowed gaze.

"And been skewered by a pole for my pains?" he managed to answer between rumbles of laughter. "Not likely. And the snow is soft."

It was, and realizing what a sight she must have made with her arms spinning like a windmill, Morgana reluctantly joined his laughter. He helped her up, and Morgana soon found herself skimming like a snowbird across the ice. Brander, of course, could skate excellently, even without the poles used to propel him forward. Morgana envied his grace, and promised herself that she would practice until she was as good as her teacher.

They stayed on the ice until Morgana was too cold to stay longer, then made their way back to the house, laughing and tumbling in the snow, throwing snowballs at each other like children. The hall, as usual, was crowded when they burst through the doors in a shower of snow and laughter, causing heads to turn, some smiling indulgently but a few, like Thorfinn, Gytha, and Erika, staring with scowls.

"So," Harald boomed from a comfortable seat near the fire, "my son sports in the weather like a seal, then stands dripping snow in my hall! Close the door, Brander, lest we all freeze."

The door was duly closed, then Brander and Morgana came to stand before the open hearth, pulling off gloves and capes, head coverings and leggings.

"Did you teach the maid to skate?" Harald asked, noting the skates Brander slung to the floor.

"Aye, and she did well. Of course, the ice on the pond is now cracked from so many falls, but 'twill freeze again soon." Brander grinned at Morgana's indignant sniff.

"I am not clumsy," she said, "just inexperienced."

"Only at skating," he teased in return, and was rewarded with a fiery blush.

Harald's laughter rumbled loudly, but Morgana noticed that Gytha and Erika were stiffly furious, so it was no surprise when Gytha spoke up.

"Ah," she said, "men must have their sport, I suppose, before turning to more serious matters. 'Tis the way of it for a virile young man like Brander. Soon he will settle down and put away his well-worn toys."

Brander frowned, sensing Gytha's not-so-subtle message behind her honeyed words.

"What are you trying to say?" he bluntly asked his stepmother. "Are you questioning my choice?"

"Nay, Brander." Gytha managed to look hurt. "I was only commending the wisdom you have shown in choosing the Celtic girl instead of one of ours for your play."

"Play?" Brander's dark brows rose. "Sport? I care not for your usage of words, mistress. Morgana is a woman, and one I cherish. It would do you well to remember that in the future."

"Of course. I never doubted that you cherished her, only the reasons." Sensing Brander's fury, Gytha rose from her chair beside Harald before Brander could speak, her voice brittle and cold. "I am not a woman to insult, Brander, with this little scene. If you wish to speak with me, I will be in your father's chambers."

Brander stared at Gytha's retreating back, furious and knowing it would offend his father to affront Gytha. Harald remained silent, taking neither side, just listening with a frown.

At the jarl's side, Thorfinn sat with clenched hands and simmering anger. He coveted the Celtic maid and begrudged Brander his free use of her. Long hours were spent watching her, thinking of her, wanting her, and he often plotted means of taking Morgana from the Viking leader.

"Perhaps the girl should be given to another," he suggested in an undertone, certain of Harald's ear, "since she is a bone of contention between the women here."

Harald waved an impatient hand. This had to stop. The conflict between Erika and this small Celt had to be ended. He decided to take matters in his own hands to bring peace to his household. If Brander took a clan woman as wife, then he could keep Morgana as mistress, as she should be, and father legal sons for the clan upon his wife. Any children from Morgana could share, of course, but there would no longer be this constant rivalry and tension. The matter would be settled. Harald's big hands clenched as he pondered exactly how to go about it with the least resistance from all. Perhaps, in this, he should ask Gytha's advice. . . .

Once more, eyes were turned curiously to Morgana, and she found herself the cause of continued discord. She stood beside Brander like a statue, waiting with head held proudly high. None would see her bow or cower, or know that she felt shame at being considered Brander's whore and not his love. But, at the very center of her hurt was the burning question she longed to ask Brander—did he love her? He'd never said, never hinted that he did, yet he treated her with kindness and consideration; and at night, lying in their bed, he made love to her with tender passion. Could he do that and not love her?

A cold, wet nose in the palm of one hand pulled Morgana from her thoughts, bringing her attention to the huge hound at her feet. He wagged tail and body, staring up at her with liquid brown eyes full of sympathy.

"The hound likes you," Harald commented into the heavy silence. Harald's eyes—so like Brander's—gazed at her as if assessing her worthiness. "He likes no one else," he added, "not even the one who feeds him. 'Tis an ill-tempered beast at best."

"I find him most courteous."

"Courteous?" Harald's brows rose. "That's an odd comment to make about a dog."

Morgana slid a wary glance toward Erika, who listened intently to the conversation.

"Aye," Morgana agreed, noting how Erika stepped forward to stand behind Brander, "it is an odd comment, but true. The dog waits patiently and never interrupts a conversation or a meal. When I feed him a tidbit, he wags his tail in appreciation, and when I give him a kind word, he returns my affection twofold. He is intelligent and loyal, and wears only one face. . . ."

"Assuming you mean there are those who wear two?" Erika cut in, unable to remain quiet any longer. "I can imagine who you would name. . . ."

"Enough!" Harald's patience snapped, and he glared at Erika. "Your imagination would interest us all, I am certain, Erika, but I can no longer abide discord and strife in my usually peaceful hall."

Morgana had the brief thought that Harald's noisy, crowded hall was anything but peaceful with its long benches weighted with Vikings, and snarling, yapping dogs fighting for scraps under tables.

"As you wish," Erika was saying stiffly to Harald, and her eyes burned with malice when she glanced at Morgana. "I only wish peace also, not like *some* who promote anger in secrecy instead of openly."

Her inference was lost on no one, yet Morgana was not

inclined to defend herself. It would do little good and only make matters worse.

Later, in her room with the barn dog curled at her feet, Morgana listened as Hlynn raged.

"Those two vipers should be left in a snowbank! Every word they say casts aspersions on you, Morgana, yet you say little in return. Don't you care what others think?—that they view you as a sneaky, sly woman out to coerce Brander into wedding you?"

"Hlynn," Morgana said, "of course it bothers me. What am I to do? Even if I defend myself, would anyone believe me? I am not one of you. I am Celtic and a stranger to these lands. . . ."

"What of Delling? He is your friend, and Disa, too. Can they not stop this?"

Hlynn stood with fists planted on her hips, glaring so fiercely that Morgana was reminded of a small badger facing tormenting hounds with defiance.

"It will stop on its own, Hlynn. All will come about in time. . . ."

"Oh!" Hlynn's foot stomped upon the hearth, and the dog raised his head to gaze in her direction. More cautiously and quietly, she continued, "Oh, I just get so angry when I think on it, Morgana, and it seems as if no one—not even Brander—comes to your defense."

"I have you, and the barn dog and my goose," Morgana reminded her with a teasing smile. "As for Brander, sometimes I wonder what he thinks. He has not come to me with any more lies to question, but neither does he seem as close." Morgana gazed at the glowing brazier on the small stone hearth, not really seeing it, just conscious of its warmth. Her relationship with Brander had subtly altered since coming to his father's house, becoming more distant, as if she stood several feet away from his warmth as she stood from the brazier. There were nuances in this house that were disturbing, affecting all the inhabitants like a cloud of dark smoke.

A chill breeze swept across the room, ruffling Morgana's hair and the hem of her skirt. Hlynn looked up, puzzled, and in the corner the barn dog lifted his great head and howled, an eerie sound that echoed through the stone and timber house like the *bean sidhe* that roamed Celtic crags and loughs, wailing outside stone walls to foretell a death. Morgana shivered.

Gytha heard the wind, too, and stepped closer to the brass brazier in her well-appointed chamber.

" 'Tis well," she said to Harald, "that you have sought my advice, husband. Men are not familiar with the ways of women and their doings, and become easily annoyed with these kinds of matters."

"Aye," Harald agreed, "but I need more specific advice, wife. Just to say that Brander should not be with the Celtic maid is not enough. We can all see that she is the cause of conflict in the household. . . ."

"But it needs to be handled carefully, or you will push him into making a hasty decision. Your son is strong-willed and stubborn. . . ."

"He comes by that honestly. . . ."

" 'Tis not a thing you need to tell me," Gytha pointed out. "I am too familiar with your moods. Now listen. I have a plan." She paused for a moment. How much did she dare tell Harald? This would require much delicacy on her part, for she could not risk telling him too much or too little.

"I think you should give Brander a bride from our clan," she proposed, "one who is young and will give him strong sons. . . ."

"Like who? Most are already wed or promised, and I cannot see Brander with a girl who squints or giggles. . . ."

"Erika."

Harald stared at his wife as if she had two heads. "Erika?" he finally echoed. "Your daughter? But that . . ."

"Is perfectly normal. Erika is no blood kin to Brander or you, and as my daughter she is well acquainted with how the mistress of a clan should behave. Do you think my daughter homely? Does she squint or giggle?"

"No . . ." was drawn out reluctantly. "Yet . . ."

"Yet it would insure that your line be carried on in high tradition, and that no foreign blood be infused with good Danish blood."

"Do you forget that my first wife, Brander's mother, was Celtic?" Harald's brow rose. "Do you suggest that she was inferior?"

"Nay," Gytha was quick to answer, "but you were fortunate to have found such a woman. Can you say with certainty that this Celtic girl is like Bevin? Remember what is said about this girl, and how she—thank the gods— betrayed her own people for your son. Would she be disloyal to Brander eventually?"

Harald frowned. He had wavered uncertainly about Morgana, liking the girl in spite of himself, but Gytha's observations were dismayingly accurate. Perhaps Brander could keep the girl on the side, but he should definitely be wed as soon as possible, and Erika seemed the most logical choice.

"You are right, wife," he said finally, not seeing the flash of triumph in Gytha's eyes. "I will talk to Brander immediately. . . ."

"Oh no, that you can't do! It must be an accomplished fact before he realizes it, or he will object." Gytha went to kneel before Harald, gazing up at him intently. "He is smitten, can't you see? And if you could manage to betroth him first, then it will not be so easy for him to go against your wishes in front of the entire clan. Especially if there are two clans involved, mine and yours. Don't you agree?''

"It smacks of duplicity," Harald half-growled, "and I mislike tricking my own son."

"Even to save him from unhappiness?" Gytha rose to her feet and stared down at Harald with a curling lip. "Let him keep the girl for a time, but when his firstborn son is laid in the cradle, he will forget her. And there will be many sons, fine and strong, because Erika is a healthy girl, unlike that small, delicate Celt who will probably die giving birth. Isn't that how Bevin died?"

The cruel reminder brought Harald's head up sharply. Aye, his wife had died giving birth to Brander, the babe was so large and she so small and fragile. . . . His eyes misted over with sudden tears that made Gytha's face sharpen. Harald didn't notice her expression. He was thinking of his lost wife, his lost love, and how the years had passed since her death; long, lonely years filled with memories . . . until at last he had taken another wife, a woman he did not love. Would he subject his son to such pain? Nay, he could not. It would be for Brander's own good if he chose a strong Viking girl who could give birth easily.

"Aye," he said. "Brander will be sent away for a while, and when he returns . . ."

Gytha smiled.

Chapter 25

The women sipped wine brought from the Rhineland, their small silver cups glittering in the smoky light from oil lamps. Disa, Delling's wife, motioned for Morgana to join her as she reclined in a carved chair near the fire with her needlework, but Morgana shook her head. Her thoughts were too dark for idle chatter.

Only that morning, news had spread through the main hall like wildfire, telling of a wedding. It was said that Brander would at last marry Erika at his father's insistence. Morgana swallowed the thick lump in her throat, wondering how she had not known. She should have, for the *bean sidhe* always foretold disaster, but she hadn't. There were no more visions in fire or smoke, no dreams that forewarned of disaster, and she wondered if the visions were suppressed because she was so far from her homeland and the sacred protection of the trees.

How could Brander do such a thing without telling her? Only a few nights before, they had slept together, cuddled in his wide bed, burrowing into the covers like field mice while the wind whistled around doors and cracks with all the fierce rage of winter. Now she found herself moved from their chamber into a much smaller one at the very back of the sprawling house, behind the kitchens.

"At Brander's request," Harald had said, unable to look at her. How could he? she asked herself again, wishing she could ask Brander. But he had been gone for three days, sent by Harald to investigate a disturbance several miles away, taking warriors with him.

A burst of laughter from the end of the long table dragged Morgana's unwilling attention to the remaining men. Delling was not among them, nor Gunther; but Thorfinn, whom she remembered from the voyage, sat regaling the others with exaggerated tales of valor and honor in Hibernia.

Even the name for my country is different and ugly here, Morgana thought. Erin was lyrical, beautiful, like its name, and the ancient name of Eire invoked visions of green hills and majestic crags. Hibernia sounded harsh and brutal, but what could one expect of Vikings?

No one seemed to pay any notice when Morgana slipped her heavy cloak from its peg and edged out the door into the cooking hall, and she breathed a sigh of relief. A deep breath of crisp fresh air should clear her thoughts.

Her booted feet made a dry, scrunching sound on crusty snow covering the path, and the dog frolicked beside Morgana like a frisky puppy. Growling in mock fury, he gripped the edge of her cloak with his teeth and tugged, making her laugh at his antics.

"Silly barn dog,'" she scolded indulgently, "you are the most lovable creature I've encountered in this harsh land!"

"It's refreshing to learn there's something here you like," a cold voice said from behind her, and Morgana whirled with a gasp to face Thorfinn.

"You followed me," she accused breathlessly, the rapid thumping of her heart pulsing like a tidal wave.

"Aye. What of it? In spite of everything, you are still a captive, Morgana." He stared at her with a cynical expression curling his mouth, hot and boldly, as if he knew what she looked like without her garments.

Thorfinn's thumbs hooked in the sword belt circling his lean waist, his fur-trimmed cape flapping slightly in the cold wind. One hand moved to stroke the side of her face in a light caress, and Morgana resisted, flinching her head away. His mood was dark and unpredictable, and she gazed at him warily. *What does he want?* she wondered uneasily, gauging the distance back to the house.

An answer was swiftly given as Thorfinn's arm moved to circle her slim waist, bringing her hard against his taut body. Their breath formed frosty clouds in front of their faces as they stood in a silent struggle, Morgana's hands trapped between them. She quivered inside, hating him, glaring into his dark blue eyes.

The entire world of pristine white was silent and still, as if waiting. It was dark yet light, the glow from torches on outside walls of the house only a faint shimmer in the distance, and the land around them glistened with crystal clarity. Morgana was more aware of her surroundings and the man who held her than she had ever been aware of anything in her entire life. Every sense seemed sharpened, and she was surprised to find that she'd been holding her breath.

Exhaling slowly, Morgana let her tensed muscles relax as she leaned away from Thorfinn's embrace.

"Release me," she said, "and I won't tell Brander about this. . . ."

Thorfinn's laughter echoed hollowly in the night. "Do you think I care if you tell him? He is to be wed, remember? What will he care if I take his leavings. In our world, a Viking is entitled to taste the pleasures of a woman if the host is willing. And Harald has not said me nay. . . ." His mouth hovered over hers, hot and encroaching upon her lips with feverish intensity until Morgana thought she would choke.

Her strangled cry alerted the barn dog, who had been watching intently, and he lunged forward, bared fangs sinking into Thorfinn's leg.

Howling with pain, the Viking immediately released Morgana and stumbled backward, clutching at his leg and swinging wildly at the dog. A menacing growl warned Thorfinn that his throat might be the next target, and he halted, half-crouching in the snow, watching as drops of bright crimson blood stained scuffled drifts.

"You will pay for this," he panted, "and your beast too! Harald does not tolerate . . ."

"Raping of guests in his home," came an unexpected voice, and both heads whirled to see the slight figure a few feet away.

"Hlynn!" Morgana moved joyfully toward her, disheveled and pale, trembling with relief and reaction.

"Are you all right, my lady?" she asked anxiously. "I saw what happened when I stepped outside to dump a pail of water, and got here as quickly as I could."

"Aye, I'm fine, in spite of all that's happened today." Morgana glared at Thorfinn in defiance.

"Loki take it, woman, you shall pay for this!" Thorfinn exploded. "I saw you watching us that day in Hibernia, standing at the edge of the battlefield, and I wanted you then. But 'twas Brander who got you before I could find you. . . . 'Tis my turn now. And I want you badly enough to defy Brander and Harald to have you!"

Shaking her head, Morgana murmured, "Nay, Viking. I

would not have you even if I didn't know Brander." Her voice broke then, and she swirled and stumbled back to the house, the dog and Hlynn close behind.

After slipping in the back way and hanging up her cloak, Morgana retreated to her chambers with the barn dog. It was only a short time until a light tap sounded on the door, and she opened it to find Disa asking admittance.

"I know 'tis late," the buxom blonde apologized as she entered, "but I had hoped to have a word with you, child."

"Of course." Morgana stepped aside as Disa swept in with a faint rustling of her silk-embroidered gown. She knew what was on Disa's mind, that Hlynn had gone straight to Delling's wife with the tale, and as the door swung softly shut she asked, "Does anyone else know what happened? It may cause talk if they do."

Disa smiled, turning to warm her hands by the fire. Nothing was said for a moment, then she quickly gave the silent Celtic girl an appraising glance. It was unnerving at times, how Morgana sensed things.

"Nay, child, none know. All are still before the fire. You are probably more aware of my words than any." A dark brow arched questioningly. "Do you love Brander?"

"Do you need to ask my feelings?" Morgana met her gaze calmly. " 'Twill not make any difference how I feel. Your clan's laws and customs prohibit it."

"They only speak against the wisdom of a marriage, not love. I have watched Brander in the past weeks, Morgana, and I have watched Erika also. He does not love her, but the look in her eyes when she gazes at him is almost frightening. She would do you an ill, I think. And Thorfinn—he may be the first of many if Brander sets you aside." She paused, adding, "I know you have probably decided how you will deal with the situation, Morgana, and I ask you to tell me your intentions."

"I didn't realize my intentions were important to anyone." A wry smile curved the soft line of Morgana's mouth.
"After all, not a day goes past that I am not reminded of my
status here, Disa. First as captive, then mistress to the jarl's
son. How am I supposed to react?"

Sighing, Disa shook her neatly coifed head, one hand
rising to press against her brow.

"I warned Delling that this might happen, that Erika
would stop at very little to accomplish what she desires, but
I had no idea that Brander was so gullible. Many of the
women are sympathetic to your plight, Morgana, believe
me. You are not disliked by everyone, though it must seem
so at times. We are a close-knit people, and it is common
for us to favor one of our own. You would do the same—but
we can still discern injustice. You have done nothing to
warrant such harsh judgment from Gytha, but she is the
chief's wife. We hardly dare to oppose her."

"I understand." Impulsively, Morgana took Disa's hands
between her own. "You are honest at least. I wonder . . . I
wonder why Brander could not have been more so himself,
why he left me to find this out when he was gone. . . ."

"Perhaps he intended to tell you but was called away. I
do not know. . . . It could be that . . . but no, surely Harald
would speak up then." Disa frowned heavily. Then her face
cleared and she said positively, "It shall soon be sorted out,
Morgana. Brander will be back soon, and there will be
explanations."

"Aye." Morgana's voice was a whisper, and her thoughts
dwelled for a moment on the woman who was promised to
Brander in marriage. Erika had offered her enmity instead of
friendship in an awkward situation—yet how could she
behave less than honorably? And Brander—would he?

Wisps of memory like curling smoke drifted through her
mind, soft and lingering, making her long for the man who

had captured her heart. Disa's voice slid between her thoughts, an intrusion into fantasy, reality cold and hard.

"Perhaps . . . perhaps you should leave this land, Morgana. I know—Delling told me—that it would be difficult for you to return to your home, but there are other places. Have you thought of it? I have relatives still in Frisia who would willingly take you." Disa stepped close, a comforting hand reaching out to lightly touch Morgana's arm. "Brander may never forget you, but once you are away he will do what must be done and honor his binding oaths. Think on it."

Morgana stared past Disa for a moment. Smoke vapors writhed upward from the fire, scenting the room with the smell of burning wood, forming wisps of cloud that hung near the high ceiling. Where were the visions that had once come without summons, helping her when she needed it and even when she didn't? Straining, Morgana tried to find answers in the smoke, but saw only the unfamiliar walls of her chamber. It was useless. There would be no help from her gods. They had abandoned her when she abandoned Erin.

Nodding, Morgana turned wearily to Disa. "If you can arrange it, I will leave this land as soon as possible."

Aye, Morgana reflected after Disa had slipped quietly out the door, *I will leave this land, but I shall be leaving a part of me behind. How can I forget the man who has stolen my heart and left me as a homeless waif? Brander has in his possession the very essence of my being. . . .*

The barn dog, sensing his adopted mistress's unhappiness, poked his cold nose beneath her hand, brown eyes staring up at her sympathetically. She knelt beside him, burying her face in his soft fur and curling her arms around his thick body.

"You are loyal and true, barn dog, as your masters are not." A warm tongue slopped the back of her hand with a loving caress. "I shall take you with me when I leave this cold land, dog." The barn dog sighed as if in understanding.

In the fireplace logs crackled and popped, occasionally hissing as smoke curled upward and flames danced like demons on the eve of Samhain, when all the spirits of the netherworld were loosed on the earth. Strange shadows seemed to fill the room, looming larger than life, cavorting on stone walls in human shape, and Morgana felt a shiver ripple up her spine. The dog whimpered and quivered and hid his great head beneath white-tipped paws.

A vision . . . a warning? Morgana's pulses raced like springtime floods. On the tapestry-lined wall over her bed Morgana watched a shadowy scene that formed, grew vague, then reformed, becoming clear as etched carvings in stone. The shapes were like those made by hands in front of a lantern light, playing over the wall rapidly. A profile, familiar yet unfamiliar . . . braids wound in a neat coil atop her head . . . Erika? And next to her, hanging alone in the air, the wicked shape of a poised dagger. . . .

Morgana's hand flew to her side. Her dagger—the one Brander had given her before coming to Harald's—she had used it at the evening meal and now it was gone. Morgana could vaguely recall having lain it upon the table beside her plate of meat after feeding scraps to the dog.

A sense of urgency filled Morgana then, and she rose to her feet to speed to the door of her chamber, turning the carved handle to jerk it open. It would not turn. The door was locked, and Morgana's struggles could not pry it open. But who—why?

Curling through the air then came a shrill scream, echoing through the halls like that of a hawk's prey caught in deadly talons. Morgana froze, heart pounding like a blacksmith's hammer against his anvil, loud and sharp.

She heard footsteps thudding against stone floors, a door

banging shut, male voices rumbling like angry bees, then an angry voice uttering a sharp exclamation. It all whirled past in the space of an instant, and even before her door was swung open long minutes later, Morgana knew what had happened.

"How is she?" she asked Harald when he stood outlined in her open portal.

The heavy wooden door slammed shut, and the outraged expression on the chief's face was the only thing that Morgana saw clearly. From her side a menacing growl sliced the air, and Harald gave a quick warning.

"If you value the dog's life, calm him."

Though she spoke no word aloud, the barn dog heard her command and he backed to a dim corner of the room.

"He will not move now. How is she?" Morgana repeated, and her throat tightened at the furious glitter in Harald's eyes.

"Erika is yet alive, Celtic witch. Your aim was amiss." Harald's mouth twisted in a harsh slant and a powerfully muscled arm shot out to grip her painfully. "Why?" His voice was a growling rasp, his breath stirring escaped strands of hair over Morgana's ear. "Why did you try to kill her, Morgana? I have felt sorry for you, attempted to defend you from my wife's ofttimes vindictive tongue even though I did not want you with my son, but you have gone too far!"

She didn't struggle against his grip but remained still, sensing Harald's barely controlled fury. He was past reason for now. Swallowing her fear, Morgana shivered slightly, unable to still the instinctive tremors.

At that moment, the door banged open as Brander stormed into her room to find Morgana gripped fast by his father. Cold, wet, weary, and dangerously near explosion, Brander demanded, "What has happened? I would like to know why

I come back from a week's journey to find the entire household in an uproar, with Morgana in another hall and Erika shrieking at the top of her lungs. . . . Why are you holding Morgana like that?''

Harald's gaze shifted uneasily, but he blustered, ''She tried to kill your intended.''

Brander stared. ''My intended—what? Morgana?'' Confusion warred with anger, then realization at his father's obvious ploy mingled with grim amusement, bewildering both Morgana and Harald.

'' 'Twas her knife . . .''

''I didn't do anything. . . .'' they said at once, and Brander waved his hands impatiently.

''One at a time, please. You first,'' he said to Harald, ''for it looks as if Morgana might faint at any moment.''

It did look as if she would faint, for her face had paled and her mouth was a thin, tight line, her green eyes big and wide with shadows.

Morgana found her knees would no longer support her, and sank to the security of her bed with a sigh.

Harald shifted from one foot to another, briefly wondering if he had listened to the wrong person and let his temper lead him astray once more.

''An attempt was made on Erika's life with a dagger—her dagger.'' His finger pointed to Morgana. ''Erika claims it was a woman, slight, with dark hair and speaking Celtic. Naturally, the evidence is against Morgana.''

''Naturally.'' Brander's sarcasm didn't go unnoticed. ''I understand your concern. Morgana?'' One brow lifted as he slanted a glance in her direction.

''I was locked in my room.'' The simple words were delivered quickly and flatly, and Brander's brow rose higher.

''Locked in your room? *This* room?''

''Aye.'' Her chin lifted at his tone. '' 'Twas locked from

the outside, and I could not open it. Someone locked me in.''

"Yes," Harald interjected, "I found it unlocked when I got here. And if she was locked in, how did she already know who had been attacked without me saying it?" His face mirrored his disbelief.

Slowly turning, Brander gazed at Morgana. Harald would not understand Morgana's gift; in truth, he did not fully understand it himself, so how could he defend her? Harald was his father and chieftain, and bound to the truth. Torn with indecision, Brander still hesitated. Morgana had never played him false, had saved his life and loved him—he was certain of that. But she was the only one who would want to kill Erika.

"I will deal with her," Brander said softly, keeping his gaze on Morgana. When Harald stepped forward, pushing something into Brander's hand, he didn't need to look down to know what it was. It was the familiar weight of a bone-handled dagger resting in his palm. He stared at Morgana's down-bent head, and at the soft, rounded profile of her cheek and jaw, the long lashes lying like a child's upon flushed cheeks. Why had she yielded to madness and attacked Erika? Now he couldn't help her. . . .

Knowing he didn't believe her, Morgana didn't protest when Brander drew her into his arms with a harsh jerk. The chamber door shut softly behind Harald, leaving them alone.

Her head fell back against his broad chest, ebony strands of hair straying from the coil at the base of her neck to drift across Brander's crimson tunic in a dark ribbon. She quivered with hurt and anger, her breath short, panting gasps as his iron embrace tightened.

Confusion battled with desire as Brander held her fast, and the delicate scent of the girl he held stirred him as much as the sight of her softly rounded breasts thrusting against the velvet of her gown. How could his betraying body desire the curving form of this Celtic enchantress—when he knew she had tried to kill a woman who had done her no actual harm?

Loki take the wench! Brander half-snarled, flinging her from him to a heap on the stone floor. Morgana remained as she landed, splayed hands holding her upright and tangled skirts pushed high on silken thighs, her emerald gaze steady and clear as she gazed at him without moving.

Brander's hand curled around the hilt of the sword at his side, his legs spread wide as he balanced lightly on the balls of feet clad in leather boots. The leggings he wore were of the softest wool, warm and covering his legs as if a second skin, outlining the lean muscles of calves and thighs. Golden hair fell across his forehead and almost into eyes of sea blue, dark now as storm clouds threatened.

"Would you kill me, mighty warrior of Odin?" Morgana taunted softly, angrily, jade eyes narrowing as his fingers tightened around the sword's hilt, lifting it from its scabbard. "Who verifies that I have attacked Erika—does she say 'twas I?"

"You must know the answer to that." The sword was jammed back into the metal and leather scabbard. " 'Tis a coward's method, to my way of thinking! Only a faint-hearted woman would attack an enemy's back."

"And you think me faint-hearted?" Morgana's mouth curled in a derisive sneer as she pushed herself to her feet. "Then you are a fool, Brander Eriksson! A fool and a braying jackal as well!" Words tumbled heedlessly from her mouth in a rush, cutting across his growling reply. "I had thought you a man struggling with honor, caught in a tangled web of your own making and unable to see a way out. Now I know you as only a selfish, arrogant lout who thinks more of passion than he does his sworn oath! Aye, stand there and frown at me, fierce Viking! You caused this snarl with your own impetuous actions—can you not find someone to blame it on besides me?''

Brander's arm flashed in a swift movement and something clattered to the floor at Morgana's feet. She knew without glancing down that it was her bone-handled dagger.

"Do you recognize the weapon? 'Twas used to attack Erika . . . !''

"Of course I recognize it. 'Tis mine.'' Her eyes held his hot gaze levelly, her tone cool as she continued, ''Does that mean my hand was the only one that could have wielded it, Viking? There are many here who could. . . .''

"You heard my father. 'Twas a woman's form Erika saw,'' he interrupted. ''A woman who struck her from behind!''

"And I am the only woman within these halls? Do you forget that my door was locked?''

"You lie. Harald himself said it opened easily, Morgana. There was no lock on your chamber door.'' He stepped closer, his hand flashing out to tangle in her thick hair, bringing her painfully closer. ''Foolish wench,'' he muttered, and his voice was hoarse with pain, ''did you think I would choose another over you? Ah, you have truly bewitched me, Morgana of Eire, for I would have broken a sworn oath to have you with me! Now . . . now I must see you punished for what you've done.''

With a soft groan of despair, Brander crushed her to him, his mouth descending upon Morgana's half-parted lips in a consuming kiss. His hands—hands that had been ready to curl around her soft golden throat and choke the life from her only moments before—lifted her tenderly from the floor and carried her to the wide bed.

He was right, Morgana thought dimly as she opened her

arms to receive him. Vows no longer mattered. There could be no more walls between them.

Somehow, she never knew quite how, their garments lay in a crumpled heap on the stone floor, and Brander's bare chest lay pressed against Morgana's trembling body. A soft sigh, an echo spiraling through the tunnels of time, uttered countless times by countless lovers, hung lightly in the air before fading beneath husky whispers of love.

Feeling the fevered caresses and burning kisses, their warm breath mingling and passion matching passion—Morgana was hardly aware of where she was and who she was; only the man above her existed. Sable hair lay spread upon fat pillows of feather-stuffed linen as her head tossed from side to side, fingers digging into Brander's back as his mouth teased a fiery path from the throbbing pulse at the base of her throat to a firm breast. The fires of passion exploded into a raging inferno as Brander's lips circled the rose-tipped crest, and Morgana arched upward.

She'd longed for him for a week, longed for this handsome Viking to coax an abandoned response from her with his sweet passion, and Morgana matched his ardor. Slim hips moved to meet him, her throaty whispers urging him on as he hesitated at her velvet entrance.

"Do you want me, Morgana?" he muttered thickly against her ear, "tell me . . ."

"Aye, I want you," and she had no chance to say more before he was thrusting against her, filling her, making her cry out. It was sweet agony, delicious torment, and Morgana held him more tightly to her. Panting, her breath coming in short gasps of air, a wave of tenderness spread through Morgana, so overpowering it almost consumed her. How could she love so much—and how would she bear the parting?

But any coherent thought was driven from her mind as

Brander began moving in rhythmic motions like those of the sea. She was drowning in sweet sensations, deliciously drowning in an ocean of sensual delight.

And when the undulating waves of passion soared to a peak and began a spiraling descent back to reality, Morgana was left in a dreamy haze of contentment. She lay beside Brander's lean body watching the glow from the fire play over his bronzed muscles and perfect features. He lay bathed in a golden aura of vitality and sensuality, kindling the fires of love as they had never been lit before.

He turned, heavy-lidded eyes hazy and languorous with satisfaction, his mouth softly smiling as his gaze met Morgana's. One hand rose to caress the gently sweeping line of her jaw, fingers lingering over lips still bruised from passion.

"You are fairer and more fragile than the first breath of spring," he murmured, and his hand traced a path from her face to a tawny shoulder, over her full breasts to the curving line of her ribs and down, trailing over the flesh of her flat belly to the swell nestled between trembling thighs. Well-formed thighs melded into shapely calves and trim ankles, and Brander lifted her legs, rising to a kneeling position on the bed.

Morgana's eyes widened as he sat back on his heels, legs bent as he rested on his haunches and stared down at her. In spite of the cool air in the chamber, Brander's skin was warm, his smooth muscles flexing as he pulled her even closer to him. The sun had frosted his skin with gold except for a whiter strip around his middle, fading now that the summer rays waited on the promise of spring to return.

Growing bold, Morgana let her eyes drift lazily over his body, greedily scanning the bulge of muscles in his arms and broad chest, sliding over the ridges of his lean belly. Dark golden hair furred his chest, tapering in a V, and her eyes followed the arrow as it pointed below. *He's beautiful*, she sighed to herself as she had many times before, a simple, primitive male beauty that could not be equaled.

This time she took the initiative, scooting back to rise to a kneeling position to match his, her hands moving over his scar-ridged chest that spoke of many battles fought, pushing at him lightly as she urged him backward on the fur-thick bed. A smile lifted the corners of his mouth as Brander obeyed her insistent hands wordlessly, and he lay stretched upon the bed with his hands folded behind his tawny head.

"You are like the gods, Brander Eriksson, more perfect than I ever dreamed," Morgana murmured, and her mouth moved to stop his reply with coaxing lips. Her tongue, warm and soft, teased, tasted, tempted, and she knew from his quickened breathing how she affected him. Passion, a coiling fire burning deep inside, flared higher and higher, threatening to consume her, and her mouth moved lower over his taut body.

For many long moments the only sounds in the chamber were those of the lovers, their soft moans and sighs mingling with the crackle of burning logs on the hearth. A log collapsed in the grate, falling in a fiery shower of sparks that went unnoticed, the brief life of the glowing ember on the hearth rug blessedly short and uneventful.

In the dim corner, a pair of canine eyes kept watch, as the ever-loyal barn dog held a silent vigil. Only his eyes noted the shadow of feet pausing at the closed chamber door, his sharp ears catching the muffled sound of an angry curse as the listener whirled and stormed away.

It was long into the night when the fires of passion and of burning logs finally lay in cooling ashes.

Chapter 26

For the next few days Brander watched Morgana with suspicious eyes, following her every movement. When she left her chamber to travel the short distance to the stone lavatory, she was bombarded with questions; and when she made the trek to the kitchen for food, she was asked where she was going and why. Exasperation battled with the longing to have him look at her as he had before. Even their nights were small, private wars.

"Did you," Brander asked once, pinning Morgana beneath his long body on the bed, "even *think* about killing Erika? Did you wish aloud that she was dead?"

Angrily she replied, "Nay! I did not! Why don't you go ask someone else if they wished to kill her, or if they picked up my dagger from the table? Why do you insist upon tormenting me?" This last was said breathlessly as she writhed beneath his weight. Near tears she implored, "Believe in me, Brander, and cease this constant badgering...."

"Don't you understand what may happen? There is to be a council, Morgana, to decide your guilt and punishment.

Do you know what could happen to you then? If found guilty of attempted murder, you could be killed by members of Erika's family. Justice . . ."

"Aye, justice." Morgana's tone was bitter as she glared up into Brander's eyes. "And I suppose it's justice for me to be falsely accused! Justice to be locked in my chambers without proof of guilt. . . ."

"Your dagger . . ."

"My door was locked!" This was almost screamed out, as she panted with rage and exhaustion from her efforts to wriggle away. "It was locked . . . locked. . . ."

"Shhh," Brander relented at last, sensing she was near to breaking. He smoothed away tumbled curls from her eyes, releasing his harsh grip on her upper arms. Purple bruises had begun to blossom on her tawny skin like large flowers from his hold. "Hush, love." He folded Morgana into his arms like one would a small child, half-kneeling on the bed, rocking her back and forth with her face pressed into his bare chest. His breath fanned gently over her ears as he murmured, "I feel so helpless to aid you. I don't know how I can. . . ."

"You can start by not crushing me to death," a disgruntled voice said into his chest, her lips moving against taut muscles. " 'Twould be much more comfortable."

A smile began at his eyes, then traveled the short distance to his mouth as he released her. She lay back upon the fat pillows, watching as Brander rocked back on his heels to gaze at her.

"I would wish that I could read minds as you do," he commented, and was rewarded with a brittle laugh.

"Read minds? Do you think I can? If I could read minds, Brander Eriksson," she said, sitting up so that her nose was only inches from his, "I would probably find an unwritten slate inside your head!"

While he was reeling from that verbal attack, she launched another one. "And if I could read minds, I would know who had actually tried to kill Erika, wouldn't I? For an intelligent man, you can be such an idiot. . . ."

"And for an intelligent woman, you can carry your game too far," Brander found his tongue to say.

Rolling one corner of a blanket over her, Morgana folded her arms across her chest and glared at him. The thin gown she wore was little protection from drafts or his gaze, and it was certainly no time to be admiring the brilliance of his blue eyes or the firm set of his still clean-shaven jaw. Why couldn't he just believe her? Why did he have to torment her continually with questions instead of making investigations to discover who might have taken her dagger and used it on Erika?

Shoulders sagged as Morgana placed both hands over her face and bent her head. It was no use. There was an impenetrable wall between them now that had never been there before, even aboard his longship. Suspicion and a sense of betrayal had been wedged between them like sharp knives, doing just as much damage.

"Sleep," Brander was saying tiredly, just as willing to relinquish the conversation as she was. "I leave early in the morning for Birka again. . . . I must," he said at her startled reaction. "It's most unusual for clans to war against one another, and Harald sends me to discover why."

"How long will you be gone?" Morgana asked sadly.

"I don't know. A week, maybe two. When I return, we will decide what is to be done."

Wonderful. A week or maybe two of waiting and wondering, of being suspected of attempted murder and ostracized, kept in her room like a chained goat.

"May I have my animals for company?" she asked

abruptly. Smoke and the barn dog had been removed from her chamber and not allowed back.

Silence, then, "Aye. I will leave instructions." The oil lamp was doused, leaving only the light from the fireplace across the room. A warm glow played over Brander's back, leaving his face in shadow, and she wondered what he was thinking. There was no way to tell even with full light upon his features, for he schooled them well. Only flashes of irritation and frustration escaped his iron control.

Hesitating, Brander swayed between staying with Morgana and returning to his own bedchamber. It was so big and empty without her bright presence, lacking the soft trill of her laughter and her teasing. Yet he still might have returned to his room if she hadn't yielded to impulse and held out her arms, longing written on her face as characters on a rune stone.

Ah, come the morrow he could resume his coolness. Tonight was cold enough without sleeping alone. . . .

Sometime during the long night Brander was awakened by Morgana. Restless, she tossed and turned, moaning low in her throat, thrashing about the bed.

"Morgana . . . ?"

"No!" Her arms flailed wildly, making him dodge a flapping hand. "Nooo . . ."

"Morgana!" He grabbed her by the shoulders, giving her a shake that snapped her head like a fragile flower on its slender stem. "Morgana, it's only a dream! Wake up!"

Long lashes fluttered and opened, revealing eyes still smoky with sleep and her own private fears. Morgana's fingers dug into his arms, nails leaving crescent marks.

"No," she gasped, "not a dream . . . real . . . and the horse . . . running, running . . . evil following me like night, like a great, dark-winged hawk . . . wings shadowing snow . . ." She looked up at him appealingly. "I saw it, Brander, like it was happening! I felt the wind, and the biting cold all around me, and we were running toward . . . toward . . ." She stopped.

"Toward what?"

"I don't know." Dark hair shimmied as she shook her head. "It was just ahead. . . ."

"Who was running? You? Trska?"

"Aye." She nodded. "I was riding him across the snow— new snow—and it was flying behind me. . . . I was alone. Then, on the crest of a hill, there was . . . was . . ." Her voice lowered to a whisper so that Brander had to strain to hear. "This . . . this *thing* . . . like a hawk, with great wings spread out like death, its shadow right behind me, chasing me; I was afraid as I have never been before."

"But it was only a dream, Morgana."

"Nay. This was no dream, Brander. I have had dreams before, and I know the difference between dreams and . . ." She halted, unwilling to tell him of the visions she'd always had, even though he knew she had premonitions.

"Between dreams and what? Reality?" he answered for her, impatiently, sleep shading his voice. "Go back to sleep. In the morn, it will be as if you had never been afraid. In the light of day, your fears will have vanished."

Morgana lay back on her pillow without argument, but she knew it had been more than a dream. For long hours she lay with her eyes wide open, staring at the black ceiling and remembering.

Days passed slowly with Brander gone, the winds of winter howling in full force outside the hilltop fort, piling drifts of snow in ever-increasing layers. Morgana whiled away the hours in her chamber off the kitchen.

The subject of Erika was a favorite with those remaining

behind, discussed over meals and the fire, at the loom, and even in the barns.

"No one believes you did it," Hlynn maintained stoutly one especially long afternoon. "Well," she added at Morgana's lifted brow and mocking expression, "*almost* no one. In truth, my lady, most think it was someone else."

"But who would wish to stab Erika? Who—beside me—has a motive?" Morgana shook her head, chin dropping back into the cup of her palm as she gazed morosely into the fire. "No, at the judgment, Harald is certain to rule that I did it." Perhaps that was the meaning of the dream. That dark, evil figure followed her still—was it doom?

Restless every night, tossing and turning, Morgana fought sleep, knowing that when she finally did yield, the dream or vision would recur. For the past week she had dreamed she was riding Trska across the snow, the stallion blending in with the huge white drifts, cantering easily across the flat heaths beyond Harald's fort. The dream always started slowly, with a sense of well-being and peace, then altered subtly to a brooding sense of disaster. First, she was cantering easily, enjoying the ride, then a dark figure appeared on the pristine white horizon, looming evilly in the distance. The ride would become a chase, with the dark figure growing closer and closer, cape whipping in the wind like a giant bird of prey, chasing her to some unknown ending. Sometimes it was so real that she could almost feel the wind in her hair and the bite of cold; sometimes there was a pervasive unreality, but it always ended the same way. Trska, running madly with foam flying from drawn-back lips, would plunge over a high precipice and fall, down and down into black oblivion.

Morgana shivered, blinking the room back into focus.

"My lady?" Hlynn was saying anxiously, "what is the matter?"

"Nothing. I am tired, 'tis all. Night shadows are falling now, and soon it will be dark." A small window, the only one in Harald's house, gave a feeble light to the tiny room through oiled skins that were almost transparent. It was not as nice a window as those in Brander's home, but it was a diversion. It looked out over the stableyard, Morgana's only entertainment besides her pets. The animals were closeted with her, the gray goose and the barn dog, and Hlynn was saddled with the task of caring for them as well as Morgana. She did it without complaining, even seeming to enjoy it except when she got too near the huge hound.

"He frightens me," she said once, "with those long wicked fangs and that ... knowing ... look in his eyes. It's almost as if he's human."

"Conn always said that animals were once human, brought back as beasts in this life to atone for some ill they had done, so that they know what is happening around them," Morgana said distractedly, only partly paying attention to the conversation. Her thoughts lingered with the dream.

"Conn?" Hlynn stood up from cleaning ashes off the stone hearth. "Who is he?"

The question startled Morgana into answering, "No one. He is dead, powerless. . . ."

"Oh." Hlynn peered at Morgana, sensing there was much more behind her explanation. Lately she had been acting so strange, as if she lived in a world of shadows, and today she had been even more distracted. It would be a good thing when Brander returned, so that the matter in everyone's mind and on everyone's tongue could be resolved. Too much suspense often deranged a person. Hlynn became uneasily aware of the brightness of Morgana's eyes, the sudden wild gleam flickering in their depths, and wondered if she had gone beyond the point of sanity.

Conn—the figure in her dream? Morgana stared into the

fire, wondering if it was the past instead of the future that intruded on her sleep. Could that be the meaning?

There was a dull ache behind her eyes, searing into her temples. She pressed her fingertips to her head and closed her eyes against it.

"My pouch, Hlynn," she said in a low tone that was almost a whimper, "please find my leather pouch. It has healing herbs in it. . . ."

Hlynn was gone in a trice, out the chamber door and down the long corridors of the house to Brander's room. She had seen the pouch many times before, had even had occasion to use some of Morgana's powerful potions for herself. She had been amazed at how quickly she had recovered.

Two pairs of eyes watched Hlynn's progress through the main hall, both vitally interested: one Viking, one Celtic. Gwyneth, sitting close to Gunther, leaned toward Erika.

"She goes to Morgana's former room. I wonder why? To steal the gifts given her by her Viking lover . . . ?"

"Shut up!" Erika snapped, eyeing the Celtic girl with distaste. "Must you remind me how Brander has made a fool of himself over the wench?"

"But you can stop it," Gwyneth said, cunning sparking in her eyes. " 'Tis simple. Take away whatever the slave brings back. It's your right; aren't you Brander's intended and isn't Morgana in disgrace?"

Erika tossed her head, turning away, but Gwyneth's words stuck in her mind. Aye, none would dare say her nay, and it still rankled her that Brander had been so generous with the selfish little witch. Brander . . . He had not paid attention to her even when she was injured, beyond asking politely how she felt. His main concern was Morgana. And she had been so brave, so noble in refusing to directly accuse Morgana of the deed! It had been at Gytha's suggestion of course, since her mother rightly felt that it would ill become her to stoop to such behavior.

Gwyneth's soft, sly words circled like hawks in Erika's mind, and she watched the archway for Hlynn's return.

It took only a few moments to find the pouch, but when Hlynn passed through the main hall on her way back to Morgana's room, she was halted by Erika.

"What do you have there?" she demanded, stepping in front of Hlynn. "That belongs to Morgana—do you steal it for her? Let me see it!"

Hlynn bravely faced the woman, noting the ashen pallor of her face and the thick bandage still circling her shoulder. It had only been a scratch after all, one of the women had told her, but Erika intended to milk as much sympathy for her plight and cause as much animosity toward Morgana as she could.

"Nay, 'tis not for you," Hlynn said. She tugged at the pouch Erika had seized by its leather thongs. "Release it, my lady."

An ugly expression creased Erika's face. "I will not! I demand that you give it to me this instant, or I will have you locked in the root cellar for a fortnight for stealing!"

Although she knew that Erika would make good her promise, Hlynn still hesitated. It was only when Erika half-turned to Gwyneth to summon assistance that she released the bag.

"'Twas a good thing for you that you did," Erika commented smugly. "What's in here?" She pulled eagerly at the strings. "Morgana's jewelry? Her rings and . . ." She stopped to glare angrily at Hlynn. "Why, there's nothing in here but some dead leaves and plants, you stupid fool!"

"I know that." Hlynn bit back a laugh at the chagrin and outrage on Erika's face.

Narrowed eyes observed the twitch of her lips, and a palm crashed across Hlynn's cheek in a loud smack.

"Do you laugh? What are these for—some kind of black magic, perhaps?"

"Nay." Hlynn stared sullenly at Erika, wishing the woman at the bottom of a deep pit. " 'Tis herbs, healing herbs for illness. Morgana has a headache and needs them." Her tone plainly said that Erika was the fool, not her.

"Herbs . . ." Gwyneth nudged Erika, and whispered into her ear as Hlynn glared. Peering thoughtfully at the pouch, Erika gave Hlynn a shove and the warning, "Don't tell anyone that I took them, or I shall see you flayed within an inch of your life, and your brother, too!" The paleness of Hlynn's face satisfied Erika that her threat had worked, and she carefully tucked the pouch into her belt.

Walking away, Hlynn wondered how two such unlikely dogs were lying together. Erika and Gwyneth? There had to be a good explanation for that.

Chapter
27

"But . . . what if they see you?" Hlynn gazed at Morgana with worried eyes. "It might look as if you were trying to escape justice, my lady."

"I can't help it. Until I know the meaning of my dream, I will not be able to sleep or eat, or even think clearly!" Morgana shrugged into a warm cape of moth-eaten white fur. It was the best Hlynn had been able to find on such short notice. "Now, if you will hold open the window for me . . ."

Moaning and muttering gloomy prospects for Morgana's expedition, Hlynn dutifully held open the window. Silver moonlight sparkled upon stark white snow. Cold blasts of frigid winter air swept into the small chamber, and the goose squawked a protest from his warm spot before the fire. Ever attentive, the dog edged close as Morgana perched upon the narrow windowsill. There was a scraping sound as she slid over and into a drift of snow, then floundered a bit.

"Are you all right, my lady?" Hlynn stuck her head out the window.

"Aye. It will take a moment to adjust." There was a pause, then, "Shut the window, Hlynn. I will return as soon as I prove to myself whether or not there is any truth to my dream."

Watching as Morgana struggled toward the barn, Hlynn shook her head. All this for a dream that probably meant nothing. It was a crazy idea, and she had objected long and heartily, but Morgana was determined. And perhaps it would be all right after all. She would only ride across the heath behind the house, then return. Morgana had promised . . .

"Oh!" Hlynn cried as a furry shape leaped at her. She flung herself away from the window, eyes wide with fright, then recognized the black form of the barn dog. He was following Morgana, and Hlynn swallowed the impulse to call him back. He would protect her as few others could.

Stumbling through thick drifts of snow, Morgana could feel the warmth of her breath escaping through the scarf she had wrapped around her head and face. She was dressed all in white so as to blend in with the landscape and escape detection. Hlynn had already arranged with Rowan, her brother, to have Trska saddled and waiting, and she would trust to luck and intuition for the rest.

The dream still haunted her, until she knew she had to lay it to rest. If she faced the circumstances surrounding the dream, then perhaps she could banish it.

Morgana sensed the dog's presence before she saw him, and half-turned. He bounded through drifts to reach her, a great black dot against white, tongue lolling from his mouth and tail wagging.

"Barn Dog," she scolded, "you were supposed to stay." An affectionate pat on his head removed any conviction from her words, and the dog trotted beside her along the path worn from house to barn.

Slivers of moonlight sparkled from crystallized snow

frosting roof and eaves, reflecting on the ground. A vague shadow flickered for a moment, and Morgana turned to look. There was nothing; no sound, no other movement distracted her. Shrugging, she slipped into the barn.

The dog waited outside, crouched on his haunches, watching for Morgana's return. There was a muffled snort and stomping of feet, and Morgana and Trska emerged from the warm barn into the frigid night air. In spite of her cumbersome clothing, Morgana needed no assistance to mount.

Hoofbeats clumped through mounds of snow as she urged Trska forward. The dog launched himself after them, brown eyes sparkling with excitement. After weeks of confinement in the house, the adventure was invigorating.

After the first few moments of apprehension, Morgana began to relax, enjoying the fresh air and brisk temperatures. It was never this cold in Erin, she'd never seen this kind of snow, but she realized that it wasn't as bad as she'd thought it would be. All that remained was to resolve her dream and the attempt on Erika's life; and in the cold air that cleared cobwebs from her brain and filled her lungs, somehow that seemed possible.

Trska snorted, clouds blowing from his nostrils, his hooves churning through the snow. He began to canter easily across the heath behind the house, leaving a wake like that of a longship behind him. The rocking motion combined with the pristine moonlight lulled Morgana's fears to a fraction of what they had been before.

They raced, shadows against the white, over undulating heath and toward the Schlei fjord. Just when Morgana was beginning to relax and enjoy the ride, thinking her dream had been just that—a dream—another shadow appeared on the horizon.

She didn't see it at first, just knew it was there, and began reining Trska to a slower pace. Her heart pounded fiercely, as though it would leap from her chest, and she turned her head to the distant dark speck.

It rode toward her as it had in the dream, cape billowing behind like huge wings, dark rider and darker horse seeming to fly across the ground without touching it.

Glints from Trska's silver-mounted bridle flashed in the still night as Morgana yanked his head around. She was powerless to do other than what had happened in the dream, moving through the time frames with agonizing certainty and slowness. There was the same feeling of impending evil, the same feeling of helplessness, and always, the inexorable rider close behind.

It was when she tried to turn Trska that the reins broke, the curbing leather strap under the stallion's chin snapping in two with a loud pop. Frightened, and feeling no firm control, the white stallion streaked across the ground like a shooting star, beautiful and bright. He raced toward a hump of ground, reins flying like banners and mane streaming into Morgana's face, whipping her cheeks with stinging cuts. She clung tightly to the saddle. Several options whirled for a moment. Should she leap free of the animal and take her chances? Or should she stay with him and hope he would soon tire and stop? And the dark, ominous figure that emanated evil—what, or who, was it?

Wind took away her breath, and her fingers were numb from the cold and gripping so tightly, so that when Trska took a final, terrible leap into the air, Morgana could not hold on. For a few frozen moments she was on a winged horse, then the downward plunge began and she felt herself falling, over and over, tumbling through empty space into dark oblivion.

The black shadow followed, coming to a halt at the edge, staring down at the shapeless bundle that was Morgana lying motionless on the ground below. Trska floundered in the snow, struggling to stand, and finally succeeded. Trembling, the stallion stood with head down for a few moments, then began to limp in the direction of Harald's hall.

A gust of wind blew the dark cape of the rider in a swirl, flapping noisily, a violent shape outlined against the moonlit winter sky. Suddenly the black stallion reared high in the air, screaming as a snarling, biting fury attacked his hind legs. Enraged, the dog charged again, sending horse and rider careening in the opposite direction in a flurry of muffled oaths and tangled cape.

Satisfied that he had protected his mistress, the barn dog trotted down the steep slope and stood whining beside Morgana. He nudged her, but she didn't move. Finally, lifting his great head, the dog howled, an eerie, shivering wail that echoed across the still land where nothing else moved. He sat back on his haunches like a statue as snow began to fall again, blanketing the ground and covering all traces of hoofprints and struggle.

Hoofs crunched through snow, the path well lit by the bright silver disc of the moon as Brander's horse plodded the last mile wearily. The others were far behind, not having the same unreasoning sense of urgency to return as he did. Morgana. He missed her. He longed to hold her slender body in his arms and nuzzle silken hair, taste her honeyed lips with sweet kisses—ah, he was besotted, he told himself. The Celtic maid had claimed his mind and heart, and he was caught as neatly as a netted herring.

A frown creased his brows as he pondered the unsettling situation he had left almost two weeks before. Harald, at Gytha's nagging, had finally agreed to a marriage between Brander and Erika, and somehow—he had his own ideas how—it had been announced to the clan that they were to be married. Harald was caught in a morass of his own making, and had left it to Brander to decry.

"I willingly admit 'twas my fault," he'd told his son, "yet it would do little good for me to renege now. 'Tis up to you to tell the clan that there has been a mistake, and I suggest that you wait. Let Erika—who claims she knew nothing about her mother's plans—save face for now. Then, in a few weeks, she can decide to have changed her mind."

It was weak and full of holes, but Brander had reluctantly agreed. Part of the deal was that he not tell Morgana the truth, "For she will tell Hlynn, who will tell everyone else," Harald had argued.

Now, riding so close to home and recalling Morgana's pain and sense of betrayal, he was wishing that he had not agreed to any of it. Her tear-misted eyes still haunted him, and he urged the bay faster.

He was almost to the house, fighting spitting snow, when a dark shape hurtled toward him, skimming low to the ground. The bay snorted and reared, eyes rolling and nostrils flared. Brander battled the animal back down, then saw what had frightened the horse. It was the barn dog, Morgana's pet, and he wondered why the dog was loose instead of with his mistress.

"Ho," he soothed the bay, patting his lathered neck. "Dog, you should be skinned for this."

The snow-covered dog barked furiously, lips drawn back from his teeth, and Brander wondered if he'd gone mad. What was the matter with the beast? Slowly, he dismounted, intending to investigate, and the dog bounded several feet away, frenzied tail whipping fallen snow into a froth.

"Come dog," he commanded, but the animal only barked more loudly, edging farther away. "Dog!" Brander pulled his sword from its scabbard, sorrowfully, knowing that the beast had gone mad and must be destroyed. It would hurt Morgana, but it had to be done.

Barn Dog leaped through the snow then paused, turning to bark before running again. It was hard to see with the wind blowing snow into his eyes, but finally it began to seep into Brander's brain that the animal wasn't mad, but excited. He decided to follow, remounting the bay and turning him in the direction the dog had taken.

A half mile away rose the hump of the Danevirke, covered with blowing snow and crusted with ice, so slippery that he had to dismount and leave his horse. It was deathly quiet except for the occasional bark of the hound and the sound of his feet scrunching into snow. His breath frosted in front of him in clouds, huffing in the silence.

Just ahead the dog began barking furiously, then reached down to tug at a bundle on the ground. Had he run to earth an animal, perhaps? Brander pulled his sword. It might be still alive and full of fight.

But when he reached the small white figure half-hidden by white drifts upon the ground, he realized it was human, not animal, and knelt to look. Sable hair tumbled in a silken pelt across his hand as he turned the body, and Brander's heart gave a lurch. *Morgana!*

Chapter 28

"She's dead," a voice said flatly, filtering through the fog surrounding Morgana. "The fall killed her."

Nay, she wanted to say, *I'm not dead. I can hear you even though I can't see you.... It's so dark and cold....*

Then a familiar voice cut through the fog, piercing Morgana's heart.

"Nay! She is not dead; she is alive! I will *not* have her die!"

Strong arms lifted her, and the pain was so intense that Morgana's fragile hold on consciousness slipped away, plunging her back into dark oblivion.

Brander cradled Morgana close as he walked toward the house, followed by the faithful dog. If it hadn't been for the barn dog, he would not have found her in time.

"The dog stays," Brander said tersely when Harald would have booted him from Morgana's room. "He stays."

A fire was rekindled in the stone hearth and Morgana was laid gently upon her fur-strewn bed. She moaned softly but did not waken, and Brander turned helplessly toward Hlynn.

"I don't know how to help her. . . ."

"I do, my lord. Please move out of the way," Hlynn said with more firmness than she'd ever used toward the Vikings. "And bring hot water and bandages, and Morgana's pouch of herbs. Erika has possession of them."

Erika? Brander frowned, wondering just how they had come into her possession, but he obeyed Hlynn's commands as if she was the mistress and he the slave. In a short length of time, he returned with hot water, bandages, the pouch of herbs, and Erika.

"I will administer the herbs," Erika insisted. "This slave has no knowledge of medicines, and I do." When Hlynn protested, she found herself overruled and shoved aside to watch anxiously. "I feel responsible," Erika explained to Brander, her face sad. "If it wasn't for what happened, she wouldn't have been driven to try an escape. I understand, and I have forgiven her in my heart. I'd like for Morgana to know this. Perhaps if she senses it, she will heal much quicker."

Distraught, and having no knowledge of medicines himself, Brander agreed. Harald and Gytha thought it a good idea, and urged him to let Erika try.

In spite of Erika's potions, Morgana remained unconscious, Hlynn muttering that it was *because of* Erika's noxious mixtures.

"I don't know much," she confided to Disa, "but I do know that she uses the belladonna too freely. Look at her—Morgana has a rash, her pulse is rapid, and even in this unnatural sleep she is delirious. I'm worried. . . ."

Frowning, Disa looked closely at Morgana. She lay still as death on the bed, her eyes closed; a rash resembling blushing gooseflesh pinked the skin of her chest, neck and arms.

"She's worse," a flat voice behind them stated, and Disa turned to see Brander standing at the end of the bed.

"Aye. Well, perhaps not worse, but not better."

"It is not common for someone who has fallen to stay unconscious this long." Brander eyed Disa as if daring her to argue. A snow-frosted cape swung from his shoulders, light from a lamp glinting in the bronze brooch pinning it at his broad shoulder.

Disa hesitated, and Brander's eyes narrowed at the glance she sliced toward Hlynn.

"Answer me!"

"I'm sorry," Disa managed to say, "I did not realize you required an answer. Aye, it is not common, but neither is it so unusual. She fell a long way, and struck her head against a rock, remember. Morgana needs rest, and . . . and all the healing arts we can combine." Disa wanted to mention Erika's potions, but did not dare. After the stabbing incident, she wasn't certain where Brander's affections lay. He coveted the Celtic maid, certainly, but did he covet Erika as wife? Disa's fingers were reddened from twisting them together, and she rubbed her moist palms against her woolen skirts.

Hlynn, watching Morgana carefully, saw the flicker of blue-veined eyelids, the transparent skin veiling her eyes quivering with motion. Was it the beginning of another bout of delirium, or was she waking? Long lashes fluttered, then lifted, and Hlynn's knees buckled with a hot wash of relief. For a moment she couldn't speak. Then she sputtered, "Brander . . . Disa . . . she wakes . . . !"

Two blond heads turned as if pulled by strings, eyes flying to the slim figure upon the bed. Brander was the first to move, his reaction swift.

Covering Morgana's small, cold hand with his own, he said softly, "How do you feel?"

There was a moment of silence before a querulous, cranky voice answered, "Like someone split my skull with a broadax. . . . How do you think I feel? Kyna?" Smoky eyes searched the faces in front of her, a scowl knitting her brows. "Where's Kyna? I want her . . . I need her. . . ."

Tension cracked Brander's composure as he clung to that small, fretful hand, staring at Morgana's pale face. She was not the same girl he'd brought from Hibernia. Too much had happened to her since arriving in Jutland, and he was the cause. His heart pained him, realizing that if it was not for him, Morgana would have remained among her own people. Guilt assailed him like dark-winged bats.

"Morgana," he said, "Kyna is . . . not here . . . right now. Are you thirsty? Or hungry?"

"No." The fretful tone again, peevish with the impatience often felt by the gravely ill. "No, I am not hungry or thirsty. I need Kyna. She said she would be here with my honeycakes. Where is she?"

Wide green eyes stared up at him as if he were a complete stranger, and Brander felt a wrenching pang. She wandered in the mists of the past instead of the present. He shrugged helplessly, and Hlynn came to his rescue.

"It was much farther than she thought, Morgana. She will be late. Now rest until Kyna returns."

As obediently as a child, Morgana closed her lids, the long lashes lying on unnaturally flushed cheeks like huge moth wings. She relaxed into sleep almost instantly, her breathing rapid and shallow.

When Brander left, Hlynn and Disa exchanged worried glances. "She will not get better if Erika keeps tending her," Hlynn insisted, and Disa was inclined to agree. But what could they do without offending the chieftain and his entire family?

*　　*　　*

Days passed with Morgana still in a semiconscious state. She grew weaker and weaker, drifting from deep sleep to light fretfulness and back to sleep. Her waking time was spent in pleas to return home, asking for Kyna and her green hills, until Brander was fraught with mixed emotions.

"Do I keep her or let her go?" he asked Gunther once, and his friend only shook his head.

"I can't tell you that, Brander, only that you must follow your own heart." Gunther's eyes were sympathetic, watching as Brander lifted a full horn of foaming mead—another of many.

Later that night Brander sat beside Morgana's bed, listening to her ramblings and wondering what to do. He had thought she would be satisfied in Jutland with him; he had not thought she would want to leave. Now she wept for her homeland and foster mother.

"Morgana," he said softly, leaning close, "it's Brander."

"Brann?" she echoed dreamily. "Brann—'tis the name for a raven. Are you the Prince Brann of legend who sailed to a sunny land in southern seas and returned a hundred years later still a young man?" Her voice drifted to a whisper, while she stared into the fire, seeing things no one else could see.

"Nay," he choked out, "Brann is a Celtic name. I am from the ancient land of Jylland, or Jutland, Morgana. I am Brander, do you not remember? Brander is our name for sword or firebrand. . . ."

Her head turned so that she was looking directly at him.

"Fire. I saw you in the fire, Viking. I saw you come to Erin in your dragon boat, with your men beside you and death in your hands, and still I perceived goodness and love. Aye, you are Brander. . . Brander, who is to wed another. . . ."

"Nay, I will not."

"Nay? But everyone knows—they all talk of it in the

halls and the kitchens and the stables.'' Her eyes closed, and for a moment he thought she was asleep again. Then, fiercely, ''And you didn't tell me!'' Eyes opened wide, accusingly, piercing him to the core. ''You didn't tell me,'' she repeated softly.

''I can explain,'' he began, determined to talk to her while she was in a lucid moment, but the door opened and Erika appeared bearing a tray filled with potions.

''I'm late,'' she said brightly, eyes narrowing at Brander perched on the edge of Morgana's bed. She swept across the room, blue silk skirts dragging over the cold stone floors and a white ermine-lined cape draped from her shoulders. She had expected to find Brander here. A crafty pair of eyes watched everything, and told her all. Now she must act solicitous and sweet, be everything Brander seemed to want, to pull his attention away from Morgana. . . .

Distracted as he was, Brander never noticed. Morgana did notice, her gaze sharpening. Pride forbade her to say a word in front of Brander, and her mouth tightened.

''Drink this,'' Erika ordered, holding out a thick clay cup.

Morgana's nose wrinkled and she pushed it away. ''Nay, I do not want it.''

''Tell her, Brander, that she must drink it in order to get well. . . .''

''But I can't tell what's in it, with all those spices and herbs you've included—is it henbane, or wolfsbane?''

''I only added spices to make it easier for you to swallow, Morgana. Trust me.'' Lips curved in a smile that reminded Morgana of a wolf smiling with all his teeth bared.

Stubbornly, ''Nay. I shall not.''

''You must,'' Brander said, pressing the cup to her lips. ''I want you well, love.''

Love. The word heartened Morgana and infuriated Erika.

The tall Viking woman bristled, arousing the enmity of the dog, who didn't like her at all. He half-rose from his constant perch by Morgana's bed, a growl rumbling deep in his throat.

"Dog!" Brander said, and the animal quieted, though he continued to glare at Erika with bright eyes.

Morgana reluctantly took the cup and drank, draining it, staring into Brander's eyes with a fathomless gaze. He was with her when the light in her eyes dimmed, growing cloudy with lethargy, and she nodded into slumber again.

"It's supposed to help her sleep—healing sleep," Erika explained. "My mother, your father's wife, prepared it for her."

The explanation was unsatisfying but unarguable. How could he dispute his father's judgment?

Chapter 29

It was night. Dark shadows lingered in Morgana's room, curling into corners to squat like beasts of prey. Her eyes were only half-open, watching the fire, her mind still drug-dazed and dreaming. Just the dog and goose were with her. Hlynn was busy in another part of the house, cooking and cleaning up after the nightly celebrations.

Long fingers curled and uncurled into the material of the quilt covering Morgana, bunching the wool then smoothing it, a rhythmic, senseless motion. Scattered impressions flitted through her mind in frustrating sequences, not lingering long enough to grow into a complete thought.

Brander . . . memories of him with her . . . laughing, loving and being loved . . . tawny hair and azure eyes . . . golden skin and taut muscles . . . Morgana closed her eyes against a sudden stab of pain, remembering Erika. Erika, tall, cool and blond, beautiful—and promised to Brander.

Erika was furious with the Viking she desired and his bedraggled little Celt. She stormed about her bedchamber, a fist curling into her open palm, planning how to rid herself of a very powerful rival.

It was the girl's fault. Everyone knew Morgana was a witch, a Celtic enchantress who had somehow snared Brander with her magic. Her magic wasn't as powerful now, here in Jutland, and Erika knew she had to strike while the girl was still weak from her injuries.

A smile curved her mouth upward. It had been so easy to find out about Morgana's plans to ride her horse that night, so very easy. And even easier to sneak into the stables and slip a dagger beneath the horse's curb bit so that it would snap in two at the first sign of stress. It still amazed her that Morgana had been so frightened, out there on the heath. She had raced away as if demons were after her, flying over snow and streams more recklessly than Erika had hoped for. It had been almost too easy.

But what now? Erika paced the floor impatiently, the cape almost like Morgana's swinging with every hard step. The ermine brushed against her ankles, and she was reminded that Brander had given Morgana a cape. Morgana, Morgana— the name tolled in Erika's mind incessantly, reminding her of a death knell.

She stopped abruptly. Death—hadn't Morgana been accused of attempting to kill her? And now, thanks to strong potions, she was considered to be very ill herself. Gwyneth's idea, suggested quietly and softly, still lingered in her brain. It would be even easier than attempting to frighten her into running away, but could she do it?

Erika had been gone with her tray of medicines for several minutes, leaving Morgana lying quietly upon her bed. Her head hurt, a throbbing like hammers against her temples, until she cried out with pain. The dog came immediately to her side, nose thrusting beneath the covers to poke at her, worry in his warm brown eyes. A muffled squawk sounded from Smoke, perched at one end of her bed, his beady eyes fastened on Morgana and the dog, whom he disliked but tolerated. 'Twas not surprising, Hlynn had muttered once, that the goose disliked the dog, since he disliked every living creature but Morgana.

With the strong potions coursing through her body the pain eased finally, leaving her weak, and Morgana felt the familiar sand of sleep scratching at her eyelids. She was almost asleep when she heard a slight, disturbing sound, a scuffling like that of field mice in the wood. The dog's head swiveled toward the door, eyes glinting in the faint light from the fire. A rumble sounded low in his throat, pricking Morgana's attention.

"What is it, Barn Dog?" she asked sleepily, hardly able to keep her eyes open. Then she heard the creak of the door opening and lifted her head to see. The dog growled again, louder, and the sliver of light shining through the partly opened door was crushed by blackness. Morgana lay tense and quiet, but the door was not reopened, and she soon succumbed to Erika's potions.

Her sleep was not peaceful but restless, filled with oddly disturbing sounds and impressions; a clanking chain and the muffled stamp of feet, the indignant squawk of a goose and the shutting of a door filtered through the fog. Then it was quiet again. Her sleep grew deeper and deeper.

Standing just outside Morgana's chamber, a robed figure waited. The dog was gone, chained in the stables and bleeding from a cuff to the head, snarling his displeasure at being removed. Very slowly, the bedchamber door creaked open.

Hoofprints carved into the unblemished sweep of snowscape

blurred with the rising wind, and the two riders disappeared over the far ridge as they rode away from Harald's hall.

"What has happened?" Gunther asked Brander, his words muffled by the warm scarf wrapped around the lower part of his face. "All I heard was that you needed me."

"Aye. I'm not certain myself what has happened. Gytha woke me with a message from my home, saying I was needed at once. 'Tis all I know." Brander nudged his bay a little faster, wondering what could have happened that would have necessitated his being summoned in the dead of night. He slanted Gunther an inquiring glance. "How did you know about it? I didn't send for you."

"There was a knock at the door, and when Gwyneth related the message I decided to help if I could."

"My thanks. You are a true friend to rise in the cold of night and ride with me."

Gunther shrugged. "You would do the same for me." There was a pause as the horses picked their way carefully across a frozen stream. When they clambered up the opposite side and stood for a moment in the silence, Gunther said, "I know 'tis none of my business, but rumor still has it that you will wed Erika. Is this true, Brander?"

Brander tugged at his warm gloves without answering for a moment, then said, "Nay. I never intended to wed her. 'Tis my father's idea, not mine."

"What of Morgana? Is she dying?"

Brander's answer was filled with anguish. "I don't know . . . she remains delirious . . . sometimes thinking she's still in Hibernia, other times accusing me of betrayal. . . ." His eyes met Gunther's. "I find it hard to keep my promise to Harald to remain silent, and intend to go to him soon enough to tell him I shall no longer do so."

Gunther nodded, recalling Gwyneth's words before he'd left. "The maid that Brander loves has eyes for another," she'd said sorrowfully, "yet I cannot bring myself to tell him." No amount of persuasion had wrung more information from her, and he'd been in a hurry, so that Gunther now wondered uneasily if he should have tried harder. There had been a strange undercurrent in Gwyneth's voice that left him wondering. . . .

"Be careful," a voice hissed, cutting through the soft folds of darkness surrounding Morgana. Consciousness returned slowly, seeping into her brain in freezing waves. Contracted muscles shuddered against a brisk draft of air that cut into her like a knife, and Morgana struggled to open her eyes. Her surroundings were dark, and she blinked but still could see nothing. When she tried to move she discovered, first with a mild impatience, then with terror, that her arms and legs would not respond to her commands. It took several moments to realize that they were bound tightly. Strips of leather cut into her wrists and ankles, and she was encased in some kind of shroud. She tried to speak, and found that a foul-tasting cloth had been stuffed into her mouth, and her throat was dry and scratchy.

Panic gripped her with sharp claws as Morgana realized that she was being hauled as unceremoniously as a bundle of old rags, thrown over a shoulder, so that with each step she was jolted and her ribs bruised. Voices flew at her in the darkness like bats, sharp and biting.

"Hurry! We shan't make it in time if you don't. . . ."

"Th' wench is heavy," a harsh male voice grumbled, "for such a small woman. . . ."

"You're big enough!" the first voice snapped, a woman's, and Morgana strained to recognize it. A shiver rippled through the shroud, and the voice said, "Hold her tight. There must be no harm to her now. . . ."

Through the thick material covering her, Morgana could

smell the sharp tang of the sea, and heard the sound of waves breaking upon the shore. The harbor? It must be, and she could hear the familiar sounds of a ship being readied for departure. Panic winged through her, and she struggled clumsily against her captors, the drugs in her system making her movements sluggish. Then she was bounced again and dropped, falling, it seemed, into a bottomless pit before stopping abruptly in a pile of something that was unexpectedly soft.

"This her?" another formless voice asked, then grunted. "If there's trouble, I'm claiming I never knew she was aboard. . . ."

"Fine," Morgana heard the voice say crisply. "Just take your silver and go." There was a solid thunk as another bundle dropped beside Morgana. She felt its presence and somehow knew that she was not alone in her troubles. The hauntingly familiar voice came again. "I don't care what you do with this," a toe nudged the form next to Morgana, "once you get out to sea. I just can't risk having it found near. Take care of things as you like."

"I will. It's been profitable doin' business with ye," the unknown voice said, growing fainter as the strangers moved away from where Morgana lay.

As she lay listening, there was a lurch and a bump, rolling Morgana against a hard surface. A moment of intense pain followed, and reality receded into gray mists of oblivion.

The
ENDING

Chapter 30

The disaster that had befallen Morgana was not as bad as it might have been. She had been kidnapped and thrust aboard a seagoing vessel, and yet perhaps it had all been for the best. The captain, who had sounded so frightening and brutal to Morgana while she was wrapped in cloth and terror, was actually a kind-hearted man, and had allowed Morgana the freedom of the ship once she'd wakened. Away from Erika's strong potions and enmity, Morgana had quickly regained strength and purpose of mind. She was overjoyed to discover her companion in misery was the faithful dog, bludgeoned but alive, wrapped in stout cords and stuffed into a sack like a pig trussed for market. The reason for his presence was obvious: Someone wanted Brander to think Morgana had left willingly.

"I got no heart for killing a blameless animal," the captain told her, "and I thought he must be your pet."

"Why did you agree to take me?" Morgana asked curiously, sitting beside a warm brazier aboard the ship. The dog nuzzled her, still weak from his injuries, and she laid her hand upon his head.

The captain, whose name, he told her, was Norbert—"In my language, 'Njorth-r-biart-r,' meaning brilliance of Njord, god of winds and seafarers"—explained that he'd taken Morgana out of human kindness. "She was desperate to see ye gone, and I thought as how she might choose another who would not be careful with an innocent soul."

"You're a good man, Norbert. Thank you." Morgana leaned back against the side of the small shelter erected upon the deck and smiled.

It had been a terrible voyage, fraught with bad winds and soaring waves, and she had huddled with the dog beneath the shelter the entire time. At least there had been more room aboard this vessel than there had been aboard the Viking longship, she commented once.

At last lay the inlet not far from Monasterboice, just beyond the mouth formed by jagged rocks thrusting from the Irish Sea. Norbert could not take the risk of beaching upon wind-tossed Irish shores, and so gave Morgana and the dog a small boat fashioned from oiled skins.

Early spring winds buffeted the small craft as she bent to the task of rowing, but Morgana paid little attention to her cramped muscles as the rocky shore drew closer. Balanced in the prow on unsteady feet, the dog lifted his head to sniff the air, as the boat bumped and ground to a scrunching halt in the shallow waters.

Morgana paused with one bare foot over the side of the boat, hearing faint, familiar sounds in the dense brush just beyond the curve of rocky beach. On each side of the tiny inlet rose sheer gray walls of rock, curling froth of waves crashed at the base, and a single, well-worn path led through the trees ahead.

Whining, the hound lurched from the boat and splashed

into the water beside Morgana, his ears pricked forward. He had heard sounds, too; it wasn't her imagination, Morgana thought with a quickening pulse.

She pressed forward through thigh-high water with her skirts held as high as she dared, the hem trailing. Slung over her back was a large square of material filled with donated clothing and boots; the only things she had brought from Jutland besides the barn dog . . . and her memories.

A shrill cry echoed through the trees and curled in the air like that of a hunting hawk, and Morgana paused to listen. The hound stiffened, stopping to shake dripping water from his thick fur, hackles rising at the sound.

" 'Tis a friend, dog," Morgana murmured softly, and her cloth burden plopped to the ground as she began to wring seawater from her skirt.

She waited calmly, patiently, knowing who would arrive, and when the figure shrouded in a woolen cloak appeared at the edge of the clearing, Morgana was not surprised. She'd known Kyna would have warning of her arrival.

"Morgana!" The old, frail voice like the crackle of dry twigs was lovingly familiar, and Morgana began to run toward her.

In moments she was wrapped in the embrace she had known since infancy, felt Kyna's warm tears upon her cheek as she was held close, and felt the tiny, fragile body quiver with emotion in her clasp. So much had happened since she'd last seen Kyna, a lifetime of emotions and events, and how would she be able to share them all with her?

But Kyna, sensing the turmoil in her foster daughter, would only shake her gray head.

"Nay, Morgana, I know what must have befallen you while with that Viking, and I swear a terrible revenge upon them all for you!" Her thin hand with curved fingers like claws rose to stop Morgana's protests, pressing against her mouth as Kyna continued, "I'm sure you think yourself in love with the Norseman, but you can see how the winds of fate dealt with you. Only if the gods ordain it will you spend your years with him—only if the gods ordain . . ."

"What of the rest, Kyna? I know you are glad to see me," Morgana said, "but when last I saw this land, all the warriors were howling for my blood because of Conn's death. Do they still?"

Kyna shook her head. "Nay. Clunaich heard Conn swear vengeance upon you for betraying him with the Viking, and, honest chieftain that he is, he swore to give you a chance to defend yourself should you ever return." Kyna smiled. "Of course, the fact that I reminded him how much you favor your lovely mother might have helped. . . ."

Morgana gave Kyna a sharp glance. Much lay between the old woman's words, like wisps of fog in early morning, lying lightly on the earth mother. Clunaich and Eibhlin? Could it be . . . ? Kyna's serene expression gave her no hint, nor would it ever. Morgana was left to her own musings.

It was a bittersweet journey for Morgana now, trodding the familiar path through thickets and wooded copses just beginning to bud with the new season. The barn dog followed at her heels, shaggy head swinging from side to side as he stayed close, and when they arrived at the tiny cottage were Morgana had lived, the dog flopped down on the welcoming stone hearth.

Standing in the doorway, Morgana visualized the room as she had last seen it, shrouded in night and Kyna asleep on her small cot while she slipped out the door. Had it been so long ago? It seemed like such a short time since she had first seen the Viking's handsome face and broad frame shadowing her dreams.

Kyna's hand curling around her arm snapped Morgana back to the present from her brooding memories of the past, her voice husky as she asked, '' 'Tis the Viking's dog you've brought with ye, Morgana? A great, fearsome beast he is.''

''Nay, 'tis now my dog, Kyna. And he is loyal to me.'' She smiled as the dog, sensing he was the subject of their conversation, lifted his head to peer at Morgana intently, brown eyes watchful and appraising.

Though Kyna snorted doubtfully, she made no comment as she bustled about the small room, and soon delicious odors filled the air. At first Morgana merely walked from one familiar object to another, letting her fingers trail over dust-covered stone carvings of the gods and intricately wrought metal bracelets and necklaces. Each piece of jewelry represented something in her past: a celebration or a lesson taught her by Conn or Kyna, a gift from someone she had healed with her potions, the lovely carved necklace in the shape of a cross that a man she had once helped had given her in thanks. All were just as she'd left them. Nothing had changed.

Nothing had changed except for her own emotions and tangled thoughts, and those were most important. . . .

Days drifted in a pattern with the changing of the seasons, and it was near the end of the lambing season when the chieftain finally came to visit the cottage.

Morgana waited, eyes steady, wondering if in spite of Kyna's assurances, Clunaich would still blame her for the death of his warriors and Conn. He stopped in front of the doorway, gazing at her.

''You are well?'' His voice was as Morgana recalled it, deep and rich, with a soothing quality that invited response.

''Aye, I am well. 'Tis good to see you again.'' A small sprig of violets tucked behind Morgana's left ear, bobbed with each motion of her head. A gentle breeze sprang up, straying across her uplifted face in a soft caress, a breeze smelling of new life and stirring with promise. Fragrant, tender blossoms swayed on fragile stems in the thick grass of the hill.

"You are different, Morgana. You are no longer a maid unaccustomed to a man." Clunaich smiled at the quick lifting of her head, the startled expression in emerald eyes clouded with sad shadows. "Did you think we would not know?—we who know all the mysteries of life? We've thought of you these nights you've been gone, my child, and we've known. . . ."

His hand, still strong in spite of his many years, reached out to grasp Morgana's chin and turn her face to his. She met his gaze steadily, relaxing, letting her mind flow like the waters of a slow summer stream. Amazingly, he understood. He did not condemn her for loving an enemy, and her mind spoke to him without words—intangible emotions soaring like seabirds in the sky—until it seemed as if she were shouting her feelings aloud.

Clunaich's words, unuttered but heard as clearly as if recited by a bard, remained in her mind and heart long after he'd left her standing alone on the slope of the hill with her dog. Brander would come for her, and when he did there would be a battle between the Vikings and the Celts. Only the gods knew the final outcome, and only the gods could be persuaded to spare her love.

Bone-chilling winter winds swept like howling warriors from Hel across the frigid waters of the North Sea, pushing the Viking longship over the choppy surface. It dipped, bobbed, and skimmed, shot through angry gray waves in lurching shudders as the determined Vikings steered the vessel with great skill toward the distant shores of Eire, ancient land of Hibernia.

Brander Eriksson stood like a stone carving of Thor at the helm, blue eyes as icy as the glittering chunks of white lining the sea's horizon. Nothing flickered in his eyes, no expression eased the grim lines of his bronzed face.

At his side, Gunther sliced wary glances at his leader, wondering at his thoughts. Delling and Gunther sat close together, watching Brander. It had been months since the Celtic girl had disappeared from Harald's hall, and since that time there had been only grim purpose in Brander's every movement. He had said little after the first shock, but in his steely gaze Gunther had recognized nothing that could be called mercy. He worried about Brander's reaction when he would once more have Morgana within his reach.

" 'Tis not far now," Harald remarked, stepping up to stand beside Brander and Gunther. "The storm pushed us off course for only a short time."

"Aye," Gunther finally replied after it became apparent that Brander would not answer. "We should be there soon."

Lost in his own thoughts, Brander paid little attention to the men. He reflected on the whirl of events and chaos he'd found when he'd returned from his short, pointless journey with Gunther to find Morgana gone. The entire house had been in an uproar, with weeping thralls and furious relatives all vying for Harald's judgment.

"Your precious Celt has flown her little nest," Gytha had shouted angrily, "to escape punishment!"

"No," Disa and Hlynn had steadfastly insisted, "it was to protect herself...."

It had taken some moments for Brander to understand that Morgana had fled Jutland. At first stunned, fury had been swift to follow, suppressing any other emotion. Tersely, between raging oaths and painful mutters, Brander had demanded to know what had taken place.

Answers had flown at him in a torrent of furious accusations from Erika and Gytha, finally ending when Brander harshly had demanded silence.

"Since none of you can agree on whether she left by ship or horse, why don't we try to find out? Perhaps it's not too late to stop her. . . ."

The expression on Erika's face had been worth a thousand words. Fortunately for the Viking woman, Brander had been too caught up in anxiety and anger to notice, but Disa had noticed.

"Why do you protest?" Disa had asked Erika when she began suggesting that they let the Celtic maid go or risk a curse. "Is it possible you know more than you're telling us?"

This exchange had caught Harald's attention, and he had stepped forward to listen. Caught, Erika had grown flustered.

"I? Why should I . . . I do not know anything! She left because I am to wed Brander . . ."

"No, you're not," Brander had said firmly. "You knew from the beginning that 'twas my father's idea, not mine, Erika, so don't look at me as if I've lied to you. I never suggested that we wed, never pretended I cared more for you than as a friend . . ."

"But 'twas understood!" Erika had ground out, glancing to Gytha for support.

"Aye," Gytha had said. "So it was."

Brander's strained temper had snapped, and he'd stormed from his father's hall, swearing not to return until he found Morgana. It had been Disa who had discovered, by meticulous, tedious questioning, how Morgana had left Jutland; and it had been Disa who had accused Erika of the deed. Denial had followed accusation, then the confrontation and tears had ended with a confession.

Disa had also confessed that she and Morgana had planned for her departure in Brander's absence. "She could no longer endure the situation," Disa had told Brander. He had been surprised at his dismay, then had grown angry. So, she had left him without a word of farewell—knowing he would wonder why she'd gone?

"By Odin, I shall find her," he'd said through clenched teeth, "and she won't ever plan to leave me again. . . ."

The confrontation with Erika had been a scene he would not want repeated, Brander reflected now as he stared over the frothing waves. Bah, women! Always conjuring up imaginary hurts to themselves—how could she have ever thought she meant more to him than she did? He'd never said or done anything that could be taken otherwise, but Erika had somehow convinced herself that without competition, Brander would wed her. And she had set out to effectively remove all in her way. . . .

"Brander?" Harald shook his son's arm. "I asked if you would not like to sit with us where we might warm ourselves." A graying eyebrow shot up as he peered at Brander. "There are coals in the brazier."

"Aye, Harald." Brander flashed a slight smile in their direction, his gaze lingering on Gunther. His friends could only guess at the depth of his feelings for Morgana, and Gunther's misery at having lost his Gwyneth still showed in his eyes. The Celtic girl had caused much enmity because of her own twisted emotions. The hatred she bore Morgana had been born of jealousy beginning on Brander's longship, and had been fueled by Erika. Because of this, Gwyneth had sought to discredit Morgana by wearing her cape and stealing her knife to stab Erika, but it had not worked out as she had hoped. Because she'd played a part in hounding Morgana and had been the one to show Erika how to use the herbs that made Morgana ill, Harald had banished Gwyneth from his clan.

Brander shared Gunther's misery of a lost love. Frustration welled as he recalled the last time he'd seen Morgana, and their last night together. Her words echoed in his mind time and again, an endless litany of meaningless syllables that tortured him. She had sworn to love him, yet she had planned to flee. Then why was he going after her? his common sense argued, and he didn't have an answer.

Lying alone in her cot, Morgana tossed and turned restlessly, a strange tingling in her body that had nothing to do with the warm weather. It was late, and the full moon was waning, a bright silver disk shining through her open window. Dust motes danced like maddened fairies on the shafts of soft light, and all was still.

From across the cottage the gentle snuffling sound of Kyna's heavy breathing eased as she shifted positions with a creaking of her rope cot, and Morgana heard the clacking of the barn dog's nails against the stones as he dreamed on the hearth. They were familiar sounds, safe sounds, yet somehow she sensed intruding forces nearby.

Rising to one elbow, Morgana glanced out the small window, but saw nothing. Her hair, the same ebony sheen as the night, streamed down her back in a flowing ribbon, catching and holding trapped moonbeams in the luxuriant strands. The light—soft, shimmering light—was all around her now, growing brighter and brighter, filling the room so that she had to shield her eyes with a hand.

She waited, hardly daring to breathe, while around her coiled whispers of night, dark and silent, whisking softly against her cheeks and hair, trembling on the sweep of her closed lashes. The room dimmed, the light fading to only a pearly glow, and when Morgana opened her eyes again she saw outlined against the mud walls of the cottage a familiar face.

Her heart leaped, but she made no sound, only watched

as the Viking longship with the breathtakingly handsome man standing like a Norse god in the prow grew sharper. She saw Brander, and with him were Gunther and Harald and Delling, and more men she could barely see. They were near now, their ship sailing like a graceful swan over the surface of the sea, gliding closer and closer, until the shadow of the sail flicked over the stone crosses of Monasterboice.

The images faded slowly and finally disappeared, and still Morgana sat propped up on her cot, staring at the blank, silent wall. Brander...He was close, not far from Newgrange, and he had come for her. Every nerve in her body was aware now, tingling and alive, and she felt a surge of energy flow through her like a bolt of lightning ripping across a summer sky.

She knew, without hearing words or seeing visions in the leaping flames of a fire, that Brander would soon be at her cottage, and Morgana rose from her bed. On the hearth the dog stretched, pink tongue curling lazily as he walked stiff-legged to his mistress. At the unspoken word from Morgana, he sat back on his haunches and watched, brown eyes alert and tongue hanging from the side of his mouth.

Raking hurried fingers through tangled strands of her hair, Morgana cast a quick glance in the bronze mirror hanging over her bed. She grimaced, and knelt to take from the small table at her bedside a stick of the charcoal used to make eyes appear larger. With a few practiced strokes she outlined her eyes, then rubbed a small amount of the color from a clay jar on her cheeks and lips. It took only a few moments to fasten a gleaming necklace in the shape of a crescent moon around her neck, and as she pushed armbands up slim arms she thought of those Brander wore.

His were shaped like serpents, while those she wore had the heads of gods carved in the ends—Celtic gods. Cernunnos, the horned god and patriarch of the tribe, adorned one end, while Dagdá, the great god of Ireland, adorned the other. The Norse gods Brander favored, Odin, Thor, and Tyr, were carved into the hilts of his sword and dagger in much the same way. Viking and Celt, they were so much alike, yet so different.

The barn dog growled low in the back of his throat, head swinging toward the closed door of the cottage, and Morgana's heart quickened its pace. He was near.

A dry shuffling in the cottage snared her attention, and Morgana's gaze sliced to the dim corner where Kyna slept. The old woman was peering at her sharply in the gloom, eyes alight with fires of anger.

" 'Tis the Viking you await, Morgana." It was not a question but a statement, her voice brittle and hard.

There was no response Morgana could make, no excuse for her actions that Kyna would understand. The old woman's hatred for the Vikings burned too hot.

Not waiting for a response, Kyna flung back the thin coverlet and rose from her bed, pausing to pull a ragged cloak about her shoulders before scurrying from the cottage. Morgana stared after her, knowing where she had gone. She could not harbor any animosity toward Kyna for her reaction, understanding the old woman's feelings.

Yet when Brander finally stood in the doorway of her simple cottage, all thoughts fled from Morgana's mind but thoughts of him. Her heart was pounding like ceremonial drums, her breath was shallow and rapid, and she trembled with longing and anxiety. He stood so near, but he remained so distant. . . .

"Brander . . ." She took a faltering step forward, one hand lifted toward him, mouth quivering as she met his stony gaze. Cold, cold eyes, like blue ice, frozen with unuttered reproaches and condemnation, seemed to pierce her soul, and she halted. He was angry with her, yet the reason was not clear. . . . Would he explain?

There was no chance for words of explanation before he strode forward, iron-hard hands gripping her arms in a vise. How had she thought his eyes cold? They were blazing now, fires raging unchecked in the azure depths, blue flame and white-hot.

The ache of his grip faded as she stared into the turbulent shadows of his guarded emotions, and Morgana sensed his pain. Guided by instinct and love, she leaned forward, letting her head fall upon his broad chest, smiling at the rhythmic pattern of his heart beneath her cheek. Its tempo told her of his reaction to her, and she could almost hear the blood singing through his veins.

Somehow they were entwined, with no word yet spoken aloud, heartbeat matching heartbeat, lips touching in a caress both light and deep, spirits attuned. It was a moment of enchantment, of discovery, and at last Brander murmured the words Morgana had often longed to hear.

"I love you, Celtic witch." His breath stirred the sable strands of hair over her ear. "You are never to leave me again, and I will not leave you."

Her answer was to pull his tawny head down further, silken arms wrapping about his neck in a surprisingly strong hold as she offered him her mouth, her heart, her life, in this one instinctive reply.

Their surroundings faded to a soft, indistinct blur as somehow they were lying upon Morgana's still-rumpled cot, oblivious to everything but each other. Velvet sighs and murmured words blended, lingered in the still air while all other sounds ceased to exist. Morgana's carefully chosen attire lay on the hard clay floor with Brander's hastily shed garments, and their bare bodies were bathed in shimmering pools of moonlight.

Gold against sable—Brander's golden head pressed close to Morgana's dark tresses, the hard muscular thighs enclosed in the satiny press of feminine ivory limbs, and the slim fingers tangling in a mat of dark, curling hairs upon a broad chest. These images were so familiar and precious that Morgana gave a soft sigh of contentment.

Her sigh stirred a silky tangle of curls on Brander's chest, moving him to murmur a soft query. "Do you sigh for me, Morgana of Eire—or do you sigh for yourself?"

"For you, Brander, and my love for you. It was a sigh of happiness you heard, not discontent."

His mouth found hers then, his lips soft and lingering, burning into hers with fire and passion, and Morgana lost herself in the ecstasy of his love. They were one again, their bodies melding in the sweetness of desire until they soared to the very heights of the night-dark skies like velvet doves.

And it was only when the fires exploded like a thousand tiny sunbursts, shooting rays of sunlit release, that Morgana slowly floated back to the reality of time and place.

Turning her head to gaze at Brander, she smiled. Ah, he was so tender at times, yet so breathtakingly strong and masculine, and she had not thought 'twas possible for a man to be both.

She lay quietly watching him, formless images stirring in her head, then as one of the images sharpened into focus, she sat up.

"Brander, tell me of Hlynn . . . Disa . . . my goose . . . and Erika?" The words would not come, yet somehow Morgana knew that Erika had been responsible for her kidnapping.

A smile flickered on his lips for a moment, then, "Aye, 'twas Erika who did it, though Gwyneth caused much trouble with her conniving," Brander muttered, feeling uncomfortable with the knowledge that he had placed Morgana in such danger. "It was good that Erika confessed when she did. I might have killed her had she not pleaded for mercy."

"Hlynn? Disa? Smoke?" she reminded, tilting her head.

"All well and looking forward to your return." A smile crooked down at her. "Hlynn guarded your goose most fiercely when I suggested eating him in your absence, so you owe her a favor...."

"Beast!" Morgana pummeled him playfully, then relaxed in a silken curve at his side.

A fine sheen covered Brander's body, and his breathing had slowed to a regular pattern as he shifted to one side, a brawny arm still curled possessively around her body. As Morgana raised a hand to stroke back some damp tendrils of his straying hair, she heard the distant clatter of hooves upon a timeworn path, and the rising chant of Celtic warriors. *Kyna!* She had forgotten the old woman's sudden departure from the cottage, but memory flooded back in a rushing torrent of fear for her Viking lover.

"Brander!" She pushed at him frantically. "You must leave at once! My warriors . . . they come to slay you!"

A tawny brow arched lazily, a crooked smile slanting the hard line of his mouth.

"Did you think I would be foolish enough to let down my guard, Morgana? My own men wait outside the cottage. I do not fear your brave Celts."

In spite of his words, Morgana rose hastily, flinging Brander's garments and sword at him in hurried motions. An unreasoning fear swept her, that she would lose her new-found love, and that she would be powerless to prevent the loss. How could he stand there so calmly—and why didn't he hurry as she bade him?

The clamor drew nearer, and still Brander dressed with slow, unhurried motions, finally buckling on his sword belt as he turned toward the closed door. The dog stood close now, ears pricked forward and hackles rising as he listened, then sent a low whine curling into the air.

"You must hurry, Brander!" She stood before him, hands lifted to caress his face, her fingers rubbing the prickly bristles on his chin before he caught them in one hand and kissed the tips. "Hide for a time, and then come back to me. . . . I will try to intercede with my warriors for you. . . ."

"Then you will return to Jutland with me, my love? I would . . ." He paused, blunt fingers tightening upon her satin shoulders as she stiffened and bit her bottom lip.

"I . . . I cannot leave my people, Brander, not now. Can you not stay in my land?"

"Why can't you leave?" His voice was cold and irritated, his face so close to hers filled with suspicion.

"I can't go now, 'tis all."

Brander growled an oath, pulling her close so quickly that she gasped and the barn dog snarled a warning.

"You will go with me when I leave, Morgana. I told you I will not allow you to be away from me again. It's no longer your choice, but mine."

For a moment an angry spark flashed in Morgana's emerald eyes, defiance apparent in the outward thrust of her rounded chin, and in the challenging tilt of her head. Then she softened.

"Aye, Viking," was her swift reply, and the corners of her mouth curved upward in a slight smile. "I yield for the moment." Argument would be pointless, and she intended for the Viking to accept her on her terms and in her time. It would be foolish to raise his ire over a matter already settled in her own mind.

A sudden pounding rattled the cottage door, and Brander pivoted to shout an answer before lifting Morgana for a final kiss and an almost painful squeeze.

"Wait for me," were his final words, and then he was gone, only the echo of his footsteps lingering.

Beside her, the barn dog stuck his cold nose in the palm of her hand, and a wet tongue caressed her as she stood without moving for a moment. Tense silence fell, then in the distance she heard shouts and bloodcurdling yells, the clang of swords upon shields, the screams of horses, and the rumble of chariot wheels. Yet, Morgana did not stir. Her earlier fear had been replaced by a calm assurance that Brander's time to die had not yet come. She would know when he was in danger; the voices would tell her.

Surely there would be a warning before he was to pass into the next life. . . .

Chapter 31

It was still early, before the sun's first rays had begun to light the world, and Morgana shivered as she stood beneath an outcropping of jagged rock, pulling her cloak more tightly around her. There was to be a ceremony to imbue the Celtic warriors with invincible strength, and Clunaich had insisted she attend.

The trickling waters of the Boyne rushed past in the first fervor of spring, and just across the water was the corbeled vault of Newgrange, a Celtic tomb for countless eons. On the winter solstice the rays of the rising sun flooded the 62-foot corridor to light the far end of the burial chamber. The Hill of Tara, another sacred site, was to the south, and Clunaich had chosen this smaller passage grave to the north as the spot for their rites.

Shadowy figures moved in solemn silence, and beside her Kyna gestured to the white-robed druids. It was time. Morgana followed the procession as it wound down unlit stone corridors going deeper and deeper into the center of the earth. It was close and damp, the sound of rushing water growing louder as they followed the vague shapes of the druids and the one oil lamp.

They stood in hushed darkness, the single lamp doused, all seeming to hold their breaths, waiting, waiting. Though she had attended many ceremonial rites, Morgana could not help but be impressed. It was a time of true communion with the gods, of stepping closer to that other life. The spring bubbling so close was a source of power, healing and life-giving, and a portal to the other world. There was no real break between life and death, the spirit merely took up residence elsewhere, going on for eternity.

Did she dare cross over? Morgana wondered, seized with the temptation to visit the other world. Would she be able to talk with her mother, to ask her advice? Eibhlin would have understood her turmoil.

She closed her eyes, letting her mind float freely somewhere above, and waited. She thought of fire, earth, water, and wind . . . the sacred elements. A small spurt of flame flared briefly in the doused oil lamp, startling the archdruid, then a gust of wind spiraled down the tunnels to snuff it out. A spray of damp earth showered down from the corridors surrounding them, splashing into suddenly boiling waters of the underground spring. *Fire, earth, water, wind. . . .*

Eibhlin, where are you? I need your advice, though I have never asked before. . . . Eibhlin . . .

Whispers, softly dark and fluttering, drifted in and out of the chamber, disembodied voices chanting ancient secrets, ancient answers to all the mysteries. Stars wheeled and soared, a dusty sprinkling of pinprick lights. And the moon, full and bright, grew brighter and brighter. . . . *Eibhlin?*

"Daughter . . . Morgana . . . follow your heart. . . ."

Was that all? Those few words, a husky whisper heard only by Morgana, and then, in a crashing return to the present, light raced along the night-dark corridors of the underground chambers to flood them with sunshine. It was dawn, the first rays of the sun illuminating the vault in blinding light that focused on the sacrificial altar at the very back of the stones.

Clunaich, the first to recover, signaled to the chief druid who then intoned the ancient chants, his ceremonial dagger flashing in a glittering arc. The ram offered in sacrifice bleated once, and was quickly drowned out by the rising litany of voices.

It was over, the warriors would be invincible, would defeat the Vikings, and Morgana trembled for Brander and his men.

"He is not to be killed," Morgana insisted, arms folded across her chest as she stood her ground. "It is written thus."

Clunaich frowned, bushy brows knitting over his aquiline nose, thin lips twisted. "I have had no sign from the gods, Morgana. I think 'tis your own fear for him that bids you beg for his life."

"Nay! I talked to Eibhlin. She told me to follow my heart. Would she say that if the Viking was not worthy?"

Clunaich's voice was dry. "Eibhlin did not follow her heart, Morgana, and yet you claim she tells you to now. P'raps she has a fondness for the Norsemen that has carried over into the next life."

"The next life gives you wisdom," Morgana countered, "is that not so? Why would she speak falsely, or allow her emotions to rule?"

Clunaich waved a weary hand. His hypnotic voice, deep and rich, was resigned. "I should know better than to question the fates, child. You are protected, as is your Viking warrior, though I don't why." He smiled, a gentle hand reaching out to cup Morgana's chin. "I can make no promises for the future, Morgana, beyond this eve. I sense changes to come, but they are blurred and distorted, so that I cannot see clearly. I am old, and my powers are dimming. Go to your Viking. He must leave our land soon or die. Go to him. . . ."

The shadowed paths through twisted oaks that blotted out the sun were deserted and quiet, and Morgana cast frequent glances over her shoulder as she hurried along. The dog was with her, close at her side, his black shape like night blending with the inky gloom.

Ancient trees, gnarled and bent into forms resembling men fleeing from certain doom, lined the leaf-strewn paths like sentinels caught in flight. It was said that long ago they had been men who'd displeased the gods, and now stood guard for all eternity.

Guide me, Morgana asked silently. *Lead me to the Vikings, ancient ones. I must find him, must convince him to flee for now.*

Dusk came swiftly, like a shrouding blanket to cover the land of mist and oaks. No light from the moon filtered through new summer leaves to illuminate the path, no torch or lantern lit the way, yet still Morgana pushed on, guided by an instinct older than time.

At last, when the moon was high in the night sky, a silver goddess against dark velvet, Morgana saw the tiny flicker of a fire through tangled branches of concealing bushes. She paused just out of sight, catching her breath, a warning hand on the barn dog's tilted head.

Firelight glinted from bronze shields and weapons, and low laughter drifted on a soft summery breeze. The dog stiffened, but made no sound, and Morgana stepped forward cautiously. One step . . . two . . . a twig snapped beneath her foot and she halted.

Barn Dog's growl alerted her just before a rough hand snaked out to jerk her arm, and a yelp rent the air as sharp fangs clamped onto the Viking sentinel's lower leg.

"Loki take it, you wretched Celtic bitch," the man groaned, kicking at the dog. "Call off your hound before I slit your throat!"

His drawn dagger was useless against Morgana, and the Viking stared in amazement at the steel blade which was knocked from his hand to a clump of leafy ferns. He stumbled backward, the wind knocked from him by the dog, eyes wide as Morgana seemed to float past like a spirit from the afterworld. The dog's eyes glowed as red as burning coals, riveting the sentinel to one spot, and he watched silently as Morgana stepped into the camp.

Brander was crouched before the small fire sharpening his sword and polishing the golden hilt carved with a likeness of Tyr, god of war and the name he had chosen for his weapon. He glanced up, then shot to his feet as he saw Morgana.

"Morgana! Why are you here now?"

He was safe and glad to see her, striding forward to take both her cold hands in his much larger ones, blue eyes lighting with pleasure, that familiar mouth curving in a welcoming smile, and Morgana's heart lurched.

"I have come to warn you," she managed to reply coolly, an answering smile lifting the corners of her mouth. "You are in danger, Brander, and must leave before morning."

Chuckling, the young Viking led Morgana away from the open stares of his men to a spot near the edge of their camp. He intercepted Harald's sharp glance and nodded as they passed.

"I have been in danger before, my love, yet I still stand before you, do I not?" Brander asked when they stood beneath the hanging branches of a gnarled tree. "Why do you fear for me now?"

"There was a ceremony...I cannot tell all, Brander, only that you must leave before first light tomorrow! Please, if you truly care for me..."

"Ah, women and their velvet traps! Of course I care for you, Morgana. I love you, but I will not bargain with that love. I will do what I must, and will love you still. Will you do the same for me?"

Morgana's arms circled his broad frame as she clung to Brander with a hint of desperation. He wouldn't listen to her pleas, but she had not really thought he would, only hoped.

"Aye," she choked out, "I will always love you, even in the next life."

Frowning, Brander tilted her chin with his forefinger and thumb and stared into green eyes swimming with unshed tears. He was uneasy, knowing the Celtic girl possessed powers of prophecy at times. Could she be right? It was not that death held any fear for him, because it did not, but he yearned for a future spent with Morgana. This life was too precious to rush into the next.

Still he was a Viking, a proud son of the North, and would not cower like a dog in this land of savage Celtic warriors and thundering horses like dragons. A sooty brow arched in amusement, and a tolerant smile curled his mouth.

"You will stay with me, Morgana. I will see that you are safe. After I defeat your warriors, we will go back to Jutland together. No," he stopped her sputtering protests, "I will hear no argument. 'Tis the way it shall be, Morgana, whether you wish it or not. I will not be parted from you again."

Nothing she said could sway Brander. He remained adamant, even when Morgana grew angry.

"You pig-headed Viking! Do you think you are immortal? My warriors will slice you to ribbons, and there will be nothing you can do!" She stood with hands braced on her hips, mouth in a tight, furious line as she glared at him in the dim light.

"I suppose you think I intend to stand like an untried lad and let your naked wild men slash at me with swords?" he half-snarled in exasperation. "What would you have me do, Morgana—run like a frightened sheep?"

She whirled in an agony of indecision, pacing in circles. If only he would listen! Perhaps if she went back to the chief, Clunaich would wait, would avoid a clash between the Celts and Vikings.

"I must go for now," she said, pivoting to face Brander. "Do not try to stop me, Viking."

Blue eyes narrowed to glittering chips of Nordic ice, and Brander's hand flashed out to grip her by a small-boned wrist.

"Loki take it, you stubborn female! I have said you will not go, and you will not."

She stared at him in astonishment. "Do you truly think you can stop me, Viking?"

"Aye, Morgana. I know I can." He met her gaze calmly, fingers tightening their grip. When she tried to jerk away she could not, and Morgana began to beat at his chest with her free hand, demanding release. Behind her the dog alternately whined and growled, torn between his former master and his chosen mistress.

"Quiet your dog before one of my men decides to," Brander commanded, ignoring her hiss of fury. Finally, seeing a Viking approach with drawn sword, Morgana sulkily complied, and the barn dog slunk to the safety of a nearby bush to keep watch.

"Release me," she ordered in her most haughty tone, bristling at Brander's obvious amusement. What had happened to them? Why couldn't he understand that she only wanted to help, that she could save him from harm if he would let her?

He was answering her unspoken question as if he'd heard her thoughts, saying coldly, "I will not hide behind a woman's skirts, Morgana, even if I join my comrades in Valhalla this hour. What will happen is to be decided by the gods and men's actions, and I would not want to spend the rest of my days knowing a woman had to protect me."

"But I am the only one who can intercede with the chief," she reminded him, "and so long ago I hid you from harm."

"Yet I did not hide behind you for protection," he cut in swiftly, "but to give me time to heal."

"You have fought my warriors before—how successful have you been, Brander Eriksson? They will kill you instead!"

"Then I will die a warrior's death and live forever in Valhalla, but I will not allow you to shield me." His jaw jutted out stubbornly, and Morgana recognized the determined glint in his eyes.

"Damn you!" she hissed in frustration. There was nothing she could say or do to alter his decision. Nor would Harald interfere, saying with a shrug of his shoulders that Brander had begun the quest and was the undisputed leader.

"I am chieftain, angry child, but my son leads his own men into battle here. I only came with him to help." In spite of his hard words Harald's tone was gentle, and his smile sympathetic and understanding.

Morgana turned her head away without answering, and

the older man sighed and left her alone on the large rock where Brander had bound her. She was filled with anger and resentment, bitterly cursing the fact that if it were not for Harald's suspicion of her and protection of Erika, not to mention his promotion of a marriage between she and Brander, few problems would exist. The natural animosity between Viking and Celt could be overcome.

Yet, a voice inside reminded, if not for Harald's actions, Brander would not have searched for her. Life was a circle, unending and constant, and all things had a reason. Hadn't she been taught that since infancy when she would rage against the fates for taking her mother from her? And hadn't Kyna and even Conn stressed that while the gods guided mortal lives, all held their own destiny?

Caught between two separate worlds, Morgana had poised on the brink too long. She must make a choice. Eibhlin had studied for years under Conn's tutelage, learning the unwritten sacred lore of the druids, yet had not realized the fullness of her powers. They had been snuffed out too early. By the law of their tribe Eibhlin was allowed to choose her own mate, the father of her children, and had chosen Morgana's father. The decision had cost Eibhlin her powers and her life, for the druid must concentrate first on knowledge, not emotion.

It was a lesson Eibhlin had learned too late. Would her daughter suffer the same fate?

The rough cords binding Morgana to the stout oak tree could not hold her, it was the invisible silken chains of her love for the Viking that rendered her helpless. All other restraints she could escape with contemptuous ease, but those links forged by her heart held her fast.

Silent tears slid down her cheeks as she sat rigidly staring into the darkened forest beyond the Viking camp. It was her choice to make—develop the budding powers within her and help her people, or choose her handsome Viking lover.

The moon had begun its final descent toward daylight when Brander once more stood before Morgana. He gestured to a tent sewn from bolts of sturdy cloth and erected a short distance from the camp.

"You will join me there, Morgana. We will talk again tomorrow when sleep has eased your anger."

A softly winging brow arched high as Morgana turned a cool stare on the Viking. "Sleep only postpones what must be done, Brander, that is all." She held up her bound wrists, her tone biting and mocking. "Do you fear my vengeance, O noble and fierce Viking warrior? Do you worry that a mere woman will send you to the next world?"

Roughly, angrily, Brander jerked Morgana to her feet, propelling her toward the tent. The barn dog, tied to a sturdy sapling, let out an enraged howl as he lunged frantically against his bonds.

"Calm him," Brander ordered, and Morgana threw him a scathing glance as she complied. With the dog lying once more in miserable silence, great head resting mournfully on white-tipped paws, Brander thrust Morgana into the tent.

It was barely tall enough to stand in, and Brander was forced to stoop so that his head did not burst through the roof. By the light of a small oil lamp, Morgana saw a large pile of furs formed into a bed in one corner, and a loaf of dark bread and a wedge of goat cheese lay upon a linen cloth in the center. Wine imported from Massalia in faraway Gaul lay in a bronze flask beside the food, and Morgana's empty stomach rumbled in a reminder that she had not eaten all day.

Pride made her clench her jaw and swallow hard as she refused Brander's offer to eat.

"I will not break bread with a man who binds me like a tethered goat!"

"You will grow weak with hunger then," he snapped, and his mouth set in a hard line. Crossing his long legs, he sat on the bed, tugging Morgana's arm sharply so that she was forced to sit beside him.

He ignored her as he cut off a chunk of the bread and goat cheese with his dagger, leaving it jabbed into the soft round of cheese when he'd finished. Morgana fidgeted, looking everywhere but at the tempting food so tantalizingly close, silently cursing the stubborn, arrogant Viking who taunted her.

How could love border so closely on hatred? she wondered miserably. Didn't Brander understand how she felt? Didn't he care? Ah, she should just slip away with her dog and leave him to the mercies of her Celtic warriors. He could go to his precious Valhalla, dying like a Viking warrior instead of letting a woman help him! She shivered at the thought, earning a sharp glance from Brander.

"This is ridiculous!" he exploded, startling her. "I won't have you making yourself ill again because you're too stubborn to follow orders. Eat, Morgana, or I shall feed you forcibly."

"I will not," she began, the rest of her words cut off by the pressure of Brander's steely fingers gripping her face in a vise. A chunk of bread was stuffed into her mouth and her jaw slammed shut by his thumb beneath her resisting chin and a hard finger hooked over her nose.

"Chew, or you will choke on it," he advised, and she had little choice but to obey. "Wine?" he asked pleasantly when she had angrily swallowed the dry morsel, holding up the flask in a menacing gesture when she began to shake her head.

A satisfied smile curled his mouth as Morgana snatched

the flask and tilted it high, but his smile faded as she took long swigs of the potent wine without lowering the container.

"Damn you, woman!" He jerked the bronze flask from her irritably, exasperation in his tone and the set of his jaw. "Don't you know how to concede gracefully?"

"Nay, Viking. Do you?" Smacking her lips, Morgana dragged her sleeve across her wine-stained mouth, meeting his narrowed gaze steadily. "It seems that I have conceded many points in the past months, while you rumbled like a speared boar whenever matters did not go to suit you. I am tired of playing your game meekly, and I am no longer your willing slave, Brander Eriksson!"

She leaned forward, eyes still trained on his carefully blank face.

"Be wary, Viking, lest you lose your manhood in this land of mine. Here men do not feel threatened by women as you seem to be. We fight beside our chosen mates, and die with them if necessary. A worthy woman is chieftain in more than just name, and leads her men into battle if she chooses."

"And do you wield a sword as well as you do your razor-sharp tongue, Celtic firebrand? If so, you would be a deadly foe indeed."

"Do you care to test me?" she retorted, stiffening indignantly at his roar of laughter.

When she drew back her hand to him, he pinned both arms to her sides, forcing her backward on the furs with the weight of his body.

"And do you test me?" he asked softly, all traces of amusement gone. "I hit back, Morgana."

Morgana met his icy gaze belligerently. Aye, she should have thought of that, but it no longer mattered. Her rage and pain needed a release. She stared up at his face without speaking, and as he lay partially stretched over her soft body, Morgana saw the frozen anger in his eyes thaw to a warmer reaction to her curves.

"No!" She struggled as he caught both her wrists in a single hand, his free hand dragging slowly over her gently rounded breasts.

"You don't want me, Morgana?" His mouth teased the sweep of her jaw, lips moving in a fiery trail down her throat.

"Aye, Viking, you know I want you," she admitted honestly, "but not when there's only passion between us instead of love."

"This is passion born of love, Morgana, not anger. I cannot deny my body as you can yours. Anger is a temporary emotion, love is lasting. I can be angry with you, and still want to feel you moving beneath me." He spoke softly, his voice caressing instead of hard and brittle as it had been only moments before, and she could feel his rising desire. When she shivered in reaction, her protests growing weaker, his mouth claimed her lips in a searing kiss.

How could he do this? she wondered wildly, an inaudible moan curling in the back of her throat. It was a surrender without resistance, an ignominious defeat of detached reason to inflamed senses. Suddenly frightened of her own response, of losing complete control to a man she had grown uncertain of, Morgana reacted impulsively.

One arm flung out to the side, and her fingers grazed the carved hilt of Brander's dagger still imbedded in the wedge of goat cheese. Without thinking, panic filling her with an overpowering need for escape from rampant emotions, she jerked the dagger loose. Her arm swung upward then paused in what was meant to be a threatening posture, but Brander's reflexes responded to menace instead of threat.

He rolled quickly to one side in a lithe motion, the heel of his hand lashing out to clip Morgana on the jaw. Stunned, she dropped the dagger as her head jerked to the side from his blow, sparks of light shooting in front of her eyes.

"You would kill me?" His fingers turned her face to his, and Morgana blinked as she tried to focus on Brander. Her jaw ached and her head pounded, and there was a taste of blood in her mouth where she had bitten her tongue.

Tears spurted as she realized what she had caused, and she shook her head slowly.

"Nay. I was only frightened of you," she whispered brokenly, "and of myself. Forgive me, Brander. . . ."

She trembled like a leaf in aimless flight on a winter wind, turning to hide her face against Brander's chest. Did he understand and forgive her?

Brander's warm lips against her bruised chin gave her the answer, and with a soft sigh Morgana raised her mouth to his in surrender. This was no defeat now, but an eager acceptance of offered love, their anger forgotten. Even the reason for her resistance faded as she answered passion with passion, her need growing to exceed his.

When their clothing lay in a tangled pile beside the pallet of fine furs, Morgana pressed close to Brander's lean frame. Her questing hands skimmed over his furred chest, fingers moving up to cradle his jaw, holding his head still for her kisses.

The fires of passion flared higher and hotter, burning with urgent intensity, until she could stand the waiting no longer.

"Brander," she urged raggedly, "please . . ."

A triumphant smile slanted his mouth as he moved to please her, and when she shuddered with moaning release, her fingers digging into his shoulders with each rolling explosion, Brander whispered honeyed words of love in her ear.

Viking and Celt, enemies yet lovers, caught in a delicious snare of sensual abandon, rushing to a thundering culmina-

tion of shared ecstasy before a slow descent to quiet satisfaction. Exhausted by the depths of their emotions as well
as physical release, they lay entwined in a languorous tangle
of pearly-sheened bodies misted with perspiration, the single oil lamp guttering to a dark hiss and leaving them
blanketed in darkness.

Tree branches overhead whispered with a fresh breeze,
the rustling of leaves a sweet melody unnoticed by the tent's
occupants. Soft words mingled and soared, and only the
barn dog marked their passing.

Chapter
32

Rising early, Morgana slipped from the tent before the first calls of the birds heralded the morning sun. She untethered the barn dog from his leash and took him with her, strolling past the posted sentinel without a word. Though the man watched her, he made no move to slow her progress as she disappeared into the thicket beyond the camp.

All was hushed and dark, Morgana's bare feet making no sound on the dew-dampened leaves carpeting the ground. Instinct guided her through the pathless woods where one spot looked much like another, and at last she came upon an ancient well. She wasn't sure how she'd known it was there, but some force had urged her to this vine-covered glen sacred to the Celts.

An aura of power surrounded the mossy stones of the well, and a tangible force emanated from the musty depths as if it were visible, hanging in the air in circling wreaths. Slowly, reciting chants older than the mountains, Morgana made a sunwise circuit of the well. She asked the gods of

the well to look with favor upon her requests, to watch over
the Viking, and to smile upon their union.

Pausing beside the weathered gray stones marked with the
hands of time, Morgana drew from the small leather pouch
at her side a strip of cloth cut from Brander's favorite tunic.
She lifted it and breathed deeply, inhaling the familiar scent
of the soap from Gaul that Brander favored, then held it
high in the air. A breeze fluttered the strip of material as she
held it, and when the first rays of the rising sun burst like
thunder over the horizon, shooting through tangled tree
branches as though they were thrown spears, one of the
well-stones began to glow like a fiery ember.

It shone first in a reddish haze, then flared to a blazing
white before beginning to fade. Just before the light died
completely, Morgana loosed the strip of material and let it
drop down the center of the well.

Standing with head bowed and arms still lifted in supplication, she felt warmed by the sun, letting it seep into her
bones, filling her with light. Light, knowledge, ancient
secrets, and untold mysteries whirled like hunting owls
above her head. Could she answer the whispering calls?
Could she forsake the brief love she had known with the
Viking for that all-consuming otherworld of life-healing
powers?

Her arms dropped to her sides and her head lifted. The
time would soon be upon her when she would have to make
that choice.

On the walk back to the Viking camp, Morgana looked
about for the dog. He had disappeared into the woods,
probably running after a rabbit, she reflected. She called to
him softly a few times, but there was no answering bark or
rustling of his approach in the bushes. He would find his
way back to the camp.

When she reached the small clearing where the Vikings

prepared for the upcoming battle, Morgana was met by Harald. One graying eyebrow rose quizzically as he surveyed her bare feet still wet from the dew and covered with leaves.

"You walk so early, Morgana?"

"Aye. There are things I have to do yet, Harald." She titled her head to stare up at this Viking who was her lover's father, and the breath caught in her throat. A fine mist covered his head and face, forming in the shape of a death mask, and she knew Harald's walk to the otherworld was at hand.

"What is it, Morgana?" He reached out, but she would not let him touch her. Puzzled, his distress showing in his eyes, Harald asked softly, "Do you hate me that much for my foolishness so long ago? I only tried to help my son. . . ."

"I know. You just did not know who to believe. . . ." She paused, needing to say the words that tumbled forth. "There are many paths to the same mountain, Harald, and not all of them lead to the top. Some are more dangerous, some smooth, but the choice belongs to each of us." She hesitated for a moment, then reached out to lightly touch him on the arm. "Your path leads to the summit. May your journey be swift and filled with sunlight."

Harald stood staring after Morgana long after she had whirled and left him standing alone beneath the spreading branches of a towering birch.

Brander was waiting for Morgana before the opened tent flap, his garments obviously hastily donned and his hair still rumpled from slumber.

"Where have you been?" he asked calmly, buckling on his sword-belt more slowly now that he saw her. "I woke to find you gone."

"I went to ask a favor of my gods, Brander. Did you

sleep well?'' The tent flap hit her in the face as she ducked to enter, and she pushed at it impatiently. Her bare toes curled into the dew-wet grass, and not waiting for his answer, she bent to find the soft kidskin boots she had not been able to find in the dark earlier. The boots were warm, and she had left them near the pallet. She grumbled to herself, frowning as she lifted pelts and furs and shook them like a terrier with a rat, but the boots remained hidden.

"What do you search for?" Brander's tone was impatient, his eyes narrowed when Morgana rocked back on her heels to stare in growing frustration.

"My boots. I have no others with me, and it is a fair distance to the hill where the sacrificial fires are to be lit. . . ."

"Oh? And did you plan to travel there without me, Morgana?" There was a faintly menacing note in his steely voice that Morgana chose to ignore, and his next words jerked her head up to glare at him. "You will remain here. We fight the Celts, and I would not have you hurt."

"You go to fight my warriors, yet you say you do not want *me* to be hurt?" she demanded indignantly. "Do you not know that these Celtic wariors are the very finest?"

"Perhaps. Yet they will lose this eve," was Brander's calm reply. "Do you doubt it, Morgana?"

"I doubt my wisdom in ever bothering to warn you of danger," she retorted bitterly, pushing to her feet to face him, momentarily forgetting her boots. Brander's head grazed the roof of the tent and he leaned slightly forward so that his face was closer to hers. A slight smile curled his lips as he watched Morgana, and she saw in the sky-blue depths of his eyes some of the same emotion she felt. "Foolish Viking," she whispered. "We are both caught in the same trap, I fear."

Some of his anger eased at the anxiety in her voice.

"Aye, but 'tis a pleasant enough trap," he agreed with a wide grin, "or it was last night." His hands moved to touch the small scratches she'd left on his chest, and the fires in his eyes burned bright with the memory.

A light flush stained her cheeks, and Morgana felt a familiar coiling fire curl in the pit of her stomach at his intense gaze. The night had been precious, the sweet words he'd murmured even more so, and she trembled at the thought of losing this fierce Viking warrior.

"'Tis the Beltane night, Brander," she whispered, "a night special to my people. Would you attack the innocents? Wait, I urge you to wait. . . ."

"Nay, Morgana. It's best to attack when there is surprise on our side, for we number few against the Celts." He paused for a moment, remembering the last feast, the Baltane night when he'd been captured by Celtic warriors and met a beautiful Celtic girl named Morgana. It was a sweet enough memory in spite of the humiliation of being captured. He wondered—as he had many times—about the direction of Morgana's loyalties. She had been with him only a small space of time, while this was her land, her people; there had to be an inner conflict raging. A brow rose as he stared at her, seeing past the pure beauty of her face to the emotional turmoil, and his voice was gentle when he asked, "Which would you choose, sweet Morgana—Celt or Viking?" One hand reached out to lift a strand of tangled hair from her shoulder, his fingers combing the silky tresses in an absent motion.

Morgana shivered in reaction. No, she could not do this, could not let him sway her. The decision must remain her own. . . .

"Choose? 'Tis not a question of choosing, Brander, but more a matter of following fate." Her chin lifted as she faced him squarely, aware of the frustration in his eyes at her noncommittal answer. "I must go for now. They will be expecting me at the hill, Brander. I am needed."

"Then that is your decision?" His mouth was tight now, deep grooves running from the corners of his nose downward, a crease knitting his brow. The warmth had faded from his eyes to leave them like the ice in Nordic fjords again, and Morgana recognized his sense of betrayal. Even while she wavered, she knew it could not be helped.

"I will return soon, Brander, I swear," she told him, hoping he might understand, but he said nothing. No word was uttered as she bent, finally finding her boots beneath a fur pelt and pulling them on.

He made no effort to stop her as Morgana left the tent and walked slowly across the littered Viking camp toward the line of bushes and trees. His thoughts were dark as she faded into the tangled undergrowth and towering trees, and he muttered a frustrated oath. A hand upon his shoulder turned him to find Harald at his side.

"You let her go, Brander? She knows of our plans for this eve."

"Even had I not told her she would know, Harald. Somehow she would know."

Sighing, Harald nodded agreement as he lowered his body to the comparative comfort of a fallen log. It was true; Morgana could command answers if she chose, could summon the future if she liked. Ah, he was growing old now, unable to withstand the rigors of warfare as he once had done; it was better to leave the problems to the young and concentrate instead upon the invigorating combat to come.

The fiery sun rolled slowly across the sky and sank in a sea of orange flame, dying splinters of light reaching out to light the hillside and sacrificial stones one last time. The celebrants hushed as the druids stepped forward to group around a large, bleached-white stone with darker stains in the center.

"Tan y'n cunys lemmyn gor uskys," a white-robed figure intoned at one side, and he swung a golden sickle in a shining arc. As dark shadows fell in smothering shrouds, a flame leaped high atop the hill, a towering pyre ablaze in a fiery beacon. Waxy green plants with small white berries were attached to the spears of several druids, and Clunaich held up a sprig of the mistletoe as he chanted over the sacrificial stone.

A white bull with horns dipped in gold was led to the spot and sacrificed, rejuvenating the life-giving sun and cleansing man and beast, its remains placed on the still-burning wood structure. Villagers lit two smaller fires of furze and drove their cattle between them, purifying the beasts with smoke before leading them out to wild pasture.

Morgana stood beside Kyna, watching the ceremony. It had not changed in all the years she had been attending the rites, and still evoked slumbering mysteries deep within her.

"Do you go with us to the monastery?" Kyna asked when the fires had died to glowing embers and white-hot ashes. "There is food and drink, and protection from the Vikings." She peered closely at Morgana's pale face. "And 'tis your feast day. Almost a score of summers have passed since you drew first breath in this life. Will you come?"

"Aye, but first I must search for the dog. He is lost, and I know he wanders in circles searching for me, Kyna. I will join you shortly." She smiled. "I will come," she repeated, pressing a swift kiss on the old woman's withered cheek before leaving.

Though the ancient rites marked the beginning of summer, it was still cool at night, and Morgana drew a dark woolen shawl over her head and shoulders as she scurried down wooded paths. Had the Vikings reconsidered—decided not to attack the Celts? No sign of them had been seen all day, and the Celt warrior sent to spy reported no unusual activity in their camp. It was just as well, for the eve of the Beltane was spent in revelry and sport, and the warriors would be distracted.

The shrill barking of foxes broke the quiet of the still night, and in the distance Morgana recognized the deeper baying of the dog. She paused for a moment, closing her eyes and trying to picture where the animal might be. A vague, formless shape clouded her mind, black against white, then the splotches rearranged to imitate the shape of the barn dog with his white chest and paws. There was the dog, tall stone crosses, moss-covered gray stones jutting into the night sky—Monasterboice.

Hurrying, Morgana retraced her steps down the path where it widened into a lane large enough for carts. Rutted tracks led to the Christian monastery, and the ruins of old roads were visible in places.

She was only a short distance from her destination when she heard the familiar whine of the barn dog. As she strained to see in the dark, a white spot seemed to leap out at her from roadside bushes, and a wet tongue was everywhere at once.

"You wretch!" she scolded, giving the dog a swift squeeze. "Where have you been? Chasing your shadow again?" His fur was damp and caked with mud, but he was not hurt, and Morgana set out swiftly for Monasterboice with the dog at her heels.

"'Tis like a remembered dream," Harald murmured as he knelt with Brander in thick-leaved bushes. "But 'twas so long ago that I was here . . . so long ago. . . ." A score of years had passed since he'd first come to this land, to this same monastery crouching like a stone megalith among

mist-shrouded trees. The very air seemed charged with
tension and a strange kind of waiting, and once more a
feeling of uneasiness swept over the older Viking. "I think
they wait, Brander," he muttered in a low tone.

"No matter. We will still defeat them," Brander answered
quietly. He wouldn't admit it to Harald, but he felt the same
uneasiness, and he'd wondered more than once about the
Celtic warriors.

Drifts of clouds like wisps of silk passed over the face of
the moon shining down on the hidden invaders, and when it
neared the ultimate hour Brander gave the signal.

He rose, a golden god bathed in pure silver light, tall and
strong, his war cry a long, wailing howl to strike terror into
the hearts of the Celts. The Vikings stormed the closed
doors of the monastery, battering them down with a fallen
log and swarming over the splintered wood into winding
stone halls.

As predicted, the Celts were ready for them. Though they
had celebrated, the warriors had been cautious, and they
met the Vikings with glittering blades and hard-flung spears.
Line-crusted hair like stiff horses' manes crowned the heads
of the men, and they wore nothing other than gold or bronze
sacred torques around their necks.

Giant boar-headed war trumpets blared and sling stones
whirred, spears thudded and swords clanged against bronze
shields as the Celtic warriors fought with fury. In the close
quarters of the monastery there was no room for their
favorite war-mounts or swift chariots, and they battled on
foot with a ferocity matched by the Vikings. Once again
there were women among the combatants, fighting with
bared teeth and huge clubs, and with great swords that
seemed too heavy to lift as they fought the invaders.

It was a terrible scene of pandemonium, screams and
fearful war cries filling the air, half-awake villagers scurry-

ing from the paths of Viking and Celt alike. Smoke rose
from overturned braziers, burning cloth, and straw sleeping
mats, making eyes stream and throats ache.

Sword swinging, Brander and Harald stood back to back
as they battled, cutting down Celtic warriors with savage
strokes. All around them were fallen men, some still alive
and wounded, some staring sightlessly at the stone ceiling
high above. Torches sputtered and flared, cries echoed in the
dimly lit halls, and the last Celt was cut down with a
chopping blow as the rest fled.

Sweat streamed from under Brander's heavy helmet, filling his eyes, and stinging a shallow cut on one cheek.
Breathing heavily, he leaned upon the hilt of his sword
wedged into a crevice in the stone floor. They had won, but
somehow he did not feel the usual flush of triumph. The
strong always conquered, while the weak were defeated, he
reminded himself; it was the way of the world. Yet . . . the
victory seemed hollow.

Morgana—where was she? What would she say to him
now that he had slain so many of her people? She was
fiercely loyal, and he admired that loyalty even while he
sought to sever her ties with this accursed land.

Harald jerked Brander from his thoughts with a large
hand clapped upon his back, his deep voice booming an
exultant speech of praise. " 'Twas as if you swung Mjollnir,
the hammer of Thor, Brander! You are a mighty warrior
without equal—a giant among men!"

All around them Vikings were tasting the spoils of victory. As they searched for gold and jeweled chalices and
ornaments, they drank wine hoarded by the Christian monks
who had hidden the villagers and Celtic warriors. At Harald's
urging, Brander took a brimming cup of wine, swallowing it
all in a single, smooth motion.

"The Valkyries are greeting many good men tonight," he

remarked, his glance sliding around halls strewn with the bodies of dead Vikings and Celts. "Valhalla will rejoice at such good fortune, Harald."

"Aye! As we rejoice!" Harald's arm swept out to indicate the defeated. "Bah, they cannot even agree on which gods to follow—how could they unite to defeat warriors such as ours!"

It was true, Brander reflected, that the Celtic people seemed to waver between the old gods and the new, sometimes merging the two. But it was becoming the same in Jutland, with old and new drawing ever closer together. Morgana's druids still held their secret, sacred rites, attended by the country folk and villagers who then raced to the Christian monastery for protection from danger.

Brander moved to a shadowy corner far from the Vikings' celebrations, his mood as dark as the night. Change was coming, he could sense it like a stag could test the wind for enemies. Morgana was not the same since her return to Hibernia, nor was he. Standing alone in her tiny bedchamber in Harald's hilltop fort, holding her discarded gown, and looking at rumpled bedclothes and the small impression in the mattress where she had lain, he realized that he loved her. Where did he go from here? He couldn't hold her if she didn't want to be held, couldn't force her to go back with him to Jutland. That had already been tried, and had ended badly.

He must have loved her, Brander mused, since the first time he had seen her standing serenely in the Celtic chieftain's hall gazing at the Viking prisoner attempting escape. Her remarkable eyes had conveyed warmth and tenderness even then, only he hadn't recognized it. Shaking his tawny head, Brander reflected on the past year. It had been a year filled with Morgana, and he couldn't envision a future

without her. Did he dare press her now, here in the homeland that she loved?

"Brander?" Gunther stepped into a pool of light shed by
a sputtering torch still in its holder on the wall, his blood
and sweat-streaked face creased with concern. "Are you
wounded?" he asked then, eyes scanning over Brander.

"Nay. I'm just a bit weary, Gunther." He gestured to the
dimly lit corridors leading into inky gloom. "It's quiet here,
and I needed to think."

Nodding, Gunther remained silently standing beside him
for a few moments, then murmured an invitation to join the
others when he felt like companionship before turning to
leave Brander alone once more. The sound of his footsteps
had barely faded away before Brander was joined by Harald.
The older man peered at his son a bit warily.

"Thinking of the girl?" he asked, then rushed on without
waiting for an answer. "Aye, 'tis what I would be doing if I
were a young man again. Time, Brander, time is not a
friend to the old. It plays nasty tricks on us, and we begin to
think we can do what young men can do." He sat heavily
upon a long wooden bench, hands resting on his knees.
"Ah, if I were young again, I would have done differently.
Much differently. I would have worried less about conquering
the world and worried more about conquering my own
rashness." Harald spoke in a low tone, as if to himself, his
words growing slurred with wine and exhaustion. "So long
ago, Brander, so long ago, and yet I still think of your
mother. I never met anyone else like her, so wild and so
sweet." He shook his head slowly, passing one hand over
his eyes. "So long ago, and her image remains in my mind
as sharp as if it were yesterday."

A cool wind swept through the hall, as though a window
had been opened to the surrounding forest, and the torch
flickered and died, leaving them in complete darkness.

Muttering an oath, Brander grabbed for the torch in an effort to rekindle the flame, but it was too late.

"There's another down the next hall," he said. "I will get it. Just wait here for me."

"Aye, I'll wait. Where else would I go when I can't see my own hand in front of my eyes?" Harald grumbled with a hint of humor.

Feeling his way along the stone walls, Brander swore when he bumped his leg against a wooden bench. This was ridiculous, he couldn't help thinking, and at the same time he wondered how the torch had been blown out when there was no window in the hall. Perhaps a door had been opened somewhere creating a strong draft.

Brander had wrested a torch from its holder and returned to the hall where he'd left his father when he heard the noise. It was little more than a whisper, a soft, velvety call like that of the night bird. He paused in the archway with the torch held high, staring toward the spot where he'd left Harald sitting. He was gone, the bench empty.

"Harald?" He frowned, then called again more loudly. "Harald—where are you?"

The sound of rushed footsteps on stone floors echoed down the hall to his left, and Brander swirled to look. Nothing, only a dim shadow that had been so swift he must have imagined it. Again that cool wind, colder now, threatening to extinguish this torch as well. Then he heard it. It was the noise again; this time a rumbling, ominous and fierce, compelling him dangerously closer.

Though an experienced warrior, Brander felt the hairs on the back of his neck stiffen, and his insides grew icy with an unnamed dread. It was the nameless, the dark shadows that coiled through the night, seeking . . . seeking . . .

"Harald!" he shouted desperately, wondering if his father was even close enough to hear him. "Don't go!"

The torch flared brighter, and in its light Brander could see Harald at the far end of the corridor, moving toward deeper shadows. He began to run, filled with an inescapable fear that he would be too late, that something was going to happen that he could not prevent.

When he turned the corner where he'd last seen Harald, Brander came to an abrupt halt. There, standing at the edge of an open courtyard surrounded by a forest thick and sinister, stood Harald, sword raised high, staring into the night. There was no wind now, and the torch burned steadily and bright, light streaming to where Harald stood.

"Come, danger," the older man was saying. "Come and taste the blade of a Viking warrior . . . !"

There was a rustling in the sigh of the wind, a peculiar grunt that was sinister and familiar to Brander. He recognized it then, and realized his father's danger.

"No!" he cried out as Harald stepped forward into the shadows. "No . . ."

It was too late. Wine-courage flowed through Harald's veins in a flood of anticipation, the recent battle still in his mind; and he saw in the rush of the wild boar yet another Celtic enemy in need of dying.

"Come," he taunted the enraged animal. Moving nimbly and swiftly in his own mind, Harald's steps were actually clumsy and slow. His movements were awkward instead of graceful, his sword held like a child would hold it, and the beast seemed to sense Harald's incapacity. Piggish little eyes glowed red in the dimness gleaming with ferocity, and the light from Brander's torch glinted on wicked, lethal tusks that curved upward over its snout.

Brander and the boar charged at the same time, but the man was too far away to help. With a shrill squeal, the huge boar ripped into Harald, laying open his unprotected abdomen with a slash of ivory tusks. Harald's sword descended a moment too late, biting into the boar's neck in a fatal stroke, and both crashed to the stones of the courtyard.

A hoarse cry of pain and rage sounded as Brander leaped forward, grabbing his father's sword to deal the final death blow to the boar. Harald lay writhing, fingers splayed over his torn stomach, but a grim smile curved his mouth.

"Nine hundred Celtic warriors and others have I slain, to be laid low by a pig," he rasped painfully. His helmet had been knocked askew, sliding over one eye, and Harald lifted a blood-soaked hand to replace it.

"Let me." Brander knelt beside his father and reached out to straighten the leather helmet. He held Harald's head on his lap, cradling it gently.

"I'm dying." Harald stated it calmly, and Brander nodded.

"Aye. 'Tis a bad wound."

"Will you take a last bit of advice from an old man?" Without waiting for assent, Harald continued, "Take the girl, Brander. I was wrong. Celt or Viking matters not as long as you are happy. I think of your mother..." He paused to cough, bright bits of blood staining his tunic. His voice shook now, and grew weaker. "Bevin was Celtic, and we disagreed about everything: religion, gods, whether the sky was blue or gray.... But through it all we loved, as Gytha and I never did. When Bevin died, I was angry and blamed all Celtic gods for taking her from me. 'Tis why I promoted a match with Erika for you... your ways were more compatible..." He suffered another rattling cough, and said, "Morgana is strong, Brander, and she... loves ...you...." Light faded in his eyes, the blue dimming to gray, and Harald's fingers curled and uncurled in a spasm of pain, his lips twitching in a grimace.

"Don't talk. Lie still," Brander pleaded, his heart wrenching. But it was unnecessary to say more, for Harald had already passed to the otherworld, his eyes still open, his muscles relaxing in a final repose.

Stunned, Brander remained holding Harald as carefully and tenderly as if he were still alive. Acceptance of his father's death was hard, and it wasn't until he felt Morgana's light touch upon his shoulder that he could move.

"I'm sorry," she said when he looked up at her.

Chapter
33

Gunther gave Brander a hard look, his jaw tight. "The men say they wish to return home. They think Harald's death is a bad omen."

"And you, Gunther? What do you think?" Brander asked with a snarl of impatience. "My warriors have turned to weak-kneed women. . . ."

"It is different when one fights shadows instead of flesh and blood, Brander!" Gunther returned hotly, his face flushing at the implied criticism of their courage. "You have a personal interest in this, which we do not."

"Losing your chieftain does not give you a personal interest?" Brander's tone was mild now, a dark brow arching derisively. "Aye, the girl is of great interest to me, but I could do as I did last time and simply take her with me if that is what I desired. I wish," he stated, one blunt forefinger spearing the air in emphasis, "to leave as victors when we leave this land!"

"There's only one way, and the Celts hide and wait." Gunther raked a hand through his thick hair, breathing a small sigh of discouragement. "Morgana could lure them to us if she would, Brander. . . ."

"Would you lure your countrymen at Gwyneth's suggestion?" Brander snapped.

"I thought . . . that since she loves you . . ."

Brander cut across Gunther's stammering words with a quick, "Love does not necessarily rob one of wits and loyalty, I hope."

"Nay, but it does fuel the desire to please," Gunther shot back, growing annoyed. "Do you not think Morgana capable of trying to please you?"

This brought Brander up short, and he stared for a long moment at Gunther.

"Aye," he said at last, "she is very capable of trying to please me, but not at the expense of others. She loves her foster mother, and she feels guilty enough about loving an enemy of her land. If I push too hard . . ." He left the sentence unfinished, but Gunther needed no more explanation to understand.

It was easier to explain to Gunther than it was to believe himself, for when Brander was once more with Morgana he found it difficult to keep the conversation from straying back to the same topic.

"Do you go with me when I leave, Morgana?" They sat beneath spreading branches of a tree not far from his camp, dappled light playing over them.

Silence lay about them in a heavy shroud, dimming the bright sunlight that gilded the green fields and trees, as Morgana struggled with conflicting emotions. She was torn; torn between the man she loved and her heritage, her legacy. The sound of steps restling through dry grasses saved her from answering his question.

Kyna interrupted them, glaring at the pair sitting so close together, shoulder to shoulder, their hands entwined. She could not accept the Viking Morgana loved, and it was evident in her strident voice.

"Go with him and you are doomed to a life of servitude, child! Did he treat you well before?" A knowing sniff accompanied her lifted brow and curled lip. " 'Twill be the same again, you'll see soon enough. . . ."

"Hush, old woman. This is not your affair—it will be decided by Morgana and me." Brander shot Kyna a cold stare, and she backed away a few steps, muttering beneath her breath. "Get gone, hag!" he growled as the old woman threw him a malevolent glare.

Kyna hesitated for a moment, ignoring Morgana's attempt at soothing words, then spun on her heel more agilely than Brander had thought possible, and strode away.

"She only tries to protect me," Morgana protested, but Brander brushed her words away with a careless shrug of his wide shoulders.

"Your dog is protection enough," he remarked, glancing down at the massive beast crouched at Morgana's feet. " 'Tis hard to believe he once belonged to my father's hall. What magic do you possess, Celtic witch, that allows you to bewitch man and beast alike?" His fingers, still curled around her arm, began to rub her tender flesh in a light caress, pushing beneath the loose sleeves of her gown to her upper arm. "What magic, Morgana?" he repeated softly, as if to himself, his icy gaze thawing to warmer lights.

"No magic, Brander, only love." Tilting her head, Morgana's breath caught in her throat as she gazed into his eyes and recognized the flaring lights of passion. He kindled the same fire within her, the spark blazing into a raging inferno that demanded quenching, and she poised on the brink of eager submission.

They lay at the edge of an open, grassy area, trees

stretching to one side, and sloping hills carpeted with thick grass and dotted with wildflowers on the others. A small stream gurgled a path through the waving grasses and fringe of trees, a summer melody to serenade two lovers. It was a rare day filled with golden sunshine and soft breezes, and Morgana yielded to desire.

No one else was near. Kyna was gone, and the Viking warriors remained in the monastery. There was no one close to hear the murmured words of love, the husky whispers of desire as Brander and Morgana wrapped themselves in fragrant summer grasses beneath the concealing branches of a tree. Time seemed to pause, a shimmering stillness filled with sensuality.

Only when the sun began to sink in a bloodred sea of light did Morgana and Brander stir, stretching lazily. It was growing late, and a rising sense of urgency pricked Morgana, calling her away.

"I must go," she murmured regretfully against his mouth, her lips brushing his as light as the wings of a moth. "My warriors might find you here and alone."

He frowned. "They have been defeated, Morgana. We hold the monastery."

A slight smile curved her mouth as she shook her head. "Do you think they care for that? The monastery belongs to Christians, not my warriors. They will come again to attack you."

"And where will you be, Morgana—leading them? Or will you be with me?"

She knelt before him, her eyes searching his in a plea for understanding.

"I'm trying, but I have not yet resolved this conflict in myself, Brander. My heart urges me to you, yet my loyalties have always been with Erin. I must make peace with myself before I am free to choose with no regrets." Her small hand lightly caressed the side of his beard-stubbled jaw. "Please—give me time, my love."

Brander gave her a coolly assessing stare for a moment, then shrugged. "I am not the keeper of time, Morgana. Do what you must, and perhaps it will not be too late."

He rose and left her there with her dog, his broad frame disappearing into the deep shadows of the trees as he strode swiftly in the direction of the monastery. For long moments after he'd gone, Morgana sat motionless, her tormented thoughts whirling like kites in the sky.

Nights came and went, drifting on padded feet like those of a straying cat, and still the Vikings remained. They drank, gamed, and quarreled, tension growing as they waited. When one of the men suggested mounting an attack on Celtic forces, it was pointed out that the warriors had already faded into the woods like the morning mist.

"How do we battle what we cannot find?" Brander asked with more than a trace of disgust in his voice. "They hide in dens like she-foxes. We will wait for them, for I believe that they come again soon."

"You are obsessed," Gunther grumbled more than once when he and Brander were alone. "I don't know what obsesses you more—the girl or the idea of complete victory."

"I will have both," was Brander's calm reply, but he had an uneasy feeling in the pit of his stomach. Would he—and which was more important to him, Morgana or a victory over this land which had taken his father?

But for now, he kept his doubts to himself. He would wait and he would watch, and when Morgana indicated a willingness to compromise, he would be ready. It was close to the time of midsummer, a lean time for the Celts. Crops were still growing in the fields and harvest was a full moon away. Existence depended upon hunting game, and with the presence of the Vikings, hunters had been too wary to venture far. Aye, he could wait.

Caught between opposing worlds, Morgana battled with herself. She walked often to the stony precipice where she had once stood talking to Conn, thinking of the past months and her visions. The dreams had returned now that she was in Erin again, and though she had been distressed at the loss of them in Jutland, she discovered that knowing the future was not as important as Conn had claimed. What had he said—that magic was stronger than love?

Even Clunaich advised a decision. A choice, Clunaich had emphasized and it was hers alone to make. Would she make the right choice? If she chose to spend her years with the Viking, she risked losing all contact with her mother's people. And if she chose to remain, like Kyna urged her to do? Then she would surely lose Brander, and that she could not bear.

"Do what you must, my child," Clunaich replied when Morgana begged for advice. "My choice is not necessarily your choice." He gestured to the druidesses close by. "Those women have studied for years and have been tattooed with the sacred markings. They have chosen their paths, as you must choose yours. But for them, there is no other life. All their energies must be concentrated on the sacred rituals and chants, the visions they can see."

Sadly, Morgana reflected that she did not have the concentration needed to commit herself. Indeed, all her thoughts were with that bold Viking. He was an invader of more than just her homeland—he had conquered her heart as well. Her course, it seemed, lay with Brander.

*   *   *

"She has chosen?" the druid asked the cloaked figure, and the head within the concealing hood nodded.

"Aye. 'Tis time." The voice was like the dry rustling of leaves when chill winds of the dying season blow them from the trees, crackling with age and sadness.

"Midsummer night," the druid replied as he turned away. "Tell those who must know."

Her long cloak swept grass wet with night dew as Kyna scurried to obey, and her heart was heavy. Morgana had chosen the Viking, not the ways of the gods, just as she had feared. The gifts were not given to many; she agreed with Conn's theories in that respect, and she feared for Morgana's future. Their religion was dying out, the new gods taking over the old, and soon there would be no druids. No druids, no sacred oak trees draped with mistletoe, no time-honored rituals to follow. There was a new god now, a more powerful god than even those the Vikings claimed, and the Christian priests who built the monasteries were luring the villagers away from ancient, familiar customs.

First the Vikings must be driven from their land somehow, Kyna reasoned. Then they could deal with the others. The order must survive in secrecy, as it had these many years past, or it would all be lost.

Kyna paused, hearing the shrill bark of foxes, and smiled to herself. Those were no foxes, but Celtic warriors who barked. The time would be soon at hand for the final destruction of the hated Vikings. On midsummer night all the powers of the spirit world would be invoked to help drive them away. Victory would belong to the strong, proud warriors of her land.

"Where have you been, old one?" Morgana asked when Kyna returned to their small cottage, but she already knew the answer. "Ah, Kyna, you knew even before I did what my answer would be, didn't you? I have struggled, but I see no other course for me to follow.''

The cloak was slowly removed, and Kyna sat heavily upon a small wooden bench. "You can only do what you must, Morgana, just as we all must. I will do what I must do. I had hoped you would listen, would use the powers you were blessed with, and would remember those who love you, but the gods ignored my pleas." Shaking her head she sighed, a whisper like the wind through the yew trees.

"No, 'tis only that my course lies in another direction, Kyna. I was not meant to keep the powers, or the gods would have removed my obstacles." She knelt beside the old woman, putting her hands over Kyna's. "One cannot evade the sight, cannot flee even to the farthest land of snow and ice to escape if it is meant to be. My fate must be with the Viking."

"I fought it, but you are right, Morgana. Your fate is entwined with the Viking's, but only in this world. When he has passed to the next, where will you go?" Kyna's hands were trembling, her mouth quivering with emotion.

Morgana's heart ached for her foster mother, and she closed her eyes. This was the most difficult decision she had ever had to make, and she hoped that one day Kyna would understand that her love for Brander was greater than her loyalty to a land and people to whom she had never felt as if she truly belonged. "I shall follow him," Morgana answered quietly, and the old woman silently bowed her head.

" 'Tis worse than I feared," she whispered after several moments of silence.

The dog whined, cocking his great head to one side as he peered at Morgana and Kyna, then rose to cross to the closed door, nails clicking against the hard clay floor.

"Someone comes . . . ?" Kyna bent her head to listen.

"Aye, it is Brander." A smile curved Morgana's mouth. She knew, as wild animals know when a storm approaches, that her lover followed the worn path to the cottage. "Do not begrudge me the Viking," Morgana pleaded when Kyna moaned, "for if you are right, we have little time."

Kyna could not answer, but could only watch with sad eyes as her foster child slipped from the cottage to meet the enemy. Vikings. They had already changed the land, and would change it even more before it would be done. These past invasions were the first of many more to come and their proud Celtic heritage would no longer be their own, but would be blended with northern traditions, becoming indistinguishable in time.

Kyna stared out the small window of the cottage. Change was in the air with the smell of summer, sharp and ripe with promise.

It was a warm night, the air sultry with the threat of rain, clouds scudding across a sickle moon. Shadows leaped and wavered, and tree branches swayed with the rising wind. Fickle moonlight glinted briefly on a golden head, and Morgana paused to wait.

"You knew I was coming," Brander murmured when he reached her, and brawny arms lifted Morgana from the ground to hold her against his broad chest. His heavy sword belt and ornately carved buckle pressed almost painfully into her soft belly, but Morgana made no murmur of protest. It had been several days since she had seen him, and she had so much to tell him.

"Brander," she blurted out when his lips left hers for a fleeting moment, "I must tell you something!"

But he paid little attention, so hungry for her kisses and her taste as he was, that it was long moments before he allowed her to speak. Breathless, her heart fluttering like the wings of a trapped bird, Morgana clung tightly to Brander, fingers curled in the soft linen of his tunic.

"What did you want to tell me, love?" Warm kisses were pressed along the sweeping line of her jaw, teased her ear, then descended the sweet curve of neck to the throbbing pulse at the base of her throat.

"Brander...I want to tell you..." She gasped as his tongue bathed her ear in hot, moist breath, then, "I will...go with you, Brander." Sighing, she offered him her lips again, eyes closed, dark head tilted back as his mouth paused against the hollow between neck and shoulder. Dreamily, holding on to him to keep from falling, "I want to go wherever you wish, wherever you go."

A shadow like that of the hunting hawk flitted over them as clouds hid the moon, then a stream of pure silver light illuminated Morgana's face. Brander pulled away to stare at her, wondering with a flash of cynicism if this was another Celtic trick before he allowed himself to react.

"I've waited a long time to hear those words," he answered carefully. He let her body slide slowly down his as he lowered her so that her feet touched the ground. "You are ready to leave your land then?"

"Nay, but if I must to stay with you, I will." She rubbed her head against the underside of his chin like a puppy, and sighed.

"Morgana, why now? What changed your mind?" His arms still circled her slim waist, locked behind her, and she leaned back in his embrace to stare up at him quizzically.

"Does it matter why?" she asked softly. "Isn't it enough that I am now willing?"

"Aye, it should be," he agreed. "Yet I find myself wondering what changed your mind."

Morgana's fingers traced the outline of his mouth and the rugged slash of his cheekbones, pausing to rub the side of his bristly chin before she placed her hands on his chest and pushed away.

"I don't know," she answered slowly. "I only know that I did finally realize what I wanted to do. Was I wrong?" *Or too late?* she wondered silently.

Recognizing the strain in her face, Brander pulled her to him, muttering fiercely against her hair, "Nay, Celtic witch, you are not wrong! This is what I want also, only I feared you would say differently." He held her as if she would melt away and disappear as spring snows fade in the bright sun.

Morgana's skirt flapped in the rising wind, making a popping sound. Then came a drop of rain and another, followed by a torrent slashing down to drench them both and make them run for the shelter of the trees. After a brief hesitation, the barn dog bounded after them to stand at their feet beneath the dripping branches of a yew.

"It shouldn't last long," Morgana remarked, and as she was once more folded into Brander's strong embrace, she ceased to care.

His mouth descended on hers in a kiss burning with passion, his hands molding her against him so tightly that she could barely draw a breath, and still Morgana pressed closer. It was as if she couldn't get enough of him, couldn't hold him close enough or feel his lips against her long enough, and reality ceased to exist as she twined her arms around Brander's neck to hold his head still.

"Do you tempt me, witch?" he teased lightly, kissing her on the top of her nose. "For I feel it only fair to warn you that I yield to some temptations very enthusiastically."

"Aye, Viking," she breathed, "I tempt you. And I welcome your response. . . ."

More words were lost in the eagerness of his reaction, in the surge of passion that swept Morgana from her feet and

found her laid on dry leaves at the base of the giant yew
tree. Few droplets of rain filtered through the thick leaves to
find them as they lay on nature's cushioning mat, and while
the storm grumbled and growled, it drowned out the soft
cries from beneath the sheltering tree.

Chapter 34

Atop the stony hill stood a white-robed druid and the Grand Bard with arms uplifted in invocation, their voices rising and blending in fervent supplication. A sprig of mistletoe was clasped by each, and a slim birch wand was waved in the still night air.

Huge stones, stark white and grouped in a sacred circle, surrounded a towering pyre of dry limbs and brush. At the center was tied a sacrifice to the gods, awaiting the next life with doomed resignation.

Green-robed druids of justice with gold-tipped spears in their hands formed two lines leading from the sacrificial altar, and lesser druids clad in robes of purple and scarlet mingled with the villagers. It was midsummer eve, and all across the land of Eire, even over the Irish Sea to the land of the Britons, fires were being lit on ancient hilltops—a chain of beacons to light the evening sky, to rejuvenate the life-giving sun, to purify man and beast, and to ensure fertility.

A young girl draped in snowy white clutched a fresh

bunch of herbs in her hand as she stood near the pyre. When flames leaped to drive away the darkness she raised the herbs high, chanting, "Thousandfold let good seed spring. Wicked weeds, fast withering, let this fire kill," then tossed them into the towering blaze, and Morgana was reminded of the years before when she had done the same.

Chants, prayers, litanies of praise rose to a crescendo, and villagers linked hands and circled right in the ritual direction of the sun as they sang. Celtic warriors, clad in torques and light armor, lifted swords and spears in tribute to their gods.

Howls rent the air, floating on the quickened evening breeze, down the hill and over treetops, echoing across the shadowed valley to the stone monastery and the Vikings within.

"They celebrate," Gunther remarked gloomily, tilting back his head to pull at the wineskin he held. He wiped his mouth on his sleeve and peered at Brander. "We should attack them now, I say!"

"While they stand on the crest of a hill and watch us come?" Brander shook his head. "We don't have the strange invincibility of the mushrooms to send us blindly into battle, Gunther."

"And I'm beginning to wish we had the mushrooms with us so we could end this waiting!"

"Aye," Delling added, "we could eat our fill of the mushrooms as do the berserkers, then rush naked into combat."

The berserkers, Viking warriors who ate a certain kind of poisonous mushroom that produced hallucinations, got their name from the fact that they often wore only a bear shirt into battle for protection and were believed invulnerable. The restless Vikings now tossed around half-joking comments as they waited for the inevitable battle to come.

"The Celts with their stiff hair like horses' manes would be no challenge for a berserker. . . ."

"I've seen a berserker make dents in his bronze shield with his teeth—can you think what he would do to a puny wooden Celtic shield?"

The man laughed, then Delling recited a poem in honor of Harald. He had learned it years before from a skald, and Brander then recalled a verse about a long-ago king named Hakon.

Mun obundinn	Freed from his bonds
a ytas jot	to the home of men,
Fenrisulfr of fara	the wolf Fenrir will run
aor jafngoor	before there comes so
a auoa troo	good a man of royal birth
konungmaor komi.	to the desolate fields.

A fitting verse for a warrior who now reposed in Valhalla, Brander reflected: Fenrir, the grey wolf who was to be the death of Odin in the last battle of the gods and men against giants and monsters, would run to the home of men before a man as good as Harald would come again. He had been a good warrior, and was sorely missed.

Bah, he was becoming womanish! It did no good to sit and brood over what was past; victory belonged to those who eagerly sought it, not sat waiting.

Brander stood abruptly and moved away from his men, lifting a silver cup encrusted with jewels and ornately carved, letting the light from torches and lamps glitter along its surface. The potent wine brought from the Rhineland swirled in the cup as he lifted it to his lips and drank, and Delling and Gunther exchanged glances. He seemed more preoccupied than usual, when they had thought matters much better.

"Didn't Morgana agree to go with us?" Gunther asked Delling in a low tone, and the older man nodded.

"Aye, that she did."

"So what is bothering him now?"

"Perhaps he questions his own reasons for staying longer." Delling paused, his brow furrowing. "It can't be just victory over the Celts, for that we have enjoyed several times. Something else gnaws at his soul. . . ."

When Brander banged his ornate cup back to a table's surface Morgana stood beside him.

"Do you enjoy the wine?" she murmured as he wiped his mouth. "Or do you simply seek forgetfulness?"

"Do you always know what's in a man's mind, Morgana? Is that another of your witch's tricks?" he asked irritably.

"Nay. Any fool can see what I see now, Brander," and in spite of her words her voice was gentle. "You boil inside at the forced inactivity, at the waiting. The time will soon be here that you can fight my warriors; then the waiting will be over."

"Aye, we all know that, but how soon?" Wine was poured from a flagon into his cup again. "I grow weary of waiting for your brave Celts to come out of hiding! If there were more of us, we would seek them out and drive them from their holes like foxes from their dens. Instead we must wait."

"The time will soon be here," she repeated, and this time Brander caught the quiet inflection in her voice.

"Ah. Do you warn me, Morgana?"

"Aye," was the low whisper, filled with guilty pain at what she considered betrayal, "I warn you, Viking." Green eyes brimming with tears gazed up at him, and he knew what those few words had cost her.

"Come with me, my sweet," he murmured then, taking her by the arm and leading her from the dim halls to the bright slivers of moonlight outside the monastery. They walked silently, winding their way around high stone crosses erected by the Christian priests who had built the monastery, letting the soft wind blow in their faces, the fragile scent of summer like a heady perfume in the air.

Brander studied her face, intrigued by her mystery as well as her beauty. He reached out to touch her, then drew back. "You are like the night, Morgana, mysterious, your light shining through the dark to guide me."

She smiled tenderly as she turned to face him, head tilted to stare into Brander's troubled eyes.

Gently, she replied, "Aye, Viking, I shall ever be willing to guide you, but would prefer walking beside you."

"Then you shall," he breathed as they halted beneath the spreading branches of a slender birch. "You shall walk beside me always, Morgana, and I will cherish you."

A shadow flickered across her sculptured features as Morgana looked up at Brander. "I hope so," she murmured in a voice tight with pain, "for by choosing you over my own land and people, I have made myself a true orphan."

"I know this is difficult for you, Morgana, and nothing I can say will lessen the pain, but I swear that I will do my best to make the rest of our days together happy." Brander drew her closer to him, his arms circling her slim form in a gentle embrace.

A voice, low and venomous, hissed from the shadows beside them, "Those days are numbered, Viking!"

As Morgana and Brander swirled around, Kyna stepped from behind a towering oak, throwing back the hood to her concealing cloak. She spared Brander a scathing glance before turning her attention to Morgana, a cold hand reaching out to her. "You are being misled, Morgana. Flee, before you are slain with these barbaric Vikings!"

"I cannot, Kyna." Morgana patted the slight hand curled

over her arm. Ah, Kyna's bones were so tiny and fragile, like those of a bird, and her thin face sagged into worried lines, gray hair straggling in wisps over her ears and down her neck. Morgana stared at that dear, loving face she had known since her earliest days, and the conflict in her heart was tearing her apart.

Tears welled in Kyna's eyes. "But if you are with him when they come . . ."

"Then I will die happy." Morgana grasped Kyna's hands in her own. "Do you recall what you once told me—how you had lost your husband and child, and dreaded the future? 'Tis how I would feel without Brander."

Dully, Kyna replied, "You really love him."

"Aye. I think I have since the day I had the vision and saw his face in the smoke and flames, Kyna. My thoughts have been with him constantly, and he owns my heart. . . ."

"But . . . your legacy—what of it? I loved your mother, and you have the potential to be as great, if not greater, than she was. I witnessed her light waxing and waning, and knew that her daughter possessed the same great gifts. Oh, not like Conn wanted, but greater, for you have kindness and humility where he did not."

"But you agree with Conn. You think I should abandon all thoughts of love and concentrate only on that which has never given me any happiness. . . ."

Kyna was quiet. She wanted to say, No, abandon only the Viking, but how could she? Didn't she remember her own lost love, and how the pain seemed to go on and on, with no end? It had been so long ago, yet the memory was still as sharp, clawing at her sometimes in the night, in her dreams, or at odd times during the day. Could she ask Morgana to endure the same pain? Kyna lifted blurred, tired eyes to her foster daughter.

"Go with him," she surprised them both by saying, "and

love the Viking until the end of your days, child. I ask only that you be happy." Kyna turned to a quietly listening Brander. Testily, "And you, Viking, had better give her the same love and devotion she gives you, or . . ." Kyna didn't finish the sentence, but he fully understood what she was trying to tell him.

"You don't need to worry on that score," he assured Kyna, "because I do love Morgana, and I'll take care of her."

Kyna stared at him for several moments, then nodded. "I think you will, Viking. I think you will. . . ."

The old woman turned, giving Morgana a long, loving look, then pulled up the hood to her cloak. She was old; she felt old and weary and ready to join her friends who had crossed into the otherworld. Morgana would be cared for by this fierce Viking, cared for much better than Kyna could care for her, and she was loved. Her worries and doubts had begun to fade as she'd heard the tenderness with which Brander spoke to Morgana, watched the way his eyes softened when he looked at her, and saw how gently he touched her. Aye, Morgana had achieved her heart's desire and no longer needed a tired old woman to look after her.

"But I do need you," Morgana said, startling Kyna from her reverie. "Don't leave me yet. Go with us. . . ."

Kyna smiled and shook her head. "No. I don't want to go to a land of snow and ice, Morgana. I want to rest upon that sunny hill with my dead husband and child. There's a time for everything, and my time has come. I wait gladly, so don't grieve. . . ." She put out a gnarled hand to wipe away the tear trembling on Morgana's lashes. "You have your love and don't need me at your shoulder. And I'll always be with you, Morgana, each time you summon me. You know that. You were taught that in your cradle. No one is truly gone who has been loved. I will be with you each time you think of me and smile.''

Morgana couldn't speak for a moment. She clung to Kyna's hand, weeping, knowing she would never see her again.

"But I'll miss you," she finally managed to say.

"Well, I certainly hope so!" Kyna's voice held a familiar sharp edge, and her eyes were suspiciously bright. "I would be surprised if you didn't miss me nagging at you, child, but nothing lasts forever. Just remember all my good advice and don't always follow your first inclinations. You get carried away sometimes. . . . Viking, you help her—and don't let her get hurt. She's her own worst enemy at times."

Kyna stepped away, back into the line of trees, her stooped, bent frame disappearing among thick bushes and vines. Morgana sobbed, pressing the backs of her fingers so hard against her mouth that her teeth left imprints in her knuckles.

"Come," Brander finally urged, holding her close. He could feel her body quiver with each harshly drawn breath. "Come with me, love. We have to hurry before your warriors find us again."

"Oh," she said, remembering. "My warriors, Brander! And there are so many of them chasing you . . . chasing us, and . . ."

"And they haven't caught us, have they?" Brander's tone was light and teasing. "I have you, Morgana, and nothing can harm me now! You are my strength, like Mjollner and the Widow-Maker. You are my weapon against all who would come against me. . . ."

A note of asperity crept into her voice. "My tongue may be sharp, but my fighting skills lack force, Viking! If, instead of behaving like a fighting cock, you would use a bit of common sense and flee, we might make it back to Jutland without mishap."

"You doubt my fighting abilities?" Brander's brows rose, but he was pulling Morgana with him, away from the line of trees and toward the Viking camp.

"You are invincible in your own mind, but there are times when Celts feel the same about themselves," she muttered, taking three steps to his one. "And we still have to get back to your ship."

"It's hidden well."

"Not well enough. I found it, and so will others."

Brander was astounded. "How did you find it? Oh, you used your sight. . . ."

"No, but even if I had, I'm not the only Celt with that gift, you know. There are others who have not been distracted by handsome Viking warriors. . . ."

Brander leaped over a small stream and turned to help Morgana, flashing her a winsome smile.

"So you admit that I'm handsome?"

"Conceited oaf, I've never denied it. I just saw no point in adding to your already inflated vanity. Especially with Erika mooning about you with calf-eyes . . ."

"Gunther intends to wed her." Brander's blunt statement was offhand, catching Morgana by surprise.

"Wed Erika? But . . . but when was this decided? And will she? And what about . . . ?"

Brander jerked Morgana beneath the hanging branches of a tree, putting two fingers over her lips to still her stream of questions.

"Shhh! I hear something." He cocked his head, but all they could hear was the gentle murmur of birds and crackling of small woodland creatures in the underbrush.

"Where are your men?" Morgana asked when he removed his fingers. "Still in camp?"

He nodded. "Aye. They are preparing to leave. The ships are ready, and loaded with treasures." His smile made

Morgana catch her breath. "But I have the most precious treasure with me." Brander's arms tightened. He nuzzled her neck with his lips, biting gently, then kissing her until she clung to him weakly.

"The men... my warriors... the time..." Her words were stopped by his mouth. Swaying beneath the hanging limbs of a willow, Morgana felt the sudden lurch of life within her, and wondered if she should tell Brander. No, it wasn't the right time. Later, when they were once more aboard his dragon ship and headed for Jutland and Hlynn and Disa, where she would see her beautiful white stallion and distraught gray goose, she would tell him of the child beneath her heart.

She hadn't told him her dream, how she had seen them around the fire in Brander's hall, seen the strong boy-child who would be born in his father's land, but there would be plenty of time on the voyage home. Home, to Jutland, where there would be a new life filled with love.

The painful dreams would cease now, for they had been banished by a magic much more powerful than any Conn had possessed. The magic was love, and that was the legacy she intended to leave her children. Theirs would be a legacy of love, not shadows.